# Christ, Man!

## A.W. Wilson

## Cover by Paul Shiers

Shiersart.com

awwilson.com

Printed and bound on demand by Amazon

ISBN: 9781731410603

*To Dunk, for saying to me, "What if all those miracles were just because they were all fucked off their heads?"*

## *What Would Jesus Do?*

"Are you fucking with me? You'd better not be fucking with me. You know who I am? Thought so. I'm the man who can't be stopped. Herod thought he could stop me. D'ya know what he got when he tried? A pile of dead kids, that's what. He didn't get me though. Wanna know why? Connections. Nobody's hooked up quite like me. What's that? You're not fucking with me? Well we might just be okay then. Here, toke on this."

Some people ask, what would Jesus do? Well this is what he would do. This is what he does best. He just owns it. Nobody in Judea can touch him and he knows it.

Jesus spreads his arms and makes it clear that although he's speaking to the new guy, this Matthew, he's really talking to everyone. "I run a tight ship here, tighter than Noah's. You want to come on board? You're welcome on board, but only if you're not fucking with me."

The new guy's eyes dart about like they're looking for the right word, but they fail and he says nothing.

"I think we can be clear he's not fucking with you."

The statement slams off the rocks and hangs amongst the dust in the evening air. Everybody looks to the west, to the speaker. It's Simon, standing slightly away from the rest of us. He's silhouetted against the low sun so everyone has to squint. Except Jesus. Jesus doesn't squint. "Thought you'd have an opinion."

Simon stares straight back. "Opinions are like asses,

1

everyone's got one."

The two of them face off in the still, warm evening.

Jesus leans over, pulls hard on the bong and stands up, inhaling through his nose and holding the bellyful of smoke down. His face, lit by the sun, is completely impassive. He stares his man down. The silence is thick, overpowering. Everybody's waiting for what's going to happen next. The only sound is the clicking of the cicadas.

Jesus erupts, an explosion of smoke and laughter. This sets Simon off and he too doubles up in hysterics. He runs at Jesus and leaps in the air. The bong's knocked flying and everyone has to get out of the way because Jesus is gripping Simon around the waist and spinning him round like a crazy bastard, both of them howling in hysterics. Matthew gets hit by Simon's flailing leg and we all end up on the floor, Matthew because he's been knocked down and the rest of us because we've fallen down from all the laughing.

This is good shit.

## Jesus and Me

We came up together, Jesus and me. My parents were friends with his mum and dad but my grandma would point out, mostly after she'd had one too many glasses of wine, that 'dad' probably wasn't the right word for Jesus' old man. She'd touch her nose and make like she was about to say something she hadn't said a hundred times before, then whisper that some funny business had gone on. She'd say the same line every time, "When Joseph married Mary he didn't know she'd come as a pair."

According to her they left Nazareth all of a sudden and had Jesus in some little backwater in secret, hoping everyone would forget about it when they got back. Then she'd babble on about how shameful it all was. Mum would always shush her and tell her she was talking nonsense, that they left because of some census. Gran's answer was always the same. "I don't remember no census."

Don't get me wrong, I respect the oldies and all that, but they don't seem to mind repeating themselves. They come out with the same old lines over and over again and it never occurs to them that maybe, just maybe, they've said it all before. Word for word. It's an insult really. They think I've got nothing better to do with my time than to listen to them churn out the same old shit. I used to give them the benefit of the doubt and put it down to their memory going tits up because of their age. I even felt a bit sorry for them. But that's bollocks. They know they've said it before, they just don't care. They even point it out sometimes. How many times have you heard an oldie start a sentence with *like I always say…*? That's your proof right there. Well if you know you always say it then stop always fucking saying it. How about that? Jesus.

I feel a bit bad for slating my Grandma, especially since she popped her sandals, but then if you tot up all the nasty stuff she said about her friends, neighbours and family members, then it becomes pretty clear that she was just not a very nice person, and being related to her didn't change that. In fact being related to her meant I saw more evidence of it. And anyway, it's not a sin to dislike your Gran. The Commandments don't say honour thy grandfather and thy grandmother do they? No they bloody well don't. And even if they did, I'd be lying if I said she was the jackal's bollocks, and by lying I'd be breaking another commandment. But come to think of it there isn't one about lying, except maybe that one about bearing false witness, but I never really knew what that one meant. There probably should have been a lying one, but God used up, like, four on stuff about Himself. Bit paranoid if you ask me, but I'm sure He knows what He's doing. He is an all-knowing deity after all.

But back to the point. Regardless of the poison my Gran spouted on a regular basis, it looked to me that as far as Jesus was concerned he was the old man's son. He was his apprentice too, just like we all were to our dads. And in the workshop our families shared, we learnt our trade together. And we got pretty bloody good at it. Even if I do say so myself. We learned what some people call life skills too, the main one being patience. You had to take your time when working with wood. *If you rush it you'll fuck it.* That's what old Joseph used to say.

We worked hard but it didn't really feel like work. It felt like time well spent. Lots of people say how they didn't really appreciate being kids when they were kids, that it was only when they looked back that they could see how good they'd had it. That's not my experience. I loved every minute of it. The workshop had a good vibe and when we weren't working, Jesus and I would have such a laugh – and sometimes even when we were working come to think of it. Over the years we built our village up from a little huddle of huts to a small town. Actually it wasn't just us, the stonemasons and thatchers had something to do with it too. We were the proper craftsmen though.

We weren't rich, nobody in the village was, but we had food, clothes and bloody good company and that was more than enough for me.

We could have stayed put, that's what everybody else did. But Jesus made it clear from an early age that he wasn't going to stick around in Nazareth forever. His was a future that lay elsewhere. When I pressed him on it he didn't give anything away. I don't think he really knew the details himself, just that he had some kind of destiny to fulfil. A destiny that would reveal itself when the time came.

The time wasn't in a hurry coming, and we carried on as we always had. We worked, we drank and we chased girls, Jesus doing the latter a lot more successfully than me. In fact he didn't even have to chase them; they'd just fall into his lap, leaving me to forage for scraps amongst his reject pile.

One morning, while we were working, Jesus had been much quieter than normal. He obviously had something on his mind but I hadn't been able to get so much as a peep out of him. Even when I'd told him my donkey goes into a bar gag, which was normally a surefire winner, it didn't crack so much as a smirk. Eventually he just came out with it. "I had an interesting talk with mum last night. She sat me down and said there were big plans for me in the family business."

"You're going to take over Joseph and Sons?"

"That's exactly what I said, but apparently my family's got

connections I never knew about. You know about that guy everyone's talking about down by the Jordan?"

"John whatsisname?"

I should tell you a bit about John.

News came to our village mostly from the traders who passed through the market, or from riders working as messengers for the Romans. At that time the only piece of news worth talking about seemed to be this John fella. Not a particularly grand name but if the stories were to be believed then people were, like, *flocking* to see him. They said he carried the word of God and if you heard him speak you'd start to see your life totally differently. To be honest, from what I'd heard, his message just sounded like common sense, not much different from what our dads had taught us. He was basically saying stuff like: *if you've got lots of food and know someone who doesn't have enough, then you should give some of yours to them.* Not catapult science, but people were lapping it up.

There were plenty of preachers around at the time but their audiences were almost entirely made up of destitutes who would buy into anything that promised a way out of their dreary lives. By all accounts this John guy was different. All kinds of people came to him, not just the poor. He had a big old thing going, and word was spreading. His followers were growing too. When I say growing, I mean they were increasing in number, not that they were growing individually. They weren't becoming giants.

The stories were coming thick and fast. Apparently this prophet, preacher, whatever, did this ritual in the river that would change your life. Obviously you had to shave off a big chunk of the hearsay to account for the fact that the further a story travelled, the more it was exaggerated. Bullshit inflation, I call that particular phenomenon. But this guy was clearly a bit special, a cut above the other so-called holy men making a noise at the time.

"What about him?" I said.

"He's my cousin, well not quite, his dad's my mum's cousin, so we're like…" he hesitated.

"Removed?"

"Yeah, we're removed."

"So you've got a celebrity in the family, cool."

"I'm going to go and work with him."

"As a preacher?"

Jesus shrugged. "I don't know to be honest, well – yeah - I guess."

"Is that a business? I mean, is there any money in it?"

"I don't really know. Mum said there's more to it, that it's a big opportunity for me and for the family. She wasn't giving much away though. I'm not sure how much she knows."

"When are you leaving."

"Tomorrow."

"Shit. How long are you going for?"

"I dunno, forever I s'pose."

I've got to be honest, I was gutted. Jesus was my best mate and now he was just fucking off.

But then he spoke again. "Fancy it?"

It never crossed my mind to say anything but yes.

The journey was properly hard going, much harder for me than for Jesus. I missed my family and the simple life I'd left behind. I'd had it comfy before. I'd had everything I needed. Now we were living on the road, just about getting by, and I stress the *just about* part. It wound me up that Jesus was always so calm about everything. We'd be in the middle of nowhere with the sun burning the lids off our eyes and there would be swarms of insects eating us alive and we'd have nothing to eat or drink and Jesus would just… smile. It was like he was in on some private joke.

We made a lot of stops on the way in the towns and villages we passed through. We'd do a bit of work - patching up fences or fixing furniture, that sort of caper - mostly for food, beer and a bed for the night. If we did get paid a few shekels then we'd do our best to save it, and we managed to get a little nest egg together. What I mean is that we put some money aside, not that we were saving up to get married.

I started to enjoy the journey more as I got into my stride and stopped missing home so much. Well it wasn't the journey I enjoyed, it was those stops. We were two young single fellas on the road, getting further and further from home, taking in the tavern culture.

We'd get a lot of attention from the girls, especially in the smaller villages where it was easy to shine if you were from anywhere other than there. I loved Nazareth, obviously. It was my home, but I knew for a fact that you couldn't ever call it exotic. But if some unattached damsel wanted to see me as a colourful traveller from some far off glamorous land then I wasn't exactly going to tell her she was wrong now was I? It wasn't just the unattached ones who showed an interest, though so we had to be careful.

I should point out that I never got first refusal. Just as they were back in Nazareth, the women were all about Jesus.

It pissed me off a bit at first. Okay, so he was better looking than me in an obvious kind of way, with what people called his noble features and unblemished skin. And yes, even I could see that his eyes were pretty special. It hadn't escaped me that they could make a woman's knees buckle at twenty paces. But I was no slouch in the looks department and my face had a lot more character than Jesus' so I'd be lying if I said it didn't get up my nose that every time a girl talked to me she would be asking what *his* story was.

So yes, at first I was bitter that Jesus was way ahead of me in the pulling pecking order but I soon saw the plus side. Being around the world's greatest pussy-lure meant richer pickings for me.

It wasn't just Jesus' looks that made the girls go gooey, it was his *way*. I've never been able to put my finger on it but Jesus has always been able to hold people's attention like nobody else I've ever known. I've thought about it a lot over the years and I still can't work out what it is, this aleph-factor of his. I've thought that maybe it's because he talks all slow and soft and never loses his cool, but I've known plenty of people like that and they tend just to get lost in the noise. Jesus always had this strange power to draw people to him. I suppose I must have fallen under whatever his spell was too, seeing as there I was, unquestioningly following him on a mission to meet some bloke who could apparently make your life better by dunking you in a river.

Our road trip grew progressively messier. We'd drink more, sleep more and work less. We'd find that people seemed willing to put us up without us having to do much at all. A few choice stories about our journey seemed to be enough to pay for a bed for the night. Sometimes, however, the welcoming attitude of the father of the house would change when he saw the way his daughter was looking at us - well okay - at Jesus. More than once we had to do a runner when the host's mood turned from *my home is your home* to *get the fuck out of here or I'll cut your nomad throats*.

All good fun.

## *Herbal Remedy*

I'd heard all the stories about the stir John was causing but I wasn't prepared for what I saw as we shambled down a hillside and the bank of the Jordan came into view. Well actually the bank of the Jordan didn't come into view at all, hidden as it was by a carpet of people.

I'd seen lively marketplaces and busy roads in and out of towns, but I'd never seen so many people packed into one place. It looked like I imagined a Roman army camp to look - pitched up outside a city it's about to fuck over - but far more chaotic and with much smaller tents. We could smell roasting, baking and something else, something herbal that I didn't recognise. And we could hear the sound, the hubbub, of a thousand voices.

Or it could have been tens of thousands. I don't know. It was a lot of voices. A lot of people. And they were all there for one reason – to see the man, Jesus' cousin, or his mum's cousin at least. This was a big deal.

"It doesn't look like we're going to get to this bloke easily," I said. "I think there might be a bit of a queue."

Jesus just shook his head, grinning. "There's no rush. It doesn't look like he's leaving anytime soon. Let's camp here tonight. We'll check it all out in the morning."

That was fine by me.

As darkness fell, the place, lit up by fires and torches, looked even more impressive. The sound of the crowd varied.

Sometimes it was just the random noises of a large number of people going about their business, but then there'd be a huge cheer, a round of applause and even singing. There was music too, harps and lutes being strummed by fingers that in some cases were highly skilled but in others were just clumsy and made a racket. Drummers supplied a constant backbeat and trumpet stabs punctuated the night air. We sat under the stars taking it all in. Sleep was a long time coming that night.

We woke at dawn and didn't hang around. We worked our way down, trying not to get our tunics snagged on all the thistles and other spiky stuff sprouting out of the hillside. We soon entered the outskirts of this makeshift town and broke bread with a group of Phoenicians who were happy to share what they had with us, and even happier to wax lyrical about the mystery man we'd come to see. Most of them had taken part in the ritual to wash their sins away – 'baptism' they said it was called, and according to them their whole outlook on life had changed ever since. They said they felt lighter, *unencumbered by sin* as one of them said. They definitely came across with a certain air of, I don't know, relaxation perhaps.

As we talked I couldn't help noticing that they were passing a clay pipe between them, with each taking a big old drag on it before passing it on. I'd seen pipes before, our dads smoked them in the evenings when the village elders got together, but these were different. Back in Nazareth they were smoked slowly - not sucked for dear life - and back home each man had his own pipe rather than everybody sharing the same one. The smell was different too. It was that same smell we'd noticed from up on the hillside.

"What's in the pipe?" Jesus asked the oldest of the group.

The old Phoenician slowly exhaled a steady stream of thin vapour and smiled knowingly. "The spirit of God." The rest of the group seemed to think this was the funniest thing they'd ever heard, but after they'd stopped laughing, which took a while, most of them glazed over and just stared into space. They still looked well-pleased with the world but as vacant as a bathhouse with a broken stall.

It was time to move on.

The herbal smell became a feature of the day, getting stronger as the groups of – I wasn't sure what to call them, pilgrims, I supposed - became more tightly packed. There were a lot of olive trees about, and olive trees have a pretty distinctive smell, but even they couldn't compete with the aroma of a thousand pipes. Or it could have been tens of thousands. I don't know. It was a lot.

Everybody seemed to be smoking the same stuff. Some had pipes like the one the Phoenicians were passing around, but others had different contraptions, glass and clay jars with curling leather tubes and water bubbling inside when they were sucked.

And all of them were having a fucking ball.

Some were giggling like children while others sat in silence, wearing huge shit-eating grins. There were those with that same look of satisfaction that had settled in the glassy eyes of the Phoenicians and others still who were holding hands, singing, swaying and clapping with excitement. What they all had in common was that they were all fucked, but in the best possible way. And it was still early.

We made slow progress, not just because it was difficult to walk through the crowds but because Jesus was loving being in amongst it all. He was fascinated by the fact that everyone we came across was completely off it. There was this one guy we came across, this tall and gangly bloke, totally off his nut and dancing like a loon. His arms and legs jerked about like they were being tugged by an invisible puppeteer. A puppeteer who was off his head too. His dancing became less spasmodic as we got closer and when he came face to face with Jesus he stopped moving completely and just stared like a tamed animal. Jesus peered into his mad wide eyes, like a doctor fascinated by a previously undiscovered condition. I half expected him to ask the guy to open wide. They kept their eyes locked together but started moving their heads from side to side like they were both trying to catch out a mirror. Suddenly they stopped whatever the hell they were doing and embraced like old mates. After they were done hugging, that was it, the wide-eyed gangly man carried on his way like nothing had happened.

We moved on.

Our slow wandering and constant stopping took up the whole morning and, knowing how unbearable the sun would be soon, we decided to go for a kip in the shade. We met a guy with a food stand and bought bread and fruit. He asked if we needed anything else and looked pretty confused when we declined. I didn't think anything of it at the time.

Everyone else seemed to have had the same idea as us so it wasn't easy to find a tree that wasn't taken. I was jealous of the ones who'd planned ahead and pitched tents in the shade. Eventually we found a space for our tired arses and sat down. I dozed off as soon as I'd finished eating.

A pain in my foot woke me and I heaved my eyes open to see a procession of people filing past. One of them must have trodden on me. Jesus was sitting with his hands wrapped around his knees watching the parade of pilgrims. "Ah, you're awake," he said. "Come on, it's showtime."

We shouldered our bags and followed the herd towards the riverbank. The air was cooler now and there was a real buzz about the place. As we got closer, those in front of us slowed down and finally stopped. We pushed our way through as far as we could until the crowd was too tightly packed for us to get any further. Without climbing over people's heads this was as close as we were going to get. To be honest I was surprised we'd not been given any grief for pushing through as far as we had.

There was no build up, just a hush that started from somewhere in front and spread backwards. A man appeared on what must have been a raised platform, although I could only guess at that because I could only see him from the shoulders up. And that was only by leaning to my right and peering through the gap between the two heads in front of me.

He looked a bit... well, skanky I suppose is the word. His beard was a mess and as for his hair, well it looked like it had insects nesting in it, but when John spoke his deep, booming voice belied his tatty appearance. "Thank you so much for taking the trouble to be here. Firstly, I must apologise for my delivery. There is such a great many of you that I must focus on volume rather than nuance, so if I sound as if I am addressing my deaf grandmother then that is not my intention."

Everybody laughed, including me.

"Some of you will be hearing me for the first time, while others have been here for a while - I recognise many faces. But whether you are an old hand or a first-timer, you are equally welcome. It fills me with cheer and good hope that so many of you are willing to hear my words. Not because I like the sound of my own voice..." he paused to allow a ripple of laughter, "...but because I think I have been given a mission, a mission to deliver a message. The fact that so many of you have gathered to hear that message is something for which I am eternally grateful." He disappeared from view, I guessed because he was bowing, and everyone clapped. Us too.

"I don't want to bore those who have seen me before but I don't want any newcomers to miss out on anything, so please bear with me, I will pitch this speech somewhere in the middle. Is everyone happy with that?"

The crowd roared their affirmation.

John put his hand to his ear theatrically. "I can't quite hear you, what was that?"

The crowd answered twice as loud.

"Look at them." Jesus whispered. "Look at how much they're digging this."

I looked around at the faces of the faithful. Their faces shared a common expression, a blend of rapt attention and unbridled joy.

The two pilgrims in front of me had been exchanging the odd comment but now were having a full scale conversation. Every time they turned their heads to speak to each other it blocked my view. I was getting sick of it. I leaned forward and hissed at them. "Can you two keep still for fuck's sake?" I expected at least one of them to tell me where to stick it but instead they both just smiled at me and said, "Sorry man."

I caught Jesus' eye.

"What?"

He shook his head. "You're such a grumpy bastard."

John spoke for a good while but fair play to him, he kept it punchy and held everybody's attention. Including mine, which is no mean feat because I've got the attention span of a locust. He spoke a lot of common sense - about everyone caring for each other, sharing stuff and all that - but then he went onto a different track. He talked about how you can have the bad things you've done washed away and just… well, start over with a clean slate. I'd heard the holy men speak in the temple every week, but they tended to focus on all the smiting that God was willing to do to folks who didn't obey him. I'd not heard anything like this before.

"Repent your sins - and be honest now - we've all sinned. And if you do, God will forgive you – it's as simple as that. God's no mug though, he does want something back, but the good news is that he doesn't ask for much. All He wants is for us to live our lives as He meant us to, and that's not so hard. We don't need to be scholars in scripture. We just need to be grateful for what we have, to look after each other. If I may put it simply my message is - don't be dicks to each other. I think we can do that, what do you guys think?"

The crowd screamed its approval.

"I've got an early start tomorrow. I'm going to be making good use of this mighty river to wash away the sins of those who wish to start their life refreshed and anew. Who's up for it?"

Another massive cheer.

"Well it sounds like we're going to have a busy day. I'll be ready at sunrise, see you there. Or I may see you sometime over the course of the evening. Either way, once again – thank you so much."

The applause went on and on.

# *Jesus and John*

Jesus was fired up, as fired up as I've ever seen him. He still carried his usual air of calm but his eyes were gleaming. As the crowd gradually scattered, we walked forward past the now visible wooden podium and sat on the bank of the river.

Jesus stared at his feet hanging over the edge, his sandals almost touching the fast-flowing water. "Well, that was something wasn't it?" He didn't look up as he spoke.

"I've never seen anything like it," I said. "He had that crowd in the palm of his hand."

He looked up at me. "You could at least pretend to be impressed."

"I was impressed. That was me being impressed."

"That was you trying to sound impressed."

He was mistaken, I was impressed by John, but I have this problem. I find it really hard to sound sincere, even when I'm genuinely feeling it. It's a condition that's blighted me all my life. People think I'm taking the piss the whole time even when I'm not. Birthdays are the worst. Try thanking someone for a gift knowing full well that you sound about as convincing as a wolf in a sheep-suit. It's really bloody hard.

"You know about my affliction," I said. "You'll just have to take my word for it."

"Oh, of course, your *affliction*."

"Yeah, actually, an affliction's exactly what it is. It's not easy being me."

"Perhaps you shouldn't take the piss, like, all the time. Then people might think you're genuine."

"I don't take the piss all the time."

Jesus raised an eyebrow.

"More often than not I'm not taking the piss."

The eyebrow crept further upwards.

"Half the time?"

I didn't think he could get it any higher but he did.

"The odd occasion?"

Jesus gave his acrobatic eyebrow a well-earned rest. "Agreed," he said.

"And this is one of those odd occasions. So you were wrong. I was being sincere, but because I knew you'd think I wasn't, I got really self-conscious and ended up sounding fake anyway."

Jesus sat back, satisfied. "So I was right."

"Were you not listening? I've just explained why you were wrong."

"I said you were trying to *sound* impressed. Whether you were actually impressed or not is irrelevant. And you've just admitted it. So I win."

"That's bollocks."

"No it's not. And my prize for winning is that I get to do this!" He kicked the heel of my sandal so it flew off my foot into the water.

I watched it drift towards the middle of the river and float away. "You're such a fucker." I didn't bother retaliating, I knew I'd end up kicking the other one in, or maybe even falling in myself, I'd been there too often.

We could hear stuff going on a little way up the bank. Merchants taking delivery of supplies to feed the economy that had sprung up here. It was quite a thing to see - traders haggling over boatloads of bread, fish, meat, rice and vegetables. And plenty of beer and wine. There was even a huge shipment of wood, I presumed for all the campfires. I hoped someone somewhere was selling sandals.

It was time to meet John.

Working our way through the pilgrims was even harder after sunset. Jesus seemed somehow to glide along while I shambled behind him holding my one sandal, tripping on tents and treading on people. I couldn't count the number of limbs I squashed but their owners were too far gone to either notice or care.

People blundered along like the walking dead, going back and forth between the different groups in loose circles around each campfire. Individual parties had annexed their neighbours, forming huge clusters of revellers. The impromptu bands amongst them banged, twanged and blew on their instruments of choice. The clatter of tambourines did battle with the rasp of horns and as we moved from one melody to the next the outgoing and incoming sounds clashed, baffling our ears.

We nearly walked straight past John. I'd expected some sort of fenced-off area with big fancy tents like those used by the preachers who brought their roadshows to Nazareth. But John and his crew were just sitting around a fire like everyone else.

Despite the lack of any status symbols, one thing that did set them apart from the rest of the happy campers was their demeanour. They seemed a bit less excitable, not sombre by any means, but not laughing and screaming like the other revellers. A bit more - I don't know – purposeful maybe.

As I was trying to decide how best to approach this inner sanctum Jesus just stomped his way over and I had to scurry to catch up. I trod on yet another hand as I did so and after apologising to its grinning owner I saw that Jesus' path had been blocked by someone who was more ox than man.

"What's your business, stranger?"

"Family business, friend."

"What name do you go by?"

"The name's Christ, Jesus Christ."

John hadn't looked like he'd been listening but when he heard this he jumped to his feet and bounded over. "My cousin joins us! We are blessed indeed. And what perfect timing, we are just about to feast."

Ox-man stepped back and muttered an apology as John, booming with delight, threw his arms around Jesus. I stood by and let them have their moment until John thrust out a hand for me to shake before getting back to the business of welcoming his long-lost cousin, who as far as I knew he had never met before.

He looked even messier close up. On closer inspection his hair wasn't full of insects, it was just really matted, and the skin on his face told the story of a man who is rarely indoors. It wasn't that he was unclean, he just seemed to have grubbiness ingrained into him, like a lump of rock carved and coloured by constant exposure to the elements. He wore a leather belt around a shabby robe, which I was to find out later was made of camel hair, a bit itchy for my taste.

"Come, take a place beside me near the fire." John's cronies shuffled along to make room. "We will dine, we will talk. We will drink."

Jesus popped the question. "And smoke?"

"Ah, you have noticed the recreational medicine doing the rounds amongst the faithful. I do not indulge myself but feel free to partake if you are of a mind. We have what you might call a supply. In fact…" he leaned between us conspiratorially and lowered his tone, "…that is why you are here."

Suddenly John was filling us in on what exactly was going on here.

He was a preacher, yes, and he had a message that he

wanted people to hear, but there was a lot more to it than that. He was actually born in Nazareth but was only there for a few months before his family went on the move. John's dad ran a small ministry and he took it out on the road, spreading the good word and all that. After some years of the roaming life the old man had decided to settle in the mountains, well away from any kind of civilisation. And that became John's life.

They lived off the land and were schooled by their mum and dad, learning to read and write, scripture mostly. John became an expert on all that holy stuff, the prophecies and all the rest of it. But a person can only study for so long so the rest of the time John and his four brothers and three sisters would hang loose, exploring the mountains that had become their home.

Apparently they got very good at recognising the local wildlife. Being kids, they were mostly interested in the bugs and lizards at first, trying to find the grossest specimens in the cracks in the rocks or deep in the cold, damp caves. But it was plants that would change their lives.

It was at this point that I realised John was in no hurry to finish his story. I wouldn't have minded - I love a good yarn, and John was a master of his craft - but I badly needed to piss. I didn't want to be rude so I just held on tight and hoped for the best.

When their dairy cow was taken ill, John's mum sent the kids out to find all the herbs they could. Like all our mums she had a decent enough understanding of using wild plants and flowers to take the edge off, or even cure, certain types of sickness. So she told the kids to bring back a selection that she could work with.

John had found a particular plant that he hadn't noticed before – a bush with bright green pointed leaves that got more tightly packed towards the top where clumps of small feathery flowers budded. Apparently what had caught his interest in the bush was where it grew; in a half-circle around a tiny pool. The pool was actually the one exposed part of an underground stream that filtered through the mountain from somewhere much higher up. Somewhere that must have caught a lot of the rain that fell during wet season.

I think I might have mentioned that I needed a wee, so you won't be surprised to learn that I wasn't particularly keen to hear about rainwater trickling through mountain streams but I knew Jesus wanted to make a good impression so I kept it shut.

The point of John's lengthy description of the happenstance of the irrigation conditions of this mystery bush, was that it had the best of both worlds. It was in full sunshine but had all the water it needed. I got the picture, the growing conditions were perfect. Unlike the content of his story, John cut off a sizeable part of the bush, which he took home to his mum.

And she didn't recognise it so she didn't use it in the concoction she was putting together for the cow.

Just before I shouted something along the lines of *well why the fuck did you tell us every bloody detail about where you found it and what it looked like then?* he got to the point, although not straight away. First he told us how the sickly cow had fared. It lived. His mother's remedy cleared a blockage in its food pipe or something. Fair play to John's mum and good luck to the cow. And *then* he got to the point. Finally. Jesus.

Once she'd saved Daisy's life, John's mum had turned her attentions to the rapidly drying bundle of leaves and buds John had brought home with him. Over the next few weeks she tried a few things, had a bit of a dabble.

And one afternoon, John and his brothers and sisters came home to find both their parents completely off their boxes.

John and his siblings had been playing in the valley at the foot of the mountains, running races mostly…. and I couldn't believe it, he'd gone off-topic again! Thankfully Jesus, who could probably see that I was doubled over in agony and was soon going to say something - the wrong kind of something - politely intervened and steered him back on track.

John's mum had separated different parts of the plant and tried burning them to see what kind of scent they gave off. She was trying to see if they were anything like the incenses she'd used in healing treatments before. Apparently she noticed that when she sniffed one part of the burning dried plant, she felt light-headed. And not in a bad way. One thing led to another and it wasn't long before she'd packed the dried buds into a clay tube and toked the whole thing down. She sounded like a pretty curious woman, and resourceful too, but I didn't ask any more about her because I was certain I was about to wet my robe.

When John's parents realised what they had, they started to cultivate the crop. They learned how and when to prune to get the best yield, when to starve them of light to shock the plants into budding and the best drying techniques. What began as a hobby quickly became a business, with John's mum and sisters focusing on production while John, his brothers and his dad took the product, which they called 'green' because they couldn't think of anything better, out into the nearby villages.

As John pointed out, people didn't have much to do back then, you didn't have circuses and chariot races like you get now, so anything that made their lives more fun - after all the work in the fields or whatever - was always going to go down well. And it went down like a fat gladiator.

So behind John's ministry, behind all the wise words from which his flock were so happily suspended, his main business was keeping his followers supplied with the product, the green.

They kept to the out-of-the-way areas because it kept them from attracting too much attention from the Romans who ran things in the bigger towns. It was a funny kind of set-up though because it wasn't like the Romans didn't know about the family's business – quite the opposite in fact. A good part of the crop was sent straight to Rome, and more to Alexandria and other cities of which a provincial boy like me could only dream.

John's family's business didn't break any laws, but it wasn't something the tribunes and prefects who took delivery of these shipments were shouting from the rooftops either. It was a kind of open secret, almost as if everyone involved had signed an agreement to keep it on the down-low and not cause any trouble, just in case.

The cash from all this, so he said, didn't just get pocketed. A lot of it went to good causes - feeding the hungry, helping lepers, that sort of thing. But for someone who'd just made a story five times longer than it needed to be it was interesting that he didn't add any detail as to what 'a lot' actually meant. I thought better of asking, and not just because I was about to explode in a shower of urine.

John's patch of the business was the furthest west, and the plan was that Jesus would open up a new market, increasing their reach in this region. It was news to Jesus that John's parents, the kingpins of this empire, had been writing to Jesus' mum regularly. Jesus' involvement had obviously been planned for a while.

All of this, apart from the pointless detail, was totally mind-blowing to me. You have to remember that I was from literally nowhere. A place where nothing ever happened and one generation followed the next in whatever trade their ancestors had got good at. Now my eyes had been opened to a world I didn't even know existed. A world of clandestine syndicates, deals with the big players in the mighty Roman Empire. At first my mind couldn't take it all in, partly because it was so huge and unimaginable, but mostly because I needed to pee so very badly.

I made my excuses and hobbled to a tree where I made like a ruptured aqueduct.

## Public Stoning

I'd been told about the city of Rome, about its paved plazas, palaces, temples and rows of houses where people lived on top of each other. It was so alien to me that it may as well have been on the moon. In Nazareth we didn't see much of the Romans. Herod Antipas, our tetrarch - which means not quite a king but for us little people he may as well have been - wasn't a Roman but he did exactly what the Romans told him, and as a result they didn't bother us.

To me they were a superhuman race, and the fact that John's family's product was shipped to the heart of their empire was huge to me, a wet-behind-the-ears young man from a tiny backwater at the arse end of nowhere. I quickly realised there was no point dwelling on the enormity of the thing. I was here now so the only thing I could do was go along with it and enjoy it. John's crew started serving up hefty portions of food and someone handed me a beer. That helped.

I asked John how come he didn't have a better set-up for himself, something a bit plusher to sleep in, better clothes, all that malarkey.

"That, my friend," he said, "is exactly the point. If I were to openly display the trappings of success then it may appear to the people that I don't consider myself to be one of them, that I am different from them, *better* than them even. That would be disastrous, not just because it is simply not true - I am a man of the people and proud of it – but purely in terms of business, I

need the people to see me as one of their own. I ne
trust. So I don't live the life of a prefect despatch
Rome, clad in silk and entertained by dancing girls. That life
would not suit me anyway. I see plenty of girls dancing of their
own accord, and they're a lot more fun to be with. I like the
dust and grime and feel of real life. And aside from my business
and my own personal tastes, there is my message to consider. I
would not be taken seriously if I were fat and rich."

"But does your message matter that much? Isn't it just a
front for the real business, the product?"

John scowled. "Careful now my young apprentice. If you
are suggesting that when I preach I am doing it for any other
reason than to touch people's hearts then you are on
treacherous ground indeed. I know you mean no harm so we
will say no more about it, but please never again accuse me of
hypocrisy."

That was me told.

I had to hand it to John, he was a cracking host. We got
talking to his cronies too, his close and trusted friends, as he
put it. They were a good crowd, and they had plenty of beer.

Simon and Thaddeus were the best of the bunch. They were
my kind of people, particularly Thaddeus, who just seemed to
want to party. I was stuffed with food and pretty well gone
from the booze when I saw him packing a pipe with green.
Simon saw me looking. "You are our distinguished guests, you
get to go first."

"Shouldn't they go after me?" Thaddeus asked. "I'd be, like,
showing them how to do it and stuff."

"No, Thad, you can bloody well wait your turn."

"But I just packed it."

"Yes, you very kindly packed it for our distinguished
guests."

"I'm first after them though."

"I apologise for my friend, he sometimes lets his hedonism obstruct his manners."

I felt like everyone was laughing at me as I had my first smoking lesson, mostly because everyone *was* laughing at me. I held the pipe in one hand and was given a long taper, burning at one end. Thaddeus told me to hold the flame to the bowl and suck on the pipe while it burned. I was crap at it. I didn't know how long I was meant to suck for and it was really hard to keep the thing burning while I was doing the sucking. I was sure I wasn't doing it right because I couldn't feel anything going in, but all the time Thaddeus was repeating his rallying call - *keep going, man, keep going* - I kept on sucking. Everyone cheered when I was done, but to be honest I felt a bit let down, nothing was different.

And then everything was different.

It's hard to explain how it felt but I'll give it a go. Everything felt smooth, like marble, but fuzzy and soft too - sort of like lambswool. When I say *felt* I don't mean to the touch, I mean like you'd feel hot or cold. I know that doesn't make any sense but that's how it was. On top of that everything became massively intense but really laid back all at the same time.

Thaddeus took the pipe off me and I stared, fascinated, as he repacked it. I swear I could see every tiny piece of the dried and shredded plant taking its place in the bowl, exactly where it should be. I watched - wondering why nobody had noticed that I suddenly had a great big moon face - as Jesus put the pipe to his lips. With the pipe in his mouth he turned his head towards me and I was sure he was trying to prod me with it for a laugh. It took a while for my messed up mind to take in what was happening: I was still holding the burning taper and he was waiting for a light. This cracked me up and then everything cracked me up. I laughed hysterically at how ridiculous it was that Jesus was always so damned cool, and because of my huge face and because of everything else that was going on in front of me and in my head.

"Stop shaking, you're wobbling it about," Jesus hissed with his mouth full of pipe. I watched the bowl chasing the flame as it danced about in the air in front of me, seemingly of its own volition. This made me laugh even more and by sheer coincidence the movement of the flame became quicker and more erratic. A hand appeared from somewhere behind me - a hand even bigger than my big face - and wrapped itself over my wrist, locking it in position.

Jesus took a big old hit. He held it down then let the smoke out real slow. There was a pause - just a moment - before his face melted into a grin. "That is definitely the spirit of God right there, fuck yeah!"

And that's when the laughter really started.

Jesus' smile was the biggest I'd ever seen. It was like it was going to burst out of the sides of his face, yet somehow it was still getting bigger. All the time I was watching I was laughing loud enough to raise the dead. It was lucky I'd had that piss not long before or it would have been like the rivers of Babylon in my loincloth. I was out of control. "Please don't make me laugh anymore, it hurts, it really fucking hurts."

Jesus pulled a puzzled face. "How am I making you laugh?"

"You know, you know exactly how. With your face, and everything."

"With my face?" He started changing his expression - from curious to confused, startled to scared, exhausted to envious - and with each new face I laughed even harder. I genuinely thought my insides were going to rupture, but my fear of that did nothing to stem my hysterics. When Jesus got to surprised I was curled into a ball and sobbing like a madman.

John's mates were loving our reaction to their product. They hadn't even had a go on the pipe yet but they were giggling nearly as much as we were. By the time they'd each taken a hit (and Thad *did* go first after us) it was chaos. Everyone around the fire was rolling around, trying to talk but not being able to because of all the laughing, which made it even funnier and – well you get the drift. We were having a good time.

The air of purpose I'd noticed about them earlier was long gone.

It was a bit like being on the beer, but more relaxed, more focused, more funny. One big difference was how much it made me want to eat. We'd literally just had a feast, but all through the evening I wanted more and more food. These guys were well stocked with tucker so I made an absolute pig of myself. Jesus was the same, worse actually. I'd never seen him eat so much.

It's difficult to say because of the state I was in but I reckon Jesus was the most off it. He couldn't get enough. He kept calling for another go on the pipe long after I'd hit my limit. If I'd been in his sandals I would have been spark out on the floor a long time ago.

"You know what this is?" Jesus was holding a crust of bread all up in my face.

"Some bread?"

"It's fucking magic. It's the bread of God." He took a massive bite then picked up a half-full bottle of wine and took a swig with his mouth still full of stodge. "And do you know what this is?" Bits of bread and wine flew out of his mouth.

"A nice drop of wine?"

"You're close." He pulled me to him so he could speak right into my ear, but he didn't whisper, in fact he shouted proper loud. "It's the wine of God. And look, look look. Look at old John over there, you know what he's chewing on?"

"No Jesus, I don't know what John's chewing on."

"The lamb of God."

John held up the wing he was eating. "Actually it's chicken, but I dig your enthusiasm." Jesus didn't register whether he'd heard him or not, or acknowledge the fact that everybody was pissing themselves, either at him or with him, I wasn't sure which. I didn't think it mattered much anyway.

It was like we were possessed by demons, but not evil ones, more like stupid ones that just wanted to have a laugh at anything and everything. Every now and again it would seem to ease off, like the laughter-imps were having a rest, but then it would kick in again. There was a good chance that this was because we kept taking hits on the pipe, but I like my demon theory better.

During one of these easing-off moments I had a bit of a chat with John. He wasn't drinking - I learned later that he didn't touch the hard stuff - but he seemed more than happy watching his crew having a scream. He was like the proud dad at a wedding.

"Jesus says you met once, but he was too small to remember."

"That's right, I met the baby Jesus, or rather, the infant Jesus. The day I arrived, he took his first steps. He walked straight into the river. It was as if he had assumed he could walk on the water. Of course he just sank. I had to pull him out. I still remember it to this day, mostly because of his reaction. Even though he had just had what must have been a terrible shock, he wasn't crying. In fact he was smiling from ear to ear - rather like the smile he is wearing right now, the one that looks as if it could very well split his face open." Jesus saw us looking and stuck his tongue out before turning back to Simon, with whom he was putting the world to rights.

I suppose I could have asked John about what my Grandma had said about Jesus' dad, but I didn't want to know. Jesus would tell me if he wanted to. And it didn't change who he was.

He was my friend. All these new people, they were my friends too. We'd, like, connected. The whole world seemed to be my friend. I was out of my fucking tree.

"I need to go wee wee." I stood up and tried to point myself in the direction of the tree I'd used as a latrine earlier.

"It's that way." John was very patient and helpful for someone who wasn't messed up. If it had been the other way round I would have sent him in the wrong direction so I could mess with him and watch him blunder about.

Jesus called out. "Wait a minute, I need to go too." He hoisted himself up onto his feet. "Show me where the magic pissing-tree is."

The tree was about thirty paces away but we walked a lot further than that because we couldn't seem to keep in a straight line. Eventually we made it and braced our backs against the tree and let fly. We decided we looked like one of those fancy Greek fountains you might see at a city bathhouse. When we were done and were staggering back Jesus grabbed my arm, his eyes were hooded and he was still wearing that massive grin. "This is amazing," he said, "amazing! I'll tell you what, I feel numb all over, like I've been stoned – but in a good way."

"Stoned, yeah, that's it!"

# The Next Big Thing

Obviously I felt horrendous the next morning. Hangovers I can handle, but this was so much more. It was like some important piece inside my head had dissolved, leaving a gaping hole. This made the business of thinking problematic. It was like my internal dialogue had lost its memory. Where previously, thoughts would trickle from one to the next, making some sort of connection as they went, now it seemed that by the time I'd reached the next idea in the sequence its predecessor would have gone walkabout and I'd be left with a seemingly random image in my head with nothing to link it back to its conception.

Looking back, what should have been more concerning to me than the dams in my stream of thought was the fact that I was aware of my own thought processes at all. I'd got through life up to that point with the contents of my head just doing their thing, like my legs or my eyes. Now I appeared to be studying the constituent parts of my perception like broken machinery on a workbench. And there's always a risk that when you take something apart you won't be able to get it back together again.

Jesus must have felt at least as bad as me, but being Jesus he carried it loads better than I did. Bastard. Some of John's mates had been to the river and filled all the pots with fresh water, so that was something. They'd picked up some fresh bread too but I couldn't face any of that. In fact I was scared to move in case everything I'd stuffed into my mouth the night before would come flying back up again. I tried not to think about it then wished I hadn't thought about trying not to think about it, because then all I could think about was how my stomach was full of sick. And because my head had lost its ability to marshal my thinking I was left lingering on that gross image for much longer than is polite. I eventually shifted onto something else but that something was even worse: the realisation that all food turns into sick once it's been eaten, but normally it doesn't get sicked up so technically we're all walking around with our stomachs full of sick all the time.

This wasn't going well.

But it wasn't just me who was feeling it. When I first woke up I could hear so much groaning it was like the Appian Way when the Romans were nailing up Spartacus and his mob.

Jesus was standing over me. "I don't want to be a pain in the arse but we're going to have to get going soon, they're all down at the river. John's going to be pissed if we're not there."

I squinted up at him. "Could you shift your head just a bit to the left?"

"That any good?"

"Bit more – that's it. Perfect." The sun was no longer in my eyes, which meant I could stop pulling a face like Methuselah threading a needle. "Did he say he wanted us to be there?"

"No, but that's not the point. We should show willing. We have to make a good impression, it being our first day and all."

"Your head has got this, like, *glow* around it."

"That'll be the sun."

"Yeah, it should be that but it looks like it's coming from - I dunno - inside you."

"You're still fucked. And don't change the subject, the point is that we've got to go and see John do his thing."

"I doubt he'll mind. He seems pretty laid back, mostly anyway, unless you put your foot in your mouth like I did last night, but he was cool after that."

"I don't care if he'd mind - I'd mind. We need to do this. He must be used to having a load of piss takers trying it on with him. We need to show him we're not like that, we're the real deal. Come on, get up." He moved his head over and I was struck in the eyes again by the sun's glare.

"You said you didn't want to be a pain in the arse."

"Exactly, I said I didn't want to be, not that I wouldn't be. You're making me act like this." He started nudging my leg with the end of his sandal. "Look what you're making me do." He stepped up the pace, kicking me over and over in the same spot. It was massively annoying and more than a bit painful. "Stop it, stop making me do this. You know how much I hate doing this." He didn't bother hiding the fact that he was finding himself highly amusing.

"Alright, I'm coming. Keep your beard on." I dragged myself off the ground and stood up. It was an ill-judged move. As I fell to my knees, Jesus - recognising this stark warning sign - lurched backwards. He was just in time to avoid the arc of puke that gushed out of me and splattered everywhere. The next heave wasn't far behind and it was quickly followed by another, and of course another - you know the drill - we've all been there. Then it was time for my favourite part: the dry heaves. My body was still going all-out to expel its demons even though there was nothing left inside me. I waited it out and when it was over I stood up - mostly so I wasn't kneeling in my own sick and rested my hands on my knees. I was there for a while, wheezing and spitting. "Jesus."

"What?"

I shook my head. "Nothing. Just…. Jesus."

"You're not talking to me are you?"

"Jesus."

"I don't get why you do that."

I couldn't answer him, not without hurling again.

Obviously nobody likes chucking their guts up, least of all me, but after a while I realised it was the best thing that could have happened. I still felt like death but at least I could move now. I'd quite literally got it out of my system.

I was suddenly as hungry as hell and His Highness deigned to let me have a few mouthfuls of bread before we went on our way.

The camp looked like Troy must have done after the siege, all eerie emptiness, smouldering ashes and corpses scattered about. Okay, so they weren't corpses, they'd just passed out. Not so much the result of siege warfare but a skinful of beer and green.

"How come you're not in as much of a state as I am?" I asked as I picked my way along, acutely aware that there must have been other puddles of vomit dotted about the place. "You were all over it last night."

"Don't remind me," Jesus answered, visibly cringing. "I think I made a massive prick of myself. I was like an excited little kid. That's why I'm so keen to show John we're not wasters."

"You weren't a *massive* prick."

"But still a prick, yeah? Thanks mate, I can always count on you to make me feel better."

"No problem, happy to help. So what about that green?"

Jesus smiled. "First go I had on that pipe I thought - where have you been all my life?"

"Did you know this was what it was all going to be about, y'know, the family business?"

"Mum never mentioned it. She only talked about the ministry part. Maybe she didn't know about the rest herself."

"Maybe, it would have been a difficult thing to explain. Look, we're nearly there."

"Look at all those people," Jesus said. "It's like you were not so long ago... heaving."

"You've been waiting to use that line all the way down here haven't you?"

"Might have been. How are the guts by the way?"

"They're fine, thanks."

"In case you get the idea that I was showing any concern for your well-being, I was just worried you might show us up by chundering in front of everyone."

"That's how people are going to remember you after you're gone - as a really caring fucker."

He was right about the heaving thing though. Everyone had come down, at least everyone who could stand after last night. I was pretty curious to see what it was all about, this baptism thing. The atmosphere was different from yesterday when John had done his turn for the crowd. It was more relaxed; less of a show and more a group activity. Everyone was sitting down, which suited me because my legs weren't playing nice that morning.

I was happy to sit at the back but Jesus grabbed my arm and led us right down to the front. I sat all hunched because I was sure it must have pissed off the people behind that we'd just plonked ourselves down in front of them. I didn't hear any tutting though.

There was a part of the river that stuck out, with a row of boulders separating it from the main channel and protecting it from the strong current. John stood in the pool that had formed, the water almost up to his chest. I need to point out at this point that in the walk down there the sun had been buried by thick cloud and even though it wasn't a cold day it was still early, so that water would have been nippy at best. I didn't know how he wasn't shivering.

A pilgrim stepped in to join him, and again, if it had been

me walking into that river I would have been jerking my feet back up after each step like I was walking on hot coals. But this guy looked like he was easing himself into a warm bath. He didn't even wince when the water reached his knackers.

Everybody was cheering.

John talked to the hardy pilgrim for a while, gave a short but grand speech about washing away his sins, then rested one hand on the guy's back and one on the top of his head before lowering him backwards into the river. As he lifted him out again the guy snorted water out of his nose and punched the air with delight. Everyone cheered.

The bloke was being helped out of the river looking chuffed to bits when John called out. "Ladies and gentlemen, we have an esteemed guest amongst us and I hope you will all make him feel welcome." The crowd applauded as Jesus stood up and did a slow full-turn, smiling and waving. Bit presumptuous, I thought, seeing as John hadn't actually said who he was talking about yet. He *could* have been talking about me.

John was clapping his hands above his head, which I guess is the only way you can clap when you're almost up to your neck in water. "Come, join me! Let's do this."

The applause grew as Jesus waded into the water. Just like the last guy, he didn't flinch at all even when his loincloth went under. John threw his arms around him then turned to the crowd, keeping one arm over Jesus' shoulder. "This is the man of whom I have spoken. He may not yet know it himself, but he will become a great man. He is the Lamb of God. John threw me a wink to mark the reference to the lamb thing from the night before. Nice touch.

With a dramatic shake of the head John's tone changed. "Hold on, hold on. Just wait a moment. This isn't right. I should not be doing this. I do not have the authority. It is this great man who should be baptising me."

Jesus spoke quietly, only those of us right near the front would have been able to hear. "No, you're alright," he said. "Let's keep it simple."

"But how can I wash away the sins of one who has never sinned?"

Jesus pulled a face and whispered even more quietly. "There might have been a few… little sins."

"Shh," John hissed through the side of his mouth before slipping back into his addressing-the-multitude persona. "I am not worthy of this but so be it. I will cleanse this man. But first let me say this… a new era will be upon us soon. The powers that be should take note - everything we know will change, and soon. This is the man who will rise to greatness in this new dawn for mankind. Today he becomes a vital part of my ministry but there will be a time when he will have a ministry of his own. Look around, see how many of you good people are gathered here. We are legion." The crowd cheered. "But this right here, great as it may be, is nothing compared to the number who will follow this man. So watch this space. Or rather, watch this face!" He raised Jesus' arm, like he was declaring the winner of a bout of the old Greco-Roman. Jesus beamed. The crowd cheered and cheered and cheered.

John put his hand on the top of Jesus' head. "I baptise you here in this place, with these good people as witnesses." He looked at the sky and weirdly, at that very moment, the sun came out. And I mean really came out. I don't know if it was just the contrast of it having been cloudy before so it seemed extra bright at that exact moment, but it was properly dramatic. Especially to a crowd that's been whipped into a near-frenzy.

"Go free from sin." John tipped Jesus backwards into the water and lifted him back out again. The crowd went fucking nuts.

# Touching the Void

We were now part of the crew, and thanks to John's very public introduction to the assembled masses, Jesus was now a big face in this off-beat community. It was more like a tribe really, and more people were joining up every day.

We quickly got into the swing of things. Most mornings we'd be at the river helping organise the pilgrims who queued patiently to be dunked in the water. There wasn't a huge amount of organisation needed if I'm honest. Everyone was cool because they loved John so much and of course because most of them were smashed off their tits. All we had to do was show them where to sit, make sure they were comfortable, knew when it was their turn and had something to dry themselves off with when they came out. That was all there was to it.

We'd be done by late morning and we'd normally have an early lunch, a cheeky pipe then sleep it off for a few hours. If John was giving a speech that evening then we'd help with that, but again, there wasn't really much to be done. It was basically just John standing on the platform and talking, it wasn't like we had to lug scenery about. We'd just stand nearby and look like we knew what we were meant to be doing. As the numbers grew it got more difficult for people at the back to hear but nobody seemed to mind. They seemed happy enough just being immersed in the good vibe.

The rest of the time I'd work the product. Simon and

Thaddeus managed that side of things, which in Thad's case seemed like putting Herod in charge of a nursery, but they looked to do a decent enough job of it. I'd be given a weight of green each day to take out and about amongst the faithful. I wasn't given scales but quickly learned how to measure it out by eye. After I'd shifted the contents and tallied it up at the end of each day I'd always only be slightly over or under, so it pretty much evened out. I never once had to actually sell the stuff, I'd just go around chatting to people, they'd soon ask if I was holding. People started recognising my face.

Jesus didn't do any selling. Instead he spent time with John, learning from the master. I deliberately avoided asking what sort of things he talked about in these private chats because I didn't want to sound like I was bothered by it. I confess I was worried that it might go to his head, being specially selected and announced as the chosen one and all, but my fears were completely unfounded. When we hooked up in the evenings he'd always be up for getting smashed and wouldn't mind making a tit of himself along with all the rest of us.

I spent a lot of time with Simon and Thad. They were an unlikely double act. Thad was tall and languid. The perma-frown etched softly into his brow implied he understood nothing, but his eyes suggested he knew a lot more than he was letting on. Simon was a more compact unit: neater, better groomed and better spoken, more comfortable being the centre of attention and more demanding of it. He was from posh stock, or at least liked to make out he was. It was difficult to tell what Thad's background was because he acted like he was stoned all the time. It was as if someone had taken Thad when he was a baby, packed him into a massive pipe of green and smoked the lot - and the effects had stayed with him ever since.

They were both good value in their own way. Simon liked to take the piss but didn't mind if you gave it right back, in fact he actively encouraged it. He was a good sparring partner. He was a demon storyteller too. He had a huge arsenal of words at his disposal and his timing was immaculate. He could make you die laughing just with a well-placed pause in a sentence. Thad was quieter but whenever he chose to speak he'd come out with pure gold. He packed a mean pipe too.

Life was good for a while, really good. I liked the people I worked with, I liked the people I met, I liked eating and drinking, and I liked getting high. I also realised that I'd started believing in John's message and buying into what he was trying to do. I was starting to appreciate what he was giving these followers of his, apart from the opportunity to have a party every night.

I managed to get hold of a new pair of sandals too. Result.

Given the choice I would have happily stayed there indefinitely but the choice, as it turned out, wasn't mine to make. It took just one night for everything to change. For everything to go to shit.

It was just like any other night. We were hammering it hard - booze, food and plenty of green. We were all over it. John came and sat between me and Jesus. "Gentlemen. How would you like to try - now, how do you youngsters say it - a whole new kind of headfuck?"

Jesus fixed him with that big old grin. "What you got?"

"What I have here, gentlemen, is the future." He held up a small wooden bowl with some shiny resin in the bottom. "It's a new kind of buzz."

Jesus stuck his face in the bowl and had a big sniff. He was like a curious dog with that hooter of his. "Smells like poppies."

John slapped him on the back and nearly knocked him into the fire. "That's quite a nose you have there, you are correct. It is indeed poppy extract, just the right part of the poppy, the part that takes you to heaven."

"Doesn't repenting your sins and leading you a good life send you to heaven?" I asked.

"Well, yes, but this does it much more quickly and you get to come back again. Are you chaps in? We'll call it training - after all, you'll be selling it when you take the business west."

Jesus grinned again. "You had me at headfuck."

John called Thaddeus over. "My dearest Thad, would you be so kind as to show our newest recruits how to make use of the contents of this bowl?" He patted us each on the back as he stood up. "Now please excuse me, I have other calls on my attention."

Thad was more than happy to oblige. He reached into his pouch and pulled out a different kind of pipe than I'd seen before. It had a longer, much narrower stem and – oh for fuck's sake the pipe's not important, what's important is what was in that bowl. Where do I start? Well it was a bit like being on the green but not at all really. It was a much heavier hit and a thousand times more intense. It wasn't as sociable as the green, but that was okay, we had all day to talk to each other. It felt like the inside of my head was a foreign land, ripe for exploring. There was all sorts going on in there - weird images, lights and stories, like dreams but dreams you could get hold of and steer wherever you wanted them to go. It was like writing and starring in your own play as you went along. Or you could just lay back and let yourself be taken on your own personal mystery tour. It was all good.

And it was all set against the overwhelming feeling that everything was cool.

But in reality everything was far from cool. Everything was pretty well fucked. While we'd been busy kissing the sky, a couple of riders had arrived in the camp and made a beeline for John. The first we heard about it was when John came hurrying over, his face noticeably pale even in the shadowy glow of the fire.

"You have to leave. The Romans are coming."

The riders were messengers, and like all messengers, they had a message. Apparently the wrong person had heard one of John's speeches, the one about this new era that was on its way and how the powers that be should take note. Either deliberately or just through the rumour mill, word had got to some very powerful people and they hadn't liked what they'd heard. Whatever John had meant about this big change, the powers that be had taken note of it. The word was that John's army would soon be under attack. It would have been funny for us, a bunch of stoners doing no harm to anybody to be thought of as an army, if it wasn't so terrifying.

John had the word put out to everyone in the camp. The message was a simple one: *run for your fucking life*.

The thing about being out of your head is that it can, up to a point, protect you from bad things. It doesn't make the bad things any better; it just makes you a lot less bothered about them. But when it's something extreme - extreme enough to cut right through that couldn't give a fuck wall - then you're in real trouble. The bad thing becomes the worst thing that there's ever been. All the good in the buzz is hijacked by whatever the bad thing is and forged into the purest, nastiest downer. This can sometimes happen even if the bad thing isn't really that bad at all, so when the bad thing is that you're about to be attacked by the most powerful army the world has ever seen, then – well – you get the picture. It's bad.

John had two horses brought over and he told us to get on. I wasn't really in control of my movements but somehow I ended up on the back of this nag. John gestured vaguely in one direction. "Go. Go now."

I wanted to say something but my mouth felt like it was on backwards. I was still trying to work out the best way to open and close it and after I'd got the hang of that my next plan was to try and get some sound to come out. Once I'd managed that I was going to have a crack at making the sounds into words.

"What about you?" Jesus asked.

"Let me worry about that," said John.

"We're not just going to bugger off and leave you to it." I marvelled at Jesus' ability to form sentences. He should have been as fucked as me. He continued to fire questions at John – why weren't we all leaving together, when we would we see him again - but John cut the conversation short by slapping Jesus' horse hard on the arse. It screamed, whinnied - whatever - and bolted off into the darkness. By the time I realised the obvious, that John was about to do the same to my ride, he'd already done it. I was off.

We were on horseback heading God knows where with God knows who on our tail. We were, as you can imagine, spinning the fuck out.

My horse seemed to be running on the spot, with the sky and the rocks and the ground and the trees all flying backwards past me, going faster and faster. I was convinced the whole world would just keep on unravelling and end up behind me, leaving me in some bottomless void. I was understandably terrified. But in amongst this nightmare of sensations a tiny little compartment of my mind was buzzing with pure euphoria, screaming over and over - *man this is cool, bring that bad boy on, let's check out the void!*

The worst thing was the moon. It was huge and fat and looking right at me, twisting its moon face into all kinds of expressions, fixing me with a crazy moon stare with its big moon eyes and screaming and laughing like all hell. But I soon came to realise that the screaming and laughing was all coming from me.

And then I realised that apart from the moon, I was alone.

Where was he? Jesus!

## From Heaven to Hell

I can't give any proper details of what happened that night, it was just a mess of shapes, colours, sounds and a medley of other sensations, some of them real and some the product of the mayhem in my head. The one thing I do know for sure is that at some point I must have stopped riding, but the only reason I know that is that I no longer had a horse.

I was alone in the wilderness.

It was early. The sun was only just creeping out so it was cold, very cold. I was thirsty and although my head wasn't spinning anymore, it still didn't feel right. In fact it felt quite wrong, like it had been kidnapped and horribly abused before being released back to its worried family, traumatised by its ordeal. I had no idea what to do, so I did the only thing I could do. I started walking.

I fixed on one piece of logic to keep me going. As far as I knew I hadn't crossed the river, which was in the east and ran north to south. That meant that if I headed east I'd hit water sooner or later, probably later, but at least it was a plan. It wasn't like I was weighed down with other options.

In case the danger of never reaching the river wasn't enough of a worry, I was lucky enough to have looming over me the threat of being found by Roman soldiers. Obviously they had no way of knowing if I was one of John's followers or not, but from what I knew of the Romans they tended to err on the side of caution when it came to crushing a perceived revolt. And by err on the side of caution I mean they would stab first and ask questions later. Very stabby bunch, the Romans.

But in the fun game of *Guess How My Imminent Death is Going to Happen* that I was playing in my head, summary execution by Roman soldiers wasn't that high on the list. Thirst was at the top followed by exhaustion, animal attack and although I'd eaten the night before, I knew that hunger was going to become a real problem within a day or so. In fact, after a little while in the hot sun with no food or water then perhaps being found by the Romans would be a mercy. Unless they chose to crucify me, which would be a right pain.

With my so-called plan in place I used the rising sun to get my bearings and walked east. The only way I can describe the experience was that it was the worst possible combination of boredom, pain and despair. My throat burned from lack of water, my body ached all over and my feet were blocks of fire. I couldn't bring myself to look at the blisters I could feel bubbling all over the soles of my feet like melting wax gnarling the stem of a burning candle. There was no point looking to see what was going on down there because there was nothing I could do about it. It wasn't like I'd packed any myrrh. To add to the fun, I seemed to be carrying passengers. All kinds of bugs had cadged a ride in my beard, hair and in all the sweaty nooks and crannies of my disgusting body.

I don't know how long I carried on like that. I kept count of the nights at first but soon lost track on account of the endless repetition. I won't try and build the tension, you know I survived, at least long enough to write all this down, so I'll get to the point. I found some water – an oasis I guess you'd call it - a pool surrounded by rocks and trees. There were even fish swimming around in it. That meant I could not only drink but eat too. Obviously I had to eat the fish raw. In fact the first one I ate may well have still been alive when I sank my teeth into its belly. I didn't have the strength to smack its head on a rock and didn't have the patience to wait for it to suffocate.

It might sound like I wasn't particularly excited about the against-the-odds discovery that without a doubt saved me from collapsing and dying in the desert, but I was far too exhausted to celebrate.

I sat in the shade of a tree with my legs in the pool, letting the water take the edge off my ruined feet. I tried to think about things logically. My body and mind were a mess, but there was no longer an immediate danger of death. In all the days and nights of walking there had been just one plan in my head – walk east, walk east, reach the river. Now I'd reached some kind of sanctuary, I had a choice to make for the first time in a long time.

Should I stay or should I go?

I decided to wait where I had food, drink and some kind of shelter, at least long enough for my wounded feet to heal and for some of my strength to return. Nothing else about my situation had changed so east would still be the way to go once I was ready.

My mind was made up. Now all there was to do was sleep like an absolute bastard.

It was a new day when I woke up, nearly the middle of the day in fact. The first thing I did was have a piss, a thick, dark piss that burnt like liquid salt, but a piss all the same, my first in ages.

I had a drink and thought about catching a fish for breakfast. They were slow-moving and easy to catch. I guessed they fed on the insects that buzzed around just above the water and dropped in when they died. My arrival had created a circular food chain: I ate the fish, the fish ate the insects, and the insects ate me. I was reminded once again of one of the main problems of leaving on the hop when a horde of Romans is coming to kill you – you don't tend to stop to pack balms and ointments. Romans wouldn't take too kindly to being called a horde though, they're always banging on about how civilised they are. But when you think about all the twisted ways they have of killing people, the word civilised doesn't quite seem to fit.

"Fuck off fuck off fuck off fuck off!" To say that the sudden sound of a man screaming made me jump is both pointless and a massive understatement. The shock felt like I'd been punched in the guts. The voice didn't sound at all friendly, but then that's another pointless thing to say - it's not really possible to shout the phrase *fuck off* in an amiable way.

It had come from behind the trees on the far side of the watering hole. I knelt down and scooped up the biggest rock I could find, well not the biggest one, the biggest one that I could actually lift and use in a fight, which because of my weakened state turned out to be quite a small stone; more of a pebble really. I was hoping it wasn't going to come to violence because I didn't fancy my chances against the owner of that voice. I'm rubbish at fighting at the best of times. And this certainly wasn't the best of times.

I walked slowly and carefully around the pool and peered through the trees. It was difficult to see any detail because the sun was behind him and I couldn't do much more than squint, but he looked like he was sitting down about thirty paces away. I say 'he', I was pretty sure it was a man. The fuck offs hadn't sounded female.

I looked around as best I could to see if anyone else was with him. He seemed to be alone. That was something.

It crossed my mind to creep up on him, but I didn't really know what I'd gain by that. It wasn't like I was going to jump on him and bash him to death with my lethal pebble. Instead I stayed behind the cover of the trees and shouted, "Who's there?"

"Fuck off fuck off fuck off fuck off!"

"Hey man, it's cool. I'm not going to do anything to you."

"Fuck off Satan. I know you're Satan. Fuck off Satan you big red cunt."

"Alright mate, settle down, you're sounding a bit wacko there. Unless you've got the actual Devil with you then I guess you're shouting that stuff at me. And if you're shouting it at me then… well it's a bit rude isn't it?"

"Fuck off fuck off fuck off fuck off!"

I gave up trying to make some kind of connection from behind the trees and stepped out into the open.

He was facing me but I couldn't see his face. I'd been mistaken about him sitting down. He was actually on his knees, with his head lowered as if in prayer. He was rocking backwards and forwards like he wasn't all there, but that wasn't really a surprise when you consider that his vocabulary seemed to comprise almost entirely of the words *fuck* and *off*. His clothes were rags and his hair was long and straggly with a halo of flies. And I'd thought I was in a bad way.

I tried to keep my voice friendly. "When did you last have a drink? There's water round here, you must want some. Hang on a minute."

He didn't answer, just kept rocking. I went back to the pool and realised I was being an idiot; I couldn't get him a drink because I had nothing to put the water in. I shouted to him. "You're going to have to come over here to drink it, just stick your face in, that's what I've been doing. It's bliss, trust me."

"Get the fuck behind me Satan, you purple bastard."

"Well that's just charming. Listen mate, if you don't have a drink soon then you're going to die. It's really that simple. It'll be better for me if you do die actually because I won't have to listen to all your abuse."

He still didn't look up, but at least he said something different. "I'll just go and sit at my dad's right hand if I die. My dad rules heaven and earth, bet your dad doesn't rule heaven and earth."

"Whatever, mate. Let's not worry about your old man just now, let's get a bit of water down you. After that we'll sort you out something to eat. You can have anything you want as long as it's fish. But one thing at a time, know what I mean?"

There was a thud, then silence.

"Mate?"

More silence.

I ran back around. He was lying with his face in the dust. He'd obviously keeled over.

I don't know how I managed it, being half dead myself, but I dragged and pushed and rolled him out of the sun to the edge of the water. I thought he might be dead already and studied him for ages until I could see that he was breathing, barely. I propped him on his side and knelt behind his head so I could splash water onto his burning face. I kept talking to him, telling him to stay with me, that he should open his mouth so I could get some water in. He didn't answer so I turned his head round, thinking if I could make him look at me, then he might take in what I was saying to him.

His hair covered his face completely, clinging to the dirt and sweat and blistering sores. I carefully peeled it back, like pulling pubes off a bar of soap.

And that's when I got the shock of my life.

It was him. There was absolutely no doubt about it. In amongst the twisted mess that barely passed for a human face, there was no mistaking those eyes.

Jesus!

## How Many Days and Nights?

"Wake up, man!" Jesus' head lolled in my hands and his tongue popped out. I thought that was it, he'd gone to meet his maker - or his dad as he'd said. But then he made a noise. It wasn't a healthy noise, in fact it was quite disgusting, like he was gargling with sick, but when you think your best mate's just died then any kind of noise he makes is a good noise. The fact that his tongue was poking out meant that I could get my fingers between his lips and prise his mouth open so I could splash a few drops of water in. My water flinging technique wasn't the best and he got a proper gobful all at once. It must have hit him right at the back of the throat because he immediately started choking and heaving. I guessed he hadn't eaten or drank anything for ages so there was nothing he could sick up. I just held onto him the best I could as he flapped about like a fish on a deck.

Eventually he went limp in my hands again. Jesus - *prising his mouth open*, *going limp in my hands* – I've got to pick my words better. What I mean is that he stopped thrashing around and calmed down. I dripped some water, just a few drops this time, onto his lips and did the same to his forehead, which was burning like the Devil's ringpiece after a hot-pepper eating contest. It seemed to take the edge off and he started breathing a bit more steadily. He seemed more asleep than unconscious, which I hoped was a good thing, although I didn't really know the difference.

53

A few times, when he hadn't moved for a while and I started to panic, I'd give him a slap. His eyes would open and he'd shout *fuck off Satan* or something similar before nodding off again. I kept on with the drops of water to the mouth and a couple of times he swallowed. I took that as a big improvement.

That went on for the rest of that day and the following night. And then the next day. And the next night too. I could go on. It felt like a month. When he started to shiver I held onto him to warm him up, but then he'd immediately start to burn up. We hardly slept at nights because he was twitching like buggery, and all the while he was burbling on about Satan. I know the Devil's not everyone's best mate, but why Jesus was going on about him so much, even in his sleep, was beyond me.

When you imagine yourself looking after a friend or relative who's at death's door - and let's face it, we all picture random stuff like that in our heads sometimes - you normally cast yourself as a stoic hero, completely focused on getting that person through their ordeal, patient, tolerant and caring. The reality's a lot different. I challenge anybody to go through that experience for real and not get massively pissed off with whoever they're looking after. And I don't just mean pissed off every now and again, I mean the whole time. Someone who's really ill is… now how can I put this? Really fucking annoying. Yes, that's it.

I'm sure that sounded harsh but I'm just being honest, and if you've ever been through it and say it's not true then you, my friend, are a liar. It doesn't make us bad people. It's not like we deliberately feel that way. In fact we try really hard not to and when we realise that's not possible we feel terribly guilty about it. But that doesn't change the fact that those noises they make, those ill faces they pull, that pained voice in which they croak at you and pretty much everything else about them while they're in that state, it's all just one huge irritation.

It's not their fault, and at first it just grates a bit. But once you've hit that point, the point of no return - the point when every single thing they do makes you want to punch them in the face until they stop doing it - that's when you know you're in for a rough ride. Then there's the resentment, ye gods man the resentment! You can't get away from it. You can't help but be aware of the amount of your time they're taking up with their sickly existence when you know you could be doing something a lot less messy and a lot less depressing. I was stranded in the wilderness with nothing but a few trees, rocks and fish to occupy me, and I still could have found a hundred things I'd rather have been doing than looking after shivery, fevery, stinky old Jesus.

Don't judge me.

Anyway, it's probably just as boring for you to hear about it as it was for me to be there, and you don't need any more references to me cuddling my mate and whether or not he swallowed. I'm going to cut out the dreary, miserable and slightly weird sounding stuff and just tell you that he got better. It took a while and it wasn't much fun but eventually he made it.

Hallelujah.

In other good news, I managed to strip enough of the dry bark from the trees to make a fire, which improved our situation no end. I'm sure everyone who survives a wilderness ordeal probably says this, but that first cooked meal was the nicest thing I'd eaten in my life, even though I did sick it up afterwards because I'd stuffed it down too fast.

Jesus and I hadn't spoken much during his recovery. We'd kept to functional stuff like *do you need any water?* and *I think that fly's laying eggs in your nostril*, we hadn't had a proper conversation yet. We were definitely due one, we had quite a bit of catching up to do, all things considered. Jesus got the ball rolling when he was strong enough. "So where do we start?"

I smiled and shook my head. "I have absolutely no idea. All I know is that I was lost in the desert, was about to die and somehow stumbled upon a bona fide oasis, I mean, what are the chances? But then I found out that this place had its own crazy-bastard-in-residence, a nearly dead crazy bastard resident who turned out to be you. Now, if I'd thought that the odds of finding a watering hole in this wilderness were huge - and just to be clear, I hadn't even considered it as a possibility, that's how huge I thought those odds were - then if I even attempt to get my head around the chances of not only finding a watering hole but finding you in it then I think my head might just turn itself inside out."

Jesus had been listening patiently to my rant. "I think my head *did* turn inside out. I can just remember being lost, not having a clue where I was and somehow ending up here, in body at least, fuck knows where my mind was. I was sure I had company. The Devil was with me, talking to me."

"Yeah, that was me. You thought I was the Devil, you were shouting all kinds of shit at me."

He laughed for the first time in a long time before thinking for a while. "Ah, I see. I get it. I remember you turning up. Well not you, not at the time anyway. You see, before I got here, when I was just wandering in the wilderness, the Devil was all up in my face giving me all this shit, all this religious stuff. He was telling me to do all kinds of miracles to stop me dying, like he tried to make me turn rocks into bread. He kept on about that. I told him he should use his imagination a bit, *enough with the fucking bread* I told him. *Man, we don't just live on bread.* He didn't like that. He kept on and on at me. At one point it was like he'd taken me up in the air, to the top of some big tower and told me I should jump off. He reckoned I'd be saved by, I dunno, angels maybe. I told him to fuck off. I think I told him to fuck off quite a lot."

"Yes, I got that bit."

"Well he was being such a prick! He kept telling me to worship him, like I was going to do that when he was being such a massive bell-end. Then he changed, looked more like a man, still all red, but without the horns and shit. He was trying to make me drink water. I thought it was another trick, like he'd taken human form and was trying to get me to drink poison. I suppose that was you."

I nodded. "Yes, that was me."

"You were really red."

"That'll be the sunburn."

He nodded. "Makes sense I suppose."

"No wonder you were freaking out so badly if you genuinely believed I was the Devil."

"Ah, mate, tell me about it. It wasn't fun. I thought it would never end."

"Do you think it was actually him, I mean before I turned up?"

"No chance. It was all a figment of my fevered mind. The poppy, the starvation, thirst, overheating, exhaustion. Something had to give. It was just one long bad trip."

"You were talking about your dad being the ruler of heaven, and earth too."

"Yeah, I remember something about that." He looked at the ground. "Let's change the subject."

"How long do you think we've been out here?"

"I can tell you how long I've been wandering about, at least until you turned up." He twisted his foot so I could see what was left of the bottom of his sandal. "Count the scratches." I could clearly make out some marks in surprisingly neat rows. "I kept track. I used the edge of a stone. Every morning I

57

scratched another mark. I could be wrong because I was in a right state, but I'm pretty sure I kept it up every morning because I can remember doing it in the devil's face, y'know, trying to show him I was on top of things, that he hadn't won. How many are there?"

The scratches were in groups of five, eight groups of five. "There's forty."

Jesus nodded. "Forty days and forty nights. Feels about right. You saved my life, mate, thanks."

"Well I wasn't going to let you die. I didn't want your corpse stinking up the place, and think of all the flies your rotting flesh would attract. It's bad enough as it is, I swear I had a family of bugs living in the folds of my plum sack. That was one of the best things about finding this place, it meant I could wash."

"Where did you wash?"

"What do you mean, where?" I pointed at the pool. "In there, where the fuck else?"

He looked appalled. "You washed your knackers in the drinking water?"

"It's not the drinking water, it's just the water, the only water we've got. In case you hadn't noticed we're in what you'd call a perilous situation, normal rules don't apply. What are you doing?"

"For your viewing displeasure, ladies and gentlemen..." He started undressing, taking his time and making sure I got a good eyeful. But there was nothing good about the eyeful. He turned his back to me and leaned forward. "Have a good look, mate, think about that crack, that dark, festering crack. Bet there's some proper ancient evil down there. You might think Pandora had a stinky old box but wait 'til you get a load of this. When this goes in the water, the communal water, I'm going to really get in there and give it a good old rinse out."

"For fuck's sake! What else was I meant to do? I needed to wash."

"Don't you worry mate, you're right, you needed to wash, just like I need to wash now. I'm not angry with you." He started wiggling his arse. "Look, I'm turning the other cheek."

To be honest I wasn't too fussed about him washing his arse in our water. Not just because I knew he hadn't had much to eat recently so his back end hadn't seen much in the way of traffic but because I'd meant what I'd said - we were lucky to be alive and had to make do with what we had. I could just drink from the other side of the pool and try not to think about it. Aside from all that it was just good to have my mate back. He was a lot more fun when he wasn't about to die.

# Good News, Bad News

There was nothing to do but sit in the shade, drink from the pool and cook and eat fish. So that's all we did. It was probably exactly what we needed, complete rest. We started to feel a lot better - loads better in fact - and in the late afternoons when it was a bit cooler, we'd walk around to build up the strength in our wasted legs. As we circumnavigated the watering hole we'd look out into the distance trying to see… anything at all really. Somewhere we could head for. But of course there was nothing, just desert stretching in all directions.

After what we'd both been through, neither of us wanted to go out into the wilderness again. We had nothing except the clothes we were wearing and they weren't much more than rags, stinky old rags at that, so we couldn't even pack any food to keep us going for a while. If we hit the desert we literally wouldn't know where our next meal was coming from.

The soles of our feet healed and our arms and legs stopped aching and our blistered, sunburned flesh peeled off to allow fresh new skin to grow in its place. There wasn't much we could do about our hair and beards apart from rinsing them in the pool and plucking off the drowned flies, but all in all we started to look and feel a lot more human. It's all relative though. If our families had seen us like that - in what we thought was a much improved condition - they wouldn't have been impressed, or even recognised us come to think of it.

It was good to see Jesus back in the land of the living. I'd been fairly sure I'd been watching him die before. I suppose you could say I saved his life, he certainly said that, but I think really I was just saving my own. If I'd been left alone I'm certain I would have gone nuts and drowned myself.

Jesus was a good person to be stuck in the desert with. Obviously, given the choice I would have taken a woman - any woman at all - over him, but if I had to be stuck with a bloke then I was glad it was him.

He was just fun to have around, it was as simple as that. Having known him for so long meant that I knew a lot of his older gags but he'd constantly surprise me. Sometimes he'd keep up a joke for days until it got really tiresome but then keep it going until somehow it got funny again, which it normally did. It passed the time if nothing else. I have to confess that a lot of his jokes - if you could call them jokes - went right over my head, but they made me laugh anyway.

Here's a for instance. One time I noticed a bit of sand in the corner of his eye and I warned him so he could get it out before it went right in and got really sore.

Instead of thanking me, his answer was just plain weird. "What about *your* eye? Full of sand, it is. Sort out your own eye before you tell me about mine."

"I haven't got anything in my eye."

He blinked. "Yes you have, you've got, like, a beam in it - a *mote*."

"It's gone right in now, you tit. That's why I tried to warn you. And what the fuck's a mote?"

His sandy eye was quickly turning an angry red. He ignored it. "You should know what a mote is - you've got one in your eye. A big one. Both eyes actually."

I put my head in my hands. "Mate, I'm not sure where you're going with this but here's the thing - there's a bit of sand in your eye and you know it's there and it must be really bloody painful so you really need to get it out. And if you'd just got it out when I warned you then you wouldn't be in agony now. There's nothing in my eye and even if there was then I'd be all, like, *oh yeah, there's something in my eye, thank you.* I wouldn't be a dick about it."

"Mote boy." He was really struggling to keep a straight face.

"I don't get it, I really don't get it."

"You don't get what? The mote, out of your eye?" His eye was really streaming now. "You should get it out."

"Jesus. You've got an audience of exactly nobody for this."

"Where have you gone? I can't see you behind that massive mote, stop hiding behind the mote."

"Wipe your fucking eye, Jesus!"

"Wipe your own eye. Get the mote out."

The more he persisted with it, the funnier I found it, despite not having a bastard clue what he was on about.

I guess you had to be there.

Then the day came. We saw what we thought was the sand whipping up in the wind somewhere to the north. We would have been happy with just that, a bit of sand blowing about, but then have to remember that we were in the middle of the desert with nothing but each other for entertainment. If one of the fish broke the surface of the pool and caught a fly in its gummy chops, it was a big event. Compared to that, a localised sandstorm was quite a show. As we watched, gripped by the windy spectacle, we noticed it was moving towards us.

Jesus called it first. "It's not the wind, it's a camel."

"It's two camels. Jesus."

"What? Why do you keep saying my name like that?"

"To get your attention."

He turned to face me, his hands on his hips. "That's bollocks. There's only the two of us here. You've got my attention so there's no reason to say it. You do it all the time.

You say it like you'd say, shit or something."

"Yeah, I guess I do. It just, I dunno, *fits* somehow."

"It's my name, stop it."

"I'll try, I can't guarantee it though, but shall we focus on what could be a bit more important. The two, no, four camels coming our way, and there's some people too. Oh my God."

"Well fuck me sideways, we're saved."

"Not if they're Romans. We're dead if they're Romans. Or they might be slave traders. That wouldn't be much fun. I'm too good-looking for slavery. Come on, get behind the trees. I'm taking no chances."

Jesus shook his head. "I'm not hiding. We're not going to get a chance like this again. I thought I was dead until you came along so all this is a bonus. I'm not going to spend the rest of my life out here. I've got things to do."

I saw his point.

We sat and watched the approach of the little camel train, caravan, whatever you call it. Two of the camels had riders, the others just had luggage.

"I don't believe it," said Jesus. "It's…"

"It's Thaddeus, and that other one."

"…Simon. Fuck me. It is!"

It was a miracle.

"Jesus Christ I presume?" Simon stepped effortlessly over his camel's lowered backside. He was obviously a good - I don't know what you call a camel rider - camelist? That doesn't sound right. He seemed less surprised to see us than we were to see him. Jesus held out his arms but Simon shook his head. "I won't embrace you if you don't mind, old boy. You look a bit on the ripe side. Would you settle for a handshake?"

Jesus hugged him anyway.

Thaddeus got down from his camel a lot more clumsily than Simon had. "Afternoon fellas." He said it like we were meeting for lunch, like he and Simon hadn't just defied unimaginable odds to find two needles in a huge sandy haystack.

"That's enough now." Simon wriggled out of Jesus' grip. "I was right, you do stink."

"Well aren't you the fucking prophet?" Jesus said. "Who would have thought that someone stranded in the desert for months would smell anything but baby fresh?"

"You've both changed your hair." Thaddeus said.

"Are you joking?" I really couldn't tell with Thad so I had to ask.

"No, straight up, it's definitely different."

Simon put his hand to the side of his mouth and made out like he was whispering but talked loud enough for us all to hear, including Thad. "I don't think he's joking."

"Why would I be joking? It is different." Thad had a perfectly straight face.

If he was winding me up then I had to admit I'd fallen for it. "Of course it's different! We've been stranded in the desert. What did you think was happening here?"

"So I was right, you have changed your hair."

"Jesus," I said.

"Stop that," said Jesus.

They had food with them and pots to cook with too. They knocked us up some rice. It was fantastic to eat something other than fish. Simon told us about their search, how they'd tried all the towns in the area surrounding the camp. When we'd not turned up they'd started criss-crossing the desert. When we asked why they'd gone to so much trouble to find us he just said it was John's orders.

"And where did John end up?" I asked the question through a mouthful of rice.

Simon's face darkened. "He ended up dead."

I spat rice all down my front. "How?"

"You know Antipas the Tetrarch, son of Herod the Great?"

"I know who he is," said Jesus flatly.

He declared that John was sowing the seeds of rebellion."
Simon swallowed hard. "He made an example of him. He cut
his head off."

"He didn't do it himself," Thad pitched in. "He got
someone else to do it. Y'know, like an executioner."

"Shut your mouth Thad," said Simon. "What the fuck?"

"Just thought I'd make it clear."

"Well it's clear enough." Simon's posh affectation seemed to
have left him for a moment. "We're talking about Jesus' cousin.
Let's think a bit before we speak, shall we?" He touched Jesus'
arm in that awkward way men do when we're trying to be...
appropriate, like he was patting a dog he thought might bite
him in the face. "I'm so sorry about John. I know he was
family. I just, well… I'm sorry."

Jesus nodded. He looked stunned, like all the life had been
knocked out of him. But he was all business. "Tell me what
happened."

"It wasn't really about rebellion," Simon said. "That's not
why they killed him at least. When John was arrested and taken
before Antipas, he faced up to him. He called him a dirty wife-
stealer. Do you know that story?" He saw from our faces that
we didn't. "Antipas took a fancy to his brother's wife. He
divorced his own wife and forced his sister-in-law to divorce
Herod…"

"Herod? His dad?" I said.

"No, his brother. I understand that the family are a little on
the competitive side. Antipas has more power than his sibling
so he used the opportunity to flout that power. It was a rotten
thing to do of course, and John told him so - right to his face.
John is the bravest man I have ever met. He could have got
away with just being locked up, but he wasn't having that. He

felt that somebody had to take Antipas to task over his actions, so he decided he would do it himself. I suppose he knew he would be spending the rest of his life rotting in a dungeon, so one could argue that he did himself a favour, got it over with quickly. But either way he's a legend."

Jesus' face was streaming with tears, and it wasn't dust in his eyes this time. "But that night when everyone fled the camp, they said it was because the Romans were coming, not Antipas."

"Antipas hasn't got any real army to speak of so he called in the Romans. He spun it to them that John was whipping up an insurrection. It's in the Romans' interests to keep order, and it's not like they're short of troops, so they were happy to lend a hand. It backfired on Antipas, though. Word soon reached the Roman bigwigs that John had been executed, and all the gory details about Antipas' real motives came to light. More importantly, they got wind of the public outcry about Antipas being such a total shit throughout the whole affair. So it's fair to say that Antipas is not flavour of the month with our beloved occupiers. And on top of all that, Antipas's ex father-in-law is on the warpath, and I don't mean that figuratively. He's looking to avenge his daughter's dishonour. He's raising an army and making no secret of his plans to take Antipas down."

"I can't say I completely understand all that," I said, "but it sounds like Antipas is fucked, and I like the poetic justice of it."

"That won't bring John back." Jesus said almost too quietly to hear.

"No," said Simon, "and I would not say he is fucked, more that his position is not as strong as it once was, and that he will think twice before calling in the Romans to fight his battles from now on."

Rather than linger on the subject of John's death, we made

plans. The first of which was that we were going to get things moving again, with Jesus as John's successor. It's what people always say when someone dies but in this case it's true; it's exactly what John would have wanted.

Simon had picked a town in Galilee where we could base our operations. "It's called Capernaum," he said, "not a metropolis by any means but it's exactly what we need. It's quiet, so nobody should bother us, but it's close enough to civilisation to allow us to ply our trade. Thad and I found a good place just outside too, perfect to grow the product."

"Are the others there too?" I said.

Simon frowned. "Others?"

"The rest of John's crew."

"Oh, I see." He shook his head gravely. "No, no others. It's just us now. In all the chaos everybody…"

"Fucked off," said Thad helpfully.

"Dispersed," said Simon, "and we have no way of contacting John's family either. So now... well I guess we're independent."

"That was John's long term plan anyway," said Jesus.

"Talking of John's plans," said Simon, "we managed to get someone on the inside to get an audience with John the night before he died. Apparently all he talked about was how you were the only man who had the balls and the charisma to take the operation to the next level. He said it brought comfort to him knowing his legacy would be in safe hands."

Jesus bristled with anger and a little pride. "John's legacy is safe with me. And that cheating murdering bastard Antipas is going to get what's coming to him. He's fucked with the wrong people."

# *Net Gains*

I'd never ridden a camel before and I quickly learned that I wasn't very good at it. I was okay at the staying on part. It was the going-in-the-right-direction bit that I had a problem with. People say they're the ships of the desert. Well if that's true then mine had a buggered rudder.

The other three were fine, striding along gracefully just like camels are meant to, with Simon in front, Jesus in the middle and Thaddeus bringing up the rear. They formed a perfect line, as if their camels - Jesus' and Thad's at least - were obsessed with the view of the arse of the one in front and would follow it to the ends of the earth.

Mine, however, was all over the place. I must have gone three times further than everyone else what with all the zig-zagging about. The others thought it was hilarious at first, especially Simon, but even he got bored of it after a while. It was probably massively annoying for them having me weaving in and out of their orderly procession, shouting abuse at the lumpy bastard that blundered along, kicking up sand beneath me. But my sympathy for the others was limited. It was far more annoying for me.

I enjoyed the stops though. Simon and Thad had brought all the gear to pitch a decent camp and had plenty of supplies. It felt like luxury after the time we'd had. The best thing was the new clothes. I could actually hear my balls sigh with relief as I tied the soft clean loincloth around them. And the fresh cotton tunic - fuck me - it felt better than a going over by the pharaoh's best concubine. It wasn't until I'd been starved of it for so long that I realised just how good the simple feeling of comfort actually was.

And to top it off, Thad had a big stash of green on him, so every night we'd get so high. Good times.

It was hard not to think about what had happened to John though. However noble and brave he undoubtedly was, he still must have been terrified in those last moments when he was dragged out of his cell towards some bastard waiting with a big axe. Who signs up for a job like that? I mean, really, who cuts someone's head off? For fuck's sake.

As enjoyable as the trip was, it was good to finally reach civilisation, or something close to it at least. Capernaum seemed to be a nice enough place, a fishing port at the edge of the Sea of Galilee. I couldn't work out why everyone called it a sea, though. It was actually a lake. A big lake, I'll grant you, but still a lake. The locals reckoned that if you were stuck in the middle when a storm blew up you'd feel like you were in the middle of the ocean. They all seemed pretty proud of that for some reason.

Simon and Thad dropped us off at a tavern on a hillside overlooking the town and gave us a bit of money to tide us over. The first thing Jesus and I did was go to the bathhouse. It was amazing to get clean after all that time in the desert. It was a massive relief to prune the beard and hair too. I was finished and dressed first so I got us a couple of beers and sat at a table outside. While I waited I found myself staring at the waitress. She was awesome. It had been a long time since I'd been active with a woman and my imagination was off and running.

"Here he is!" I pushed a beer towards Jesus as he approached the table.

He wasn't as enthusiastic as I'd hoped. "What are you doing

out here?"

"Having a beer, what does it look like?"

"Well we can't stick around. We've got work to do."

"Jesus, we've only just been saved from death or madness in the desert, remember? Surely we can mark the occasion with a few jars. It's not like we have pressing business is it?"

"It's exactly like we have pressing business. We've got to recruit. And we've got to do it now. Simon and Thad have kept everything going. They searched the fucking desert for us. How would it look if we just sat here and got drunk?"

"I think they'd approve, they'd probably join us. I thought that was the plan."

"The plan is to get this business back on track and take over where John left off. Remember John, the guy who got his head cut off?"

"I can't believe you're making out that I'm in some way besmirching John's memory by suggesting we have a few beers."

"You've been listening to Simon too much. You'd never have said *besmirching* before."

"Whatever." I folded my arms and sat back.

"Alright, one beer."

"Well I've nearly finished this one, and you've not started yours yet, so it would be daft if I didn't get another one. I'd just be sitting here watching you drink yours."

"Get yourself another beer, but just you, I'm happy with this one."

I ordered two more beers.

Jesus finished his really quickly, the bastard, and wouldn't let me order any more. We were off to work, against my better judgement. Simon had said that two of John's followers, brothers, were fishermen here in the town. Apparently they'd been at the camp in Jordan almost from day one so we made them our first target.

Jesus and I asked around at the docks and some old gnarly bloke who was plucking bits of weed out of some particularly stinky nets told us where the brothers' boat was. When we got there it looked like it was just about to set sail, cast off, whatever. One of them was on the shore untying the rope that kept it, like, moored while the other was on the deck, doing something with the nets at the back.

Jesus spoke to the one on dry land. "I am looking for the brothers, Simon and Andrew."

"I'm Andrew. He's Simon."

"Pleased to meet you, Andrew." Jesus shook his hand, which wasn't easy because the guy was holding a lot of rope.

"I know you," the one on the boat called out. "You're the chosen one. You're Jesus! I saw John baptise you, and the sun, wow! It was like a lightning bolt from heaven." He stepped off the boat and shook Jesus' hand. "It's an honour to meet you. My name is Simon." He was chunkier than his brother, not fat exactly but he obviously knew where the pie-tray was.

"It's a pleasure to meet you Simon."

"So to what do we owe the honour of your visit?" Even though I'd never met him before I could tell that this new Simon was phrasing his words carefully, adding pomp to suit the status of this unlikely visitor.

Jesus didn't beat about the burning bush. "I want you to follow me."

"What does that involve?"

"I presume you heard what happened to John?" They both bowed their heads respectfully. Jesus carried straight on. "Yes it's a bad business, but there's no point dwelling on it. John's wish before he was butchered was that I should take over and continue his work. To do that I need good people, people who can get other good people on board."

"On board the boat?" Andrew obviously wasn't the sharpest of the two.

Simon smiled, not unkindly. "He means he wants us to recruit people for his ministry." He looked at Jesus hopefully. "That's right isn't it?"

"That's exactly right."

"But we're just fishermen," said Simon. "We wouldn't know the first thing about it."

"You'll still be fishing, but instead of fish you'll be fishers of men."

Simon winced. "When you're fishing you use a big net and drag it behind the boat in the hope that lots of fish get caught up in it. You don't want to be catching people in a big net do you? You want them to follow of their own free will, like they did with John."

Jesus glanced towards heaven. "Obviously I wasn't suggesting that we actually catch them in nets, but okay, it wasn't the best analogy. I still think you'd be perfect."

"I'm not so sure, what you need are salesmen. We're not salesmen. Don't get me wrong, it's a real honour to be asked, but I don't think we'd be right for what you want."

Jesus was showing remarkable patience. "What I need are people who can talk honestly, and it's clear from this conversation right here that you can do that. You'll be among the first to join us and you'll do really well, I know it. We have an important message, a death to avenge and plenty of green. What do you say? It's better than the constant smell of fish isn't it?"

Simon looked at his brother and shrugged. Andrew shrugged back. "Plenty of green, eh? Fair enough. We're in. If you think we're worthy of serving you."

"More than worthy." Jesus shook their hands again to seal the deal. "One more thing," he said. "We've kind of already got a Simon. I don't want it to get confusing so do you go by any other names?"

"My gran sometimes calls me Peter because she's going a bit batty and thinks I'm my dead granddad."

"Peter it is then."

"Whatever you say boss." They got back onto their boat and started packing their stuff.

When they re-emerged Peter was rubbing his hands together eagerly. "Did you want to get started straight away?"

"Do we have to?" I whined. "Aren't we going for some beers to celebrate our first successful recruitment?"

Jesus gave me a withering look before turning to Peter. "Yes, we're getting started straight away."

"Okay, well there's a couple of people who I think might be interested. If you don't mind another pair of brothers that is. And another pair of fishermen."

"What do the brothers do?" I asked.

Peter frowned. "I don't get you."

"I mean, what do they do for a living, what's their occupation?"

His frown turned into a smile then back into a frown again. "They're fishermen, just like us."

I sighed impatiently. "You said the other two were fishermen, the ones that weren't brothers."

Peter nervously looked at Jesus then back at me. "Are you joking?"

Jesus shouted in my face. "For the love of God, they're the same! There's only two people. He meant they're brothers *and* fishermen."

"I know!" I said. "I was joking." I knew full well I wasn't fooling anybody.

Peter led us round the dock to a much bigger boat with its nets laid out on the shore. It was net central round there. Two men were attending to the sea-weedy masses of wet twine.

The taller of the two men spoke, "Simon, Andrew, how are you doing fellas?"

"Good to see you James," Peter said. He nodded at the shorter one. "You too, John. But I'm not Simon anymore, I'm Peter now. This man here just gave me a new name."

"That's nice, I guess." James sounded doubtful.

"Actually it is," Peter's chest inflated. "To be named by Jesus himself - I'd say that was quite a thing. What do you think?"

At the mention of Jesus, both James and John stood visibly straighter and looked at him like he was royalty.

I'm sure I'm going to sound a bit moany here but… Okay, so it made sense that word had got out about Jesus, especially after John (the Baptist, that is, not this new John) had given him such a big-up in front of his followers. And I understood that very little of interest went on in backwaters like Capernaum, so when people hear about some new celebrity then they take notice. I got all that, really I did. But what I didn't get was this: why were they looking straight at Jesus? How come it didn't cross their minds that I might have been the great man they'd heard so much about?

But fair play to him, Jesus knew how to carry it. He fixed them with a look that said *I'm the real deal*, and then he spoke. "I want you to follow me."

What I've described won't sound like much but it was one of the most intense moments I've ever experienced. I guess you had to be there, but it was as if the wind changed. Or the wind stopped. Or everything stopped. Or everything started – yes, that's the one.

Maybe he had some sort of power, maybe I just hadn't noticed it because I'd grown up with it and didn't know a time when I wasn't under its influence. One thing was clear - there was no way these two newbies were going to turn him down.

"We have to tell our father," one of them said. I forget which.

They walked up the wotsit plank onto the boat and came out with an older man, obviously their dad. He walked straight over to Jesus and didn't even shake his hand. Instead he bowed his head.

"It is a pleasure to meet you sir," Jesus said.

"The pleasure, the privilege and the honour are all mine."

"You have begat fine sons sir," Jesus was talking in his Sunday best, "and I would love it if they could join my ministry. There is much to do and I know they have a vital role to play." He was acting all humble, like he didn't know damn well it was already a done deal.

The old man raised his head. "I am of the understanding that they are resolved to this course. Nothing I could say would change their minds, but I would not wish to anyway. They have my blessing."

"Thank you sir. That means a lot."

"Please call me Zebedee."

The fact that it was a solemn and moving moment wasn't lost on me. Honest. Here was a loving father who relied on his two strapping sons to man the fishing boat - the family's livelihood no less - and he was agreeing to let those very same sons drop everything to follow a complete stranger, not so much on a wing but definitely on a prayer. It was a big deal, a life changing moment for him, his sons and the rest of his family - his whole community.

But how am I meant to keep a straight face when someone says his name is Zebedee?

Jesus covered it up well. He was respectful enough for the both of us and we were soon off looking for more recruits.

I was starting to think that everyone in Galilee hung around with his brother but the next two weren't related. They weren't fishermen either. I forget what Philip and Nathanael actually did for a living and I don't remember how we came across them. What I do remember is that Philip got my back up straight away. I'd probably have despised Nathanael too but Philip hogged all my hatred for himself. I didn't like his face, especially when he talked. He had this expression that could have been a smile or could have been a wince, it was impossible to tell. Either way it just came across like he thought you were a twat and whatever he was saying was the most important thing in the world. His voice was whiny too, like he was talking through his nose all the time. That didn't help.

But on the whole we'd done well. We had a roll call of Peter, Andrew, James, John, Nathanael and last and definitely least, Philip. Add all those to Simon and Thad (and of course me and Jesus) and we'd made it to X - a nice solid numeral. Okay, so we weren't, like, legion but we had the makings of a crew.

## Sermon in the Pub

Jesus and I were sitting outside the tavern waiting for the others to arrive so we could have our first proper meeting. I was really starting to fall for the place and hadn't spent nearly enough time in it for my liking. It was called *Magdalene's*. It was pretty basic but had everything we needed. The tables outside were in the perfect spot overlooking the town and it was a great place to sit and drink while the sun went down. And then to carry on drinking long after it had set.

It made me nostalgic for those times we were out on the road, stopping at random towns and villages and getting up to all sorts with the local girls. It seemed a world away. That's not saying that times weren't good now, they were just different, especially to someone like me who was used to just drifting along. We had a purpose now, and that meant we had to plan, we had to get things done. And it wasn't just Jesus and me anymore.

I'd liked it when it was just Jesus and me.

We finished our beer and Jesus ordered two more. The girl serving us was the one who'd caught my eye the day we arrived. I knew it was game over for me as soon as I saw the way she looked at Jesus. She was lost somewhere in his eyes, just like all the others. She went to get our drinks while all I could do was hope she had a sister.

Jesus put his head in his hands, cringing. "Oh man," he said. "I so nearly fucked that up with those first two. Fishers of men!

What was I thinking?"

"Mate, you've got a way with words, probably better than anyone I know, but yeah, when you came out with that one I thought you'd been possessed."

"I was trying to sound like John but just sounded like a dick."

"Don't beat yourself up over it, it was more their fault really. They don't seem like the sharpest scriptures in the scroll. And you learned from your mistake. You pulled it right out of the bag straight after with the other two, James and John. I've got to say it - that was something to behold. You, like, ordered them to follow you."

"Yeah, that was pretty cool. You nearly blew it though, laughing at their old man. You've got to keep it together, mate. This is real now."

It occurred to me that I was being told off by my boss. "Can I point out one thing in my defence?"

"You're going to anyway, so go on."

"His name was Zebedee."

Jesus laughed through a mouthful of beer and then went into a coughing fit. He waited it out then took another swig. "Yeah, fair play, he was called Zebedee."

"So, these newbies, how do you think they're going to get on? We seem to be pretty heavy on fishermen. And what Peter said about not thinking he had the skills you needed, well that was pretty honest. It might have been pretty accurate too."

"He'll be fine. He just doesn't know it yet. That's the only danger. If they don't think they've got what it takes then they're going to keep on asking what they should be doing and that's not what I need. I need them to take responsibility. I can't keep telling them what to do. Give a man a fish and all that."

"I think they're okay for fish."

Jesus laughed again. "They're fishers of men now!" He put

his head in his hands once more. "What the fuck?"

"Try not to dwell on the dickness, mate. You turned it around, you're on your game now."

Jesus shrugged. Let's hope so. Talking of which, they'll be here soon. Our first meeting. Could be interesting."

"You nervous?"

"No, not at all. Well maybe a little. I've never hosted a meeting before. I don't think I've ever even *been* to a meeting before."

"You're Jesus. They all love you. They'll be hanging on your every word."

"Maybe," he looked at our almost empty glasses. "Let's get some more of these. Where's that minx of a waitress, I'm liking the look of her."

That was it. I knew it was a done deal.

We needed a bit of privacy for the meeting and so we'd arranged with the owner to use a room upstairs. When the others turned up, the waitress showed us, leading Jesus by the arm of course, inside to what was obviously the owner's dining room. Most of the space was filled by a long table. Jesus and I sat at each end while the others sat in a row of four down each side.

After the introductions Jesus stood up. "I called this meeting so I could make it clear what we're trying to achieve and what's expected of everyone. But first of all I want to say a big thank you to each and every one of you for agreeing to come on this journey with me."

"No problem at all, it's good to be aboard."

"Thanks Peter. So, I have two aims and it may be confusing to some but they are equally important. I need you all to keep that in mind. Peter started to chip in again but Jesus made it look like he hadn't noticed and talked over him. "The first aim is to continue to spread John's message," he looked at John. "I mean John the Baptist's message. The message of having each other's backs, of protecting those who can't protect themselves, the message of redemption, of rebirth – all that good stuff. I want people to know that whatever they've been up to before, they can have a fresh start if they follow me. And that's right, I did say *if they follow me*, sounds pretty arrogant doesn't it? It's like I've got some sort of messiah complex. Well maybe I have, but I make no apology for the heights I'm aiming at. I'm not pissing around here. John meant a lot to a lot of people. He changed lives. I want to take what he had and run with it, bring it to the next level – and the one after that. If I need to be seen as a messiah then that's what I'll do. I'd like to say I'm not in it for the personal glory, that I'm just carrying out some kind of duty but let's face it, that's bollocks. Of course I'll enjoy the personal glory. I won't insult any of you by pretending otherwise."

"Refreshingly honest, we can dig that." Peter again – right old teacher's pet he was turning out to be.

"Yes, well, thanks Peter. Now, the other aim is to move the product. Those of you who spent any time with John down by the Jordan will have sampled the green, and those who wanted a bigger and stronger buzz would have tried the poppy too. Anyone who wasn't there will have heard all about it because let's be honest, that's why you're all here." There were a lot of knowing nods but he didn't give anyone a chance to interrupt. "Up until very recently we were a small part of a bigger business back east, but now we're on our own and we're going to be bigger than the bigger business ever was."

"I like it. We'll be the biggest of the biggest!" Oh for fuck's sake Peter.

"The one drawback of not being hooked up with the eastern branch is that they were our supply line so now we've got to source the product ourselves. We're okay for the green," he nodded towards Thad and Simon. "Do you want to say a few words about that, fellas?"

Simon stood up. "Certainly old boy. We're growing it in a valley nearby. It's not easy to get to, the slopes are treacherous and the shrubbery surrounding it is overgrown to buggery but that suits our needs because it means we won't be bothered by passers-by or the more traditional farmers. Thad here has what you might call a nose for the product, and he is confident that the growing conditions are absolutely spot-on." He looked at Thaddeus.

Thaddeus was silent for a while before the shekel dropped. "Oh, you want me to say something? I see. Well, erm…" he was somewhere between standing and sitting and his awkwardness was tangible. He glanced at Jesus, fiddled with his glass then looked at Simon. "Yes, the growing conditions are… what was the word you used?"

"I used two words, spot-on."

"Well I don't really know what that means, but yeah, the growing conditions are good."

Simon geed him along. "There's plentiful light, and abundant irrigation."

"Yeah, it gets a lot of sun, and there's a stream there."

"Thanks you two, great work," said Jesus, "but we do need to get a regular source of the harder stuff. Peter and Andrew, I'm putting you in charge of that."

"I'm sorry? What was that?" It was like Andrew had been slapped awake.

"I'm putting you and your brother in charge of growing the poppies and extracting the key ingredients." Andrew went to speak again but Jesus held up a hand. "It's okay, don't fret, you won't be on your own." He nodded in my direction.

"Yes," I said. "I'll be helping you to get going… apparently."

Jesus nodded. "So there you go Andrew. You and your brother will have a fully trained expert showing you the ropes."

"Well I wouldn't say expert exactly..."

Jesus cut me off with a smile and a wave of the hand. "Too modest. Far too modest." The glance he shot in my direction said it all. He wanted me to shut my mouth. I decided not to point out that *fully trained* meant that I'd spent an afternoon with Thad while he showed me the sort of places where poppies might grow (we didn't find any, although we didn't search for very long), and being told (in theory because he didn't have any plants on him at the time) how to milk the poppy. As knowledgeable as Thad was on his specialist subject, he was awful at imparting that knowledge to others and easily distracted by other activities.

In other words, Thad was an awful teacher and we'd just got stoned.

So I knew I was going to be no help at all to Peter and Andrew so I had a crack at wriggling out of it. "I won't be offended if Thad would rather take the lead on this one."

Jesus wasn't having any of it. "Thad's busy growing the green, that's our core business."

So that was that, the boss had spoken. I had to put up or shut up. I had to train Andrew, who was obviously shitting himself at the prospect of such responsibility, and Peter, who I was sure wouldn't stop talking long enough to hear anything I had to say.

James and John were put in charge of distribution and Philip and Nathanael were given a much more general but as Jesus said, no less important job of planning and organising. Jesus was going to be making appearances, meeting the people, preaching the good word, not just in one place like John had done but taking his message - and just as importantly, his product - out and about. He needed someone to keep on top of all that and apparently Phil and Nat were the men to do it. Phil was beaming all over his git-face but luckily he kept his whiny mouth shut.

"I have a question." My voice went all wobbly because for some reason I felt really nervous speaking in front of everyone. "What about me? What's my role? Apart from helping Andrew and Peter find poppies. What am I doing after that?"

Jesus shrugged. "What a daft question. You're my right hand man, same as always. I can't do this without you by my side." Completely beyond my control my chest swelled with pride and I blushed a deep red. What can I say? It felt good to be the chosen one's chosen one.

"Now," Jesus continued, "I want to talk a little about the other product we're pushing, and for those of you who haven't already worked it out, that product is me. People didn't just flock to John because he talked perfect sense, although that obviously helped. The real reason people followed John - in their droves I might add - was because he had something special. Anyone who heard him speak was hooked on his charisma, his message, his honesty. The formula couldn't be more simple, a strong figurehead, an even stronger message, and loads and loads of drugs. Any questions so far? James, you don't need to put your hand up, just speak mate."

"When can we get stoned? If I'm going to sell this stuff then I want to try it out."

Jesus smiled. "That's a very good question. As soon as we're done here we will, I promise. We'll get smashed off our faces and we'll laugh until it hurts, but first we have to sort out all this sensible stuff. Sound reasonable?"

James leaned back, nodding enthusiastically. "More than reasonable."

"Good to hear. Right, it just so happens that we've now got all the sensible stuff sorted." He rubbed his hands together.

"Let's get stoned."

Simon sorted out some beers to go and we filed out of the tavern. It was a short hike to a quiet spot further up the hill where we proceeded to get smashed off our faces and laughed until it hurt.

We really took care of business.

# Project Management

It was like Samson leading the… I don't know, I can't think of any other famous blind people but you get my point. As per the action I'd been assigned at the meeting, I was out with Peter and Andrew, looking for something I didn't have a clue how to find. I say looking, as if I was following some sort of procedure, checking for tell-tale signs and the like. But I wasn't. Because I didn't know what I was looking for. I was just leading them in random directions hoping to stumble upon a field full of poppies.

We don't seem to say it like we do with horses but we were on donkeyback. I'd recently taken ownership of a trusty new steed and he was the absolute business. I called him Maximus. It suited his noble posture and great big face.

We went a long way out over the hills and deep into the next valley. None of us was having a good time. It was hot, it was sticky and the donkeys (apart from my Maximus of course) were far from fresh-smelling. Andrew and Peter were as frustrated as I was, and because I'd been deemed to be in charge I became the target of their rage. It wasn't quite full blown yet but the signs of its early rumblings were clear in their strained voices and in the increasing volume of their cursing as they swatted away yet another fly.

I had to keep their spirits up. It didn't bother me that they were having a bad time but I knew I'd get enough grief as it was if we went back empty handed. I didn't want those two seasoning the shit-pot with their own pinches of criticism. I had to make them think we were making progress, that I could tell by - I don't know, the feel of the soil or something - that we were getting close. Every now and then I actually stopped, dismounted Maximus and knelt on the ground. I'd pick up a handful of dirt and feign a deep in thought expression as I rubbed it with my thumb and watched it carefully as it crumbled through my fingers as if it meant something. I think I might even have sniffed it at one point. I couldn't tell if they were buying it or not.

We'd set off early to try and miss the worst of the sun but we'd been out for hours and it was really starting to heat up. I was running out of ways to say, *not far now*, so I tried to distract them with a bit of the old chit-chat.

"Do you miss it, the fishing?"

Surprisingly Andrew rather than Peter answered. "Fuck yeah, especially compared to this. We could be out on the water in a nice cool breeze, dead quiet, no flies."

I was regretting picking that particular topic, I'd meant to take their minds off our crappy situation, not remind them of it. "Bet you don't miss the smell of fish though."

Andrew's eyes narrowed. "Jesus. Do you know many times I've had to listen to some lame gag line about the smell of fish? Fucking loads, that's how many." He put on a high-pitched voice. "*Ooh you're a fisherman, fish are smelly aren't they?* For fuck's sake."

"I know what you mean," I said.

"No you don't, what were you before this?"

"Carpenter."

"And does everyone you meet make jokes about splinters? I bet they don't."

I couldn't resist. "No, but here's one. I'm never going to get a splinter again," I paused before hitting them with the punchline, "touch wood!"

I swear I saw the faintest flicker of a smile on Andrew's face.

"You thought that was funny, go on admit it. You're laughing."

"I'm not laughing." His face broke into a grin. "Okay, fuck it, that wasn't half bad."

"I couldn't help noticing something you said just then," I said to Andrew, "something I've found myself doing. When you were getting all pissy with me, you said *Jesus*."

Andrew nodded, slowly. "Yeah. I did, you're right. I've noticed you doing that. Didn't realise I'd started doing it too. I don't know why, it just…"

"Fits?"

"Yeah, it fits."

"I do it too," said Peter, "seems like it's contagious."

"Well don't do it in front of the man himself," I said. "He's not too keen. He's forever having a go at me about it."

Peter pulled his donkey round and pointed at a clump of trees further into the valley. "It's going to be roasting soon, let's go and get some shade."

It was a good spot, five or six good-sized trees with a clearing in the middle where it was much cooler. I had a drink of water and made myself comfy, laying back with my head resting on the trunk of tree. It was covered in moss so it was soft, like a cushion. I lay back and closed my eyes.

"So how long before we find something?" Andrew asked.

I kept my eyes closed. "Shouldn't be too far now. The soil content is starting to look good."

"Do you want us to keep pretending we believe all that bullshit?" I was starting to like Andrew. I kept my eyes closed and kept the smile off my face.

"Believe what you want mate, it doesn't matter to me. I'm

the expert, remember."

"What colour is it?"

"What colour is what?"

"The poppy."

"Red. Or maybe pink, I'll know it when I see it. But I'm trying to snooze here, so a bit of quiet wouldn't go amiss."

Andrew ignored my appeal. "How big is each flower?"

"Still trying to sleep, less of the noise please... what do you mean, how big?"

"I mean, what size is it? Like, compared to those ones."

"Which ones?"

"The ones in the field over there. The reddy pinky ones. The ones that cover the entire valley."

I opened my eyes and looked where he was pointing. "Fuck me! I mean... told you! I knew we were getting close."

I know it's normally just something people say but I genuinely could not believe my eyes. It was like someone had carpeted half the valley with flowers and each and every one of them looked suspiciously like the sample poppy that I'd finally got off Thad. I rummaged in my bag and plucked it out, just to be sure. I held it up by its broken stem and looked out into the valley. It was a perfect match. Its size, shape and colour were repeated in front of me a million times over, *as far as the eye could see*, as they say.

Peter looked as amazed as I was pretending not to be. "God is definitely smiling on us," he said.

"I don't want to take anything away from God but this wasn't His work, this was all me. I used logic, followed the signs, tested the soil, all that technical stuff".

The two brothers swapped looks that said *he's talking rubbish again.* "Whatever," said Peter, "but we have to thank God for creating all this. I mean, apart from anything else they're just so beautiful, the way they ripple in the breeze, the colours shifting.

Amazing."

Now I liked God as much as the next man, and in my case the next man was normally Jesus of Nazareth, so... well, you get the picture, I was a big fan of God. But I didn't see why Peter had to be such a pussy about it. Yes, it was an impressive sight, but this was no place for comments like that. He was on a scouting mission with his crew, not on a picnic trying to get under some bird's tunic.

It was pretty awesome though, and he had a point, when they all moved in the wind it did look pretty cool. It was like a sea – a sea of poppies. I tried to work out how many there were in total. I settled on a figure of a fuckload times ten.

"How are we going to pick them all?" said Peter.

"How are we going to carry them all?" said Andrew.

"I'm sure you'll think of something, I've done my bit. Now, about that snooze..."

My non-interventionist policy bore fruit, the brothers came up with a solution that was elegant, simple or just plain obvious depending on your point of view. They decided we should build something right there in the valley, where the poppies could be processed and stored. Yes, I know, I could have thought of that, but fair play to them anyway.

The success of our mission made the return journey much more bearable but it was still a huge relief to get back to Magdelene's. I filled Jesus in over some well-earned beers.

"So how did they fare?"

"Not bad at all," I said. "Bit whiny at first, bit of a respect issue - like they couldn't accept that I was the expert."

Jesus smiled knowingly. "You're not an expert."

"Yeah, but they didn't know that."

"Do you think they'll do okay though?" said Jesus. "Do you reckon they can use a bit of initiative?"

I thought for a while before answering. "Yeah, I reckon."

"Good. I don't want us to be wiping their arses all the time. I want them to have their own ideas, not depend on me."

"Give a man a fish and all that."

Jesus took a suck on the pipe and breathed it out slowly. "I think they're okay for fish."

"Using my jokes now?"

"Whatever." He emptied out the pipe and starting packing it with fresh green.

My prediction had come true, Jesus had nailed the waitress. Her uncle owned the tavern; Bartholomew was his name, a quiet fella mostly but that all changed once he'd had a skinful. He had this rule, he didn't drink until the sun set, but once he started it was like he was making up for lost time. I was amazed at how much he could put away but put it down to years of practice. After he'd been on the sauce a while he'd just laugh and laugh. It sounded like I'd imagine a bear to laugh, if bears could laugh. When he was in that state I'd always tell him jokes because I knew he'd react the same regardless of whether they were good or not, and anyone in earshot would think I was the funniest guy in town.

Back to the waitress, well technically she wasn't a waitress, not according to her. She said she was just helping out while she was deciding what to do with her life. That was a new one on me. Girls didn't – and still don't - decide what to do with their lives, they just get married when the right bloke comes along. The right bloke in their dad's eyes that is. Maybe because her dad wasn't in the picture things were different for her.

I warned Jesus, both as a friend and as his professional advisor, not to shit on his own doorstep. If things went according to plan then he was going to be big news, and having a regular squeeze so close to home could be a real problem. Jesus' answer was as clear and as simple as always. "Be cool, she's cool. Everything's cool."

When I looked at her the word that came to mind was the complete opposite of cool. She was hot, hot as the fires of hell. Even if Jesus was right about her not being a problem for him, I knew she was going to be a problem for me. A big one. I couldn't take my eyes off her. Oh man I just wanted to take a big juicy bite.

I conceded eventually that Jesus was right, she was pretty cool. She wasn't clingy like so many are, at least it didn't look that way to me. She seemed to understand that Jesus wasn't your average schmuck who was going to be tied down to anything serious, not for the foreseeable future anyway. And even though she lived at Magdelene's too, she didn't expect to share his bed every night, and she didn't kick up a fuss when he got back really late. Or didn't get back at all.

Her name was Mary – same as his mum.

# Being Thad

Simon's main role in proceedings, apart from making sure Thad stayed upright, was looking after the finances. He'd been John's treasurer and still had what was left of the cash from the Jordan operation. Fair play to Simon, when it all went tits up he could have easily bolted with the loot. Nobody would have known in all the confusion. But I guess he believed in the cause. Or maybe he was a man of means as his manner suggested and didn't need the money. I thought about asking him but it wasn't really any of my business.

What I seem to be taking ages to say is that we had the cash to cover day to day costs; board and lodging, beer and the like. Jesus even kicked some back to the parents of those in the crew who'd given up work that had previously put food on the family table. I was sure Zebedee was pleased about that.

We didn't live like kings but we had enough not to have to do anything else to get by. That was important to Jesus. He wanted everyone completely focused on the business of the crew without other commitments getting in the way.

It became a regular thing for Jesus and me to sit at our favourite table outside Magdalene's, looking down at the town and enjoying the last knockings of the day. You could say it was business - the boss and his right hand man recapping on the events of the day, planning the next moves.

Things were rolling along nicely. Thad was working his magic, producing plenty of green, and James and John were doing a grand job of shifting it. It wasn't flying out of the sacks but that wasn't the plan. We were all about the slow and steady approach; getting long-term customers on board who'd keep coming back and would tell all their friends.

"It's all about forging lasting business relationships," Jesus had said.

"You can talk proper bollocks sometimes." It was okay for me to talk to him like that as long as nobody else was around.

On the other side of the business, Nat and Phil had started arranging low-key events starring the man himself. Nothing formal, just enough to let the punters catch a glimpse of Jesus and what he was all about. The plan was to get people talking, loosen them up for the next stage. That's what Phil said anyway. It didn't seem to me that they were actually doing anything much, except letting Jesus go out and do his thing, which he would have done anyway, but what did I know? Phil even had a name for these little walk and talks: *teaser tasters* he called them. Tempting as it was to call him out for spouting such flatulence, I played the bigger man and stayed out of it.

Talking of staying out of things, I had a right result. Because the green farming had gone so well and because we were still building up a customer base and hadn't shifted our backlog, Thad and Simon had plenty of time on their hands and offered to show Peter and Andrew the ins and outs of poppy extraction. Thad told me he was worried about treading on my toes after Jesus had said I was the expert trainer but I very kindly granted them permission to take the responsibility off me. I'm good like that.

Instead I was more than happy to take the lead in building the factory in Poppy Valley. It had been a while since I'd used my carpentry skills and it was fun to get back into it. Jesus was well up for getting involved and that was the first time I can say that I felt like a proper advisor with an eye on the bigger picture. I pointed out that a figurehead like him needed to keep a bit of mystery about him. He was a man of the people, sure, but he had to set himself apart from the rest of us, keep a distance from certain things. Hauling and nailing lumber definitely fell into the *distancing from* category. It took a while to convince him. I even had to throw a strop about how he wasn't taking my views on board but he saw sense in the end.

If I'm not mistaken, Jesus started to carry himself a bit differently after that, a bit more, I don't know, regal maybe. My instinct was to rip the piss out of him for it but I remembered the bollocking he'd given me for not taking things seriously enough. I was learning to shut my mouth.

So with me in charge of the project and using the trees we'd been sitting under when we first discovered the poppies, we knocked up a tidy little cabin, even if I do say so myself. The idea to build there had been because of convenience but it also solved a couple of problems that hadn't even occurred to us. The first was security. We could have someone on site all the time to keep guard on the place. The second was land ownership. The valley didn't officially belong to anyone but the law, according to Simon anyway, 'tended to recognise an owner as someone who was showing working use of the land'. Having our factory slap bang in the middle did us no harm at all on that front.

We planned a little opening ceremony but waited until after we'd processed the first harvest. The reason for waiting was obvious, it meant the bash we had after the ceremony had a much better standard of party-fuel. I took the opportunity to settle a score with myself. The first and only time I'd done the harder stuff it hadn't gone well, what with us having to ride off into the night on horseback and all, so I was keen to have a proper go. I wasn't sure if Jesus was going to dabble because he'd had an even worse experience than me last time around.

But he wasn't going to let the small matter of being visited by the Devil put him off. In fact he was first in the queue. He really did like to get high, that boy.

Mary was all over it too. It was the first time I'd seen her outside of her uncle's place and it didn't go well for me. I wouldn't say she was a buzz-kill, quite the opposite really, she intensified the buzz. But that was the problem. I could feel myself getting more and more into her, like she was at the heart of my whole trip. No matter where I looked or who I was talking to I'd find my gaze veering in her direction. Self-consciousness was starting to smother me. The last thing she needed was my big spazzed-up face staring at her all night. And the last thing I needed was to look like an unwanked cock in front of the whole crew.

Luckily there was a safe harbour to park my crazy-ship. Luckily there was Thad.

I was really getting to like Thad, particularly the fact that he didn't care what anybody thought about him. Unfettered by the fussy considerations that burdened the rest of us, Thad was just there to have a leviathan of a time.

Take his attitude to women (and I wished I could have taken his attitude to women). Whilst the likes of me would be standing on our heads to get a girl to look our way, Thad wouldn't even notice she was there, focused as he was on wringing every last drop of fun out of the here and now. It's not like he wasn't interested in women, he just never fell into the honey trap that claimed the dignity of so many of the rest of us. This cool detachment wasn't something he was conscious of. He wasn't playing any kind of game, he was just being Thad. Yet still, more often than not he wouldn't go home alone at the end of the night.

If it sounds like I was a wee bit jealous of Thad then it's because I was, completely. I wished I could breeze through life like he did, not trying to score points, not caring if anyone was impressed or even if anybody noticed me. But my jealousy didn't make me like him any less, and even though I knew I could never emulate him, I could at least tap into the vein of casual indifference that pulsed through him.

Thad was my only hope of escaping the deep hole into which I was sliding. The hole that was soft and wet and smooth and smelt of Mary. I knew Thad would be on a whole different level and I wanted to latch onto it, go wherever he was going in that uniquely fucked up head of his. I wanted a buzz that was unencumbered by sexual desire. A fun buzz.

Thad had set himself up in the corner, hunched over a table cluttered with tiny little bowls and bottles. A shrine of candles lit his face from all angles, making shadows dance around his eyes, nose and mouth. He looked like a happy devil - and I don't mean that like - *ooh he's a happy devil* - I mean he looked like I'd imagine the actual Devil to look if he took time out from all that brooding malevolence and cracked a smile once in a while.

"What you up to Thad?" It wasn't easy to get those words out. I was messed up.

He looked up at me with his usual crazy eyes but his voice was different than I was used to. He sounded almost as refined as Simon. "I'm putting all the key ingredients in place." He waved a hand at the rows of bowls in front of him. "I've assembled perfect doses to navigate the trip. Contained in these vessels are spirits. Spirit guides you could call them. They all have different roles to play, different advice to give. They help keep things smooth, keep things moving. There's method to this. There is a path to follow. Can you see the path?"

I peered aimlessly at the table. I wanted more than anything to see a path but of course I couldn't. "Sorry mate, no."

Thad smiled. "It doesn't matter. I have a map." He tapped

his head. "Up here."

I could feel myself starting to sink again. I'd pinned my hopes on Thad and in the world of my head, the world of green and poppy, he was deserting me. He was casting off and drifting away. Losing Thad would bring my world crashing down around me and all would be lost. Ridiculous, I know. Melodramatic and self-indulgent, absolutely. But a cast-iron truth to me at the time.

The hole opened and I slid downwards.

"You still with me?" I felt a hand on my arm. I was back in the room. I don't know if my eyes had been closed but now all I could see was Thad's wise, open face looking at me intently.

My response was meant to be a nod but more closely resembled the twitch of a prey animal, frightened out of its wits and with nowhere left to run.

He gripped my arm a little harder, he didn't know it but he was holding me over a bottomless pit of despair. Or maybe he did know it. "As I was saying," he said quietly, "I have a map. I can show you where the path goes." He let go of my arm and left me hanging. I knew I could drop at any moment. He opened a pouch and took out two gleaming gold pipes. He handed one to me. "Shall we go?"

Everything changed. I was no longer dangling over the precipice of disaster and he was no longer drifting away. I was at the wheel with Captain Thad, setting sail for uncharted seas.

I couldn't tell you much about the rest of the night but I was no longer distracted by Mary. Everything was cool.

# *Showtime*

"Now this is the part I don't understand. Those olives were delicious, each one more succulent, more tender, more tasty than the last." Simon was in full flow as he, along with Jesus, Thaddeus and me, took a late afternoon wander around Galilee.

"I can't stand olives."

Simon reacted like I'd offered to stick a pilum up his arse. "I beg your pardon? How can you not like olives? How can anybody not like olives?"

"I just don't, it's really that simple".

"I bet you do really, you just haven't tried the right ones. We'll source you some good quality olives and you can have a taste."

"What is it with people who like olives?" I snapped. "Why do they think it's their mission to convert non olive-likers? Why do you feel the need to spread the good word of the olive? What does it matter to you if I like olives or not?"

"I just think you need to try one."

"I've tried loads! I'm not five years old. I know what olives taste like and I know for sure I don't like them. I'm not being unreasonable, in fact I'd prefer it if I did like them, I mean, they grow everywhere so it'd be handy if I did. But I don't. I'm sorry but I don't like olives. Actually I'm not sorry. Why should I be sorry?"

"I still think you should try a nice olive."

"Tell your story before I punch you in your olive-loving

98

head."

"Well if you're dying to hear my story then I'll get back to it. Where was I? Ah yes, I was eating olives, and incidentally, if it sounded like I was stuffing them down like a gannet then that is not the case. I had a small bowl, perhaps a dozen olives. When I had finished I disposed of the stones and rinsed the bowl. My repast was complete."

"I've heard this one," said Thad. "It ends with you getting the shits."

"Well, thank you, Thaddeus. Please accept my heartfelt gratitude for truncating my story for me. I was, as I'm sure you could tell, finding the ordeal of relating it almost unbearable, despising as I do the cadences of my own articulations. But in point of fact you have not *heard* it before. You saw it. You witnessed the event. It was yesterday."

Thaddeus looked at me and Jesus with a big grin on his face. "It ends with him getting the shits."

"But surely it's not the destination that matters. It is the pleasure of the journey."

Jesus piped up. "You're obviously going to tell this story regardless so you may as well just get on with it."

"Thank you. So, it wasn't until sunset that I felt something deep inside me, something untoward."

"I'll give you something untoward deep inside you," said Thaddeus.

"Are you threatening to stick a pilum up my backside?"

"Just tell the fucking story," said Jesus.

"I'm trying to. So as I was saying, I felt that something was afoot. It was just a bit of discomfort at first but it quickly progressed to stabbing pains. I was in very real distress, doubled over in agony."

"He don't look good."

"No, Thaddeus, I didn't look good at all."

"Not you, him." For someone whose eyes were perpetually bloodshot, Thad must have had pretty good vision. I couldn't even tell who he was pointing at, let alone see what sort of state they were in. After much squinting I could just about make out the rough shape of someone walking towards us. It was a little while before I could see enough detail to realise that Thad had a point, he wasn't quite right. I don't mean Thad, by the way. We all know he's not quite right. I mean the bloke who was walking in our direction. It wasn't that he was wobbling all over the place, like me on a camel. It was more that he was trying a little too hard to keep himself steady. The closer he got to us the more we could see that this guy was definitely a few rocks short of a stoning. He was tall, gangly you might say, and had crazy wide eyes.

He came right up to us and stood face to face with Jesus. The rest of us straightened up, ready to step in if it looked like trouble. The wide-eyed gangly man was staring into Jesus' eyes and Jesus was staring straight back.

Keeping their eyes locked, they started moving their heads from side to side.

Thad looked as confused as the rest of us. "What are they up to? It's like they're doing that mirror trick."

A bell rang in my head and I remembered. It was the wide-eyed gangly man we'd met on the first night in John's camp. He and Jesus had done the same routine but it had seemed a lot friendlier back then. In fact if I remember rightly it had ended with a man-hug. Not this time. The wide-eyed man suddenly stepped a few paces back and for no reason at all started howling like an animal.

"That's not appropriate behaviour." Simon.

"What the fuck, man?" Thad.

"Jesus!" Me.

"I've got this." Jesus.

The wide-eyed gangly man howled for a while longer, long enough for a crowd to form to see what the hell was going on. Then he stopped. He pointed a gangly arm at Jesus. "It's you, you're *him*. You're Jesus of Nazareth."

"Yes, that's me, how can I…"

Jesus didn't get a chance to finish because the wide-eyed gangly man went berserk. "Leave me alone, leave all of us alone. You've come to kill us all!" His eyes looked like they were going to burst out of his head as he screamed and ranted and waved his arms. "You've come to destroy us!" His crazy eyes flashed around the growing crowd. "He has, you know, he's come to destroy us!"

"Enough!" Jesus' voice caught me off guard. It caught everybody off guard. It wasn't like his voice; it was like the boom of a cannon. Everything stopped. There was nothing anyone could do but pay attention. Jesus was in charge.

He faced the gangly man, whose eyes weren't quite as wide as they had been a few moments before. Jesus spoke softly. "Give me your hand." Without hesitation the gangly man did as he was told. Jesus put his free hand on top of the man's head. He didn't raise his voice. "Evil spirits, leave this man, you have no place here. He does not want you. You must depart and make way for the good. Leave him." He gripped more tightly and then he was using the cannon-voice again: "Leave him. Leave him *now*!"

The man jolted as if struck by lightning and Jesus released his grip. He fell to his knees – the gangly man, not Jesus. The crowd were totally hooked on the action, me included. There was total silence and we all carefully watched the man crouching motionless at Jesus' feet. As if waking from a stupor he lifted his head sharply, blinking like the daylight had been suddenly turned up. He held out his arms and looked at them as if he'd never seen them before. He stared at his hands, turning them over so he could check both sides. He looked up into Jesus' eyes and when he spoke his voice was totally different than it had been before. It was, well, not mad is the best way to describe it.

"My lord, you have saved me. You have plucked out the evil and now I can live again. You despatched the darkness and now I see only light. You are the chosen one and I am forever in your debt." He lowered his head.

There was a shout from somewhere in the crowd. "He cast out that poor wretch's demons, it's a miracle!" The voice sounded familiar but I couldn't place it. Then I heard another shout, saying something pretty similar but in a much more whiny voice, which I had no doubt belonged to Phil.

The crowd started cheering and shouting. *Miracle* seemed to be the key word.

"Who is this man?" Phil's voice again. "Who is this great healer with the power to cast out evil spirits?"

The reply, which I now realised had to be Nat's voice, came from the other side of the crowd, they'd obviously split up to make their show more convincing. "This man is Jesus Christ, and casting out demons is the least of what he can do. He is the chosen one. Let him speak."

The crowd hushed and everybody stared at Jesus. The wide-eyed gangly man was still on his knees with his head bowed. Jesus took a deep breath. He had the crowd dangling from his fingertips. He could have whispered and still have been heard. "I am nothing. I merely invited the spirits to leave this man so they could make room for the spirit of God. Demons will not stand in God's way, they cannot. They do not know how."

"He carries the spirit of God!" Nat called from the back.

Jesus held his hands up in front of him as if batting away the suggestion. "To say I carry the spirit of God is correct. But to say I am special is not. We all have the spirit of God inside us, or at least we can if we invite him to be inside us."

"We don't know how. Show us how." This was an actual punter in the crowd, not one of ours.

"You already know, but I am happy to show you. Today I am merely out walking with my friends, but I will be willing to speak to anybody who cares to listen. If you wish to change your life, if you wish to be happy and make those around you happy, then you may find it interesting. Otherwise this is not for you. At sundown tomorrow I shall be…" he looked around him, "…is this as good a place as any?"

More than a few people shouted in agreement.

"Then here is where I shall be. Come along. Bring your friends, bring your family, all are welcome." He raised an arm, bringing the show to a close. "Thank you friends, see you tomorrow."

Phil and Nat were on Jesus straight away, ahead of a load of others trying to get close to him. Nat played the role of an excited fan, gushing praise into Jesus' face while Phil whispered at us through the side of his mouth. You don't know us, right? Get tight around Jesus and tell us we've got to leave, that he needs space."

Simon carried out Phil's instructions and addressed the huddle around him. "Please, such a… *happening* is very draining for Jesus, he needs time to recover. He needs space, please respect this."

Nat nodded and answered loudly, maybe a little too loudly. "I respect his wishes and will give him the space he requires. I will come tomorrow at sundown to see more." He looked around at the crowd behind him. "Let us leave the man in peace, he has worked a wonder, we will let him rest."

Phil whispered again. "Get him out. We've got to leave them wanting more. See you back at Mags."

Phil and Nat scattered with the rest of the crowd while we

led Jesus away in what must have looked like one of those Roman attack formations, the turtle or whatever, but less impressive because there were only four of us. And we didn't have helmets or armour.

"So do you want to fill us in on what the fuck just happened?" I asked Jesus when we were clear of the crowd.

"I'm sure you've worked it out but we'll talk when everyone gets back. I'm looking forward to a beer. This casting out of demons is thirsty work."

## Post-Match Analysis

At Magdelene's, the four of us sat in near-silence. All we wanted to talk about was the whole demon casting out thing, and Jesus had already said he wasn't going to discuss it until the others got back so there wasn't much in the way of chat. On top of this, I for one wasn't particularly happy at having been left out of such a big operation and having had to watch it unfold with the rest of the plebs.

I wasn't sure exactly what had gone on but I had a rough idea. It was obvious that Phil and Nat were in on it. And Jesus of course. If Thad and Simon were anything like me then they must have felt aggrieved too, like they'd been left out of some big private joke.

Mary put a jug of wine and four glasses down on the table. Jesus leaned over and kissed her. It was only a peck on the cheek but the way they looked at each other was like they were properly at it. "We're going to need some more glasses babe, another three. Better bring another jug too, we're celebrating."

"No problem, honey."

I must have been distracted by the sight of Mary's arse as it oozed away but Thad, always sharper than anyone gives him credit for, picked up on what Jesus had just said. "Three glasses? Who else is coming apart from Phil and Nat?"

Jesus smiled. "All will be revealed."

When Phil and Nat turned up they were trading high-fives and doing that fist pumping thing that idiots do when they're excited.

"We're all here now," I said, "so I'll repeat my question from earlier. "What the fuck just happened?"

Jesus downed half his glass. "Not yet, we're one missing. He won't be long."

"Who?"

"Thomas."

"Should I know who you're talking about?"

"You should have no trouble recognising him. In fact, here he is now. Tom! Get over here you crazy bastard!"

I looked over my shoulder and there was the wide-eyed gangly man, swaggering his way over, grinning like the Devil himself. Jesus jumped up and hugged him, almost picking him up. "How are you feeling? Demons all gone?"

Thomas, along with Phil and Nat, doubled up with laughter.

I cleared my throat, loudly. "I don't want to be a killjoy but you haven't answered my question."

"I'll let my two marketing geniuses field that one if you don't mind." He bowed his head. "Philip, Nathanael?"

Phil looked at me. "You've probably worked it out already haven't you? You're a sharp enough fella."

The compliment put me in a better mood. "I've got to say I did think something was up when you and Nat appeared from out of nowhere – well you didn't even appear, I just heard you shouting." I looked at Thomas, shaking my head. "I thought this guy was for real though, I was close to slapping him when he started screaming."

"Yeah," said Jesus. "Sorry for keeping you lot in the dark but it had to look good. You had to look as surprised as everyone else."

Thad spoke up. "Well you got what you wanted, I was surprised."

Simon snorted. "Well that's no biggie is it? I've seen you

surprised by your own face when you've been inebriated, which happens to be most of the time."

"I'll surprise *your* face in a minute," said Thad.

"I am really sorry for keeping you three out of this," said Jesus. "It had to look natural, and I think it did. But it wasn't my plan. I just did as I was told." He nodded at Phil. "He's the brains behind the operation, the one to Phil you in."

"I see what you did there!" Phil was nearly coming in his loincloth. I could hardly bear to listen to him. "There's not much to tell, really. It was a big fat set-up, but you know that already. The only bit you don't know is that I met Tom a few days ago. He saw one of the teaser taster walkabouts, recognised the big guy and we got talking. He was well up for getting involved. And it couldn't have worked better. Everyone did a fantastic job. This was massive, we really got noticed."

Nat took over. "Tom, you were priceless, absolutely bang-on. You pitched it just right. And Jesus, well what can I say? I don't want to suck dick but you're a pro. That speech after you'd cast out the demons - everything about it was perfect. I loved the way you made out like you were playing yourself down, being all humble, but nobody was in any doubt what the real message was - *I'm the man, I can do all kinds of shit, you'd better not miss out on this.* And when you did the voice, fuck me man! You nailed it. All that practice was well worth it. You scared the shit out of me to be honest. It sounded like God Himself was talking. There'll definitely be a crowd tomorrow night." I'd never heard Nat talk this much before, or this excitedly. He'd obviously found his calling.

Jesus yawned and stretched. "Talking of tomorrow night, I need to be fresh, so I'd better get my beauty sleep. You lot should do the same."

The collective disappointment was audible. The evening had had that mad-night-about-to-kick-off feel about it but now the boss was telling us all to turn in. Our candles were well and truly pissed on.

Jesus raised his glass and grinned. "Got you, suckers! Come on, let's get fucked up."

And so we did. Phil assumed it was a celebration of the event he'd orchestrated and spent the whole evening blathering on to everyone about how carefully planned it had been and how well it had gone. I personally saw the night as a welcoming party for Tom. He seemed like a decent enough bloke. At first I'd assumed from the wide eyes and how I remembered him from before that he was cut from the same cloth as Thad, but it turned out that he wasn't as… eccentric as our Thaddeus.

It was a good night but I couldn't get into it like I normally could. It felt that things were changing a bit too fast for little old me.

After everyone else had crawled back to their lodgings it was just me and Jesus left. Even Mary had gone to bed. If I was in Jesus' sandals I would have followed her straight there, but then if I was in his sandals I wouldn't ever have been wearing sandals, because I'd always be in bed. With Mary.

But for once I had other things on my mind.

Jesus broke the silence. "Come on then, out with it. There's something you want to say. You've wanted to say it all night whatever it is."

All of a sudden I was stone cold sober. "I just wondered if this is how it's going to be now."

"You're going to have to be a bit more specific."

"Cheap tricks, conning people. I thought there was a bit more to us than that."

He looked angry but checked himself and sighed. "You're right. Of course you're right. It's not something I was particularly happy with."

"You looked happy enough. You were partying pretty hard

with the rest of them."

"Listen, if I'm going to be the boss of this crew and take it where it needs to go then I can't show any doubts about anything. Once I've made a decision I've got to stand by it. They've got to see that I'm rock solid."

"Makes sense, but why make that decision in the first place?"

"I've thought about this a lot mate, trust me. And no, it's not ideal. But here's how I see it. The people around here don't have much. They spend most of their time working and the rest getting shat on by whoever's in charge, and at the moment that cunt Antipas is in charge. If by putting on a bit of show I can fire up their imaginations and get their attention then what harm can it do?"

"It can fill their heads with shit, that's pretty harmful."

"I'm not filling their heads with shit. I'm filling their heads with hope. And you can be damn sure that everything I say - however much it might be tarted up with a display like this afternoon's - is something I believe in. That stuff about casting out the evil and letting the good in? I meant that. Okay, so Tom was faking and I don't believe in actual demons, but I do think that people spend too much time focusing on the bad shit in their lives when if they just looked a bit closer they'd see that there's a lot more good shit. And it's a lot more satisfying to wallow in good shit than it is in bad shit." He saw me smiling and that set him off, he couldn't keep a straight face anymore. "Yeah, I know, I'm talking about wallowing in shit now, I've just been burbling on haven't I? I forgot how drunk I was. Jesus."

I raised my arms triumphantly. "You did it! You fucking did it!"

"Did what?"

"You took your name in vain."

He put his hands to his mouth like a little girl who'd just said 'poo'. "I don't believe it. How did that happen? It just…"

"Fits?"

"Yes! It just fits. Oh for fuck's sake."

"If it makes you feel any better, what you were saying before, yes you were burbling but there was some sense in there. I wouldn't be able to repeat it back to you because I'm as arseholed as you are but there was definitely something in all that stuff about hope and… good and bad shit… and, whatever."

His face went serious again and he looked me in the eyes. "Listen mate, we might be bullshitting people but we're never going to… *bullshit* them, you get me?"

I nodded. "So," I said, "that voice you did today, that mad loud voice?"

"Yeah?"

"What the fuck?"

"I've got to say I was pretty pleased with how that went."

"Nat said you'd been practicing?"

"Yeah, it takes a bit of work. When I've been over at Poppy Valley where nobody can hear me I've been getting it down."

"Peter and Simon would have heard you, so I guess they knew about it too?"

Jesus nodded.

"Where are they tonight anyway?"

"They're staying in the valley, keeping an eye on things." He leaned over and gripped my shoulder like a drunken uncle at a wedding. "Listen mate, I'm glad we had this talk tonight. I'm glad I can count on you to speak your mind, that's why it's so important you're here. I've said it before and I hope I say it again - I couldn't do this without you."

I was pleased but embarrassed like any mate would be. I shuffled on my stool. "Cheers mate."

And if I do start acting like a prick I know you'll be there to say, Jesus, you're being a prick. You will, won't you?"

"Trust me, I'll call you a prick until the camels come home."

His eyes narrowed. "But not in front of the others, never in front of the others."

"I get it. Jesus."

"Stop doing that!"

"You can't tell me not to anymore, you've started doing it yourself. It's open season now."

"Fuck it," he said, "whatever." He raised his glass. "To the good shit, may it keep out all the bad shit."

## Customer Base

Jesus' first proper, organised – I don't know what to call it really - performance maybe, was a pretty straightforward affair. I was in on the pep-talk beforehand. I'm pretty sure they made a point of including me because I'd made such a fuss last time. Phil stressed that there'd be nothing supernatural, just Jesus, his message and most importantly of all, his charisma.

"We've got to manage people's expectations," he'd told us through his nose. "If we do something mind-blowing every time then people are going to expect it every time, and that's unsustainable."

Like we hadn't worked that out for ourselves.

"It's a coordinated strategy," Nat had added.

"Yeah, thanks Nat," said Phil. "It's coordinated, long term. We've got to keep the fuse burning. Every now and again we'll throw something big at them to stir up a bit of a buzz - get people talking - but for the most part we'll stick to the simple stuff. Our man sells himself just fine without any fancy business anyway."

It sticks in my throat to say something positive about Phil - and to a lesser extent, Nat - but it was amazing how quickly they'd taken to this business. The roles had been thrown at them pretty much at random but the way they talked you'd think they'd been born into the trade. I say trade, you can't really call the business of bullshit a trade but I wasn't going to tell either of them that. They were probably just blagging it mostly but they did seem to be doing a decent job of it. Just as Nat had predicted the day before, there was a big old crowd.

A nice touch was to have Thomas introduce Jesus. He was all *I'm living proof of what this guy can do*, and he played it well. As Phil had said, there was no more trickery after that and I was glad of it. Even though Jesus had won me over on the need to spice up the truth to make an impact it still felt more comfortable keeping it simple, if only because there was less chance of being found out that way.

It's no disrespect to Jesus to say that he wasn't playing to the toughest of crowds. Nothing much happened in this town and when it did it was pretty predictable stuff so it wasn't too hard to impress for someone who knew what he was doing. And Jesus knew exactly what he was doing. His message was refreshingly simple, a departure from the usual diet of endless detail - scripture, prophecies, lists and rules – that folks were used to. He was passionate and funny, the guys found him endearing and the girls found him extremely easy on the eye. He was easy on the ear too, putting things in a way that made you feel like you were working it out for yourself rather than just being told what you should and shouldn't be doing.

What surprised me most was the material he'd come up with. I'd spent more time than anyone with Jesus but I hadn't heard any of this stuff before. I didn't know if he'd practised it or not but he just seemed to reel it out off the top of his head. The message was in a similar furrow to that ploughed by John but it wasn't at all like he'd ripped it off. It was all Jesus, and all good. I really enjoyed it, not as one of his crew but just as a punter. And of course he went down a storm with the crowd.

The audience was less hysterical than before, which was to be expected because there was no casting out of demons this time, but they were just as enthusiastic.

Jesus did a bit of a Q and A at the end and he dealt with

every question smoothly. The only wobble was when he was asked, "How do we follow you?" Tricky one really, I wouldn't have known what to say if I'd been asked that. It wasn't like you signed up to be in the official Jesus club.

There was a long pause before he answered. "Stay close and keep your eyes and ears open." Later on, in the inevitable celebration, Nat singled that comment out for special praise, pointing out that to have the confidence to hesitate, almost like he was off guard and look like he was really thinking before answering, "Was an example of a master orator at work". He'd looked at Jesus with proud eyes. "When you finally sprang the answer on them it was even more powerful. Obviously the pause was all for show, you knew exactly what you were going to say."

"I had no fucking clue," Jesus told me later. "I was caught cold and my mind went blank. To be honest I can't even remember what I ended up saying."

Whether Nat was right and Jesus was just being modest or if he had pulled it out of the bag at the last minute, it had done the trick. Plenty of the adoring crowd had taken the advice to stay close to heart and piled back to Magdalene's with us. It was the perfect moment for James and John to do their thing. As our sales department, they had the job of taking all these excited punters and turning them into customers. It wasn't difficult, the stuff sold itself, but like Phil and Nat, our self-styled marketing whiz-kids, James and John wanted to show they were on top of it all.

They hurriedly got us together before the drinks started flowing and gave us our instructions. "Please just smoke like you would normally. Don't say anything, just get nicely high."

Thad pulled a face. "I was gonna do that anyway. I'm doing it now."

"Yeah, well that's no surprise Thad. But you didn't let me

finish. If anyone asks you about it then just say they should talk to me or James."

"And who are you?"

"You know who I am. I'm John."

"James' brother?"

"Yes."

"You don't look like John."

"I *am* John."

"You don't look like James then."

John looked like he was thinking carefully how to word his answer before settling on what he'd probably thought of in the first place. "What the fuck, Thad? Just do it."

"Okay." Thad leaned down and took a huge pull on the bong wedged between his knees under the table.

John's plan hadn't seemed like much but it worked a treat. We got high, all casual, like, and loads of Jesus' new-found fans were curious enough to get involved. We did take a bit of a detour from our instructions, though. When they showed an interest in what we were doing we didn't send them straight to John or James, instead we let them sample the product. If Thad had got his way we would have given them freebies all night but I played the wise-guy and pointed out that when somebody's overdone it on the green, the last thing they want to do is buy more green. Everybody else saw the sense in that. Except Thad.

"You can't overdo it on the green," he argued. "If you could then I'd know about it. It would have happened to me."

Simon put him straight. "My dear Thaddeus, your own experiences can't be taken into consideration here. Granted, you have probably indulged in this particular medicine more than anybody else in the world, perhaps more than everybody else in the world *put together*, and yet, as you say, you have never overdone it. That can be taken as fact. However, what you need to remember, my friend, is that you are an aberration. In your case the normal rules do not apply."

"An abberwhatnow?"

"You're a freak."

"Fair enough. I'll send them to James or to that other one just before their eyes go all like mine."

"A little bit before that if you don't mind old boy, but yes, that's the way to go."

Business was, as they say, brisk, not just for us but for Uncle Bart, who was suddenly running the busiest bar in town. I passed him on my way back from the first of my many visits to the latrine. "A few more nights like this and you could retire," I said.

He finished pouring a beer and squeezed it onto the bar in front of him. "Maybe not retire but I'm not going to complain." He nodded at the dozen or so beers that sat on the counter waiting to be collected. "These are going down like the Walls of Jericho. I know it's because of you lot, so cheers for that. Seems like there's some kind of new fad going on too, everyone's smoking that funny stuff." He looked at me almost interrogatively. "That's got something to do with you lot too I s'pose?"

I thought about denying it but realised I would have made fools of us both if I tried. The sun hadn't quite set outside so this was pre-drink Bart, his wits still about him. I knew he'd spot bullshit a mile off and I didn't want to deceive him anyway. "Yep, that's us."

"I'm not knocking it but if it's going on in my place then I should know what I'm into. Be good if someone could fill me in sometime." He started pouring another beer. "Y'know, when it's less busy."

I felt a hand on arm and turned to see Mary. She was easing her way past me to get to the bar, and my heart, which had lifted to my throat at that touch, dropped to my guts. She scooped up four of the beers from the counter and with a smile turned to take them out to the thirsty faithful. She had a good system going. There was no time to take payment each time she served a batch of drinks so she marked in chalk on the table so the punters could settle up later. Her method relied heavily on honesty of course, but the assumption was that Jesus' followers weren't likely to steal a few beers.

"Hello?" Bart had stopped pouring and was facing me with both hands on the counter. The smirk on his face said it all. "Distracted were we?"

Again, I would have been fooling us both if I tried to say anything other than what he could see with his own eyes so I chose to ignore the question, statement, whatever. "So anyway Bart, back to what you were saying, yes, it's only right that we fill you in on this new fad as you called it."

Bart was pouring again but he was still smiling. "Sounds good, you know where I am. Just for now though, whatever it is, does it make you hungry when you smoke it?"

"That is a side effect, yes."

"Ah, that'll be why. Everyone's been ordering food. I've had to send my daughter out to get more stuff in."

"I thought she was your niece."

"No she's definitely my daughter."

"She wasn't gone long."

He stopped pouring again. "Who are you talking about?"

"Mary. If you sent her out for provisions then she got back bloody quickly."

"I'm not talking about Mary. I'm talking about my daughter."

"I don't think I've met your daughter."

"She's here every day."

"Oh."

"And you've never noticed her?"

"No."

"She doesn't look like Mary. That'll be why." He put the latest beer on the counter and started pouring again. There was no trace of a smile anymore.

I hurried back to our table.

I was disappointed to find Phil holding court and even more disappointed that most of the crew seemed to be listening to what he had to say. "Tonight was big, but we need to go bigger next time. We should take it out of town, make it different. Make it an event."

It didn't seem like anyone else was going to stop him running away with himself so I did the honours. "But it's a pain for people to get out of town."

"Exactly, that's what makes it an event. If they feel like they've had to go to a bit of effort then they'll feel more invested in it, like they're in on something."

"They are in on something."

"Exactly."

Twat.

# How You Going to Feed That Lot?

It was late morning when I got to the site of Phil's big out of town event. By the time I'd got up, everyone had left so I'd had to go by the directions on the posters dotted around town. 'Head north', they said. That was all. One of Phil's strokes of communication genius, I imagined.

Actually it wasn't a bad idea and I found the place easily, although it was quite a walk.

I had to begrudgingly accept that Phil had chosen the location well, apart from it being so far out. It was a natural amphitheatre, in fact it was so perfectly formed you'd think it had been dug out and smoothed by Egyptian slaves. The crowds weren't due for a while yet and I could see most of the crew around and about, along with a few dozen volunteers who'd jumped on the band-chariot and offered to help set up.

They'd all been busy in my absence. About two-thirds of the way up the western slope there was the mouth of a cave, one of those dark scary ones that give you the heebie-jeebies when you think about what might be inside. In front of that was a wooden stage, not big but a tidy enough job. On the southern side of the dip there was a long counter with barrels behind it. I could see Mary arranging jugs and cups along its length. A big flat rock on the slope just above this makeshift bar bore the legend, 'your cup may runneth over but bring it back, you'll need it again'.

Along the opposite side ran several rows of latrines, again, makeshift is the best description but they looked functional enough. Privacy wasn't the order of the day but there were a few trees dotted about for anyone who was shy.

It was quite a set-up.

"You made it then?" My view of pits dug to accommodate bodily waste was replaced with that of Mary, smiling and shielding her eyes from the sun. I nearly melted in the glow of that smile. "Hey you," I said weakly.

"Hey to you, too."

I nodded in the direction of the bar. "That's impressive work."

"Not too shabby is it? I can't take all the credit though, Uncle Bart was in charge and we had more than half the volunteers on it. It was a lot of heaving and hoisting but we got there. I'm pretty good at erecting things."

I tried not to react just in case she had said it innocently, which I'm more than sure she hadn't. "How did you get all the wood here?"

"You're saying you don't know how to get wood?"

I didn't know what her game was. If it had been anyone else I could have happily played along, but not with her. I could feel my tongue tying itself in a big fat knot. I steered away from the conversational traps. "How many of you are going to be running the bar?"

"There's room for about twenty behind there. We're on a mission to keep the beer flowing."

"Will you have enough?" I couldn't take my eyes off the red pendant that rose up and down with her breathing, hoisted by those wonderful bags of fun on her chest.

"Uncle Bart's taken the cart back to pick up more barrels. He's gone back and forth I don't know how many times today. He'll probably do at least one more trip after this one. If you're about when he gets back you can help us unload."

"Will do. But do you think it's going to be that busy?"

"Definitely, Phil's all over this."

I had to stop myself from saying something cutting about Phil in case I looked like a bitter and twisted fucker. Even though I was starting to accept that I *was* a bitter and twisted fucker.

"Anyway, better see what else I'm needed for." Mary danced off in Jesus' direction.

I could see Phil loving being in charge of a group of volunteers, waving his arms about and talking out of that face of his. They dispersed in smaller groups, presumably burdened with fresh orders. I took a wide berth in an attempt to get to Thad and Simon on Phil's far side without him seeing me, but his head was darting about like a meerkat's as he busily surveyed what he saw as his master plan coming to fruition so I had no chance. As soon as he saw me sneaking past he was on me like a plague of locusts. "Ah, you're alive after all. Come to help out? The day's not over, not quite anyway."

I swallowed the obvious two-word response. "If I'm needed, yes." I pointed up at the cave. "What's up there? I just saw someone move."

"There's nobody up there now but that's where the big man's going to do his thing. It's the perfect spot, having the cave behind will beef his voice up - make it carry further. We're going to need that 'cause there's going to be a shitload of people here today."

"I get that bit. I meant, what's happening in the cave?"

"Nothing, it's just providing the acoustics."

"I just saw someone inside."

"There's nobody inside. And you know what they say, mate, curiosity killed the camel."

"No they don't. Nobody says that."

"I do. I say it. Anyway, like I say mate, don't worry about it.

It's all good."

He was as good as patting me on the head like I was an over-inquisitive child. It was becoming increasingly difficult not to punch his stupid face. "I'm going to go and help Thad and Simon," I said.

"Do they need help then?"

"I don't care. I'm going to help them anyway."

Jesus' star had risen in the last few months. After every public appearance he'd picked up more followers, and always the enthusiastic kind who were bursting to tell their friends what they'd seen. There hadn't been much need for any of the supernatural stuff recently. Jesus' reputation had taken on a life of its own and plenty of people were going around telling anyone who'd listen how he'd cast out their demons, healed their sickness and even cured their blindness or given them the ability to walk again. Whether anyone believed them or not didn't really matter, it was fantastic publicity either way.

It could be said that it was the green-infused parties that caught the public imagination but I wasn't so sure. Without Jesus people would still have come to us for what we sold but not in such numbers, and they certainly wouldn't have stuck around. With Jesus' passion, showmanship and most importantly of all, his message, *just be nice to each other for fuck's sake*, we stood for something, something that people wanted to be part of. We were what you might call a movement. We just happened to be making money off it, which is no bad thing. Everyone's got to make a shekel or two.

So Jesus was the hottest ticket in town, and at every event I'd become used to seeing a bigger crowd than the last. Today was no exception, in fact today was a monster. The crowds started to trickle, flow and then flood into this natural arena, and once again I had to give Phil the credit for having been right. Well, I didn't actually give him the credit to his face, I just thought it, and even that was more than he deserved.

There was a real carnival feeling in the air. Entertainers bounced through the crowd doing a variety of turns; dancing, singing and somersaulting in return for a handful of shekels. We were happy to let them do their thing. It all helped keep the punters occupied in the build-up to the main event and generate an atmosphere. The one thing we did have to clamp down on was preaching. Quite a few had come along to release their dogma into the world. This was our crowd and we couldn't let our message be diluted or distorted by just anyone with a loud voice and a need for attention. Thad and Thomas were perfect for the job of shutting up these street-preachers. They didn't get rough but they were imposing and insistent. It was all in the eyes.

When the time came, Jesus nailed it. I could try and describe what he said and how he said it but I wouldn't do it justice. He just did his thing and the punters loved it. Phil was – oh for fuck's sake – right again, Jesus' voice did really carry, but what he said wasn't the important thing, it was the way he said it, the way he held himself up there on that slope with the sun beaming over the crest of the ridge above him. You couldn't take your eyes off him.

I didn't feel like I was watching my best mate anymore, it felt like I was watching a genius at work, although that doesn't really cover it. I'd been impressed by him before but maybe the detachment of watching him from further away allowed me to take in the full impact. I'd got used to seeing the look of wonder on the faces of the audience as they fell under his spell, and now I could feel that same look sprouting all over my own face like a fungus. It was so weird, standing there, soppy faced and choking up, not like a father bursting with pride at his child's performance, but the other way around. I was the child and he was the father. And it wasn't pride I felt. It was something close to hero-worship.

After Jesus worked his magic the party really kicked off. Bart and Mary's crew were dishing out beer like it was going out of fashion and the collective cloud of smoke from the cornucopia of contraptions engulfed us like, well, like a big cloud of smoke.

And then everyone got hungry.

I hadn't thought about that. We were stuck out in the middle of nowhere, off our boxes and with nothing to eat. I took a note to give Phil an earful for dragging us out there and not thinking about feeding us. To be fair I could have thought of it myself and brought something to keep me going but I didn't feel like being fair, not to Phil. And besides, if I'd been seen eating food I reckon I would have been set upon by the angry mob and had it stolen off me. I say angry mob, nobody was really angry, what with them all being off their tits. They were more of a hungry mob.

And then I saw Phil up by the mouth of the cave next to Jesus. He was holding up both hands, two fish dangled from one, and in the other was a basket holding some loaves of bread. He called out to the crowd. "Is anybody hungry?"

Everyone answered, that was an easy one.

Phil did his fake smile, his cheeks tightening into shiny little balls. "But this is all we have, two fish and these five loaves."

"What the fuck?" More than one person called out.

"It would take a miracle to feed everyone with what we've got here. Do we know anyone with any previous in performing miracles?" The crowd bellowed Jesus' name.

Jesus stepped onto the platform. Phil passed him the basket and the fish and Jesus set it all down in front of him. He looked at the crowd. They were silent, expectant. "Hungry, anyone?"

After the obvious answer, Jesus reached down, pulled up a loaf and threw it to the crowd. He did it again, this time with a fish, then another loaf, then two fish and more loaves. He repeated the process a few times and it took a few moments for people to twig that we were now well past the five loaves and two fish that we'd started with. But when it did sink in they went crazy. Jesus stood up and fixed them with that look, that *I got this* look. He nodded as the cheers grew louder then held up a hand, cutting the sound dead. "Better get some fires lit," he said. "These fish aren't going to cook themselves." The noise was deafening as Jesus kept it coming, reaching down and flinging out fish and bread over and over.

I don't know how many people were actually there that day but it had to be a thousand. Or it could have been five thousand. I don't know. It was a lot of people.

# Fall Out

"You dug a tunnel?"

"No, we're not that good. There was one already there, I think it must have been a stream once and now it's just a hole. We put the platform on top of that, with a gap so Bart could pass the stuff up through."

"Bit of a cheap trick."

Phil let out a long sigh before answering me. "Listen mate, I know you think I'm an arsehole and you're probably right, I'm a cocky little gobshite when I get going. But all I'm trying to do is get the job done. I know you and the big man go way back and I know you don't trust some of us latecomers, well you don't trust me that's for sure. But nobody's trying to fuck anything up. Except Thad, but he's only trying to fuck himself up, and for some reason that seems to work out okay for him. I'm not saying you and me are ever going to be close friends, and feel free to think I'm an arsehole as much as you want, but there's no point in us constantly niggling at each other."

The stunt with the fish and bread had left a bad taste in my mouth (pun intended). I could see why they'd done it and wasn't angry about it, not with Jesus anyway, but it didn't feel right so I'd avoided all the back-slapping that took place afterwards. Phil had obviously noticed and the morning after, while I sat outside Magdalene's enjoying a fruit juice and my own company, he'd sought me out. Arguing with Phil was well within my field of expertise but I wasn't used to such sincerity from him. Him attempting to make peace was more than I could handle.

I didn't really know what to say so I thought I'd try being honest. "But sometimes, you're a bit..."

"A bit what?"

"It doesn't matter."

"No, tell me, I'm a bit what?"

"A bit of a prick."

Phil put his hands behind his head and leaned back. "Okay, I'll tell you what, how about fuck you? You're only here because you happen to be Jesus' mate. You're not actually getting anything done, not like the rest of us. Bart's an *innkeeper* and he's contributed more than you, and that's with Jesus shagging his favourite niece."

"His only niece."

"Trust you to know the family tree. You don't need the wisdom of Solomon to work out what your motives are there. You're always leering at her, dribbling and shit. It's embarrassing. Word of advice, mate…"

"I don't want your advice."

"Yeah, well you're going to get it anyway, because, like I'm sure you've pointed out when you've been bitching about me behind my back, I fucking love the sound of my own voice. So here it is. When you're the right hand man to a guy like Jesus you get plenty of birds falling into your lap. So why don't you take advantage of the enviable position you've somehow found yourself in and get your own pussy. And when your boss's missus is around, put your tongue away. Prick."

It didn't seem appropriate to throw a punch so I jabbed him in the eye.

He clamped a hand over one side of his face. "Really? That's your answer? You poke me in the fucking eye?"

"Yep, that's it." I poked his other eye.

He did a little girly squeal and his other hand flew up to his face. He looked like he was *it* in a game of hide and seek. "You're a joke, you know that?"

I kicked him under the table, making sure the front edge of my sandal caught him nicely on the shin.

He took his hands away from his face and looked at me through bloodshot eyes. "Do that again and I'll mess you up."

It would have been really funny to slap him but I thought it might be a bit much. "No, Phil, you're not going to mess me up, I'll tell you what you're going to do, you're going to fuck off."

Thad appeared and sat down on my side of the table. He studied Phil with that deadpan expression he constantly wore. "What's wrong with him?"

"He's got a mote in his eye, both eyes, motes."

"What's a mote?"

Phil was trying to keep cool but wasn't carrying it off very well. "I haven't got motes in my eyes. I just had his fucking fingers in my eyes. He poked me, like a child, like a girl. And he kicked me, for fuck's sake."

Thad nodded like it all made perfect sense. "You probably had it coming."

"Fuck the both of you." Phil limped off to a different table.

"You haven't got a beer," Thad said to me. You could be stark naked and Thad might not notice, but if you didn't have a drink he was all over it.

I picked up my juice. "It's a bit early for beer don't you think? No, of course you don't think that."

Thad stood up. "I'll get you one."

"I really don't want one."

He gripped the edge of the table and looked at me, waiting for me to change my mind. I didn't say anything.

"I'll get you one," he repeated and headed for the bar.

Phil's lecture, particularly the part about Mary, was sinking in like piss on sand. I started wondering how obvious I'd been. If Phil had noticed then everybody else must have done too. I wondered if the little innuendos she'd dropped the last time we spoke were hints that she knew what I was thinking. I vowed under my breath to try and keep it under control. I wouldn't leer any more. I would only look at her when it was absolutely necessary, when I was talking to her for example. I'd have to look at her then or she'd think I'd lost it; holding a conversation with my eyes darting about all over the place but never in her direction. She'd think I'd gone mad. Or maybe blind, blind people's eyes whirl about a lot. Actually, I did sometimes think I might lose my eyesight from all the times I'd thought very vigorously about Mary when I was alone.

Thad returned with beer and Simon.

"So, what's going on chaps?" Simon always looked so fresh. It was afternoon but it felt like early morning after what we put away the night before and everyone else looked as groggy as they must have felt, but Simon was pristine, like he was a guest at Caesar's Palace.

Thad's face wore a puzzled look. "I'm still trying to work out where all that bread and fish came from."

We both looked at him, trying to work out if he was joking or not. Simon glanced at me with a cross between a smile and a puzzled frown on his face. He turned to Thad. "Where do you think it came from?"

"I don't know where it came from. If I knew that then I wouldn't have said I was trying to work it out."

"Don't make out like I'm the stupid one here," Simon answered. "You know where the fish and bread came from. We talked about it. Bart was passing it up from underneath. The cave was full of fish and bread."

"Yeah I know that, but where did it come from?"

"From the tunnel, from the cave!"

"Yeah, I know that, we just talked about that."

Simon threw his hands up in the eternal *Lord give me strength* gesture. "So what are you asking?"

"Where all the bread and fish came from." Thad's voice kept at the same level, quiet, patient. He had all the time in the world.

Simon soldiered on. "Bart took them up there earlier, before everyone arrived."

"Yeah, I know that. But where did they come from?"

A look of realisation and disappointment came over Simon's face. "Really? That's what you've been asking all along? Where the fish and the bread came from originally? They came from the sea, and a bakery! Where the fuck else?"

Thad looked thoughtful and took a sip of his beer. "Oh."

"You didn't know that?"

"I hadn't really thought about it."

Simon rolled his eyes. "Jesus!"

"Someone call?" It was the man himself. And I take back what I said about everyone except Simon looking groggy. Jesus looked immaculate. He sat down opposite me and I was taken back to how I'd felt the previous day when I'd been completely - I can't think of a word that doesn't sound over the top - spellbound, mesmerised, whatever. It felt like something had changed, that he wasn't the same old Jesus anymore. I knew it wasn't logical but I had no idea how to act around him.

Thad stood up and went inside.

Jesus shrugged, "Something I said?"

I forced a laugh and looked at Simon, expecting him to say something about Thad just being Thad, but he didn't say anything at all. He just looked at his hands as they fidgeted in front of him.

Jesus' eyes darted between Simon and me as the silence

grew deafening. "What's up?" he eventually said.

"Nothing's up," I said.

"So why aren't we talking?"

He had me there. He had both of us there. "I don't know, it feels different now," I offered.

"What do you mean, different?"

"I don't mean in a bad way, and I can only speak for myself, but you're Jesus Christ. You're this, like, legend."

"What the hell are you talking about?"

I could only shrug. I looked at Simon. He was offering no help at all. Simon was never silent, he always had an opinion. It dawned on me that he must have been feeling exactly the same as I did.

Jesus looked worried now. "What's this *legend* bullshit? And what difference does it make? I'm still me. I'm still your mate. You told me ages ago that I should distance myself a bit, keep a bit of mystery going for the punters. I've tried to do that, but I don't think I've done it too much have I? Have I been an arsehole? Please tell me if I've been an arsehole.

"No you haven't. Really, you've done nothing wrong. But it's different, there's no way round it. You should take it as a compliment. I guess we're like, a bit in awe of you now."

"In case you didn't notice, I didn't really magic up that bread and those fish."

"It's not about that." The image of him delivering his speech, his head silhouetted against the sun came into my head. "It's not about the bread and fish."

Thad returned. He solemnly placed a beer in front of Jesus.

"Cheers Thad, nice one mate."

Thad smiled politely and sat down.

"Not you as well! Stop it, the lot of you. Stop being so serious. Stop being dicks. Let's have a beer, let's have a smoke, let's have a laugh. Thad, you got a pipe on the go?"

"Can do." Thad looked relieved to be given something on which to focus his attention. He took out his pipe and started filling it with green.

Jesus took it off him. "I can pack it myself Thad. Right, you lot. Stop it. Take the piss out of me or something."

Thad and Simon looked down at the table. "Fat lot of use you two are," I said. I looked at Jesus and forced a laugh. "Hey, how about when you said *fishers of men* to Andrew and Peter?" I cleared my throat. "That fell on its arse didn't it?"

Jesus shook his head. "Jesus, you're right, even your piss-taking's gone lame. What the fuck is wrong with you lot?"

Simon spoke at last. "Nothing is wrong. It's just the way it is. You have stepped up. You have already gone further than John ever did. This is when things start to change. We cannot fight it. And we shouldn't want to. It's just how things are. You wanted to go all the way. Well you're well on the way my friend…." he paused, and I thought that maybe a punch line was coming, that Simon had just been playing along, perhaps Thad too and it was just me who was seeing Jesus differently. But then he finished his sentence.

"…my lord."

## Floor in the Plan

Andrew and Peter had been conspicuous by their absence of late and I'd felt bad that they'd missed out on everything that had been going on. I had an image of them studiously guarding the poppy crops; a pair of monks toiling, steadfast, working their fingers to the bone in their holy labours to turn the plants into something smokeable and sellable. But the sight that greeted Simon and me when we visited the valley was Andrew, standing on his head and wearing nothing but a blank expression.

Peter, also bollock-naked, lay on his back a few feet away, screeching with laughter. He saw us and tried to stand up but didn't even make it to a sitting position. As soon as he looked at Andrew, who was shaking from the strain of holding himself in his upside down position, his fishing tackle dangling onto his belly, Peter was seized by another laughing fit and fell flat on his back again. "I was doing them earlier," he shouted. "You should have seen me, I was, like, on my head. Which is funny when you think about it cos I'm also *off* my head!" He made a token effort to prove to us that he was better at headstands than his brother but gave up almost as quickly as he'd started.

Admittedly it was pretty funny, if a little strange, but Simon and I both knew why Peter found it quite so hilarious. It was because he was completely off his tits. His surprisingly floppy man-tits. Andrew was the same, albeit less floppy.

Simon and I hadn't tethered the donkeys and Maximus went

wandering over and started nosing around in Andrew's inverted nethers. This was enough to break him out of whatever flight he was on inside his poppy-infected head and bring him crashing back to earth. I mean that literally; as soon as Maximus' snout made contact with Andrew's parts he screamed and toppled backwards into the dust, where he lay laughing even harder than his still-shrieking brother.

"Well it just goes to show," I said, "don't get high on your own supply."

"I would disagree with you there old boy," said Simon. "I'd say they make an exemplary case for it. When their mortal life's done and they're about to step through heaven's gates they're not going to look back on their lives and say, "I wish we hadn't got completely mashed and done those naked headstands."

"Fuck, no!" Peter shouted from his prone position. "I'll tell them at the gate that I did the best naked-headstands and they'll definitely let me in. Who's on the gate anyway? I want that job! I want to be, like, the gatekeeper to Heaven. I'll be there and the dead will arrive trying to get in, and I'll be all like, *well let's have a look then shall we? What sort of good stuff did you do in your life?* And I'll be able to see everything they've done and if they've done too much bad shit then I'll be all, like, *sorry mate*, and I'll pull this massive lever and they'll drop down and join Satan's crew. I'd be the best at being the gatekeeper. I'm the best at two things, naked headstands and being the gatekeeper of Heaven." His whole body shuddered with laughter.

I don't know if it's just me but when I see something awful - like a seething mass of cockroaches or a dead jackal being eaten by maggots - I find I can't tear my eyes away. I'm repelled by the sight but feel some compulsion to keep looking, fascinated by the awfulness. And that's how it was with Peter lying in the dust, his flabby body wobbling with every giggle. All I could do was stare.

"Shall we join them?" Simon said.

"I'd rather keep my clothes on, thanks."

"I mean shall we get high?"

"Did someone say, *get high*?" Thad emerged from the hut, that big dopey grin plastered over his face like wet mud.

"Jesus," I said.

"That explains everything," said Simon.

Andrew pointed at Thad like he was shopping a burglar. "That's him. He's the one who made us like this". He curled into a ball and started sobbing with laughter. That set Peter off again. Not that he'd really stopped.

Simon looked at Thad. "Firstly," he said, "what are you doing here? I thought you were still in bed when we left, and secondly…" He didn't need to say any more, he just turned towards the two brothers, twitching in the dust. He held his hands in front of him, palms up; the universal *what the fuck* gesture.

Thad shrugged. "I came over last night."

Simon looked confused. "But I was with you last night."

"Not all night."

"You mean you walked here in darkness?"

"I don't think there's any point debating it," I said. "He's here, that's proof enough. Is there any water around? Maximus is hot."

Thaddeus watched me tether Max in the shady side of the hut. "Maximus is cool."

"He's as cool as they come, but he still needs a drink."

Simon tethered his own mount, Jeroboam, next to Maximus. We watered them and pulled up handfuls of long dry grass for them to chomp on. Thaddeus and the brothers stared, transfixed by the movement of the animals' mouths, so much so that they started mimicking it, chomping slowly, rolling their teeth round and round, their lips smacking at the end of each cycle. Simon looked at me, a knowing smile on his face. "We have no choice do we? We simply must get high."

I nodded. "Be rude not to."

Thad was only too pleased to cater to our needs and I soon felt that feeling wash over me, the feeling that I can never fully remember while I'm straight - try as I might - but is so blissfully familiar when it arrives. The five of us lay in a row. "We're like a catch of fish on a deck," said Andrew.

"You sir," said Simon, "talk about fishing far too much. You really need to let it go."

"Cast it adrift," said Thad.

"Nice one," said Simon.

I spoke up. "Has anyone else noticed how the sun has just been hanging there for ages? It hasn't budged. It's either got stuck or time hasn't moved for a while."

"That's not possible old boy," Simon said.

"Which?"

"Well, either, but I mean the latter."

"Which one was that?" said Thad.

"The second one." Simon's brow furrowed as he tried to keep on top of the thought process in his mangled mind. His face flickered as he found his thread again. "The time thing. If time has stopped then it can't have stopped *for a while* because there would be no *while* because there would be no time. If time stopped then nobody would ever know because they would have no way of tracking it, no point of reference. It might happen all the time and we would never know."

There was a pause while we all lay there thinking about it.

Eventually Peter spoke. "I think it just happened then."

"Shut up and put some clothes on," said Andrew.

"You should both put something on," I said.

"I'm wearing something," said Andrew. "I'm wearing a blank expression."

I sat up and looked at Andrew. "That's too weird. Did I say that out loud?"

"What?"

"When we got here and you were standing on your head I remember thinking that all you were wearing was a blank expression, and now you've said exactly what I was thinking. I'm certain I didn't say it out loud, I just thought it. So how come you just said it?"

Andrew looked confused. "Just said what?"

"That you were wearing a blank expression."

"I haven't said anything, not for ages, not since before you were going on about the sun being stuck."

"Are you trying to fuck with my head?"

"We've all fucked with our heads," said Simon. "Not that I'm complaining."

Thaddeus sat up and looked around. "My head's fine."

"Shall we go for a walk?" said Peter.

The consensus was that Peter's suggestion was a good one, but when you're all off your heads it's difficult to put any kind of plan into action and the more people involved, the more difficult it is. Five doesn't seem like a big number, but when each person's thoughts are wandering about like drunken donkeys, it takes some work to get those five donkeys to point in the same direction at the same time. There was no chance of getting Andrew's thought-donkey to point forwards, he was too far gone, so we took it in turns to keep him somewhere close to our world. I say we took it in turns, that's not strictly true, it suggests some kind of schedule or rota. What actually happened was that when one of us had a moment of lucidity and was able to remember, we'd give Andrew a prod to make sure he was still with us and not wandering off or about to lie down in the dust.

We did eventually manage to get it together enough to start

walking and as we went, the sun seemed to start racing across the sky like it was making up for lost time. My head wasn't ready for the strain of any further deep analysis from Simon so I chose not to mention it.

The strangest thing about the whole afternoon was that we made it back to the hut. Admittedly it hadn't occurred to us at any point while we were out that we should have been thinking of heading back, even though the afternoon had long become evening, which had in turn stepped aside to let night do its thing. Thad had kept us topped up with poppy and green so we'd maintained our less than dagger-sharp states of mind, although the impact of the later hits had been waning steadily.

It was a full moon that night, which was lucky because otherwise we wouldn't have known we'd made it back at all. We probably would have just kept on walking to Jesus knows where. Even with the moonlight we still might have missed it if it hadn't been for Thad.

"There's Maximus!" he shouted. "And the less good one."

None of us noticed that the donkeys were no longer tethered, probably because they were still really close to the hut. It wasn't until we saw the door hanging off its hinges that we realised something wasn't right. I have to say that the first feeling I had when I realised we'd been robbed was relief that the thieves hadn't done any harm to Max, and to a lesser extent, to Jeroboam.

We could tell it was a mess inside even before we'd got any lamps lit. Shelves had been torn down, their contents strewn across the floor, lying amongst shards of broken porcelain. Tables weren't just upended but smashed to bits. Everything that could be destroyed had been destroyed.

"Apart from all the damage, how much has actually been taken?" I said.

Andrew was whimpering. "We should have been here. This

wouldn't have happened if we'd been here."

"Let's try to focus," I said. "It's shit, but it's happened now and there's no point dwelling on what might have been. What exactly did you have in here that's not here now?"

"You think it's our fault don't you?" Peter said.

"It doesn't matter whose fault it is."

"I knew it. You do think it's our fault. And you're right, it is our fault. Mine mostly. We've let everyone down."

I knew where this was going. Whenever someone apologises there's always a clause - either stated up front or kept on standby, ready to be let loose at just the right moment - that the fault of which the passive-aggressor is passionately claiming responsibility should at least in part be shared by someone else. This clause, when revealed, is normally delivered in the form of a question.

"Was it my idea to go for a walk?" Peter asked.

*Here we go*, I thought.

Peter continued. "Did everyone else think that was a good idea? I was in a bit of a state after all. I'm not suggesting anyone else did anything wrong, I'm just saying."

Simon rounded on him. "When somebody declares that they're just saying something, they're never actually just saying it otherwise what would be the purpose of saying it? We all know what you're *just saying*." He seemed to have read my mind.

I made an effort to stop myself from shouting. "As I've been trying to say, it doesn't matter whose fault it is, what matters is that we deal with it. Now tell me, what exactly did you have in here? What's been taken? Thad, what are you doing?"

Thad was kneeling in the far corner, wedging his fingers into a groove in the wooden floor and prising a section free. He slid it aside and lowered a lamp into the exposed hole, casting an eerie light from beneath onto his curious face. It was reminiscent of the night of the party when he'd sat in that same corner surrounded by his potions, pots and candles, and invited me to set sail with him on his voyage to oblivion. He nodded but his face remained impassive. "The stash is safe. We're cool."

"When did you put that in?" I was more than a little put-out that they hadn't asked me to get involved with any building modifications, and a secret underfloor hideaway was quite a modification. I was the one with the skills.

"It was Thad's idea," said Simon. He's pretty fastidious when it comes to you-know-what. Andrew and Peter did all the work though."

"Bloody right we did," said Andrew. "We're not sitting on our arses out here you know."

"You're standing on your heads from what I could see. How much space is down there?"

"It's about waist deep and runs under half of the floor," said Andrew.

"There's a great deal of space and almost all of it used," said Simon. "We are extremely lucky our intruders failed to find it."

Thad slid the board back over the hole and stood up. "Yeah, we got lucky this time. But this won't be the last of it." His matter of fact delivery gave the statement an extra air of menace. "They'll be back."

## Unholy Alliance

I woke up with a sore face. My hand instinctively moved to my cheek and brushed at the source of the pain; several splinters of porcelain that I'd apparently used as a pillow. I felt blood oozing out of the scratches inflicted by my sleepy hand. "What is this stuff anyway?" I asked nobody in particular.

"It's bits of pestle." I recognised Peter's voice.

"And mortar." Andrew.

"Oh." I didn't know what those words meant. I strained my eyes until they were something close to open and looked around. "Where are the others?"

"They're seeing to the donkeys."

Simon came in looking like he'd slept in silk sheets and bathed in ass's milk. "Gentlemen," he said. "It's time to commence the clean-up operation."

"I need to get back to the big man and let him know what's going on."

Simon looked at me, arms folded. "Excuse my Gaulish but - like fuck you are. You're helping us here. You can go afterwards."

"It was worth a try."

There was nothing to eat. The intruders had raided Peter and Andrew's supply cupboard, presumably for no other reason than to be as cuntish as possible. There was water, which was a blessing, but that was it. We all felt rotten and none of us was in the mood for it but with all the furniture smashed it wasn't the comfiest place in which to hang around, so we just got on with the job. We sifted through the debris to find anything worth salvaging, which was almost nothing, and swept and scraped and scooped up all the rubbish, which was almost everything, into poppy sacks. By the time we'd finished almost the entire contents of the cabin were piled outside.

I took Maximus - or rather Maximus took me - back to Magdalene's to fill the big man in while the others stayed to keep an eye on the place. Whether they'd be able to do anything about it if our intruders returned was questionable, but it was the most sensible option we could think of.

The journey back was horrible. Every part of me ached from sleeping on the floor, my head was numb from the caning I'd given it the previous day and my stomach was begging me to feed it.

When I got to Magdalene's I went straight up to Jesus' room and banged on the door. I've already pointed out that my head wasn't as sharp as it should have been and that should go some way to explaining why I went ahead and opened the door without thinking to wait for an answer.

I didn't get past the doorway. I just stood gripping the knob, staring in shock and awe at the wonderful contours of Mary's back and shoulders, her hair sweeping down to the most flawless peaches I'd ever seen. Even the soles of her feet looked astonishing. She was kneeling with her back to me, facing the edge of Jesus' bed. For a moment I was too intoxicated by the unexpected rush of that delicious skin and immaculate curves, moving so rhythmically, sensuously, that I didn't take in what was obviously happening. It was the sight of Jesus' hairy knees poking out from either side of Mary's toned thighs and his still-sandaled feet pointing in my direction that brought me crashing down to reality.

Mary instinctively turned her head to face me, revealing,

next to the perfect circle of her lips, Jesus' loincloth-serpent gripped tightly in her fist. I was looking straight into its fat purple eye. I swear it winked at me.

I left the room, closing the door carefully behind me.

To say it was awkward when Jesus finally came down to meet me is like saying David was a bit tasty with a sling-shot. We both took the same pretend-it-didn't-happen approach but acted so uncomfortably that we may as well have been shouting *I saw Mary giving you a blow job - you saw Mary giving me a blow job* back and forth at each other.

His face grew increasingly pained as I told him what had happened at the poppy factory. I felt guilty for dumping such bad news on him, especially as his day had obviously been going so well until I'd turned up.

"So they didn't get any of the product, but what about the unharvested crop?"

"Unharvested?"

"The stuff that's still growing."

"Oh. I didn't think of that. Sorry."

He held up a hand. "Don't worry about it. From what Peter told me they'd already got most of it up anyway so we should be okay." He leaned back and narrowed his eyes. I knew enough about this new Jesus to just shut up and let him work through the problem.

"Shit," he said. "I knew this was coming."

"It's comforting to hear that you knew all about it. When were you going to tell us?"

"There are things in motion, things that will change everything. We're at the final stages. I was going to tell you when it was all in place."

"What things?"

"I'm making a deal, making an ally."

"Why do we need an ally?"

"For two reasons, security and distribution, and from what's happened today, the first can't come soon enough."

"You sound like you know who we should be worrying about."

"Don't you?" He started peeling an orange. "Who's the most obvious person? Think what happened to John."

"Antipas. Shit. We're all fucked then."

"Nobody's fucked. I told you, things are in motion."

"Fancy giving me a bit more detail?"

He tore off a segment and held it out to me, I shook my head. "No?" He said. "It's really ripe, really juicy." I shook my head again, not knowing where his hands had been recently. "Suit yourself. Was it just you who came back?"

"Yes, we thought it best to leave as many bodies there as we could in case they come back. I should get back too. I promised to take them some food. They'll be really pissed at me if I take too long."

"Yes, you better had. Get some bread and fruit from Bart, he'll sort you out. When you get there just sit tight and keep an eye on things. You'll all be relieved before nightfall."

"Relieved? Are we soldiers now?"

"Something like that."

"You're not going tell me those details are you?"

"Don't worry about that for now mate. Just get back there, wait for the relief."

"I hope you got some relief. After I'd left the room I mean."

Jesus didn't smile.

"Sorry, couldn't resist it."

Still nothing.

"I'll get my robe," I said.

When I got back to the others they couldn't get the food off me quickly enough. Peter denied it later but I swear he bit my finger in his haste to feed his face.

"Save some for me," I said. "I've not had any yet".

Bits of crust flew out of Andrew's mouth as he snapped at me, "Bollocks, you haven't."

"I haven't. I was in too much of a rush, I didn't want to keep you lot waiting."

Andrew swallowed and tore himself another piece. "You're such a liar."

"Alright, but I didn't have much, so give us a bit."

I was dying to regale everyone with what I'd seen in Jesus' room but from his reaction to my rather innocent joke I thought it best to keep it to myself. I told them what he'd said about Antipas though.

"Sounds a bit far-fetched to me," said Andrew. "Why would Antipas give a shit about us?"

"He cared enough to take the head of our former leader," said Simon without looking up.

Andrew shrugged. "So we're all fucked then?"

"Nobody's fucked," I said. "I told you what the big man told me. Things are in motion."

Andrew wrapped his arms around himself. "Since you told me Antipas wants our blood, the only thing that's in motion is my guts. Excuse me, fellas."

We sat tight, as instructed, not speaking much and juggling two feelings: fear and boredom.

"We're technically on guard duty here," I said to Simon, both of us propped up against a shady tree-trunk, "but what if they come back? What are we actually going to do?"

"The obvious course of action would be to fight them off."

"Yeah, I get that. That's what we'll try and do but look at us." I nodded towards Thad, Andrew and Peter lying under the tree opposite. "Look at the three wise men over there - do you think we've got it in us to fight off a mob of Antipas' men?"

Simon smirked. "Do you really want me to answer that?"

I remembered Jesus' question about the unharvested poppies. "The stuff growing in the far corner of the field, is that all that was left before?"

"You mean did the thieves take any? No, I don't think so. They obviously didn't have time to pick flowers. They…"

"Shut up a minute."

"You shut up."

"I didn't mean it like that, shh, I can hear something." Simon sat up and cocked his head. "It sounds like a lot of people walking."

"I'll tell you what it sounds like," I said. "It sounds like soldiers marching."

"In this direction."

"Shit."

We jumped to our feet and saw that the others had done the same. Without a word we stood in a defensive line in front of the hut. It occurred to me that instead of sitting around in the shade we should have been preparing ourselves, at least found things to use as weapons but then all we had were bits of broken furniture and a couple of shovels, and that would have been laughable.

"I need to go wee," said Thaddeus, and despite our impending massacre I had to stifle a smile.

The first we saw of them was sunlight glinting off their armour; the unmistakable full battle armour of Roman soldiers. My first instinct was to turn and run and my second was to throw up. I'm sure I wasn't the only one of us to feel those urges but we stood firm, well not firm, but there's no such phrase as *stood flimsy*.

We could see them more clearly as they descended the slope into the less wooded valley. There were twenty legionaries marching two abreast, with two figures walking behind. One was clearly a centurion or some other kind of senior officer, my knowledge of the Roman army hierarchy has never been the best. The other was a civilian, if his plain tunic was anything to go by.

"Is that Phil?" Peter asked. "It is, you know. Shit, they've got Phil."

"I'm not sure about *got*," Andrew answered. "He's walking pretty freely, doesn't look like a prisoner."

In my head everything fell into place. "He's sold us out! I bloody knew it, there was always something wrong about him."

They were close now and we could see the faces of the soldiers at the vanguard, narrowed by the brass cheek plates of their crested helmets. The pilum each carried was terrifying, not just because it was a lethal piece of kit but because it was obvious that any arm that could carry that heavy weapon over such distances had to be as strong as the sharpened iron at its business end.

The commanding officer gave the order and they stopped as one.

Philip, our betrayer, strode forward. "Hi fellas, this lot will take it from here."

"Not without a fight." I knew it was a futile gesture but I wasn't going to let them just take what was ours. The others obviously felt the same and we all stood as imposingly as we could, which was not very imposingly at all.

Phil's eyes widened. He looked at me, at the soldiers, then back at me. "Shit, no! God, no. They're on our side. They're the relief, they're our protection. The big man sorted it."

"Jesus hired Roman soldiers?"

"Well not hired, exactly. I don't really know the details, I'm just the go-to guy, but I know arrangements have been made. I'm sure he'll fill you in." A look of shock blanched his face. "But wait a minute, if you thought they were here to take over then you must have thought I was in on it, that I was some kind of traitor."

I looked at my sandals. "Not *traitor* exactly," I muttered. "We thought that maybe you were their prisoner, that you'd been forced to give us up."

"Listen, mate, I know you think I'm an arsehole, and I'm still pissed at you for poking me in the eye and kicking me by the way, but the one thing you can't doubt about me is my loyalty. They'd have to kill me before I gave any of us up."

"I'm sorry." The words felt like my own balls were in my mouth.

"That guy doesn't say much does he?" Thad was gesturing towards the commanding officer standing motionless at the side of his troops and staring straight ahead.

"It's unnerving isn't it?" said Phil. "I tried talking to him on the way down but he was having none of it. I think this is a *no questions asked* kind of deal."

"Can we just, like, go then?" I said. "We can just leave them to it?"

"Yes, the big man wants us all back at Mags."

Walking away from a pack of deadly Roman soldiers is not something any of us was used to and we all sidled off, almost on tiptoes, as if at any moment we could make the wrong move. In which case they'd decide we were their enemy after all, and do what the Romans do to their enemies.

Simon and I untethered Max and Jeroboam and we filed slowly away, glancing over our shoulders all the while, fully expecting the sound of rushing boots, unsheathing metal and the feel of a blade in the back.

## Dance With the Devil

The camels stationed outside Magdalene's told us we had guests, well they didn't literally tell us, they weren't talking camels. You know what I mean. The silk throws and ornate saddles gracing the aforementioned beasts indicated that these guests weren't short of a few denarii.

The bar was empty when the five of us stomped in, except for Bart wiping the bar down. "Ah you're here," he said. "They're all upstairs. I said I'd come up with you when you got here."

"Who's up there?" I asked.

"Everyone - John, James, Philip, Nat, Thomas. And Jesus of course. And then there's the others."

"That's who I was asking about."

"I don't know who they are. There's four of them and they look - well I dunno - they don't look like this joint is their sort of place. I think they're used to something a bit more… palatial."

"Did they just turn up?"

"Yeah, but I don't think it was a surprise to Jesus. When they got here he just asked me to get some posh wine. I told him my wine's always posh but he said to get something posher if I could."

"So it's someone important?" I said.

"I'd say. Shall we go up?"

"Can't we have a beer first?" Thad asked.

149

Bart led us upstairs to the room in which we'd had our first meeting. At one end sat Jesus and at the opposite end - my seat really – sat a man for whom the best description was exactly as Bart had said; he looked like he belonged anywhere but in these basic, humble surroundings. He was draped in silk and jewels and his sculpted beard framed a face that could have been chiselled from a slab of pure ebony. His right hand man sat… to his right, in much more simple garb but still obviously used to the good life. The remaining two members of the entourage stood behind their master, their eyes fixed ahead like the stoic Roman centurion earlier that day. We latecomers took the remaining seats down the sides but stool availability was at a premium so Thad and Peter stood, either deliberately or otherwise, exactly opposite the two standing members of the visiting dignitaries.

I sat down. The presence of these regal visitors kept me from releasing the torrent of questions from inside my head.

Jesus waited until everyone was settled before speaking. "Gentlemen, it's good to see you. I understand you have had a trying day. Please let me introduce you to our esteemed guest. This is Aretas the Fourth, King of the Nabataeans, friend of his people."

Most of us saw ourselves as outsiders, rebels, even. The notion of dynastic rule was something we'd seen as an injustice since we were first able to form opinions. In our eyes, birthright to a throne was no right at all. But firmly held convictions are all very well. Sitting at the same table as an actual king was another matter entirely.

We all stared at this man from another world.

"Holy shit," said Thaddeus.

We were impressed, no doubt about it, but hot on the heels of our initial dose of awe was another more natural feeling; suspicion. I didn't know much about Aretas, in fact I didn't know anything about Aretas, but I knew that kings didn't keep their thrones by playing nice. I'd lived under two kings, well one of them was just a tetrarch but it was all the same to me. The first butchered a load of babies, while the other, his son, our very own Antipas, beheaded our spiritual leader. I guessed I wasn't alone in those thoughts because our distinguished guest had obviously picked up on something of a vibe.

"I can see in your eyes, my friends…" the king's voice was deep and confident. He made a point of making eye contact with each one of us, "…that my presence here does not fill you with warmth, with affection. I admit that we are from different worlds, worlds that in normal circumstances would not meet. I do not know what you think of me but I am here because I was invited by this man." He gestured expansively towards Jesus, "This man has my utmost respect. I have the title of king but it will not be long before he will be hailed as such, and he is far more worthy of the label than I. He is already a king amongst men. So even if you harbour trepidations about my presence you should trust the judgement of your own king." By the end of this rousing sermon he was standing, his arms stretched wide. Slowly he sat back down, letting his words impress upon us. He nodded at Jesus, opening the floor to him once more.

"Thank you for your carefully considered words, King Aretas. I accept your gracious compliments." It was weird hearing Jesus talking so formally, playing the head of state. "If I may, I would like to share with my men the purpose of your welcome visit, which has coincided with an incident that epitomises the need for your assistance. I refer of course to the recent events at the factory. It won't come as a surprise to the more astute of you that it was the work of our old friend Antipas. He is, if I may put it simply, making a move on our action." He let the murmurs die down before carrying on. "Our guest, King Aretas…"

The king raised a hand. "It is acceptable for you just to call me Aretas."

Jesus smiled. "That will save time. Aretas has been wronged by Antipas, just as we have. We do not need to go into details but he has good reason to wish Antipas to fail. He also has a great deal of knowledge of our tetrarch's intentions. Antipas' plan was to take what product we had at the factory, not so much to sell it himself but to hamstring our operation. We understand that he also intended to take Peter and Andrew for their knowledge of growing and processing the poppy." The brothers exchanged terrified looks. "His plan failed of course. His actions were no more than an inconvenience to us…" he paused. "Yes Thaddeus?"

"I've got a question." Simon put his head in his hands, pre-empting his despair at whatever was going to come out of his best mate's mouth. Thad regarded King Aretas. "How come you're so pissed at Antipas?"

A look of confusion flickered across the monarch's face. He obviously wasn't used to being on the receiving end of such impertinent questions. "That is not something with which you need to concern yourself."

"Leave it Thad." Simon's words were a whispered hiss, not meant for anyone but Thad to hear, but we all heard it, including our visitors.

"Excuse me, gentlemen." I turned to see Mary leaning into the room. "I'm sorry to interrupt, but I need some help with something important. Thaddeus, could you spare a moment please?"

It was obvious to everybody what she was doing; she was getting him out of there before his lack of tact blew whatever deal Jesus was working on. Obvious to everyone except Thad, that is. "Okay," he said, as if it was perfectly natural that Mary should need him urgently enough to interrupt the meeting. He obediently left the room.

Aretas looked at Jesus, his expression saying *I like what you did there.*

Jesus nodded and carried on. "So Antipas' plan failed but we should not celebrate too much. He wants us gone. He has the means and we all know he has the motivation. I am telling you this because it's important that you know it. You have all given up everything to be at my side so it is only fair that you know exactly what we are up against. If anybody wishes to leave then they can do so now. Nobody will judge you, lest they be judged themselves. If you leave now then Antipas will not catch up with you. He's not that close to us, not yet anyway, so now is the time to stand down if you are that way inclined."

None of us moved. We were never going to. Jesus must have known that. This had to be a deliberate ploy to show Aretas that our crew weren't pussies. If it was, then it seemed to have worked. Aretas clasped his hands together, beaming. "I applaud every one of you. You are my kind of men. However, even if you were burdened by fear I could relieve that burden. I have resources I can put at your disposal. Firstly I can provide protection...."

"A number of us have seen what this protection entails," said Jesus. "There are currently two dozen soldiers guarding the poppy factory and more where that came from."

I felt myself raising my hand. "I have a question."

"Go ahead," said Jesus.

I glanced at the door, half expecting Mary to come in and take me on a fool's errand like she had with Thad. "How come they're Roman soldiers?"

Aretas laughed. "Good question sir! Why are your oppressors suddenly your protectors? The answer is that I would have sent my own troops but they are occupied at this time. But you want the best don't you? The Romans, much as I hate to admit it, are the best. The Spartans could give them a run for their money but in terms of training and discipline, you simply cannot beat the Romans."

"But how did they come to work for you?"

"I have connections." Aretas stood up. "That leads us smoothly onto the second part of what my resources can give you. I can provide pipelines into every corner of the Roman Empire, pipelines through which your product will flow. And your profits will flow right back. Since the tragedy of John's execution and his family's business being scattered to the four winds there has been little supply, but the demand has not gone away. If anything it has increased. With my help you can feed that demand. Of course I will divert some of the return into my own coffers - I am not running a charity - but when the money starts to flood back in your direction you will find me cheap at twice the price."

Phil spoke, surprisingly for the first time. "If you don't mind me asking, what's your cut of the deal?"

"I have had lengthy discussions with your master and we have settled on an arrangement. We do not need to go into tiresome details now."

"Fair enough," said Phil. Our so-called master had obviously made the deal already. This meeting was for information only.

"On the subject of money," Aretas continued, "I know financial reward is not the primary aim of your organisation but it is only sensible that you make as much as you can, and think of the good you can do with it all. You can feed and clothe the poor, you can help the needy. You can change the world. Ah, refreshment!"

Mary came in carrying a huge tray of wine and glasses. She set it down on the table and started pouring. Bart, arms folded, mouthed the word *posh* at me.

"Thank you Mary." Jesus stood up. "Supplying the entire Roman Empire with the means to get high while at the same time defending ourselves against a tetrarch who wants us all dead is no mean feat. It will take detailed discussion, plans, action, more discussion, more plans and even more action. Our work is only just beginning, but now is a good time to mark our agreement in principle." He raised his glass. "We welcome you, Aretas the Fourth, King of the Nabataeans, friend of his people. We look forward to a long and healthy relationship where all parties reap the plump fruits of our endeavours." It really was something to behold, Jesus playing this role. I could see exactly why he was doing it. Aretas must have been used to cutting deals with tetrarchs, prefects, monarchs, even Caesars, so Jesus had to show him he could mix it with the best of them. And he was doing a damned good job of it.

Aretas stood, followed by his right hand man and the rest of us. "I am grateful for your welcome, Jesus of Nazareth, the anointed one, The Christ. I am honoured by your hospitality and I commit to protecting the personal safety of you and your men and to growing our respective business interests." He raised his glass. "I toast this alliance, may it be long, may it be mutually beneficial." He drank. We followed. "As you say, Lord Jesus, there is a great deal of further discussion to be had, weeks, months, perhaps years. As you will appreciate, I have a kingdom to run. The reason I came here in person was to show my commitment to this arrangement. However, now we have met, talked, drank together, I am satisfied that we are reciting from the same prayer book and my presence is no longer necessary. I will leave my aide here, my right hand, to work alongside you. He speaks for me and will give you everything you need. His name is Matthew."

The guy sitting to Aretas' right stood self-consciously and gave us a crumpled smile.

155

A few more diplomatic platitudes were exchanged, some stuff about the *relationship bearing fruit*, and *a bedrock of trust being laid*, and the meeting was over.

Aretas, along with his two bodyguards - I can't think of anything else to call them - mounted their camels and, with the setting sun on their backs, rode east.

Thad was polishing glasses at the counter. "Did he answer my question?" he asked as we filed past.

"No," said Jesus, "but I can. Antipas took his half-brother's wife, remember? That's the main reason John was executed, because he spoke up against it. To marry this new one he dumped the woman he was already married to. And the woman he was already married to was Aretas' daughter. He humiliated her, brought shame on his family. And King Aretas is not a happy camel."

"Fair enough," said Thad, picking up another glass and buffing it with a cloth. "I don't know why these needed doing so urgently though."

# *Welcome Matt*

It was weird having Matthew around. Despite all the grand statements from our respective 'masters', we weren't completely certain of where we stood with each other. Regardless of what he'd said - and he'd said it very well - Aretas was part of the evil empire, pure and simple. Just because he hadn't done anything to us directly, it didn't mean he hadn't been responsible for some pretty heinous things in the pursuit and protection of his power.

But I could see why we needed the arrangement. Without him we would have all ended up a good head shorter.

Jesus had been right to point out just how much work there was to do and the more I thought about it the more came out of the woodwork. To reach the scale that Aretas was talking about, everything would have to be stepped up. Most obviously we'd have to grow a lot more of the product, which sounds simple, but that meant bigger farms, which in turn meant more land, buildings, security, delivery and a pile of other things that I couldn't even begin to think about.

Aside from all that what we needed most was people and I'm not talking about Aretas' borrowed soldiers or his network of middlemen spanning the Roman Empire, I mean people we could trust.

Despite all the big words, all the diplomacy, all the posturing, Aretas was still an unknown quantity. It was only sensible for us to hold onto a few reservations about him. I wouldn't say we didn't trust him, but then I wouldn't say we did either, not completely.

So hanging out with this new guy, this Matthew who'd been left with us, was a little bit strained at first. We didn't feel we could talk freely in case we said the wrong thing and it got back to Aretas. For starters it didn't feel right taking the piss out of each other in front of him, in case he took it at face value and thought we all hated each other. Jesus had made a point of showing Aretas that solidarity was a big feature of our group and we didn't want to undermine that.

But we didn't want to come across as too relaxed, too playful, either, not if there was a chance our behaviour was being reported back to Jesus' new business partner. Basically we didn't want Aretas thinking he'd hooked up with a bunch of jokers. This meant, for some of us especially, that we had to act somewhat against our nature.

I wasn't particularly happy with how things were panning out. I knew change was natural, necessary, we were entering yet another new phase, we were developing. I got all that. But I wanted it to be a laugh again.

For a unique perspective I consulted a man with a powerful capacity to think outside the sack to overcome any obstacle standing in the way of his pursuit of pleasure.

That's right, I consulted Thad.

"It all seems to hinge on this Matt fella," he said. "If he's like us then you don't need to worry. It's only if he's an uptight sort that you've got a problem. What you need to do is get to know him, and you only truly know a man when you've been off your head with him."

"You're suggesting I get him fucked up?"

"Exactly, but you need to get fucked up too."

"Well," I said, "if you think it'll help."

"Course it will. But just one thing."

"What's that?"

"I want in."

It was agreed.

Thad told Matthew that he wanted him to come and look at possible growing conditions on the land up the hill from Magdalene's. We weren't trying to trick him. We would have just asked him outright but that day he was having back to back meetings about different aspects of the business, so we couldn't get him on his own. The subterfuge was aimed at everyone else. I wanted to keep the numbers down. More people meant more chance of the wrong thing being said and if it turned out that he wasn't *like us* then it could have been damaging. It occurred to me pretty quickly that I was completely contradicting my own logic because if anyone was going to say the wrong thing then it was going to be Thad. But he was so up for going, like a dog that's been told it's going walkies and is already bouncing about in excited anticipation. You can't just change your mind and bugger off without it when it's in that state. You'd break its doggy-heart.

Thad was a lot like a dog. A big floppy dog.

So early that evening the three of us made our way to higher ground.

"What's in the bag?" Matthew asked Thad, as we weaved between the olive trees.

"Oh don't worry yourself about that, pal, you'll find out soon enough."

Matthew answered straight away. "I'd like to find out now."

Thad patted him on the back. "All in good time, my friend, patience is a virtue and all that."

Matthew turned to me. "What's in the bag?"

"Tools," I answered.

"What sort of tools?"

Thad stepped in. "The kind that fuck a person up."

159

Matthew stopped walking. "What's going on?"

"What are you stopping for?" Thad put his arm around Matthew and guided him gently but firmly forward. "There's a good spot a bit further up. Nice and secluded."

Matthew shook himself out of Thad's grasp, a look of desperation on his face. "Come on then. Just get it over with."

Thad looked offended. "What are you talking about? I just said we're not there yet. We need the right spot. I reckon this is going to be messy."

Matthew's face was as white as a shroud.

It was obvious to me what was going on in Matthew's head even if it wasn't to Thad. I was tempted to keep it going for a bit for a laugh but thought there was a very real chance of him soiling himself so I did the decent thing. "Thad's talking about a good spot for getting high. That's what this is about. It's been pretty much all business up to now, we thought we'd get to know each other a bit - not in *that* way but, well, y'know."

Matthew sighed. "No I didn't bloody know. I thought…"

"Yes, I know exactly what you thought. Why would we want to do that? What do you think we are, monsters?"

Thad looked blank. "What did he think?"

"He thought we were going to kill him."

"Why would we want to kill him?"

"That's what *I* said."

"What's in the bag?" Matthew asked again.

"Some wine, some green. Oh, and a bong." Thad sounded disappointed at having to blow the surprise.

Matthew folded his arms. "Let me see."

Thad handed him the bag.

He peered inside, then back at us, his previously drained face now refilled with a flush of embarrassment. "Sorry."

"What did you think was in there?" I asked.

"I don't know, a knife, an axe, a hammer maybe."

"But why?"

"It's just something that happens in this business. It could be any reason. You might not trust me. You might've done a deal with Antipas. You might have wanted to send some kind of message to Aretas. I don't know."

"I think you need a drink," I said.

"And a smoke," Thad added.

We sat down on the grass and I handed them a bottle of wine each, taking one for myself. "Is straight out the bottle okay? Don't bother answering that, we haven't got any glasses, so unless you want to cup your hands…"

Thad gleefully prepared the bong. "Have you ever done one of these?"

Matthew looked at the contraption. "Not really. No. Not at all."

I peered into Matthew's face. "You've gone all white again, like you were before."

"I very much doubt that," said Matthew. "It's one thing to be a bit nervous about getting out of your head, it's another thing entirely to think you're going to be stabbed, chopped or beaten to death and left to rot on some unknown hillside."

"Fair enough." I didn't bother arguing.

"Are we smoking or what?" Thad only ever got impatient when drugs were involved. "Who's going first?"

"You are," I said. "I don't know why you bother asking."

"Well I did pack it, it's kind of a rule, the one who packs it has first go."

"Have first go then."

"Not because I'm being greedy, just because it's the tradition."

"Whatever, just smoke the damn thing."

He lit up. The bong bubbled as he pulled on it. Matthew looked on and despite what he'd just said, he did look as scared as he had when he thought he was going to get whacked. Fair play to him though, when it was his turn he leapt right in, sucking down as much as he could before breaking into a coughing fit. He held the bong out for someone to take it off him.

"Cover it up, there's still some left!" Thad dived to cover the ground and stop all that virgin smoke escaping.

Thad only ever got flustered when drugs were involved.

I'd been a bit worried that Matthew might have had a bad one after having such a scare right before taking the hit, although admittedly I couldn't have been that concerned or I would have stopped him. I'm of the belief that a bad go on drugs is something everyone should experience at some time in their lives, it teaches us something about ourselves, shows us what our minds are capable of.

Matthew was fine anyway, quiet but fine. There were no giggles, not even much of a grin, but there was an unmistakable look of contentment. This was a man who was a long way from home who'd had a lot of responsibility thrust upon him. Now he was finally getting to relax, and relax with an intensity he'd never experienced before. It was as if a cork had been plucked out of the top of his head and the stress was gushing out like a vapour. I could as good as see it, and after I'd taken a hit of my own I really could see it.

I opened the conversation. "So what's it like being the right hand man to a king?"

"He has lots of right hands, but it's okay. The palace is comfortable, the food's good and there's plenty of wine."

"What's his palace like?"

Matthew said nothing.

I studied his face. "Are you thinking it over or did you not hear me?"

His eyes moved in my direction but they weren't focused.

"Awesome."

"The palace?"

"If you like. This, everything. Awesome."

Thad looked up from repacking the bong. "We have a winner!" There was only one thing Thad loved as much as getting off his head - almost as much anyway - and that was being responsible for other people getting off their heads.

It was obvious I wasn't going to get anything meaningful out of Matthew, for a while at least. Not that this was an interrogation. I didn't have specific questions I needed answering. I didn't know what I wanted to be honest, just to get to know the guy and get a feel for how solid this arrangement was with his boss. I wasn't following a plan, which was lucky because we shouldn't forget that I was pretty far gone too. Thad packed a mean bong.

The wine wasn't the posh stuff but it went down nicely and there were far worse ways to spend the early evening. I took several hits of the bong and Thad took several more. We were both surprised when Matthew spoke.

"Can I have another go?"

"Of course." Thad couldn't answer quickly enough. He handed the bong to Matthew who took a pull on it, more carefully than before.

After the coughs subsided - only a few this time, and to Thad's delight he even remembered to put his hand over the top to save what he didn't use - Matthew smiled. "You've got a good life out here. I like your style."

"Nice to have you back." I took a swig of wine. "It's not bad is it? It's been more hectic than normal recently, for obvious reasons but yes, there's plenty worse ways to live."

"He's very impressed with your set-up, you know."

"Who is?"

"Aretas. He'd heard a lot of good things - we'd all heard a

lot of good things - and he wasn't disappointed after meeting you."

The compliment added to the comfy cushion of my nicely dazed state of mind. "So what's his angle?" I said. "Everything he said made sense, and yes, he'll make a good return on his investment, but level with me, there's something else going on here isn't there?"

"Well yes, and he as good as said so. He wants to mess up Antipas. He hates him. Antipas wants your business and wants you dead, so Aretas wants the opposite."

Thad's big dog-face loomed between us. "Why doesn't Aretas just take our business by force? He'd still be fucking up Antipasti and he'd get to keep all the profits."

"Thanks Thad," I said. "Great plan telling Aretas' chief advisor that his boss would be better off robbing our business off us."

Matthew was beaming, slapping Thad on the back. "I'm liking this guy! He's something else. But don't worry. Aretas isn't like Antipas, he likes to keep things simple and he's not too fond of having blood on his hands. If he took it off you he'd have to find someone else to run it, and as far as he's concerned he's already got the best people running it. The more time I spend here the more I think he's right. That's the only thing I'm going to be reporting back to him."

Thad smirked. "Ain't this just a great big love-in?"

"How did you end up at Aretas' palace?" I asked.

"Believe it or not I used to work for Antipas, as... no, it doesn't matter."

"As what?" I said.

"It's embarrassing."

"You know full well you're going to tell us, otherwise we'll stab you to death as planned."

"With a hammer!" Thad shouted, snorting with laughter.

"I don't know why that's so funny, I was genuinely scared, but okay. I'll tell you. I was a tax collector."

"Fuck off," we both answered.

"I told you it was embarrassing. I didn't actually go out and collect the money. I was more of a bean counter. It was before the two of them fell out. They had a joint venture going, investing their money in some building projects for Caesar. We're talking major returns. I was sent to Aretas' palace to work with his people there and ended up staying. I don't think Antipas even noticed my absence."

"So you change sides easily then? Sorry, that came out wrong, but you know what I mean."

"I wouldn't say I changed sides, like I say it was before they fell out. I couldn't go back now even if I wanted to. Antipas would probably send me back to Aretas in little pieces. But maybe you're onto something, maybe I do like to take advantage when I see an opportunity for a better life. I like what Jesus has going here, what you've all got going here, and I wouldn't object to making it permanent."

Thad passed him the repacked bong. "I'm sure that could be arranged."

# Who's Your Daddy?

It turned into quite a session. The wine ran out pretty quickly but we had plenty of green. There was always plenty of green. Matthew had made the transition from completely vegged-out stoned, to giggly and chatty stoned, and although the former was much funnier for Thad and me, Matthew was much better company now he could speak, so in the overall picture it was an improvement.

His stories of life in the palace were fascinating to me. Thad was a lot better travelled than I was; it seemed that he and Simon had been everywhere from Arcadia to Zion, so he was less awestruck than me. But all the time Matthew was talking it meant we could carry on getting smashed, so Thad was happy with that. It sounded like Aretas wasn't such a bad king; fair and just and all that, but his court was full of politics and backstabbing. Matthew said he stayed out of that side of things and just kept his head down so as not to make himself a target.

Our mission had been a resounding success and I was looking forward to telling the rest of the crew that Matthew was just like us, that we could all relax around him. As it turned out, that wasn't going to be the most prominent thing on my mind when I got back because Matthew was about to drop a huge cannonball.

There'd been a lull in the conversation, one of several as our green-addled heads turned in on themselves, our thoughts meandering down random pathways, starting perhaps with something we'd been talking about but quickly mutating into something disconnected and downright bizarre. It was a bit like when you lie in bed drifting off and as you start to doze your thoughts become dreams. Exactly like that in fact, except without the falling asleep part. It was a very temporary state and if someone spoke we were pulled back out of our heads and into the group again, sometimes taking a few moments to shake off the flotsam of our internal imagery.

But when Matthew spoke this time, all the fluff clinging to my trippy thoughts was shorn away as I was yanked back to reality.

"So what's it like being best mates with the Son of God?" he said, looking at me as if he was asking me what I'd had for breakfast.

"What - erm -what?"

"I've been sitting here blathering on about living with a king and you've not told me anything about growing up with someone who's been referred to more than once as the King of all kings."

"Yeah, he's special, but - but what was that thing about God?"

"What do you mean?" Matthew had half a smile on his face, the face of someone who thinks he's on the sticky end of a wind-up. Looking back, I probably wore the same expression.

"You said he was the Son of God."

He hesitated. "Well, yes, the fulfilment of a load of prophecies apparently."

"I'm not sure what you're getting at," I said. "People say he speaks the word of God, which is great, it all adds to his, like, aura, but he's just got a good message. He wouldn't ever say he was a relation."

"Are you shitting me? You must have heard the stories."

"I've heard the stories." Thaddeus was lying on his back, his

167

hands folded over his chest, like a corpse but with his eyes wide open, staring up at the darkening sky.

I shifted my glance between the two of them. "What stories?"

"The virgin birth," said Thad.

"The visits from the three kings," said Matthew.

"King Herod having all those babies killed," said Thad.

"I knew about Herod and the babies, but that was just Herod being Herod. It had nothing to do with Jesus. And virgins can't have kids and... what was the other one again?"

"You tell him," said Thad, enjoying himself.

Matthew looked confused, like he was being asked to explain to a baker how to make dough. With a shrug that said *oh well, fuck it*, he told me what he was sure I already knew, that Jesus' mum hadn't lain down with Joseph when she fell pregnant and that the child she was carrying was, in fact, sired by the man upstairs. At this point my thoughts turned to my bitter old grandmother and her sniping gossip and I zoned out for a bit. When I got back into the story Jesus had been born and was having lots of visitors; some shepherds first, and then some kings who'd travelled for miles to get there and bring him gifts.

"They followed a star, so they reckon," said Thad as if that was a perfectly sensible conclusion to the story.

"So let me get this straight," I said. "The son of God was born in some cowshed somewhere..."

"It was a stable, and the place is called Bethlehem," said Matthew.

"Never heard of it," I said. "And if it was the birthplace of the Son of God then I think I would have done. And if everything happened like you say it did, what happened next? Everyone just... fucked off? The wandering star moved on, perhaps to usher in another deity over, I dunno, a pig sty somewhere? Joseph looked at his wife and said *good work, you've given birth to God's son, now let's go back to Nazareth and I'll get on with my carpentry business, we've got a few orders to fill?"*

Thad turned his head towards Matthew. "He makes a good point."

Matthew shook his head. "They couldn't shout about it. It was too dangerous. They had to go back and live normal lives until he was ready. He was too much of a threat to the status quo. I mean, look at the lengths Herod went to."

"So you're saying Herod killed all those kids because he was trying to whack the baby Jesus?"

"It wasn't the most elegant of solutions but that was Herod the Great for you. And it was all for nothing because…"

"Because Jesus got away." Thad had sat up and was peering into the cloth bag. "I reckon we've got enough for one more each, everyone in?" We both nodded.

"Everyone knows the story of Herod the Great Baby Butcher," I said, "but if the Son of God was born in a stable to a mother who hadn't even had sex, how come I haven't heard about it?"

Matthew shrugged. "Probably because of what you said earlier, because there wasn't any follow up, Jesus just disappeared, so all that was left was the testimony of a few shepherds. The kings told their story though, and that's how I know it, and how Aretas knows it. There's a lot of stuff that kings and Caesers get to know that your average punter isn't privy to. And it was in Herod's interest to keep it contained. Obviously he couldn't hide the fact that he was having all those babies killed…"

"But he could keep it quiet that he was shitting himself about some new king being born." Thad lit the bong and had a go on it before continuing, talking through the smoke escaping through his nose. "And Antipas is a shit off the old cock."

Matthew and I leaned towards Thad, as if by studying him more closely we could work out what the on earth he'd just said.

"What?" said Thad.

"What do you mean, what?" I answered. "What did you just say?"

"That Antipas is like his dad, paranoid, bloodthirsty, all that stuff."

Matthew was giggling. "Chip off the old block!"

"That's what I said."

Thad handed me the bong and I sucked on it hungrily. I closed my eyes and my head started showing me pictures; memories of Jesus as if building a case in support of what I'd just heard. The evidence that laid itself in front of me included Jesus leaving Nazareth because his mum was sending him on a mission for the family business, a family business that I'd never heard about before, even though I'd known him all my life. There was John declaring that he wasn't worthy to baptise him, that he was bound for greatness. Then of course that thing Jesus had about him, when he was nailing it - when people would just stop and listen, or drop everything to follow him. Finally I pictured Jesus' delirious rant in the wilderness, about the Devil getting up in his face and his dad being in charge of heaven and earth. It all started to make sense - far-fetched, ridiculous, ludicrous sense - but some kind of sense all the same.

"Jesus," said Thad.

I passed the bong to Matthew. "I know what you mean Thad, this has blown my mind."

"No, I mean Jesus, as in here he is, here's Jesus."

I looked behind me to where Thad was staring down the hill. The man himself was approaching.

He sat down on the grass. "Find some good growing

grounds did you? Or are you just getting fucked? Any left for me?"

"You can have mine, it's the last bit," said Matthew, handing him the bong.

"If you're sure?"

"No problem."

"Don't mind if I do, cheers." Jesus lit up and sucked slowly and steadily. It could have just been that I'd been on it for hours, but I swear the stream of vapour that eased out of his mouth spiralled above him and caught the moonlight in a perfect circle. A halo.

"Ah, yes! That's the business, the first of the day. You sure there's no more?" There were a few head shakes but nobody spoke. "I don't want to sound paranoid," he said, "but either you've all been sitting here in silence or you all just stopped talking when I got here."

"The second one," said Thad, King of Tact. "We were talking about you."

I shifted my seating position so I was facing him. "We were talking about when you were born. Matthew's been telling me some stories, Thad already knew them."

Jesus just smiled.

"So you know what I'm talking about?"

"Have you got anything to drink?" He answered his own question with a glance at the empty bottles. He shrugged. "Yeah, I think I know what you're talking about, I've heard those stories too."

"So you were born in a stable?"

"Only because the inns were all full."

"And you had," I said, "visitors?"

"Apparently. Obviously I was too young to remember but I'm told that people started turning up. Some shepherds first."

Matthew interjected triumphantly, "Who'd been told to go

there by an angel no less."

"So they said, and then three more blokes. They'd brought gifts."

"They weren't three more blokes!" I said, almost shouting. "They were kings, kings who'd travelled some crazy distance to get to you. And those gifts weren't new pairs of sandals were they? One of them brought gold."

"Yeah alright, one of them brought gold."

"What did the others bring?"

"I forget. Bath stuff for my mum I think."

"And how did these blokes with the gold and the bath smellies find you?"

Jesus cleared his throat. "Oh yes, I wondered if you'd get to that. They said they followed a star."

"One that magically stopped right over the stable," I said.

"So I was told," said Jesus. "But let's be honest, it all sounds a bit far-fetched doesn't it?"

"You're not denying it." Matthew looked shocked that I was grilling the big man like this but I thought I was well within my rights to push for answers from my best mate who everyone but me seemed to know was God's representative to mankind.

"Look," he said, "you can believe what you want. Everyone's allowed to believe what they want."

I stared at him. "Just answer me straight. Are you the Son of God?"

"Let's go and get some beers," said Jesus.

# Turning the Tables

I had to accept that if Jesus had spent a lifetime not telling me the secrets of his past, and perhaps his future, there was no reason he was going to start now just because I'd heard it from a third party. There was no point pushing him on it so I left it to him to tell me if he wanted to. I didn't know what to believe but I knew enough to know more than ever that he was... special.

Matthew, though still technically Aretas' man, quickly became a member of the crew. We even had a swearing-in ceremony to welcome both him and Bart into the fold. I say swearing-in ceremony, that makes it sound pretty formal. What actually happened was that we all went to the mountains and got totally messed up, but that counts as a ceremony on my tablet. Jesus was on fine form that day, playing the crazy gang-boss. I'm not sure if Matthew really got the joke but that was okay. I hadn't laughed so much in ages.

Jesus announced afterwards that twelve was enough of a crew. The top table was at full capacity and anyone else who got involved from then on would just be a hired hand. We had plenty of hands to hire in the months that followed. Business started to grow as Aretas opened up all the channels he'd promised. We looked to Jesus' growing flock for recruits to help with all the extra work. The selection process was simple: pick those who'd shown the most commitment and dig a bit deeper to see if they had the aptitude for a specific role. "You can be the most loyal man in the world but if you're shit, you're shit," Jesus had said, emphasising the importance of the latter part of this two-tiered recruitment process.

There was a limit to how fast we could grow because there was a limit to how much product we could, well… grow. Most of the money we did make went back into the business. Jesus made security the first priority, keen not to be beholden to Aretas for protection any longer than he had to. He never came out and said it but we all knew that however solid the relationship with Aretas was, things had a way of changing and loyalties with them.

Next was infrastructure. There were so many different strands to the whole thing it would have been easy to end up with a huge tangled mess. Simply keeping track of all the deals was a task in itself. There was a growing number of middlemen, mostly Aretas' people and, as I pointed out to Jesus, "You can be damned sure Aretas will be charging them for the privilege, he's making a lot more off this than whatever we're paying him."

Jesus answered with a calm smile. "I know the cost of doing business with a man like Aretas. It's already in the numbers, don't you worry your face over it."

The last of the strands, the major ones at least, were getting the stuff out to where it should go and getting the money back safely. It all had to be carefully managed.

We became more noticeable as a crew, mostly because growing that much gear takes up a lot of space, and that meant we had to play politics with the right people to get the land we needed. The elders in Galilee were technically under the yoke of Antipas and they needed certain assurances that their bloodthirsty tetrarch wouldn't hold them to account. It was funny how their fears seemed to subside when a sack of money landed in their lap.

We all kept the roles we'd been given, but our responsibilities grew. James and John were now joint heads of the biggest narcotic distribution concern in the Roman Empire. Not bad for a couple of fishermen with a stupidly named father.

Phil and Nat, the public relations boys, now had a much bigger public to make relations with. They'd enlisted Thomas, which made sense seeing as he'd been the stooge for one of their most successful schemes, or scams depending on your point of view.

As a crew, we were a lot less hands-on with the growing because Thad, Simon, Peter and Andrew simply couldn't cover all that ground. They each took up more of a consultancy role, hooking up with the growers and, like, consulting I guess.

I was finding that I didn't really have much to do, which was great in a way, but I kind of wanted to be the go-to guy from time to time. For that reason it felt good when Jesus asked me to go on a trip with him. He was going to Jerusalem to meet our distributor there; a guy called Nicodemus who as well as selling our product in the city was looking to push for sales further west. He was quite a player, sitting on at least one of the councils that effectively ran the city. He'd been picked to represent us because of his clout and his connections. Matthew came too, along with four guards. They weren't dressed for battle like the Roman soldiers we'd been assigned before but they had pretty nasty looking daggers on them and could obviously look after themselves. I was happy to assume they could look after us too.

The journey took two days and turned out to be a blast. Our security didn't have to show their skills at head-cracking or gut-slicing because there was no sign of trouble and we had a warm welcome in the hostelries along the way. We were used to being recognised in Capernaum, so it felt weird that nobody knew who we were, but a good kind of weird. It was the time of the festival so there were plenty of people headed for the city and plenty more who'd already arrived when we got there. The whole place was rammed.

We pushed our way through the crowds towards the temple; the venue for the planned meeting. The grounds within its outer walls suggested more of a place of business than a place of worship, with market stalls catering for the thousands congregating for the festival.

Getting to the door to the temple proper wasn't easy. There was a bottleneck of people all trying to get in, although they were trying to get to the service that was about to start inside, while we had other intentions. Eventually inside the huge arched doorway which opened up into a wide chamber, we stepped off to the side. This was more to get out of the rush of the crowd pouring past than anything else but it turned out to be a wise move. A man stood, arms folded, outside a door a few paces to our left.

"Can I help you, gentlemen?" His relaxed countenance was in sharp contrast to the frenzy all around. "Don't tell me, you are Jesus, the Christ."

I'd given up questioning how people who'd never seen Jesus could identify him so easily.

"That's me." Jesus offered a hand.

"It's an honour to meet you." Rather than shaking it, the man clasped Jesus' hand in both of his own and lowered himself into a clumsy bow. "Step this way please." He shouldered the heavy door open. It led to the foot of a narrow spiral staircase. At the top of the stairs we turned right into a large office, well lit by the huge window overlooking the temple grounds we'd spent so long working our way through. The crowds were starting to thin out as more people headed inside for the impending service. At a desk beneath the window sat a small hairy man.

He stood and came round to greet us, introducing himself. This was Nicodemus, the man we'd come to see. We'd never met in person before, all our business had been through messengers, but of course he picked out Jesus straight away. He bowed more competently than his assistant. "It is an honour to meet the Christ."

Jesus took his hand briefly. "You are most kind. Please sit."

Nicodemus returned to his window seat behind the desk. The rest of us remained standing.

Jesus got to business. "So you want to open up some new markets, Liberia and Gaul as I understand it."

Nicodemus nodded. "Yes my lord, but there is another matter to which I would like to draw your attention,"

Jesus stared vaguely over his head. "Go ahead."

"You are looking at the problem right now. The vendors with their market stands."

"Selling the sacrificial doves, changing the pilgrims' money?"

"That's not all they are doing. They are agents for Tetrarch Antipas. They are selling their product here. They know my affiliation and are sending a message, a message directly from Antipas himself. I have approached them, I have threatened force, but they have threatened to return that force tenfold."

"Did they mention Antipas by name?"

"No, but they left me in no doubt that he was their backer."

Jesus was out of the room before Nicodemus had finished the sentence. Our security crew hesitated at first, not sure what to do but eventually went out after him. Matthew and I stayed put.

"What's going on?" Matthew asked quietly.

A look out of the window answered his question. Jesus was in the courtyard, striding towards the trading stands. Without warning he grabbed the nearest one and flung it over, scattering its contents everywhere. He leaned over the upended table, getting right up in the face of the trembling man behind it and roared. "What are you doing peddling your shit here? This is your father's house, your daddy's house. And do you know who the daddy is? I'm the fucking daddy. This is my house." He gripped handfuls of the man's tunic and pulled him towards him, his spit flew as he screamed in his face. "Take your shit and get the fuck out." He released the man with a shove, knocking him onto the ground. He looked around at the other dealers. "What are you fucking looking at? Get the fuck out of it. Tell your boss, tell Antipas, tell him he needs to stay the fuck out of my house."

The last stragglers who'd been making their way into the temple had all but forgotten the service as they stood, dumbstruck, as Jesus flipped another table and kicked at one more. Our security had caught up with him now and stood around him; a human shield. But they weren't needed. The message had already been heard. The dealers were hurrying out of the gate.

Nicodemus stared out of the window and back at us. His eyes were wide with shock. He shook his head and muttered under his breath, "Christ."

## Fuck You

"I don't know how I'm going to spin this. We've been selling Jesus as a man of peace, but now he's gone and kicked off in public."

I couldn't believe what I was hearing but I had to consider my words carefully. "Phil, mate, I know we've never been close…"

"Never been close? You hate my guts, you bloody kicked me."

"Yeah, well, sorry about that. But I'm hoping we can put all that behind us, this is all a bit bigger than our petty squabbles."

"I never had a squabble with you. You've just hated me right from the off."

"Yeah, well, sorry about that."

"Stop saying *yeah, well*."

"Yeah, well… okay, anyway." I winced inwardly. "I'm sorry for hating you. I mean, I don't hate you. Look, I'm sorry for being such a tosser is what I'm trying to say. I'm trying to get over my shit and put our shit behind us, because shit's got real now."

"That's a lot of shit."

"Fuck you then."

Phil looked pained. "I was trying to have a joke with you. All I meant was that you said shit a lot of times."

"I suppose I did, sorry about the fuck you."

Phil shrugged. "There's always going to be a fuck you just

around the corner."

"I think we can live with the odd fuck you. The point I'm trying to make is that we've got to back each other. We're in the same crew. We don't have to be bezzie mates but we can get along well enough to do what's needed."

"Didn't I say the exact same thing to you a little while back? In fact, didn't I offer you an olive branch? And if I remember rightly you took that olive branch and poked me in the eye with it."

"I see what you did there. That's quite good, fair play. Okay, you've got me, I've been a twat and I'm sorry."

Phil paused before speaking, I'm sure he was loving having the moral high ground. I, of course, was hating every moment of this, but I knew I had to make it up with Phil. Since the poking and kicking incident we'd avoided each other as much as possible but it couldn't stay that way forever, particularly not now Jesus had effectively declared war on Antipas. Finally he nodded. "I guess so. Okay."

"Good man," I said as we shook hands awkwardly, like brothers who haven't spoken for years meeting at an aunt's funeral. "Now we can talk freely without you thinking I'm having a pop at you the whole time."

"Which is pretty much what you've been doing up to now."

I gritted my teeth. "Do I have to keep apologising, or can we get on with business?"

"Yeah alright, go on."

"Right, what I wanted to say is that if your biggest worry is how are we going to spin this to make Jesus look soft and fluffy then you've not been paying attention. The biggest problem - in fact it's so big it's the only problem - is that Jesus has sent a direct message to Antipas. You remember Antipas, son of Herod the baby killer, chopper offer of heads? Yes, I'm sure you do, well Jesus sent that very same Antipas a message, and that message was fuck you."

Phil smiled. "Everything comes down to fuck you."

"Absolutely, and the fuck you that Jesus sent to Antipas is bigger than all of mine put together. And that's what we should be focusing on."

"Yes," he said. "I suppose we should. Has anyone spoken to him about it?"

I hesitated, "No, nobody's spoken to him about it."

"Well you need to step up, mate. Surely if anyone should talk to him - and someone definitely should - then it's you."

He was right of course. I was always bemoaning my marginalised role in the organisation and now here was an important task that fell squarely in my remit. And besides, I was one of the few people who'd actually seen Jesus go off his nut, the few of our lot anyway, there were plenty of other witnesses. Of all the crew, I was in a unique position to talk to the big man and see what was going on in his head. Phil being right wouldn't normally have bothered me, my standard response would have been a big fuck you, but I had to use those sparingly now. I did have to step up. I had a role to play. "I'll talk to him."

I caught up with Jesus in his room where he'd spent most of his time since the strained and silent trip back from Jerusalem. He was standing at the window with his back to me. The atmosphere felt different from the last time I was in there, that is, he wasn't getting a blow job off the girl of my dreams.

He turned round and for only the second time ever I saw tears in his eyes. "I don't know what to do, mate."

In that moment all his confidence, all his power seemed to have been stripped away. All that remained was a man clearly in way above his head, burdened by responsibility and scared out of his wits. I did what I thought was the right and proper thing to do under the circumstances. I stepped forward and put my arms around him.

"What are you doing? Get off me you big pussy."

I quickly pulled away. "Believe me, mate, I didn't want to hug you, but you're all, like, crying and stuff. You're the big pussy."

"I wasn't crying, I just had a mote in my eye."

"Again with the mote! Christ, that gag didn't work when we were both half dead in the wilderness."

Jesus smiled. "It's *Christ* now is it?"

"It does have a certain ring to it."

He shrugged. "I suppose it does."

"So are we going to talk about it or what?"

He feigned ignorance. "What?"

"Oh come on. I come in the room and you're crying. You tell me you don't know what to do."

"Oh, that. Yeah. I suppose we should talk about that…" he left the sentence hanging.

"Go on then," I prompted.

"Go on then what?"

"Talk about it."

"You mean now?" He looked genuinely surprised. "Oh. Alright then, yeah, I suppose now's as good a time as any…"

"You just tailed off again! Okay I'll go first. What did you mean when you said you don't know what to do?"

"Well it was pretty much self-contained in the statement but if you must have the details," he sat on the edge of the bed. "Here I am, some kind of spiritual leader…"

"And head of a drug operation."

"Yeah, that too, but I see it as the same thing. Anyway, people listen to me, people rely on me, people depend on me…"

"Kind of the same thing as *rely* but go on."

He punched me on the arm. "You're such a fucker! Do you

want to talk about this or not?"

"Not really, but we kind of have to."

"Well stop interrupting me then. Right, so people rely, depend on me, whatever, and I was put in a position where if I made one choice I'd look weak - and in our game we can't look weak - and if I made the other choice then I'd invoke the wrath of an evil despot, our sworn enemy, and put all our lives at risk."

"I see what you mean, damned if you do, damned if you don't."

"If you believe all those stories, then I don't think damnation's an option for me."

"Are they true? Is the man upstairs your dad?"

"Leave it alone, I was joking! So what do I do?"

"You could apologise to Antipas."

"Now it's you who's joking. I've already said we can't look weak. If I apologise to that tosser, which I wouldn't do out of principle anyway, we'll look like pussies, we'll make ourselves targets for every two-denarii operation in Judea."

"Alright, I wasn't married to the idea. I was just starting to list options."

"Saying sorry to Antipas is not an option."

"Yeah, I'm getting that. So the only other option as far as I can see is that we use our resources, and our best resource for this kind of thing is Aretas. We tell him that things have," I rummaged around in my head for the right word, "escalated."

"I don't want Aretas thinking we need help."

"Jesus! The only reason Aretas is involved with us at all is because we needed his help."

"Yeah, but I don't want to keep asking him to fight my battles for me."

"But he's got a fucking army! And apart from a few heavies that we've brought in, we haven't. And anyway, Aretas hates

Antipas, he's going to war with him, that's why he's backing us. He must have known something like this was going to happen. It's probably part of his plan. We have to tell him."

"Maybe, but we have to find a way of doing it that doesn't make us look weak."

I smiled. "I think I know just the man to come up with something."

"You mean Phil? You hate Phil. In fact I've been meaning to talk to you about that. You need to sort out whatever your problem is with him. Everybody's noticed. It's not good for business. We need to be solid. There's no place for in-fighting."

"I've already talked to him, we're cool."

"Don't shit me."

"I did, honest I did."

"Anyone who says *honest* isn't being honest."

"Well I am. I realised I needed to fix things with Phil and so I fixed them. I'm all, like, grown up."

"Well I'll be damned."

"I thought damnation wasn't an option."

"Whatever. Get Phil up here."

"How about we go downstairs and get a nice beer? If you entertain any more men in your room people are going to start talking."

"Have you found me entertaining then?"

"Just come downstairs."

Phil was sitting at the bar with Nat, chatting to Bart. "Get us some beers and come outside will you, Phil?" I said. Bart started pouring as Jesus and I headed to the garden. Phil joined us soon after, carefully hugging three beers to his chest.

"Cheers," Jesus said, lifting his glass and taking a sip. "Ah, that's good. So, you two are mates now are you?"

Phil glanced at me. "Apart from the occasional fuck you."

"Good to hear it," said Jesus. "Now, Antipas has no choice

but to come down hard on us for that business in the temple. We can do what we can and we've got some muscle now but what we really need is an army. We've got to get a message to Aretas but we can't look like we're begging for help. I don't want us to look like pussies."

"Not pussies, right, got it," said Phil.

We all took a sip of our beer.

We took another one.

"So," said Jesus, "how's it going?"

"Not bad, thanks," said Phil. "I've just moved to a new place. It's small, but it's much closer to here. There's a really nice garden and…"

"I mean how's coming up with a solution to our problem going?"

"Oh that," said Phil. "Working on it."

We all sipped of our beer.

Jesus looked at Phil then at me and back at Phil again. "Shall I… leave it with you?" He downed his beer and stood up.

"Yep, leave it with us, we're all over it." He waited until Jesus was back inside before speaking. "Well I don't think we covered ourselves in glory there."

Tempting though it was to remind Phil that he was meant to be the ideas man, so technically it was him and not us who'd failed to cover himself in glory, I thought it might upset our new-found pax-romana so I thought better of it. "I'll get some more beers," I said.

When I got back Phil was leaning back on his stool, his arms behind his head, a show of satisfaction.

I put the beers on the table and sat down. "You got something?"

"Absolutely."

"Look, I'm really trying not to think of you as a dick, so perhaps if you could be less smug and just tell me, that would be great."

"Fair call." He sat forward. "What we do is we use Matthew. We send him to see Aretas, because he's worried about Jesus."

"Worried about what exactly?"

"Worried that Jesus has got this crazy side. That he's going to make a move on Antipas. He can say that everyone's warned Jesus how dangerous Antipas is but he won't listen, that he just keeps saying he's going to run Antipas off his patch and avenge John's murder into the bargain. Aretas won't want everything going to shit because of a rash move by Jesus, he's onto a good thing here, he's bound to send reinforcements, lots of them. We get the army, Jesus doesn't lose face. In fact he'll look proper hard."

"That's… that's actually not half bad."

"Not half bad? It's two halves fucking good."

"Okay, I'll give you that, it is good. I can sort of see what he sees in you now."

"That's the best I'm going to get isn't it?"

"I think you'd feel a bit uncomfortable if I was any more glowing than that, it would be weird."

Phil smiled. "I guess so. I suppose we'd better toast this flimsy little pact we seem to have made."

"I suppose we should, to the obvious?"

"Of course." Phil raised his glass. I raised mine.

We spoke together, "To fuck you!"

## Water Water Everywhere

Matthew was well up for Phil's plan, and, with a couple of heavies in tow, saddled up (or whatever it is you do with camels) and headed east. We knew he had a long journey ahead of him but hoped he would return as quickly as possible with a big chunk of Aretas' army under his command.

We had to take steps to cover our backs against Antipas in the meantime. Phil had a plan for that too. He said we should work harder than ever to push Jesus in the eyes of the public, making him so popular that it would be hard for Antipas to take him down without causing unrest. Antipas was ruthless and bloodthirsty but even he knew that killing John hadn't gone down well, either with the public or more importantly for him, with the Romans. Our occupiers were, on the whole, happy to leave Antipas to get on with running his little slice of their Empire but wouldn't think twice about intervening if the actions of their provincial puppet ruler caused even a whiff of a popular uprising.

So we went all-out to make Jesus the people's favourite, which wasn't the hardest thing in the world to do because he was well on the way to that position already. The people simply adored him. I don't know if Phil leaked it, or if the whispers were circulating of their own accord, but the whole Son of God thing had started to spread, sitting comfortably alongside the terms *Messiah* and *Saviour*.

We did more public appearances than ever, in Capernaum

and all around Galilee. He even did a few stints in the temple at Jerusalem where we were pleased to find that Antipas' dealers had taken Jesus' message on board from the last time and stayed away.

The public appearances were a great success and we did it all without any trickery. Well maybe not completely, there was this one time…

We'd had word that there was a wedding in a village not too far away. I forget the name of it but the bloke getting married was the son, or maybe nephew, of an old family friend of Jesus' folks. This meant that Jesus' mum was going to be there. There was no way he was going to turn down a chance to see her, and Mary was dead excited by the prospect of meeting the woman who was her… well she didn't actually say *future mother-in-law* but you could tell that's how she saw it.

We didn't go empty-handed; Jesus had Bart bring six huge barrels of wine as a wedding gift. Along with the four of us and a few security, Phil and Nat came too. This would have appalled me not too long before but things were different with Phil now. I could still see that he was a bit of a knob, but at least he was our knob. I wasn't too sure about Nat though, bit of a dullard if you ask me. But nobody was asking me.

It was a horrible journey, the heavens, as they say, opened and it pissed it down the whole way. I asked Jesus a few times if he could have a word with the man upstairs but when he told me to fuck off for the third time I gave it a rest. I felt bad for Maximus, he was soaked, but he kept on plodding onwards. Good old Max. We camped out for the first night. I didn't bother pitching my tent, opting instead to sleep under the wine cart. To be honest I was glad to be as far away as possible from the all too imaginable things that were bound to be going on in Jesus and Mary's tent.

The rain had eased up by the next morning but trudging

through the mud was slow going. The sun was setting when we arrived and the wedding party was quite the spectacle; all lit by a ring of torches with clusters of candles throughout. Jesus and the others went into the throng to find his mum while I gave Bart a hand parking the cart round the side behind what was obviously the refreshment tent. The huge jars inside made us think that perhaps they were okay for wine but we unloaded anyway.

We lapped the venue a few times, not deliberately but because we struggled to find the others. One thing that stood out a mile was that everyone was hammered. We'd have to go some to catch up, but I fancied our chances. Eventually we found them. They'd caught up with Jesus' mum and he'd obviously done the introductions because everyone was in a half moon around her, talking or listening intently. There was no way in without being rude so Bart and I stood on the outskirts waiting for someone to notice and bring us into the conversation. Mary - Jesus' mum that is - looked fantastic and in case that came out wrong, I mean she looked very well, nicely turned out, healthy, confident.

I found my eyes settle on Mary, the other Mary, and this time when I say she looked fantastic I mean she looked amazing, delicious, soft, firm, wonderful. She looked like the mother of my children. She was side on to me, her eyes fixed on her namesake, fascinated as anyone would be by the woman who gave birth to her lover, but presumably in this case - if she believed the stories - fascinated even more by the woman chosen by God to bear His child.

My eyes were torn from an intent study of Mary's slightly flushed left cheek and where it made the transition to delicately parted moist lips, when Jesus' mum called my name.

She was a whirlwind of greetings: *it's been so long, it's sooo good to see you, you have been looking after my baby haven't you?* It was great

189

to see her and brought all the memories of home flooding back. All those simple pleasures. All that laughter. She told me how well my family were doing and how much they missed me. I was a bit choked to be honest.

We were introduced to the bride, her father and the groom, and I'm ashamed to say I forgot their names almost as soon as I heard them so there's no chance of me remembering now. I had wondered how the bride's father would feel about us all turning up, because I was sure we hadn't been invited, but he couldn't have been more welcoming. Drunk on happiness, and pride for his daughter, as well as being drunk in the more traditional sense, he conjured up some stools for us. As we sat down he leaned in between me and Phil. His hands were heavy on our shoulders and his breath stank of booze and whatever they'd had for the feast. He was close enough to whisper but talked loudly enough for everybody to hear. Phil and I both winced as his hoarse, excitable chatter assaulted our ears.

"I... I hope I've made you comfortable at least cos I got a concession... confession to make." I was released as he leaned more heavily on Phil and raised himself up to gesture towards our surroundings. "There's loads... loads..." he immediately lowered himself between us again and my right shoulder took the strain once more, "...loads of people here. Loads. Loads more than I thought would come. And that's because I've got such a wonderful daughter and she's..." his eyes were rheumy with tears, "... she's married her prince. He's gonna make her happy." He stood as upright as he could whilst still using me to brace most of his weight and gripped his free hand into a fist. "Well he'd better make her happy or I'll have him." His scowl was replaced with a look of contentment as he either reminded himself that there was a good chance the groom was going to make his daughter very happy, or he'd simply forgotten what he'd just been saying.

He leaned his head back between me and Phil, who were both keeping our gazes fixed straight ahead so as not to catch his eye and become a target for further burbling. I stole a quick glance at his close-up face and saw that he was staring through heavy-lidded eyes at Jesus and his mum opposite. They were looking back at him, straight faced but with matching pairs of smiling eyes.

"Was that the confession?" said Jesus.

The father of the bride swayed his head from side to side as he answered, not immediately of course, a day of drinking was all but shutting down his ability to make the connection between thoughts and speech. "No. No. That wasn't the concession." He paused once again and then seemed to be overcome with lucidity. His grip on my shoulder eased and his head became still. "We're out of wine."

Before any of us could point out that we'd brought six barrels of the stuff, Mary turned to her son. "You can sort that out can't you dear?"

Jesus played the sulky teenager. "Do I have to do everything?" He *harrumphed* himself to his feet.

Our host turned his head to watch Jesus heading away and then looked back at his mum who just winked and said, "My son will make it right."

Bart went after Jesus and the father of the bride slumped onto the vacated stool muttering to himself. "Everyone came to see my princess, everyone came and drank all the wine and now all we've got is water. It's good water, clean fresh water, but water's not a party drink. Everyone came. Water." He dozed off.

"He's had a busy day," said Jesus' mum, like she was speaking fondly about an over-tired infant. The other Mary was watching her in unconcealed awe and I could see why. I was seeing her in a new light too. To me she'd always just been

Jesus' mum, I hardly even noticed her, but now I could see her for what she really was, a sharp, funny, beautiful woman. She seemed to be answering all of the younger Mary's questions just by simply being herself.

The rest of the crew had just been sitting quietly too but I could see that Phil was craning his neck to see if Jesus was on his way back. And soon he was, holding a cup almost overflowing with wine. Jesus crouched in front of the father of the bride and tapped him gently on the shoulder. His head jerked upwards and then lowered slowly, his eyes working overtime to focus. He was face to face with a smiling Jesus who said, "Here you go, you've probably had enough but one more won't hurt, it's your daughter's wedding day after all."

The man looked as if Jesus had just risen from the dead. "Where did you get that?"

Jesus pointed. "Over there."

The father staggered to his feet, using Nat as a crutch this time. He looked where Jesus was pointing. A not so orderly queue had formed past the huge jars and Bart was doling out wine, filling everyone's cup. "It was water!" the bride's father screamed. "It was water and you made it into wine." He took the cup from Jesus, spilled half of it on Nat and glugged it back. "You turned it into wine, you wonderful bastard!"

"No I didn't, I…"

I've never seen Phil move so fast, before or since. He jumped to his feet and took hold of Jesus' shoulders, rocking them as he spoke. "You have blessed us once again with your kindness, with your gentle but awesome power. Thank you, oh Lord." He glanced at the father of the bride, who was busy raising his cup to the crowd of people outside Bart's impromptu bar and roaring with laughter. Phil put his finger to Jesus' lips. "Don't deny anything," he whispered. He turned to me and Nat. "You got that? Don't deny anything. Let him believe. Let them all believe." He made a hasty dash in Bart's direction, presumably to make sure he was singing from the same hymn sheet.

So as I've said, as a rule we didn't employ cheap stunts to further fan the flames of Jesus' legend.

But we made damn sure we got those barrels out of sight well before morning.

# Self-Fulfilling Prophecy

"I haven't read any of it. I'm not too hot on reading, and besides, only a few places have the parchments." Peter spent a lot more time at Magdalene's nowadays. "I've heard all the stories though."

Thad had been, as usual, not quite there, but this subject matter seemed to rouse him from his reverie. "The whole thing's fucking nuts."

Peter looked distinctly uncomfortable. "You... you shouldn't talk that way."

"Why not?"

Peter looked confused by the question. "Because it's blasphemy."

"I'll take my chances." Thad poured himself more wine from the jug and looked around to see if any of the rest of us wanted a top up. Peter put his hand over his own glass.

"What's that about?" Simon snapped. "You won't take a drink off Thad in case his scepticism infects you?"

Peter lifted his hand but kept his glass guarded. "I don't know what you mean."

"Yes you do, there was no other reason to cover your glass."

"No, I mean I didn't understand what you said - that word, septizizum, whatever."

"It means someone who doesn't believe," said Simon.

"I reckon," said Thad, "that the more you read that thing,

the less you'll actually believe in the stuff it says."

"I believe all of it," said Peter proudly. "I observe all the teachings of the Testament."

"But you haven't read it yourself?" Simon said.

"No, I'm not too hot on reading, like I said."

"Have you asked someone to read it to you?"

Peter scratched his beard. "Well, no. That would be ridiculous."

Simon wasn't letting this go. "So you've been told the general gist of selected parts - selected by a preacher."

"Yes. That's what preachers are for isn't it?"

"How old was Noah when he died?"

"I don't know, seventy?"

"You're nine hundred years out."

"He never lived that long."

"That's what it says in the Testament. And how about God killing all those babies?"

"God didn't kill any babies," said Peter.

Simon looked well-pleased with himself. "It's right there in Exodus, all the firstborn of Egypt, all at once."

"Just because they were firstborn, doesn't mean they were babies," said Thad. "I mean, I'm a firstborn and I've got a beard. Babies don't have beards."

"Yes, well, thank you Thaddeus. My point stands though. If you believe the Testament, then the man we know as God seems rather keen on casting people out, casting them down, raining fire upon them, besetting them with plagues, slaughtering them," he looked at Thad, "particularly babies and children, the more innocent the better. Generally he seemed to go around invoking his wrath at the slightest provocation. He was, is, quite an insecure chap too, gets very jealous if there's any worshiping going on that isn't pointed in his direction."

Peter shifted himself backwards on his stool, shooting

furtive glances at the ceiling as if expecting a shaft of fire to burst through and consume Simon. "You shouldn't talk that way. You should believe. If you don't, then…"

Simon filled the dead air. "Then what? What will happen?"

"I don't know. Bad things."

"So you are saying that I should believe in everything it says in the scriptures to ensure that I'm not on the end of some violent retribution from a vengeful deity? Believing is believing, you either do or you don't. One cannot make oneself believe something just because one is threatened with eternal damnation. I could try and make myself believe that I have frogs instead of toes, but I would always know that they are not really frogs, they are toes. You can't believe something because of fear. You can only *say* you believe something. There is a rather large difference."

"Well *I* believe," said Peter. "And if you don't, then what are you doing here?"

"I didn't say I didn't believe. I said I didn't believe everything a preacher tells me, and definitely not everything that's written in the Testament."

I wanted to give poor Peter a bit of a break. "Simon, how come you know the scriptures so well?"

"He's a bit of a zealot is our Simon," said Thad.

"I'm only zealous about acquiring knowledge. I find it important to arm oneself with as much information as possible so one can make a proper judgement on things, cut through all the bullshit."

"I tell you what they should do," said Thad. "They should write a fresh one, a *new* Testament. Leave all the weird shit out this time." He poured himself some more wine.

"If Jesus' star keeps rising then they're going to have to write a new one, and it'll be all about him," said Phil. "Which takes us back to the purpose of this meeting. What's in there that we can use? You lot seem to be experts on it, what have you got?"

"I'm still not quite sure what it is you're after," I said.

"I don't know how I could have put it any more simply."

"Indulge me. Tell me again. Pretend I wasn't listening and was chatting to James when you said all that stuff at the start. And tell James again too. Pretend that he wasn't listening either, because he was chatting to me."

"Yes," said James, smiling, "pretend that."

"Jesus," Phil rolled his eyes. "Okay, is everybody listening? Yes? Good. Right, we're at a stage now where Jesus is hot stuff, people think he's the Messiah, the Son of God..."

 Peter interrupted. "He *is* the Messiah. He *is* the Son of God."

Phil didn't try to hide his impatience. "I didn't say he wasn't."

"You didn't say he was either. You just said that people think he is."

"But what people think is all that matters."

Peter folded his arms, silently lodging his disapproval.

"Right, where was I? Oh yes, the Testament. What I'm asking is this... is there anything in the scriptures that we can use to our advantage? It's rammed with prophecies, can you think of any that we can..."

"Make it look like they've come true?" I said.

"I was going to say fulfil, but yes."

"You mean, like, there's going to be a big flood?" said James.

Phil sighed. "No, I don't mean like, *there's going to be a big flood*, I mean something a bit more..."

Thad interrupted him. "I think that one's been and gone anyway."

"You could say we missed the boat on that one!" I said,

high-fiving James.

Phil put his head in his hands. "For the love of God."

"Something more… what?" I said.

"More relevant, more personal."

I felt I should give him a hand before his blood started to boil. "Is there anything written about the coming of the Messiah?"

Phil peeped up from under his hands, a glimmer of hope in his weary eyes. "Yeah," he said, "that. Is there anything about that?"

"Oh yes," said Thad, "plenty."

Phil bit his lower lip. "Well would you care to edify the rest of us?"

Simon talked over Thad's baffled expression. "Thad won't know what the word means so I'll take care of the edifying. If you want messianic prophecies then the scroll of choice is that of Isaiah. I can't remember all of them, I'm not that anal, but there's the obvious big one that we can't use because he's already done it."

Phil was sitting upright again. "Who, Isaiah?"

Simon looked baffled. "What do you mean?"

"I mean, who's already done it?"

"Isaiah's not going to fulfil his own prophesy now is he? I mean Jesus. Obviously."

"Obviously," agreed Thad.

Phil's eyes no longer looked weary. "What do you mean? What prophecy?"

Simon looked at Phil as if he was joking, realised he wasn't and pressed on. "*The Lord shall give a sign, a virgin shall conceive and bear a son.* I'm paraphrasing but it's along those lines. There's probably a *behold* in there somewhere."

"Isaiah foretold a virgin birth?" Phil's mouth hung open, a look that was repeated by the rest of us around the table with the exception of Thad, who was presumably a holy book scholar by proxy from hanging out with Simon for so long.

Simon grinned. "I don't know how I could have put it any more simply. You didn't know?"

"No I didn't bloody know!"

"I didn't know either," I said meekly.

"Me neither," said James.

"Nor me," said Peter.

Andrew shook his head. "News to me."

Simon looked at us as if we were idiots. "How can you not know that? You've been following the guy for God knows how long."

"We're not all experts in scripture." Phil sounded more exasperated than he did when I'd poked him in the eye. "You two could have said something."

"It never came up," said Thad.

Phil put his hands on top of his head and leaned back, "Jesus!"

"So obviously we can't use that one," said Simon, you're after one that has yet to be fulfilled. Let me think." He drained his glass. "I'm going to need some more wine. It will help refresh my memory."

"I'll go," said Thad. "I'm going to get my gear anyway." We watched him walk away, our eyes still wide from Simon's revelation.

"Come to think of it," Simon said, "the rest of Isaiah's prophecies are a little on the vague side. There is a mention of Galilee, we could probably get something out of that, but it is murky at best. There must be something more solid."

"What does it say about Galilee?" I said.

"There's something about an affliction in Jordan and Galilee and how the people that walked in darkness that live in the land of the shadow of death, upon them light has shined or something similar."

"That's us," said Peter. "We're the ones walking in darkness, Jesus is the light."

"You could read it that way I suppose," said Simon, "but it's stretching it a little. It's less straightforward when you read it in context. How about this? It might sound a bit odd but it's specific and it's do-able. It's not from Isaiah, it's from…" he rubbed his eye, screwing up his face, "…Zechariah, that's the one. I don't know Zechariah too well but I remember one part because it struck me as a strange scene - the king riding victorious into Jerusalem on a donkey."

Peter jumped in excitedly. "Aretas said Jesus would be called King one day."

Phil frowned. "Can't you think of any others?"

"If we go back to Isaiah there's a big passage about suffering and dying."

"Let's go with the donkey one then." Phil's business head was firmly back on.

"What's that?" Thad was back with a lot of wine.

"We're going to get Jesus to do a victory parade into Jerusalem on a donkey," said Simon.

"Fair enough." Thad starting pouring.

"I'm not sure about this," said Peter. "I don't want to say I told you so but I did, didn't I? I said he was the Son of God. Not only was his mother a virgin but a holy book said it was going to happen. It was foretold."

"Well firstly," said Simon. "The holy books foretold a lot of things, and plenty of them didn't make much in the way of sense. And plenty more that did make sense haven't shown any sign of being fulfilled in the centuries since they were predicted. And secondly, you obviously do want to say I told you so because you just said it, and you looked rather smug while you were doing it."

Peter's face looked like a smacked arse.

"The point is," said Phil, "that people think Jesus is the Son of God, and it's my job is to make sure they keep on thinking that."

"Is that all this is to you, a job?" Peter looked at Phil expectantly but didn't get an answer. "Whatever, it's not right just to pick a prophecy and act it out."

"John did it." Jesus' voice caught us all by surprise. We looked round to see him leaning casually in the doorway.

"How long have you been standing there?" I said.

"Long enough."

"What was that you said about John?" said Phil.

"That he did the same thing, perhaps not as directly, but he allowed people to believe he was the fulfilment of a prophecy. To many he was Elijah, returned to the world," he looked at Simon, "as foretold in the scroll of Malachi."

Simon grinned. "Who had ascended to Heaven four hundred years earlier. Good knowledge sir!"

"I'm struggling to keep up here," said Phil. "What exactly happened?"

"I don't know if any of it actually happened," said Jesus, "but according to scripture, Elijah was a prophet and a bit of a miracle worker as I understand it. When his time came, he flew up to heaven in a flaming chariot."

"How did the chariot fly?" said Phil.

"On a whirlwind apparently."

"No horses then?"

Simon pitched in. "Oh yes, there were horses. They were on fire too."

Thad looked satisfied. "Told you it was fucking nuts." Peter threw him a look of disapproval.

"Anyway," said Jesus, "in the scroll of Malachi it's foretold that Elijah will return some day. When John was doing his thing a few people asked if he, like, embodied the return of Elijah. He denied it of course. He would have looked like a bit of a knob if he went around shouting, *Look at me, I'm Elijah - my flaming chariot's being fixed so you can't see it but I'm definitely him*, but he was more than happy to keep the idea in people's minds."

"Clever," said Phil. "That's how I would have done it."

"Absolutely," said Jesus. "It's right out of Phil's big book of public relations."

"I'm not sure if I should take that as a compliment or not."

"But you're going to anyway," I said.

Phil shrugged. "But how do you know John did this?"

"Because he told me," said Jesus. "That's why he dressed like he did. He let people believe that he was Elijah returned."

"So this Elijah," said Phil, "what was his deal?"

"His deal," said Simon, "was that when he returned he would pave the way for the new Messiah".

I spoke up, "Is that why he said all that stuff about you when he dunked your head in the water? About the new era and how you would rise to greatness?"

Jesus shrugged. "Well, yes, obviously."

Phil's voice was pitching upwards with excitement. "If people think that John was this Elijah, who would usher in the new Messiah, and John pretty much ushered you in as exactly that, then, well, why aren't we using this?"

"How do you mean, use it?" said Peter.

Phil bunched his hands into fists in frustration. "To make people think that Jesus is the Messiah. How the fuck else?"

"He is the Messiah," Peter insisted.

Jesus patted him on the arm. "Thank you Peter, that's very kind of you to say. But Phil, in answer to your point, we kind of, like, already are. Not directly, maybe, but we know people have already made the link. Why do you think that particular word started getting thrown in my direction in the first place?

Like I said before about John, I'd look like a bit of a knob if I went around saying it, so let's just let people think it if they want to."

I couldn't resist it. "Missed the ark on that one didn't you Phil?"

"Piss off."

Jesus wagged a finger at the two of us. "Play nicely now, boys. "Anyway, we're getting off the point. What we're discussing here is the donkey thing and whether it's acceptable to act out a prophecy. My view is that if it was good enough for John then it's good enough for me."

"Well if you're cool with it." Peter's mutter was almost inaudible.

"I think it'll be fun," said Thaddeus. "We can make a day of it. We can get Jeroboam a nice rug for Jesus to sit on and…"

I cut him off. "What do you mean, Jeroboam? There's only one donkey in these parts worthy of fulfilling a holy prophecy and that's Maximus."

Jesus smiled. "Let's do it."

# Barstool Confessional

Even under the impending threat of a move by Antipas, we kept the business going and kept it growing. Apart from the wedding trip we'd stayed close to Magdalene's. All the crew had moved in and the rest of Bart's vacant rooms, along with some tents outside, were taken up by our security. We managed the empire from there, providing heavily armed travelling companions for our messengers and any of the crew who had to make a trip outside.

There was more downtime than ever before and mostly we filled it with parties. On arrival each guest had to be checked for weapons. This wasn't something either us or the guests were happy with but it was a necessary evil given our security situation. Once inside, everybody had a blast and Jesus seemed more relaxed than ever before.

Jesus and I had a lot less one-on-one time and I have to confess that it did bother me a little. I couldn't help but feel that my right hand man status was more of an honorary position than anything else. He didn't seem to confide in me on the big decisions anymore and that, apart from being a blow to my ego, made me wonder what I was doing there sometimes.

In terms of a social group I had the rest of the crew now. I'd hang out mostly with Thad, Simon, Bart, James, Thomas and even Phil. Peter and Andrew were nice guys but their piety got a bit much sometimes, and John, James' brother, was okay but he hardly spoke so he wasn't much in the way of value. I find those quiet types difficult to be with, not because I find them offensive - John definitely wasn't that - but because I feel obliged to try and draw them into the conversation. It takes the edge off a night on the beers when you have to keep throwing conversational bones out to the bloke who's been sitting in silence all night because you feel sorry for him. It was only really Nat who bothered me at all but I couldn't tell you why exactly. I just didn't like him. Perhaps I'm a bad person.

So despite our confinement, things weren't half bad. Of course it helped that we lived in a bar and had a limitless supply of green and poppy, but on the whole life was good. It was nothing at all like I'd planned it to be but come to think of it I hadn't actually planned my life anyway. I'd just gone along with whatever came up. I couldn't complain, although I'm sure I often did.

The biggest fly in the myrrh was Mary. Oh Mary, Mary, Mary. She haunted my heart and my head. For a couple of weeks she was the first person I saw every morning when I came out of the bathhouse. It always seemed to be her who was next to go in. She would just have a sheet wrapped around her, one forbidden shoulder on display and more of her thighs than it was safe to look at, particularly if I wanted to think of anything else at all for the rest of the day (and the following night for that matter). She wouldn't have gone out in public like that, she'd have been stoned for it - and not in a good way - but she seemed to think it was okay in front of me. It was like she saw me as a family member or perhaps a eunuch. But I wasn't her brother and I was definitely no eunuch, the javelin in my loincloth making the latter point abundantly clear.

I envied the jar of oil, freshly pressed from a nearby olive grove, that she always had tucked under one flawless arm as she waited for her turn in the tub. I knew it was destined for the most divine of tasks and I'd imagine her letting it trickle onto

her soft cupped palm before spreading it sensuously over her…
well you get the picture.

I had to change my morning routine.

But avoiding Mary was impossible. We lived in the same
house, bar, whatever, and she was dating my best friend. The
biggest problem was that she was so damned nice. Anybody
who spoke to Mary felt uplifted somehow. To say she was a
breath of the freshest spring air is cheesy but it's also true. I felt
that breezy springy uplifting thing just like everybody else, but
for me it was tainted, combined as it was with crushing
heartache. Spending time with Mary was like coming down off
the poppy at the exact same time as coming up.

I had no shortage of women and they were all lovely but
none of them had Mary's way. I would lie in bed, my squeeze
for that particular week sleeping beside me, and I'd find myself
thinking about Mary. I felt bad about it but I didn't think it was
my fault. I felt like the victim.

When I didn't have female company, I would tend to be the
last at the bar. That setting - the last knockings of the night, the
silence punctuated only by the barman washing glasses and
wiping down the counter top - it should have been the perfect
place and time to unburden myself of my feelings. Barmen
expect their punters to unload on them their tales of unrequited
love. It's part of the job. But when the barman happens to be
the uncle of the girl in question then it changes the dynamic
somewhat.

I wondered what he must have thought as I physically bit
down on my tongue to keep it from vocalising my dark secret.
At best he must have assumed that I'd get a weird twitch in the
mouth after a night on the sauce.

Sometimes Bart would finish his cleaning and leave me to it,
and I would sit alone, listening to the clicks and creaks of the
building as I supped on what was intended to be a nightcap, but

as the assumed definition of nightcap is the last one of the night, the drink in hand would often lose that title when I'd replace it with another. Well I was sitting in a bar for Christ's sake. What else was I going to do?

And yes, technically it was for Christ's sake that I was there.

"What are you smiling at?" Hearing a female voice on one of those late night solo sessions caught me off-guard. It was Mary, as if thinking of her had summoned her like a magic spell, but that notion was undermined by statistics; if she'd appeared every time I thought of her then she wouldn't have been able to do anything else.

"Erm... just funny thoughts I suppose."

She climbed onto the stool beside me. "What are you doing?"

"I'm building a scale model of Noah's Ark out of corks."

Mary just looked at me, cupping her chin in her palm, her elbow propped on the counter.

"Sorry, that sounded really sarcastic. Well it didn't just sound sarcastic, it was sarcastic. I thought I was being funny but I was just being rude, sorry."

"That's okay, it was a daft question. I guess I meant hello."

"Hello," I said.

"Mind if I join you?" There was that red pendant again, in pride of place on that perfect chest, the lucky chain clinging to the soft flesh of her neck.

"I think you already have, oh, you mean a drink, sorry." I slid myself off the stool and went behind the counter, taking the most recently washed glass and pouring her some wine.

"You do this a lot don't you?"

I hoisted myself back onto my stool. "I'm not much of a sleeper." That was a lie. I was a champion sleeper, the King of Sleep. I just started a lot later than most. "How come you're up?"

"Couldn't sleep either." She picked up her glass and took a sip. "Thanks for this by the way."

"No problem, I'm glad of the company." It felt like the right thing to say.

"Really?" She shifted her position so she was sitting more upright and facing me.

"Of course. What do you mean?"

"I mean you haven't seemed glad of my company much recently. If I didn't know any better I'd say you were avoiding me."

"No, course not. No, not at all. Avoiding you? No. Course not."

She smiled; a window into heaven. "Well that clear and well-worded answer has put my mind at rest." She studied my blank face. "Just in case it's not obvious, I was being sarcastic."

"Yes," I looked down at my glass. "I get it."

"So what's going on?"

"What do you want from me Mary?" Saying her name directly to her felt strange on my tongue.

"I don't get you."

"Come on. I'm trying, really I'm trying, but I can't… well you know. Of course you know." I hadn't meant it to come out like that but at least it was out, admittedly in some unspecified code, but neither of us was in any doubt what I had meant.

Mary looked into her lap. "Oh. Yes, I see." Fair play to her, she could have chosen to play it dumb, pretended to misunderstand me in the way that beautiful women so often do to spare the feelings of yet another adoring fool.

I'd left the jug of wine on the counter and I leaned forward and refilled my glass, Mary tilted hers forward for a top-up. I obliged. "Look, I said. It's nothing. You and Jesus are amazing together. I really couldn't be…" my last swig repeated on me causing me literally to choke on my words, "…happier for you."

"Oh well, if it's nothing then that's fine, problem solved." She shook her head and swivelled in her seat so she was facing the bar.

"Mary," without thinking I reached out and touched her wrist. It was the first time I'd ever touched her skin and it was like being struck by soft lightning. "You're right, it's not nothing but it's not something either. It's not like I'm ever going to make a move on you - for so many reasons."

"I know that. You've been the perfect gentleman, really you have. I know how loyal you are - and I know you'd never betray Jesus - but you and I have got to get past this. We're probably the two most important people in his life, big parts of this whole… operation, and more important than all that, you and I are friends, and that means something. We have to get past this."

We sat in silence for a while, a surprisingly comfortable silence. I'd been bursting to tell somebody about this and even though the person I'd ended up telling had turned out to be the last person I wanted to hear about it, I felt a huge relief. And not just because I'd just eased out an enormous but miraculously odourless fart that had been building up whilst we'd been talking.

"So what do we do?" she said at last.

"I reckon I can get it together," I said. "It's right that we talked about it. It's been a real help."

Her face darkened. "Now you're just taking the piss."

"Not at all, that's just another example of my curse to walk the earth, forever sounding insincere."

She nodded. "Ah, yes, Jesus told me about that but he called it…"

"My affliction?"

"That's the one."

"And I bet he said I brought it on myself by…"

She grinned, "By taking the piss the whole time, yes."

I shrugged. "So, you and me, are we cool?"

"We were always cool as far as I was concerned. I guess it's all down to you. Can you stop avoiding me? Can we be… mates again?"

"Yeah, I reckon I can manage that." And even though we hadn't actually done anything at all to fix the situation - not come up with a single way for me to control my feelings for the angel sitting next to me - I did think I could manage it. Maybe it is as good to talk as everyone says it is.

As soon as one issue in my life was solved, or at least painted over, another one came floating to the surface. "You mentioned earlier," I said, "that you and I are the most important people in his life."

She knocked back the rest of her wine. "Yes, that's true."

"I think you're half right, right about you at least, but me? I'm not so sure these days."

"What makes you say that?"

"I seem to be the last to know about things. He said once that I was his right hand man. Well a lot of the time this right hand doesn't know what the rest of the body's doing." I immediately regretted bringing this up. It made me sound like a whining little pussy and it was pointless anyway; she was just going to tell me what she thought I needed to hear, not because she was deceitful but because she would never offend me on Jesus' behalf.

"You're wrong to think that. He couldn't do any of this without you. He says so all the time. If he doesn't tell you something it's for a very good reason. It doesn't in any way suggest that he thinks you're less important. There's plenty of stuff he doesn't tell me and I know I'm important to him."

Yes but you're a girl, you're important for different reasons. I bit my tongue before that came out.

# The Law is an Ass

"What I want to know is how come Antipas hasn't made a move yet?" Bart was cleaning up after what was meant to be a lunch but had taken up all of the afternoon. I like those lunches. Bart himself hadn't touched a drop because of his daylight rule, but if I were him, having watched us lot sink more and more beers and having to actually bring us those beers, I'd have been getting ready to catch up as soon as possible.

"I suppose Phil was right with his plan," I said.

"To make Jesus so popular with the public that he's untouchable? It sounds sensible, but that can only last so long. Soon enough Antipas is going to think that we're rubbing his nose in it, which isn't a problem in itself. It's when he thinks that other people think we're rubbing his nose in it, that's when the real trouble starts. That's when he's got to be seen to be doing something. That's what it's all about in this business, what people think of you, and making it clear that you aren't going to take any shit."

"You sound like Phil."

Bart scowled. "No I don't, I talk through my mouth, Phil talks through his nose and when he's not doing that he talks out of his arse."

I ventured a joke. "I did wonder why his breath smells so bad."

"I've never noticed his breath. Has he got bad breath?"

I wished I hadn't bothered. "No, his breath is fine. It was

meant to be a joke, y'know, talking out of his arse, bad breath?"

"I see," said Bart. "Good one, I s'pose."

If I'd done that gag when he'd had a skinful, or even just a few, he'd have been on the floor by now. I made a note to myself to choose my moments in future.

I looked at the stack of glasses, the empty wine jugs and the dishes encrusted with remnants of food. "Can I do anything to help?"

"Jesus," Bart muttered under his breath.

"What?"

"If there's one thing that gets on my wick it's people offering to help. If you were going to help you would have just come round here and helped. It's not complicated, it's not like I'm working on a cure for leprosy and you need special instructions. When people ask if they can help, what they really mean is, *can you say no that's alright I'm okay thanks so I can get a guilt-free pass and carry on sitting on my arse while you clean up my shit?* You can see the water, you can see the cloths. You can see the mess, why do you need to ask?"

He was definitely more fun when he'd had a few but part of me had to concede that what he'd said was exactly what I'd been doing. I reluctantly walked round to join him and started scraping the plates into the slop bucket.

Suddenly Bart was screaming at me. "Stop it! What are you doing?"

"Helping?"

"You're chucking old bits of food into my mop bucket. How's that helping?"

I fished out the biggest bits and started again with a different bucket. I tried to get the conversation going again.

"So you think we're on borrowed time then? With Antipas I mean?"

"Don't you? Doesn't everyone?"

212

"Fair point. What do we do about it then?"

"I'm sure the big man has a plan," he said.

"If he has it would be nice if he shared it with us."

"He'll tell who he needs to tell. I'm surprised you don't know all his plans. He tells you all his moves doesn't he?"

"Used to."

Bart put on a baby voice. "Poor liddle boy not gedding enough attention from daddy?"

"I'll tell you what? Fuck you and your dishes, that's what." I stomped outside in a shameless sulk, realising before I'd even got through the door that I didn't really have anywhere to stomp to. I couldn't go up to my room because I'd have to pass Bart on the way to the stairs and I'd look ridiculous. My only option was to sit outside on my own. I couldn't even get a drink what with just having just told the landlord to go fuck himself.

My unlikely saviour was Phil, flanked by two security guards.

"What are you doing out here?" he said.

"Just getting some air, it's a nice evening."

"It's alright I suppose. Where's everyone else?"

"Sleeping it off. We had a big lunch."

"So I'm the only one who's been working? Nothing new there." He turned to the guards. "It's okay fellas, you can go in, cheers." He sat down and spoke gravely. "I think I know what Antipas is up to."

I looked at him expectantly.

"He's trying a different approach, different from what you'd expect from someone like him anyway." He paused, waiting for a response. This was a common trait of Phil's. Instead of just coming out and saying what he had to say, he liked to maximise the impact by punctuating it with pauses and solemn expressions.

I put on my best solemn expression in response, conscious

that my eyes were weighed down from an afternoon on the beer. "Tell me."

"He's working through the Pharisees."

I nodded. "I see, the Pharisees, hmmm."

"You have no idea what I'm talking about do you?"

"No."

"Have you heard of the Pharisees?"

"Yes, I've heard of them but I didn't pay much attention."

"Attention's not your strong point is it? I'll tell you what, get me a beer and I'll fill you in."

"Can't you go?"

"I've been on my feet all day. You've been relaxing here. It won't kill you."

"Bart might."

He rolled his eyes. "What have you said to piss off Bart?"

"Nothing, nothing, I was helping him tidy up but you know what Bart's like, he's really particular, really fussy. I think I got under his feet."

Phil's raised eyebrow said he knew there was more to the my story, but he went inside.

I looked out onto the town below, wondering once again how I ended up so far from home.

When Phil came out, a jug of wine in one hand and two glasses in the other, he was grinning like a jackal. "Got under his feet did you? You're priceless you are."

"Alright, you've had your fun, tell me what Antipas is up to."

He was still smiling. "Why'd you get so pissy with Bart?"

"He was being a twat. Anyway, we're having an important meeting. Let's get on with it shall we?"

"I thought I just bumped into you, but you can call it an important meeting if you want. Right, where were we?"

I poured the wine. "You were about to tell me what the

Pharisees is."

He put his business face back on. "The Pharisees call themselves the keepers of God's law. But they're more like interpreters. They take the rules written in the Holy Scriptures and convert them into something meaningful, a guide to how people should live their lives."

"Give me a *for instance*."

He thought for a moment. "Right, in one of the scrolls, I dunno, Jeramiah or something, it says that you can't carry a burden out of your house on the Sabbath. People like eating with their neighbours on the Sabbath, it's pretty much their only day off and the easiest way for lots of people to share a meal is for everyone to bring something along. This is a problem, because, according to the scrolls, a plate of food is a burden, so you can't take it out of your house. To get round this, the Pharisees decided, decreed, whatever, that if you put up posts and use some tarp, then you can make a group of houses into one…"

"We did that back in Nazareth! I never knew why. It's so everyone can carry stuff between the houses and not break God's law?"

"Exactly."

"Isn't that cheating?"

Phil shrugged. "I don't know, maybe.

"So the Pharisees are like tax advisors, they tell people what they can get away with?"

"That's one way of putting it, but they don't just do that, they're priests and all the rest of it. They're pretty bloody powerful. Anyway, from what I'm hearing, the Pharisees are pissed at Jesus. They reckon he's breaking all the laws and that his teachings are encouraging others to break them too."

"Do we care what a few stuck up preachers think? Aren't they just one of God knows how many religious orders knocking about, telling us all how we should live, and presumably getting rich off it?"

"We might not care what they think but they've got a lot of clout, people listen to them. People look up to them. You're right, there are plenty of different groups like them around but they're by far the most important, around here at least."

"So where does Antipas come in?"

"I think he's behind it all. He's got the Pharisees in his pouch, using them to make Jesus unpopular. It's hard for him to take out a champion of the people - but if everyone thinks he's a blasphemer..."

"Jesus is no blasphemer. He's only got good things to say about God."

"I know that and you know that, but public opinion is a different thing entirely. If Antipas plays this right, then he'll not only be able to take out Jesus without a problem but he'll be thanked for it."

"How do you know all this?"

"I've been talking to the community elders, the people in the know. I hook up with them pretty regularly, get a feel for what's going down."

I was impressed. "I didn't know you were so connected."

He shrugged. "I have to be." He took a swig of his wine. "The main guy Antipas is working through is some high priest, Caiaphus is his name. From what I hear he reckons that sucking Antipas' arse is a good way to get on. He's leading all the moves against us."

"Any idea how we stop him?" I said, hoping he wasn't expecting me to think of anything.

Phil shook his head. "Nothing springs to mind."

"We need to talk to Jesus, make a plan."

"Yes," he agreed. "Did Mary go up to his room with him?"

I nodded.

"I'll leave it a bit then."

We both finished our wine and I refilled our glasses. Phil looked like he was thinking, working the problem through in his head. I had a go too but didn't really know where to start.

Eventually he spoke. "You might have hit on something there."

"I didn't say anything."

"No, not just now, before. You said about the Pharisees getting rich off the back of what they do."

"I did mention that, yes." I didn't know where this was leading but I was happy to take any credit that was going.

"We can use that. If they're going to throw muck then why shouldn't we throw it back? If we can discredit them then it doesn't matter what they say about Jesus, he'll still be the people's champion. In fact, them coming for us could help us. It gives us a cause that people can relate to. We're challenging the out of touch duffers who've had their way for too long."

"You're quite good at this aren't you?"

Phil shrugged. "It was your idea mate."

"Fuck you."

"What was that for?"

"It was getting weird again. I'm still not completely comfortable with us being so bloody nice to each other."

He nodded. "Fair enough, it was getting a bit weird. So do you think Jesus has finished giving Mary one?"

"He might not stop at one. Would you?"

"You seem a bit less gaga over her these days, have you got it out of your system?"

"I was never gaga over her."

The memory of the last time we'd talked on this subject loomed large in my head, as I'm sure it did in Phil's, so just to keep the peace I made an attempt at a proper answer. "Yeah, alright, I was a bit confused for a bit but it's all cool now. I'm not going to deny that she's crazy fit but there's plenty more birds around." In my keenness to trivialise the whole thing I might have gone a little overboard with the male bravado.

Phil poured the rest of the wine. "She is quite something. I'm surprised Jesus ever leaves his room."

I changed the subject. "Realistically, what do you think our chances are in all this stuff with Antipas and the Pharisees."

"What do I think? Honestly?"

I topped our glasses up. "Honestly."

"Okay. My honest answer is," he downed his wine in one, "if we get through this it'll be a fucking miracle."

# Mount Improbable

We were back out in the hills. The same place we'd done the stunt with the fish and the bread but there were to be no tricks, no trapdoors this time, just Jesus sticking it to the Pharisees.

"The angle we need," Phil had said to Jesus in his pep-talk, "is that the Pharisees' version of the law doesn't go far enough. You've got to drown them in piety. You're the one who's preaching God's Word and it's them who are straying from the good path. If anything, they're the blasphemers."

Jesus' reply had been short and simple. "I can do that."

We stood on the hillside in front of the mouth of the cave that would amplify Jesus' words to the assembled masses below. It looked to be our biggest crowd yet and they were ready; up for it. The food and drink vendors had done a good trade and there was a proper festive atmosphere

"What the fuck is that?" It was an open question and I'm surprised I managed to say it clearly enough for anyone to hear because my whole body was gripped by a run-for-the-hills-screaming kind of fear. But we were already in the hills and there was nowhere to run. I didn't need a response to my question although plenty of the crew gave me one: *Romans*.

They lined the ridge at the back and if I hadn't been so sick with terror I would have been impressed by the spectacle of at least a hundred men, rigidly upright, polished armour glinting in the sun, standards fluttering in the breeze. Putting on a show was part of how the Romans did their thing, how they stripped their opponents of any morale, any vague hope that they had a chance. The message was loud and it was clear:

*Look how organised we are.*

*Look how disciplined we are.*

*Look how fucked you are.*

The crowd below, a giant flock of birds waiting to be fed by Jesus' words of wisdom, were blissfully unaware of the killing machine behind them.

I looked round at the rest of the crew, at the mouths flapping open, the faces drained of colour. Everyone was reciting a breathless prayer.

Everyone except Jesus that is.

Jesus was smiling.

"Got a few extra guests today, boys." He rubbed his hands together like he was about to tuck into a hearty meal. "I hope they enjoy the show."

"Do you think they'll just slit our throats and get it over with?" I don't remember who said that. It might even have been me.

Someone answered. "No, they'll just maim us for now, they'll kill us later, take their time, make a big show of it."

Jesus continued to look up to the ridge, his eyes scanning back and forth along the row of soldiers. He was still smiling. "Nobody's getting maimed, nobody's getting killed."

"So you're saying we just… carry on?" I said.

"Would you rather we just sloped off?"

"I was thinking more about running. We could hide in the cave."

"They'd have us trapped if we did that," said Bart.

"How about we climb further up, escape into the desert behind us?"

"It's completely open back there," Bart again. "They'd hunt us down easily. They'd have fun doing it too."

"We could leg it into the crowd and split up. We'd be impossible to find." If I was sounding desperate it's because I was.

"If they are here to kill us," said Jesus, "do you think that would do it? Do you think they'd just slap their helmets and say *d'oh, we've lost them, oh well, let's go home*? We all know that's not how the Romans roll. They'd probably start burning people until we came out."

"Or boiling them," said Thad.

"My dear Thaddeus," said Simon, "have you considered what is involved in boiling a person? Would you not agree that it would take excessive effort to set up even just one boiling station all the way out here?"

"They might have planned it, they might already have all their boiling needs catered for, out of sight, over the ridge," said Thad.

"Nobody's getting boiled," said Jesus.

"But we might get burned?" I said.

"All I said was that if they'd come to kill us then hiding in the crowd isn't an option. But I really don't think they've come to kill us."

"Well I don't think they've come here to fly kites," said Simon.

"What's a kite?" said Thad.

Simon sighed. "Remember when we were in Alexandria? Those children with squares made of papyrus. They were on long lengths of twine and flew in the wind."

"I thought they were birds."

"Really? You actually thought they were birds?"

"Shut up about kites." I turned to Jesus. "Why are you so sure they're not here to kill us? Are they on our side, like the ones that came to guard the poppy factory? Is this another one of those secret deals you don't tell us about?"

"No," he said. "They're not ours. I just know that they'd be daft to kill us in front of all these people. They're just here to let us know, to let everyone know that they're in charge."

"It's all about appearances in this business," said Bart.

"Well if you don't mind," I didn't care how petulant I sounded, "I'm going to carry on shitting myself, because I think that's bollocks."

Jesus' smile had gone. "What did you mean by secret deals?"

"You know exactly what I meant."

Phil clapped his hands. "Come on now people, we've got a show to do. We've got a crowd to entertain. There's no point speculating about what the Romans are here for, they're here, we can't change that and if they have come to kill us then there's nothing any of us can do to stop them. So let's just get on with what we came to do, shall we?"

"Yes, let's do that," said Jesus.

And so we did, well Jesus did. We stood back and let him have the floor, or more precisely, the bit of mountainside. Now I know I've said it a lot, but Christ, that boy could hold an audience.

He started with a list of bite-sized statements - *blessed are those that...*, *blessed are they who…* - the poor, the meek, bereaved, hungry, all good stuff the crowd could relate to. When he got to blessing the merciful he made a point of looking up at the soldiers. He repeated the gesture when he blessed those who were persecuted for the sake of righteousness. The crowd had all noticed the Romans by now but nobody had left. Either they were scared of being picked off individually on their way out, or they felt somehow protected by their spiritual leader, their *saviour.*

After blessing all and sundry, Jesus changed tack. "We all know we should get along with our friends and neighbours, that's a given. But try this for size." He once again turned his gaze to the soldiers. "Love your enemies. Love anyone who has it in for you. Do you think you can do that?" There was a murmur of acknowledgement from the crowd. He then went to work on Phil's plan. "Talking of enemies, I have been criticised from certain quarters. They say I am here to abolish the Law, to undermine the Word. The truth is that I am here to fulfil it. I am saying we should stop finding ways around the commandments and just get on and heed them. A lot of people don't want to hear this but if you want to get into Heaven then you'll need to be more righteous than the Pharisees, the so-called Keepers of the Law who'd have you believe their watered-down, convenient version of things."

I glanced at Phil who was nodding, fists clenched, like a gladiator trainer watching his man stick it to the other guy.

"Take adultery," said Jesus, "we all know the commandments say we shouldn't do it, but let's face it, thinking about it is as bad as doing it and who hasn't thought about it? The point I'm making is this, it's easy to get bogged down in the rules, in the laws, but surely it's better that we just try and lead good lives. We shouldn't be doing it to prove anything to anyone, we should just do it because it's right. If you give to the needy then don't make a big fuss so everyone hears about it, just do it because you want to. Don't be like the hypocrites who go around wearing their piety like a gold chain. Don't be like those who think they know better than anyone else just because they have a fancy hem on their robes and get the best seats at the feasts. Don't believe everything the Pharisees tell you. Make up your own mind."

The show had a very different feel to it than usual. Jesus talked for longer for starters, and in a lot more detail. The crowd loved it of course, but instead of cheering, like we were used to, they just listened attentively, patiently.

As Jesus finished, to rapturous applause, Phil as good as

leapt on him, slapping his back and pumping his hand. "That was awesome, perfect. You had the crowd totally hooked, and all that stuff about the Pharisees was spot-on."

"Do you think there were any here?" I said.

"Without a doubt," said Phil. "I doubt Caiaphus would have been here himself, he wouldn't want to sully his sandals, but there'll be some here. They're keeping a close eye on our man. They would have heard every word."

"They would have heard a great big fuck you," I said, "less violent than the one to Antipas' dealers in the temple but probably even more effective."

"Absolutely," said Phil, "great stuff."

"I didn't say it was necessarily a good thing," I said, "but to be honest it's not my biggest concern right now. What worries me is that lot." I nodded towards the Romans. "What's the plan here?"

"Don't look at me," said Phil. "I do public relations, not escape acts. Any ideas, big man?"

"They'll probably wait for the crowd to clear then massacre us," said Jesus.

I looked at him, waiting for the smile, for the *just kidding it's all under control*, but it never came. He just looked back at me.

"Excuse me?" I said. "What happened to *nobody's getting killed?*"

Jesus shrugged. "I had to say something or you'd have just run off."

I couldn't believe what I was hearing. "Too right I would have run off."

"Exactly, you would have started a panic and loads of people would have got killed, including you."

"It would have been nice to have had the choice."

"Course you had a choice! I didn't order you to stay. I just said they weren't here to kill us, which was just my opinion, not a statement of fact."

"But it wasn't your opinion, you only said it to stop me running off, you just said so."

"But you didn't know that. As far as you knew it was just my opinion."

"Here they come," said Phil. We looked up to see the Romans advancing down the slope. They didn't seem interested in the crowd, who parted like the Red Sea to let them through and left hastily in their wake.

I looked at Jesus. "Well that's just fucking priceless, cheers mate. Thanks for dragging me out of Nazareth for this. I've always wanted to be slaughtered by Roman soldiers."

It was too late to run. All we could do was stand and watch as a legion of the most efficient fighting force ever assembled made its way towards us.

And then, with a call from their centurion, they stopped.

The crowd were all but gone now. The dustbowl was emptying like a draining latrine. What was left was the most eerie, terrifying sight I've ever witnessed. The valley beneath us slashed across the middle by the rigid chain of soldiers, helmets cocked as they stared upwards in our direction.

I became aware of something moving at my feet, it could well have been happening for a while but I'd been too transfixed on the soldiers to notice. Dust was streaming down the slope around me. A small rock bounced past and something hit the back of my knee. I turned, we all did, and looked up the slope behind us, knowing full well what it was; the heavy footfall of another legion of Romans, the other half of the pincer movement. We were about to be crushed.

We were half right. It was soldiers, lots of them, but they definitely weren't Romans. These men were a lot darker and they didn't have uniforms, just light robes. They didn't carry shields, swords or javelins, not so much as a pilum. Instead each man carried a broad knife, curved like a sickle, but much bigger and much sharper at the end. Whoever they were they looked proper hard.

"What have I missed?" The breathless voice was Matthew's, appearing from behind two extremely scary looking men.

"You missed a fine speech," Jesus spoke to Matt like he'd just turned up late to a dinner party, "even if I do say so myself." His smile was back.

The soldiers lined up in front of us, less rigid and organised than the Romans in the bowl beneath us but no less impressive.

I was slower on the uptake than most because my natural instinct is to be terrified by anyone who arrives unannounced with a deadly weapon and the obvious ability and inclination to use it. But then it dawned on me and I nearly collapsed with relief.

Our odds of survival had just got a lot better.

## Shudder to Think

With the two armies facing off against each other I looked down the ranks of Aretas' men and realised they outnumbered the legionaries by at least two to one. I still wouldn't have bet against the Romans, they had history on their side but we clearly had the upper hand, as well as the upper ground.

With a thump and a clank the Romans shifted their positions but stayed rooted to the spot. I think the term is 'presented arms'. Their centurion walked thirty paces ahead of his men and stopped.

Jesus walked towards him with Aretas' soldiers shuffling down behind, keeping the same thirty paces back. The two men were now face to face in the no man's land between the two sets of troops. We could see that they were talking but none of us could hear what was being discussed.

Almost casually, the centurion turned and signalled to his men. We watched in disbelief as they marched away.

I couldn't believe what I was seeing. "They're retreating. They're actually retreating."

"They're not retreating," said Jesus, climbing back up the slope towards us. Don't use that word again." He made sure he had everybody's attention. "You all got that? The Romans didn't retreat, they weren't here to attack. They were here because it was such a large public assembly and they needed to make sure order was maintained."

"What have you been smoking?" I snorted. "They were

marching towards us! If Matt hadn't turned up with Aretas' men we'd have been cut down like weeds."

"There's more to it," said Bart. "It's all about appearances in this game."

I was losing patience with Bart. "Will you stop saying that all the fucking time?"

"Bart's right," said Jesus. "And so are you. Yes, there was a good chance they were about to kill us, or perhaps it was just a show of strength. We'll never know. But think about it. Their centurion had to make a call. Taking on this lot," he gestured towards Aretas' men, "would have meant losing half or perhaps all of his men, but turning and running would have meant the end of his career and probably his life. So he made a sensible decision."

"What did he say to you?"

"That he was satisfied the event had passed without incident and that he and his men were returning to their garrison."

"They bottled it," I said. "They ran away."

"What did I just say? There's to be no talk of running away, or retreating, or backing down, or giving ground, or yielding. Basically there'll be no talk of anything that sounds like they pulled out of a fight. If anything like that gets out then they'll be forced to make a move, because, as Bart says, they can't be seen to have bottled it. And the next time they'll make sure they finish it."

I wasn't convinced. "They're probably going to do that anyway. This is the Romans we're talking about."

Phil obviously had an opinion. "I'm not so sure. The Romans aren't backing Antipas. They're still pissed at him for all the unrest he caused when he took out John. They were here because they've been told about a man sowing discord amongst the people, calling out the old laws and traditions." He turned to Jesus. "That's you by the way." Jesus nodded. "The Romans don't care about the old laws and traditions, they worship about a million different gods, what they do care about is keeping order, so after what they heard about this rabble rouser here they took the easiest option and sent an army to get rid of him."

"But it was Antipas who told them about Jesus," I said.

"Not directly," said Phil. "As far as the Romans are concerned it came from their network of spies and whisperers. They didn't know they were doing Antipas' bidding, they were acting on intelligence."

"That's one of them oxi-wotsits," said Thad.

"Sorry?" said Phil, clearly not happy at being interrupted.

"Roman intelligence."

"He's saying it's an oxymoron" said Simon wearily.

Phil thought for a moment. He smiled. "Not bad. Not bad at all."

"So you think we're safe?" I said. "You don't think they're coming back?"

"I can't say never, but we've definitely given them something to think about. Killing us is no longer the easy option, not because they'll be worried about losing men if they take us on, but because they won't want it to... what's the word?"

"I think the term is escalate," I said.

"That's it, if they go all-in it could *escalate*, people will start to take sides and the whole thing could grow into something much bigger. They won't shy away from taking action if it does come to that - they're not pussies - but they'd much rather keep a lid on it."

"I think we should take a step back," said Jesus, "and thank this man here." He grabbed Matt by the shoulders and shook him. "Come here you leave-it-to-the-last-moment motherfucker!" He was laughing his head off, and Matt's head nearly fell off from all the shaking.

"Pretty close wasn't it? It's a good job we didn't stop for that last piss-break or we'd have found you lot in a big messy pile."

We headed back to Magdalene's but instead of having a party to celebrate the fact that we'd made it back from the brink of death we had work to do. Aretas' men needed somewhere to pitch camp so we had to clear the hillside above the tavern. I was gutted, not just because cutting down trees and shifting rocks was bloody hard work but because I'd had some good times up there. It wasn't going to be a great place to go and get caned anymore. It was going to be a military base.

We worked under the bright moon until late into the evening. Aretas' men didn't say much, not to us at least. It wasn't that they were unfriendly; they just didn't go out of their way to chat to us. I suppose it's part of being a soldier. You train, live, eat and sleep with your legion - or whatever the Nabataean equivalent of legion is - and you just get used to sticking to your own. We didn't understand their weird dialect anyway. They sounded to me like they were clearing their throats the whole time.

I somehow got roped into helping dig the latrines. Latrines for two hundred men is a very big hole. We didn't get involved in pitching the actual camp, the soldiers had their own way of doing it and we would have only got in the way. I was more than happy with that and even happier when we finally got to the bar. The phrase well-earned beer had never been so appropriate.

Matthew was the toast of the night of course but I got to thinking about how he'd arrived in what could only be described as the nick of time, and how Jesus had been so unruffled by the whole thing when the rest of us had been scared witless. If it had been a piece of planned brinkmanship on Jesus' part then it was pretty irresponsible to say the least. It could easily have gone wrong. And if it had then we would have all been killed.

I was tempted to ask him outright but if my suspicions were true then he'd obviously chosen to keep me in the dark about it, which meant all I'd be doing was creating a situation where he was forced to lie to me. I didn't like being lied to.

So I had to keep my thoughts to myself, which wasn't easy because if Jesus had taken to gambling with our lives for the sake of a good set-piece, then everything in the garden was far from rosy.

Nobody else seemed to have any qualms about what had happened. They were all content to keep going over the same conversation about facing certain death before being delivered at the last by a miraculous turn of events. Each time we re-lived the scene my mind drifted to a picture of what would have happened if Aretas' men hadn't turned up when they did; the Romans continuing their march towards us; the sound of their boots, the smell of our fear. The uncompromising certainty of what was about to happen…

"You okay, old boy?" Simon woke me from my day-dream, day-nightmare… day-mare? "Your whole body just trembled."

"I can't stop thinking about how it could have ended today."

"So you literally shuddered to think of it."

"I suppose I did."

"That's something I've been thinking about a lot recently."

"Your own mortality?" I asked. "The amount of danger we're in every single day?"

"No, not that. I meant the word literally. We all know it gets misused, people saying they literally did this and they literally felt that when what they actually mean is they *figuratively* did this or they *metaphorically* felt that. I know I'm not making a new observation here, in fact people make the point so often that it's become as annoying as the thing they're describing. So before you say I'm going over old ground, I'll explain my new angle."

"I wasn't going to say you were going over old ground. I was going to say that I'm not really in the..."

"Well I'll explain anyway. When people say that seeing this or seeing that made them sick, they tend to be speaking figuratively. It is generally understood that they do not mean that whatever they saw actually made them eject the contents of their stomach through their mouth, not usually anyway. So what, then, do we do when we want to say it literally? What if you saw something that actually made you vomit? If you said it made you sick, people would assume you were just stressing that the thing you saw was unpleasant, they wouldn't think you actually threw up. So what do you do? You can't say that it *literally* made you sick because the word *literally* has been undermined and lost its meaning."

I realised he wasn't going to let up until he'd seen this through. "I'd say *physically*."

"Exactly!" said Simon. "You would say physically, as in, that made me physically sick, and everyone would know what you meant. We have all come to accept that the word physically, when used in this context, points out to the listener that actual rather than figurative nausea occurred. But now the *literally* criminals have messed it all up again. People have started to say *that made me physically sick*, when the thing they're talking about didn't actually make them sick. They are just trying to add weight to what they are saying. And so we are buggered again."

"And you thought you'd bring that up now, right after me telling you how messed up I was about what happened today?"

"Well, yes," said Simon. "It was relevant."

"How was it relevant?"

"Because you used the word *literally* in its proper context."

"No I didn't, you brought that whole thing up. All I did was tell you how shaken up I'd been by what happened."

"Yes, and it literally made you shudder."

"Thank you so much for all your help and support during this difficult time."

Simon smiled. "No problem old boy."

# *Advance Party*

There was a knock at the door to my room. That almost never happened. "Who is it?" I threw on my tunic.

"It's Phil."

"What do you want?"

"We're going to Jerusalem."

"Okay. Have a good time."

"No, I mean you and me. We're going."

I opened the door.

He barged past me. "How come your room's bigger than mine?"

"Please do come in, oh you have. My room's bigger because it reflects my status both in the organisation and in terms of mankind generally."

"You do talk shit sometimes."

"Only sometimes? I'll try harder from now on. So what do you mean about Jerusalem?"

Phil walked to the window and peered out. "The view's better too. The big man wants us to go and prepare the way for the big event, drum up a bit of interest."

"Get a buzz going?"

"Now you're talking my language." He sat on the bed.

"Yes I am. Awful isn't it? The view's not as good as it used to be, not since an army – what's the word? - *garrisoned* itself outside."

"If it wasn't for that army we'd have been cut into little

pieces by now."

"Or boiled."

"Or cut into little pieces and then boiled."

I was still standing in the doorway. "Shall we take this conversation outside? It's a bit weird having you in here. Especially as for some reason you've got into my bed."

"I'm not in your bed, I'm on it."

"Whatever. Get off my bed and we'll go downstairs so you can buy me a beer."

Phil stretched out on the bed. "Ah, you like to be shown a good time before you put out."

"I'll put your face out in a minute."

"What does that even mean?" He walked past me through the doorway.

"Something offensive?" I closed the door behind me.

It was late afternoon, fairly cool but still warm enough to sit outside. I waited for Phil to bring the beers out, nodding a hello to a big group of Aretas' men who were well into a session. They were definitely making the most of life in Capernaum, not least because the women loved them. As Jesus and I had learned when we first hit the road all that time ago, there's nothing like a taste of the unusual to loosen a girl's loincloth.

"Here's to an unholy alliance." Phil handed me a beer and sat down.

"Cheers. How come it's just me and you going?"

"Well it won't just be us. We'll be taking a load of these boys with us." He raised his glass towards Aretas' men. "Cheers fellas!" There were a couple of grunts in return but not much else. "Hopefully we'll get some sober ones," he said more quietly, "but yes, me and you. It's not the most obvious choice."

"Maybe it's a reward for us stopping being dicks to each other," I ventured.

235

Phil rolled his eyes. "For Christ's sake, how many times? We weren't dicks to each other, it was you, just you, being a dick to me. We've been through this."

"Yeah alright, point taken, I'll rephrase it. Maybe Jesus is, y'know, checking us out, making sure we can work together after all our… problems."

"You're over-thinking it. Has it not occurred to you that he might have just thought we were the right people to make the trip?"

"I don't know anymore, not with everything that's happened."

"Between us?"

"No, I mean that thing the other day, when Matt turned up with Aretas' soldiers."

He put his beer down, frowning. "What's that got to do with anything?"

"Well, nothing really, but didn't you think it was a little… convenient?"

"That's a bit of an understatement. I'd say more like fucking lucky."

I hadn't meant to slip into this line of conversation. I didn't want to be seen as cynical or suspicious, particularly as Phil had Jesus' ear, probably more so than I did. I tried to pull out. "I guess so."

But Phil wasn't letting it go that easily. "Are you saying that us being saved from being massacred was somehow a bad thing?"

"Not at all, just forget it."

"I'm obviously not going to forget it. Come on, what's on your mind?" He folded his arms, a mother waiting for an explanation from a guilty child.

"Well if you're not going to drop it," I sighed. "Don't you think there might be more to it than lucky timing? I don't know the way to Aretas' palace, but it would be quite a coincidence if the route back brought Matt and his men past the exact spot where we were holding an event. And even more of a coincidence that it was at the exact time the Romans were making their final push."

Phil thought for a while. "Are you saying Jesus planned it?"

"I'm saying it's a striking coincidence."

"How would he arrange something like that? He'd have to get word to Matt, have to get the timing bang-on."

"Yes," I gulped on my beer. "He would."

"But what would he gain from it? It couldn't have been meant as a show for the crowd, they'd all gone by that point."

"Maybe he didn't want the crowd to know we had an army at our disposal. Maybe that wouldn't fit with the image you're selling."

Phil flinched. "Are you saying I was something to do with it?"

I raised my hands placatingly. "No, I'm not saying that," I paused, "well maybe. I really don't know to be honest."

"Well I bloody didn't."

"Fair enough, you didn't have anything to do with it, but for you to say that, it sort of implies that you agree that something was going on."

He threw his hands up. "Woah, hold it right there. Just back it up a bit, will you?"

"Okay." It hadn't occurred to me that Phil might have been involved, but from his reaction I was pretty sure he wasn't, unless he was a bloody good actor. It was obvious that I'd planted some doubt in his head though, and now it was charging around in there like a bull in a terracotta shop. I sat back and took a leisurely sip of my beer, giving him time with his thoughts.

"You're just being paranoid," he said at last.

I shrugged. "Maybe, but how about you?"

"I don't know." He rubbed his eyes. "I don't know. But even if the big man did play with our lives to make whatever point he wanted to make, there's not much we can do about it. It's not like we can challenge him. He'll just deny it, and I don't particularly want to stir everyone else up."

"My sentiment exactly," I said. "I didn't mean to bring it up anyway."

We drained our beers in a silence that marked the subject as closed.

"We're leaving tomorrow morning," Phil said eventually. "We can take a couple of camels."

"I don't get on with camels, or they don't get on with me. Either way, I'm taking Max. You can take Jeroboam."

"It'll be a lot slower going on donkeys, and besides, the soldiers are going to have camels. We can't expect them to crawl along at snail's-pace just because you've got an ass fixation."

"Alright, we'll take bloody camels then."

"Good man. It's your round, or have you pissed Bart off again?" He grinned.

I picked up our glasses and stood up. "You're hilarious, you know that?"

When I came out with fresh beers Thad was sitting in my seat.

Phil looked up. "I was just telling Thad about our trip."

"When are you leaving?" said Thad.

"Tomorrow morning." I put the beers on the table and sat down. "Sorry Thad, didn't know you were around or I would have got you one."

"That's okay. Have you been to Jerusalem before?"

"Do you not remember?" I said. "We went a little while back and there was that whole thing with Jesus having a go at the dealers in the temple."

"It was a huge deal," said Phil.

Thad looked like he was struggling to answer a question in a school test. "Don't think I remember that."

"Well it happened," I said. "We were all shitting ourselves. In fact we're still shitting ourselves. You sure you don't remember?"

Thad looked away, his normal dog-face a puppy this time, one that's been shut outside by its owner. "It's been ages since I've been to Jerusalem."

"Oh well," Phil said, I'm sure you'll get to go back there again sometime."

Thad's face sagged even closer to the ground. "I really like Jerusalem."

"We'll bring you back something nice," I said. "Perhaps a little amphora with *I love Jerusalem* written on it."

"It's shit being cooped up here. I feel like a prisoner." He rested his face on his hands.

I glanced at Phil, who answered my unspoken question with a nod and a thinly concealed smile. "For fuck's sake Thad," I said. "Do you want to come to Jerusalem with us?"

It was like all his Passovers had come at once. "Really?" I swear I could see a tail wagging.

"Yeah, why not?"

"Do you think the big man will be okay with it?" said Phil. "Do you think he'll mind us inviting someone else along?"

Thad's face drooped again. He looked at me expectantly. I had the ball. He was waiting to see if I would throw it for him.

"This is Thad we're talking about, Phil. Thad's a law unto himself. Everyone knows that, even Jesus. Especially Jesus. Thad just, y'know, gets away with it."

"Gets away with what?" Thad said.

"Everything!" I said. "You drift along, and things just fall into place for you without you having to worry about any of it. The rest of us have to deal with all the usual shit, like anxiety and self-consciousness, and have to be organised so we don't forget stuff. You don't have to worry about any of it, especially forgetting stuff because you don't care if you forget anything. You know someone else will sort it out. I'm not saying it's a bad thing. If anything I'm jealous."

James emerged from the bar, a foaming pint in his hand. "Hi Thad, having some beers inside and saw you were out here without one. Here you go mate."

"Cheers, James," said Thad.

James went back inside.

Phil sniggered.

"Do I need to say any more?" I said.

Neither of us had seen Thad blush before.

Camels are bastards. That's not just my opinion. It's a cold hard fact. If anyone ever tells you otherwise then you have my blessing to punch them hard in the face. If I could have reached that far I would have punched the camel - the one that staggered and jolted its way to Jerusalem with me on its back - hard in the face too. Just as with my previous camel nightmare, everybody else's camel-toed the line, all straight and orderly, while mine lurched around like it had hornets up its arse. I wouldn't have had that problem if I'd been allowed to let Maximus take me. Max was slow. Max was steady. Max was comfortable.

For security reasons, we'd been told not go anywhere in the city without our armed guard, and because it would have been difficult to move freely with a dozen soldiers in tow, Phil had arranged a series of meetings in one place; the temple where Jesus had flipped out on Antipas' dealers. Nicodemus had sorted it out for us. He gave us his office and Phil and I (and Thad every now and again when he could be bothered) hosted a succession of appointments with the great and good of the city.

It was testament to Jesus' standing, or at least to the legends that were spreading like syphilis about him, that these men gave their time to see us. I also had no doubt that the impression Jesus must have left on Nicodemus on our last visit had been passed on and had its own part to play in the interest being shown in the big man.

We met with the community leaders, holy men, innkeepers, anyone with influence, and told them our news: the Messiah was making a grand entry into the city the following Sunday. We held back on the detail, it wouldn't have done to point out that we were shamelessly contriving to make an ancient prophecy come true, but we did point out - well Phil did anyway - that this would be Jesus' last public appearance in Jerusalem. This had no basis in fact; it was just Phil's way of cranking up interest.

But it would turn out to be true.

It was a joy to see the last man leave. Listening to Phil deliver his patter all day had taken its toll. I needed some time away from that voice. I knew Thad would be up for it and I had a good idea that Phil wouldn't, so I suggested we sneak out for some beers. I got the responses I wanted, a *God yes* from Thad and a *we've been told not to go anywhere without Aretas' men* from Phil. Here was a man who underneath all the swagger and self-belief was a stickler for the rules.

But he knew better than to try and tell us we couldn't go, so Thad and I sought out somewhere suitable whilst trying to stay as discreet as possible as we weaved through the narrow streets of the darkening city. Our *somewhere suitable* turned out to be a place near the docks, full of travellers coming from and going to every part of the civilised world, and when I say civilised I mean occupied by the Romans. The hotchpotch of nationalities in the heaving tavern made it easier for us to blend in. The place was full of outsiders, and we were just two more. I was on my guard anyway, not so much against arousing questioning of who we were, or where we were from, but against an outbreak of sudden extreme violence for absolutely no reason. It was that sort of place.

My hackles went down as quickly as the beers though, and before too long I was having a damned good time. There's something about drinking in a strange place that makes the drink taste smoother, the conversation more entertaining and the girls more appetising. Not that there were any girls in this dockside bar, but the point stands. There was also something about drinking with Thad. He was probably the easiest company in the world. With Thad you didn't have to be on your game. You could just sit and say nothing if you wanted, but that seldom happened because he had a way of looking at the world that illuminated even the most banal of topics. He made me feel that he actually cared what I said too, rather than seizing on a key word and using that to steer the conversation back to himself, like so many other people do. It felt like he was actually engaging with me. How he gave that impression was a mystery to me, because at the same time his vacant expression suggested he wasn't listening to me at all.

That's how I remember it anyway. And in case that didn't sound like it made any sense at all, we did smoke an awful lot that night.

Thad got talking to a couple of Greek merchants, spice I think their trade was, but it was so noisy in there I could barely hear what they said. I just let Thad get on with it. I was happy sitting in a fug of green and beer, listening to the sound of a hundred conversions barked out in a hundred different drunken dialects. I let myself float on the haze.

I lurched back to life, like in one of those dreams where

you're falling and the collision with the ground wakes you up so fast you almost shit yourself. A voice in my ear was saying my name. I turned to look, screwing up my eyes to focus on the face swimming in front of me. It wasn't someone I recognised, but he obviously knew me, or knew of me at least.

"I need to talk to you, would you mind stepping outside?"

## Max Exposure

"Who's going to fulfil an ancient prophecy then?" I laid my palm on the top of Max's head, loving the contrast of the soft fur against his solid skull. "Who's going to carry the Messiah into the city, eh?" I squeezed, gritting my teeth as I did so, an attempt to divert the force of my affection and stop myself from gripping too hard. "Who's the best boy? Who's the best? It's you, you're the best boy. Oh yesh you are, oh yesh you are!"

I was crazy about Maximus. My world had changed beyond recognition, and as far as I could tell was just going to keep on changing, but Maximus was a rock. He was always happy to see me, always up for a carrot or a bit of fruit, loved a bit of a pat and somehow managed to convey a whole range of emotions in that same impassive look. I never worked out how he did that. He could have been the star of a one-donkey play: 'The changing yet unchanging faces of Max'.

I gave him a big hug around his massive neck and he returned the gesture by pressing his head sideways into me. I loved it when he did that. Making Maximus happy was my favourite hobby. "They're going to write about you, Max." I kissed him over and over. "Oh yesh they are, oh yesh they are!"

"Am I interrupting something?" I extracted myself from Max's face - the best face - and looked up to see Nat - one of the worst faces. He was probably still pissed that I'd attended the meetings with Phil the week before instead of him. "Why are you talking to your donkey like it's a baby?"

"Well the answer to your first question is yes, you are interrupting something and the answer to the other one is fuck off, knob-head."

Nat shrugged and held out a bundle in front of me. "I've got the blanket it's meant to wear."

"He's Maximus, he's a *he*, not an *it*. Give me that." I snatched the blanket from his sticky hand. It was enormous, the blanket that is, not Nat's hand. I folded it in half and then in half again before placing it carefully across Max's back, who stood just that little bit more upright. I was so proud. He looked like royalty. I turned to Nat. "You can fuck off now."

Nat fucked off.

We were camped just outside Jerusalem; the whole crew, along with more than a few of Aretas' soldiers, ready to make the big entrance into the city. It was mid-morning and I'd been awake since well before dawn. If Phil's pitching to the bigwigs of the city had done its job then it was going to be a big occasion. But that wasn't what had kept me from sleeping.

The man who'd talked to me outside the bar had said he was a messenger for somebody, but either he was deliberately vague with the details or I was too hammered to remember. He'd said his boss wanted to arrange a meeting with me to discuss a proposal. That's all I could remember, except that I'd be contacted soon, and - I remember him stressing this part - that I couldn't discuss it with anybody else.

I don't remember getting back to the temple from the bar but I remember waking up the next day. I felt like death, and tasted that familiar tang of regret, created usually out of the assumption of some awful drunken impropriety carried out the night before. As every drinker knows, even if there has been no such gaffe, the mind is trained from bitter and regular experience to expect the worse, but this time the regret was more intense, more deeply rooted. And the word *regret* didn't really cut it. The feeling was an overwhelming sense of negativity. I had done something bad or something bad was going to happen. Or perhaps a mixture of the two.

When I'd seen Phil in the morning he'd loved the fact that I was such a wreck after he'd chosen to be the goody-two-sandals and stay in, but after my response to his attempts at crowing about my prospects of a camel ride back to Capernaum on a hangover, even he sensed that I wasn't in the mood for playing.

I'd kept to myself in the days between getting back to Magdalene's and travelling back out to Jerusalem with the rest of the crew. I had no idea who the mystery man had been but it was pretty much a given that whoever he worked for wasn't about to give me good tidings of great joy. I had a fairly good idea who the man's employer was, but didn't want to think about it. I just blocked it out and hoped it would all go away.

All I knew for sure was that I was tired, tired of being scared for my life, homesick and pining for the simple existence I'd known before.

But there was nothing I could do about any of it. I was still part of a crew and had a role to play, and besides, it was Maximus' special day and I couldn't let him down. I held out a handful of oats and he slowly chomped them down, his whiskery lips tickling my palm. Despite the flood of fear and confusion in my head, I couldn't help but smile. "You're a great big smile-maker aren't you, Max? Oh yesh you are, oh yesh you are!"

My hand was clean of oats but Max continued to chomp, seeing off what was still clinging to his gums and huge tongue. I put my hands on either side of his head and looked him in his big soppy eyes. "I wish I had your life Max," I whispered. "You look like you've got it sussed."

I filled Max's water bucket and wandered back to the group,

where Phil was taking charge. "It's nearly go time," he said. "Everyone should know the plan by now. It's a simple one. Us lot, soldiers and all, will go ahead and line up on either side of the road into the city. Jesus will follow on the donkey."

"On *Maximus*," I said.

"Whatever. When we see him coming all we have to do is go completely nuts. Shout, scream, whistle, anything you want. The louder the better. Make sure everybody knows the Messiah is coming, that they should get excited."

"Isn't it a bit dangerous for Jesus to be on his own?" said Peter.

"He won't be on his own very long." Phil looked at Jesus. "Are you alright with it?"

"You know I am. What I'm actually worried about is looking like a complete bell-end."

"How do you mean?" said Phil.

"I mean, riding into the city like I'm some all-conquering hero but sitting on a fucking donkey."

"On *Maximus*," I said.

"Whatever," said Jesus, "and on feasting weekend too, it'll be packed. I'll be a laughing stock."

"But you were into it before." Phil sounded disappointed.

"I know I was, but now we're here it's dawned on me how much of a dick I'm going to look."

"But it has to be a donkey," said Phil. "It's in the prophecy."

"But what if no-one gets it? We could look like a bunch of nutters, you lot screaming on the roadside while I come plodding past like I'm delivering bloody olives."

"People will get it." Phil's voice had an edge of desperation. "They love you."

"I suppose we'll find that out won't we?" said Jesus. "I just wish Zechariah had prophesied something a bit less daft."

"I don't know what to tell you," said Phil, his impatience

starting to show.

"You could tell me I'm not going to make a total prick of myself."

"You're not going to a make a prick of yourself." Phil looked around at us. "Anyone want to pitch in here and help out?"

We all murmured that he'd be fine, that it would go really well, but we didn't sound very convincing. Since he'd mentioned it we'd all seen Jesus' point.

Jesus smiled grimly. "Thanks for that overwhelming vote of confidence, fellas."

"Shall we do it?" said Phil.

"If we must," said Jesus.

I went to get Max and as I was leading him back I didn't notice that the blanket had slipped half off him and was dragging along the ground. When I finally realised, I gathered it up, but it was already covered in grit and thistles. It was no longer any use to anyone, so I dropped it to the ground. "Give me your robes," I said to James and John as I reached the others. "His blanket's been on the floor, it's fucked."

"Can't you just give it a brush off?" said Phil.

"Do you think that didn't occur to me? Do you think I'm a complete penis? It's obviously too dirty to brush off or I would have just brushed it off."

"Do you want me to have a look?" said Nat, clearly not averse to a punch in the face.

"No, Nat, I don't want you to have a look, unless you've got magical blanket cleaning powers. Have you got magical blanket cleaning powers, Nat?"

Nat looked at the ground.

"Thought not," I said.

James and John took off their robes and handed them to me. "Sorry about this, mate," I said as I placed them over Max's back.

Matt mustered the fifty or so soldiers and we entered the gates of the city, lining the road on either side as planned. We stood and waited and I could tell that a few of the crew were trying not to laugh as Max and Jesus lumbered into view. "You'd better not be laughing at Maximus," I hissed through gritted teeth.

They stopped laughing.

"Everyone ready?" said Phil in a half-whisper. "Make some noise!"

We did as we were told, some more convincingly than others. I was rubbish of course, feeling far too self-conscious to get more than a few cheers out. Peter and Andrew were the business though, and Thomas wasn't half bad either. They adopted weird high voices and chanted *hosanna*. That was more than enough to get us noticed, and heads started to turn in the busy street. Unbelievably, people started to join in and the cheering and chanting grew and spread. Phil took off his cloak and with a flourish, laid it on the ground at Maximus' feet. The rest of us followed his example and random strangers in the crowd started doing it too. Bart pulled up a clump of palm leaves, laid all but one on the road in front of Jesus and started waving the remaining one like a flag. Again this caught on with the rapidly growing crowd.

I have to say that even to my cynical eyes it was something to behold. The road lined with cloaks and palm leaves, the chanting and singing and most of all, the sheer volume of people. They herded to the roadside, weight of numbers narrowing the thoroughfare in half. What was amazing was how quickly their interest shifted from trying to see what all the fuss was about, to full on fervour, rapture even. We were used to this kind of response back in Capernaum; they were our home crowd, fed on miracles and plenty of stirring performances by the big man. This was something very different. We were playing away to a whole new audience. I knew that the stories about Jesus' exploits - some true, some exaggerated and some simply made up - had spread to places like this, and our meetings from the week before had drummed up some good publicity, but I hadn't expected a reception like this.

The whole place was going batshit crazy.

Fears of Jesus making a fool of himself were long-forgotten and it showed on the big man's face. His beard surrounded an enormous grin as he made his one-man, one-donkey procession into the city, waving at the crowd, fanned by leaves and adoring words.

Maximus was smiling too of course but only I could tell.

The road led us to a square near the temple, and that's where Jesus brought Max to a halt. He leaned forward, kissed him between the ears and disembarked. The crowd were all around him as he raised his arms and said, "Thank you for such a wonderful welcome. I won't flatter myself - much as I'd like to - I know this isn't about me, this is about the message I carry."

Phil, grinning his face off, turned to me and winked. "I love that," he whispered, "playing himself down. It just makes them more up for him, such a smart move."

Jesus looked around slowly and deliberately, acknowledging the size of the crowd. "What I think we have here," he said, "is all the ingredients for one great big fuck off party! Who's up for it?"

Everybody was up for it.

## Name Drops Keep Falling on my Head

The party just… happened. It sprouted around us where we stood, like fast-growing, very excited mushrooms. Shopkeepers and innkeepers opened their doors to meet the demand of the excited punters. Food, beer and wine appeared, and musicians showed up from all parts of the city, taking up corners of the town square and the alleyways around where the crowd - far too big for the square to hold - spilled outwards.

My first concern was Max. I knew the noise and the crowds would be stressing him out even though he was putting a big brave face on it. We'd left Jeroboam at a stable in the temple grounds and I was looking forward to getting Max back there where it was quiet and he would have some donkey company. It wasn't easy to navigate him through the crush of people, all of them patting him as we made our way through, fanning him with the leaves they still held.

It got easier to move when we were out of the square, and with the excited clamour fading behind me, we made our way to the temple. One of Nicodemus' men let us through a side gate to the stable and Max's ears pricked up when he saw Jeroboam. After a bit of face-nuzzling with his friend, he had a big drink of water and chomped down some oats and vegetables. I stayed with them for a good while, making sure they were settled and comfortable, before deciding it was time to join the party. I gave Max one last sloppy kiss. "I'll be drinking to you, Max."

As I headed for the main gate to the temple grounds I was intercepted by a man I didn't recognise, until he spoke that is. "My boss is ready to meet." It was the mystery man from the dockside tavern.

He led me back into the temple and we took the now familiar steps to the office. Nicodemus wasn't there, someone else filled the chair behind his desk and a line of soldiers blocked the light from the big window. They definitely weren't Roman, and their loose robes, although similar, did not match those of Aretas' legions. They jerked to attention as I entered.

These soldiers, I was about to learn, were the personal guard of Antipas, ruler of Galilee and Perea, son of Herod the Great, beheader of John the Baptist. I learnt this because the man they guarded so zealously and ruthlessly was standing to greet me.

"Mister Iscariot, I presume."

I was face to face with our arch enemy. And all I could do was shake his outstretched hand.

"Do sit down," he said, lowering himself into the chair behind the desk. I did so, half expecting to fall through a hatch into a nest of enraged vipers - I'd heard the stories - but it was a standard chair on standard floorboards.

The gems on Antipas' wrists rattled on the wood of the desktop as he meshed his hands together in front of him. "Do you mind if I call you Judas?"

"You may as well. It's my name after all."

"It is indeed. You are probably wondering why I wanted to talk to you so I will dispense with the formalities and hasten to the point."

"I think it's pretty obvious why you want to talk to me."

He nodded, keeping his eyes on me, the whites thick with intensity. "Yes I suppose it is obvious when one thinks about it. You should know first that it is extremely rare that I go to the trouble of meeting somebody face to face, particularly somewhere like this, with somebody like you."

"You flatter me," I said.

"I meant no offence but I will not pretend to care if you take any. I am not here to win your friendship. I am only here in person because I knew you would not come to my palace willingly, or even if you did, you would struggle to find a strong enough story to explain your absence to your..." he deliberately paused before forming the word, "...associates. It was also convenient for me to meet you here as I am returning from an audience with Caesar Tiberius. The route brought me in this direction..."

He waited, presumably for me to register that I was impressed by his clumsy reference but I tried not to even blink.

He carried on. "...but I said I would dispense with the formalities so I will return to the purpose of our discussion. Things cannot go on as they are. The band of agitators to which you have affiliated yourself is becoming something of an irritation to several of my business interests."

"I wouldn't call us agitators exactly."

"Let us not quibble over terminology. I had thought that the demise of your previous leader would have put an end to my problem, but it seems that with this Christ figure in charge, your little operation has become stronger than ever. I will not bore you with the detail but your primary business conflicts with my own. And on a purely political level, your man is stirring people up - something which if left unchecked could eventually undermine my position. I do not fear an uprising, that is extremely unlikely and even if it were to happen," he looked proudly at his soldiers, "I could crush it very quickly, very easily. My concern is purely with our masters in Rome. I am left to run my little portion of the Empire as I see fit, without external interference. I desire for it to stay that way. I could of course, crush..." he seemed to enjoy saying that word

"...your operation without exerting too much effort but the same point stands - it would attract unnecessary and unwelcome interest. So I am going to take the action that leads to the minimum of fuss and the least bloodshed."

"That's very big of you." It probably sounds like I was putting up a pretty good show of bravery by talking back to this dispenser of death, but the truth is I was so scared that I'd passed through fear into some numb void beyond.

"I have already pointed out that I do not care if I offend you, and I certainly do not care if you despise me, so you may as well keep your comments to yourself. I have told you more of my decision-making process than I needed to. This was to convey to you where I stand, and subsequently where you stand."

"Come on, out with it. What exactly do you want from me?"

"I want you to bring me Jesus."

"I think he's a bit busy at the moment."

"Do not test my patience."

I shrugged.

"You would not be here had you not passed my test."

I said nothing. I wanted to know what he was talking about but I didn't want to give him the satisfaction of showing it.

"When you were approached seven days ago you were told not to speak of your conversation to anybody. And you did not, did you?"

"Didn't what?"

"Did not speak of the approach, not to anybody."

I shook my head.

"Does that mean, 'no' you didn't speak of it, or 'no' you didn't *not* speak of it?"

"The first one."

"That is what I suspected, and that gives me an insight into your position. If you were wholly on board with your associates, you would have informed them of the fact that you were approached by the agent of an unnamed individual, in secret and under cover of darkness. You would have discussed with them what it might have meant, who the unnamed individual might have been and agreed on the best action to take in response to the situation. You did none of those things."

"How do you know I'm not lying about that?"

Antipas' face broke into the most charmless smile I had ever seen. "Do not worry about how I know, just accept that I do."

I immediately made the assumption that there was a spy in our operation and, almost as immediately, I made the counter assumption that Antipas was bluffing. This train of thought led me quickly to the idea that he could even have been double-bluffing. Whichever it was, my head was all over the place. Which I'm sure is exactly where he wanted it to be.

"So despite what you are willing to admit, even to yourself," Antipas leaned forward, only slightly, but enough to step up the intensity of his delivery, "you are already considering the benefits of helping me."

"Whatever the benefits of helping you might be, they're not going to be enough to make me betray my... friend." I stopped myself from saying best friend because that would have sounded pretty childish in the circumstances, even though it was true.

"I do not think you are giving due consideration to my definition of the word *benefits*. You are probably making the assumption that I will reward you financially for your assistance - and that is true - but the most attractive benefit to you is this: if you do what I ask, then you and your associates will stay alive. Let me be clear on this. I do not wish to make a scene, for the reasons I have explained, but I will do so if necessary. If it does come to that, then you, your fellows and that apology for an army you have borrowed, will all be killed. In a deeply unpleasant manner, I might add." He sat back, letting me soak up this threat.

"What about Jesus?"

"If you play along? He will be imprisoned."

"I don't believe you. You'll have him killed."

"I wish no harm to the man. I just need him to stop functioning. He cannot function from a cell."

"The same could have been said for John but you took his head."

"There were other factors involved in that decision and although I never regret any of my actions, I do learn from them and apply what I have learned to future decisions."

"So you realise you went too far with John, pissed off too many people, and don't want to make the same mistake again."

"I am Antipas, ruler of Galilee and Perea, son of…"

"Yes, you've said."

The only thing that gave away his rage at my interruption was a brief whitening of his clasped knuckles. He controlled it and smiled that awful smile once more. "My dear Judas, I am not here to debate with you. I am here to tell you that you have two choices. You make it easy for me to find this Jesus, and all of you live. Or you choose not to assist me and all of you die." He leaned forward and his face became a leer. "And that includes your master's lady-friend. She will be kept around for a while, my men like to enjoy themselves, and they would find much to enjoy with her. Unfortunately they do have a way of wearing out their toys from playing too roughly with them." The soldiers maintained their fixed expressions but their eyes were smiling.

I wanted to throw up, but all I could do was sit there and look at his smug, evil face.

"So here is what you have to do to prevent a bloodbath. The arrest will be made a few days from now, somewhere private. I do not wish to appear to be directly involved, so it will be handled by some local Roman soldiers acting in the name of someone very powerful in these parts, someone who is a close ally of mine. Your kind all look the same to our Roman friends, so the soldiers will need to be directed to the right man. This is where you come in. When they approach, you will give them a sign. You will kiss your master. That will identify him. The soldiers will do the rest. That is all you have to do."

I knew I had no choice. I also knew that he was lying though his gold-capped teeth when he said Jesus wasn't going to be executed. Even so, it was one life against all of our lives, including whatever unspeakable brutality he had lined up for Mary. I had no option but to agree to what he was proposing.

But I took a different option. "Go fuck yourself, you pompous cunt."

# An Offer I Can't Refuse

I didn't know how I got out of that room alive. I just stood up and walked out, and somehow nobody cut my throat. Technically I had the satisfaction of having got to say the *that's what I should have said* line, but that satisfaction was way down the pecking order, on a list of emotions that was led (by some margin) by arse-moistening fear.

At the time, I guessed that Antipas' guards didn't understand my dialect, and so hadn't realised I had insulted their master, but that didn't really hold water. All it would have taken was a nod from the man himself and I would have been dead before you could say 'Nebuchadnezzar'. As I was soon to find out, Antipas had simply chosen not to take any action. He had probably expected me to react exactly as I did, but his threat-laden approach was only phase one of his plan to convince me to do his bidding. Phase two was a more practical illustration of what he was capable of.

After leaving the temple grounds, I went back to the party, which was even bigger than when I'd left it. Of course I had a rotten time. It's difficult to let your hair down when you know the lives of everybody close to you are in grave peril.

I didn't tell anybody about the meeting, not least because everybody was completely shit-faced and so wouldn't have been at their most receptive to such knee-trembling news.

We had brought tents with us, but were given places to sleep by the people of the city. I ended up in a room in a tavern close to the centre of town. I'm not sure how the landlord squeezed me in because, on feast weekend, every room was taken. I was grateful for his generosity but I'm sure he regretted it after what was to happen.

I woke up early, dry-mouthed and bleary-eyed. Despite not being in a party mood I hadn't turned down too many offers of drinks the night before. I lay staring at the unfamiliar ceiling as the memory of my meeting with Antipas washed into my head like a stubborn turd that wouldn't sink. On top of the fear that chilled my bones, I became aware of a nasty smell, and could feel wetness on one side of me. I turned to see.

I found myself looking into cold, dead eyes.

I leapt out of bed. On the blood-soaked mattress was the severed head of a donkey. I looked long and hard at it, scared, confused and sick to my stomach. I eventually identified the remains as that of Jeroboam.

I don't know how long I stood there staring, my thoughts focused not on the awfulness of the act but on the physicality of it; the question of how somebody could cut the head off an animal that size, and carry it into a person's bed without waking them up or rousing anybody else in the building. I assumed the latter, because if anybody in this fully-booked tavern had heard, they would have raised the alarm before now. Either the people who did it were extremely stealthy or anybody who saw them had been silenced. There was of course a third, more terrifying but far more likely scenario: the perpetrators had been seen but the witnesses hadn't needed to be silenced because they'd been complicit in the proceedings.

I puked, of course, a spouting cocktail of disgust, horror and fear. I was in no doubt that this was a message from Antipas. The disembodied head was an obvious reference to John the Baptist's demise, but somehow more chilling than that, the choice of victim was a clear message that he knew things about me, that I had been watched.

I'm ashamed to say that in amongst all the terror, the dread and all the rest of it, one feeling stood out more than any other: relief that it wasn't Maximus. Antipas had somehow managed to learn that I adored my donkey. He'd obviously picked that barbaric act to spell out to me that he could do anything he chose in order to bend me to his will, but he, or his men at least, had made a mistake. They'd got the wrong donkey. This didn't help my immediate or long term situation - I was still totally fucked - but it was heartening to know he wasn't infallible.

That's when I noticed the final flourish he'd arranged for me, a little extra statement to leave me in no doubt over how far he was willing to go. I could barely see through my streaming eyes, but in the dark of Jeroboam's fur, matted with so much thick, red blood, another red gleamed out at me, its sparkle muted but still unmistakable. Mary's pendant.

I threw up again and when it was over I heaved my broken spirit into action. I needed to know if Mary was alive, dead or missing and I knew from what Antipas had said the previous afternoon, that the last of those three possibilities was by far the worst. I peeled the necklace out from the goo. I imagined that their plan may well have been to put it around what remained of poor Jeroboam's neck but it was obviously far too short for that, so it had just been placed across it. I felt another wave of sickness as I pictured the men who'd done this, stooped in the glow of a lantern over my sleeping form, putting this hideous finishing touch in place. I cleaned the chain and the pendant as best I could on the blanket, rinsed most of the blood off my hands in the bowl of water by the bed, puked once more for good measure, dressed and left.

I didn't know where anybody was, so just wandered the streets of Jerusalem looking for a familiar face amongst those who had emerged from the city-wide party, their eyes carrying the burden of the night before. The burden of wine, beer and the contents of James and John's sacks. We were an empire now, no longer dabbling in petty dealing, but it had seemed rude not to bring a good stock of supplies along.

I walked in circles, not by accident, but covering the taverns closest to the main square, waiting for one of the crew to appear. I was hoping of course to see Mary, so I could immediately shut down the panicked feeling in my gut, but the first person I stumbled upon was Thomas. In the aftermath of every bender where the members of the group are scattered by drunkenness and circumstance, everybody has their own story to tell. Thomas' story was that he'd been dancing with two girls, sisters apparently, who'd made it clear that they wanted to make him the meat in their kebab. According to him they took him back to their shared room but he'd been too out of it to take advantage of the golden opportunity. He'd recently woken up, still fully dressed - cringing at his lack of prowess and the missed chance of a lifetime - and snuck out past the bed where the two siblings were spooned together. His regret was tempered only by the fact that the cold light of day had done the girls no favours in the looks department. Doubting Thomas' story at first, I'd become convinced that he was telling the truth by the end. My thoughts were that if he had gone to the trouble of making up a pair of horny sisters, he would have gone the whole hog and pretended he'd given them the night of their lives, not admitted that he'd failed to get it up. And he would have left out the part about them turning out to be dogs too.

In the circumstances, I wasn't interested in Thomas' story, and finding him didn't actually help me in my mission to find Mary, but it was good to have some company. I didn't tell him about my rude awakening, or that I was looking for Mary specifically, just that I wanted to find the others because it wasn't safe for us all to be separated like this. He agreed and we circled the city-centre together.

We passed a place selling bread, an impromptu stall set up by a Babylonian merchant cashing in on the feast weekend. Thomas pointed out that we may as well stop and get something in our stomachs, because we were just as likely to see one of our crew from that vantage point as we were by wandering around. I went along with his suggestion, mostly because my stomach was so empty from having repeatedly spilled its contents that I was close to passing out.

After we'd eaten our breakfast, we saw Matthew, or rather he saw us. He'd been searching the city, rounding up the crew. He had ten of Aretas' soldiers with him. Apparently he'd been a lot more successful than we had. He'd found everybody except Thad and Simon.

"So you found Jesus, and Mary?" I asked.

"Didn't have to, they stayed at the temple."

"You've seen them?"

"No, I slept on the floor of the last bar I was in but I know they went there. Apparently there's some sleeping quarters in one of the outbuildings."

"Are you going there now?"

"That's where I've been sending everyone. I'm going to carry on looking for Thad and Simon. I could do with some help though, you know what those two are like. They could be anywhere."

"I need to get back. I want to check on Maximus." I said.

"You and that bloody donkey! Fair enough I guess. Tom, do you fancy helping out? Unless you've got, I don't know, a camel to cuddle or something."

Thomas laughed. "No, I'll give you a hand."

After what I'd been through, I was dying to pour out my

story to someone, anyone, and it was tempting to do so with these two. But I held my tongue, mainly because if I'd told them my actual 'bloody donkey' experience then it would have prompted a long discussion. I was in a hurry to get to the temple. I knew Mary had stayed there but didn't know if she'd made it through the night.

The other reason for not telling them was that I wasn't yet sure what to say exactly. I would have to tell them about Jeroboam's head because it was bound to come out at some point. Everyone would guess whose handiwork it was, but the harsh truth was that Antipas had got his way. Phase two of his plan had worked. He'd scared me enough to convince me to betray Jesus. I had to do it, not to save my own life but the lives of the whole crew, including Mary's if she wasn't dead - or worse - already. Now I was Antipas' errand boy, however unwilling I might have been. I had to watch what I said. If anyone suspected my motives or even that Antipas had targeted me personally, rather than picking me out at random from Jesus' followers, then steps would be taken to stop me. As much as I wanted to be stopped, as much as I wanted to save Jesus, I couldn't be responsible for all those deaths.

Thomas joined Matt and the soldiers in the hunt for Thad and Simon, and I headed back to the temple. My thoughts were focused on the question of Mary, but I considered whether Nicodemus would be there and how I would be able to act around him if he was. He'd obviously brokered the meeting between me and Antipas' agent, and he'd given up his chambers for that fateful meeting. Whether he'd been got at, or had done it for money I wasn't sure. All I knew was that I wanted to tear his head from his shoulders, but for all the reasons I've just pointed out, I couldn't let on.

The sight of the place filled me with dread. I'd worked myself into a frenzy, thinking about what would be happening to Mary if she'd been taken, and by then I was certain that she definitely had been taken. I hurried up the steps to Nicodemus' office guessing, correctly, that that's where they'd be. My eyes swept the room as I opened the door, seeing the blurred faces of the crew as I sought her out. At last I saw her and nearly ran up and hugged her, but I masked my relief, relief that was replaced with a sense of misery and shame when I looked into the smiling face of Jesus.

"Good to see you, mate," he said. "How's your head? Mine's still fucked, what a night!"

All the petty concerns and suspicions that I'd had about him not so long ago seemed trivial now, pointless even. Whatever we'd been through and whatever he'd become - drug kingpin, Messiah, Son of God - it didn't matter. He was my mate. And now I had no choice but to betray him to his sworn enemy.

# Suspicious Minds

I'd assumed we'd be going straight back to Capernaum, but as I found out after checking that Max was okay, we were headed elsewhere. Thankfully Max was fine, although I'm sure he was traumatised at having his stablemate dragged away from him in the dead of night. I had feared that he'd seen Jeroboam being butchered in front of him, but there was no sign of his decapitated body or even any blood. In spite of everything I was grateful for that.

I spent quite a while with Max, giving him plenty of loving and carrots, and by the time I got back into the office, Matt and Tom had returned. They'd obviously found Thad and Simon fairly quickly because they were back too. Thad looked as dead-eyed as he always did, but even Simon, normally so good at masking the effects of a heavy night, was looking pretty forlorn.

There was an extra man present. He may have been there when I first arrived but in my haste to see Mary I hadn't noticed. He looked familiar but I couldn't quite place him.

"This is Joseph," said Jesus. "He's from Arimathea apparently, but I'm showing my ignorance here, I have no idea where that is."

I realised where I'd seen him before. Phil and I had met him in that very office when we'd come to advertise Jesus' triumphant entry into the city. Thad may have been there too, depending on whether or not he'd graced us with his presence for that particular meeting. The fact that this guy had been one of Phil's appointments implied that he was influential, but it was obvious just by looking at him that he had wealth, and with wealth, power tends to follow. He wasn't flashy like Antipas or even Aretas. He wasn't dripping with jewels, although his clothes looked expensive, both in fabric and cut. Just the way he carried himself screamed to the world that he'd done alright for himself.

"It's okay, my Lord, nobody knows where Arimathea is," Joseph answered, smiling. "I share my name with a good many others so people tend to suffix *of Arimathea* to my name to make the distinction. Your mother's husband is called Joseph as I understand it, so I am in fine company."

"You mean my father," said Jesus.

"Forgive me, my lord, yes, I mean your father, your earthly father at least, and a great man I am sure. But I am aware that your genealogy includes somebody even greater, the greatest of all."

Jesus waved his hand dismissively. "Joseph here is a well-respected man. He sits on this city's Great Council. I should point out that many on the council do not approve of my teachings, or my... activities so it is no small thing that he is here with us."

I couldn't help but keep stealing glances at Mary, not in the hungry way I had in the past but out of the sheer satisfaction of seeing her alive and well.

Joseph was speaking again. "It is an honour to be here with you and your fellows, my lord. You are right to say that you have some critics on the council, upon which the Pharisees hold a strong influence, but speaking for myself, I am a huge admirer of your words and deeds. Yesterday's outpouring of love from the residents of this fair city shows that I am far from alone in that opinion."

Jesus was a statesman now, well used to having these

glowing platitudes heaped upon him by other men of stature and perhaps a little tired of it. "Your support is warmly received," he said, before addressing the rest of us. "Joseph has kindly offered to put us up in his home for a few days. So if everyone is happy with that, I'd like to take him up on his generous gesture. Apart from anything else, I don't think any of us is in a state to start the trudge back to Capernaum."

"Does he have space for us all?" said Peter.

"He's right here, you can ask him yourself."

Joseph smiled again. "You will find that I have plenty of room."

"For Maximus too?" I knew I was going to get laughed at for this but I didn't care. I was going to make damn sure no harm came to my baby boy.

"Ah, Maximus, the prophecy fulfilling donkey! Yes, my friend, your furry companion will be well catered for."

"How about Jeroboam?" said Thad.

"There is ample room for any animals in your travelling party."

My stomach lurched at the mention of Jeroboam. I still hadn't told anyone my awful news and it was going to be hardest of all to tell Simon who, despite not being as doting an owner as I was, would still be understandably gutted to learn of Jeroboam's tragic fate. Thad too, would be more upset than most, the fact that it was he and not Simon who'd asked if Joseph had room for 'Boam was testament to that. This wasn't the time to talk about it though, I didn't trust anyone after all I'd been through and didn't want to blurt anything out in front of this new guy. But I knew I was going to have to say something before we left. Someone was bound to notice we only had the one donkey.

I waited until everyone was getting their stuff ready to leave and asked Jesus, Phil, Simon and Thad for a quiet word. I led them out the back.

"What's all this about?" Phil asked as we neared the stable where Max stood, looking delighted to see me.

"Something terrible has happened," I said.

"Where's 'Boam?" said Simon.

I explained what had happened, leaving out the part about Mary's necklace, and of course my meeting with Antipas the previous day. And then I burst into tears.

I didn't mean to. It just came flooding out. I cried for Jeroboam - for what he'd been through, for the shock of waking up with his severed head, for the terrible images that had been flying through my own head since I'd thought Mary had been taken. But most of all I cried for my best friend, for the position I'd been put in and what I knew I had to do.

And he's the only one who didn't stand in an awkward silence, not knowing what to do when confronted with a crying man. He put his arm around me, and instead of saying the standard *it's okay, it'll be okay*, he just said, "I'm so sorry mate, I can't imagine what you've been through. You're safe now. You're with us, we're together. Nobody can fuck with us when we're together."

It was exactly the right thing to say, at least it would have been under normal circumstances, but because of all the other factors that I hadn't told him about, it was exactly the wrong thing to say. His genuine sympathy, his reminder that we looked out for each other, and most of all, him telling me I was safe, just made the sobs and the snot flow even harder. When this was all over, once I'd carried out Antipas' unspeakable deed, there was a good chance that we would all be safe. All except Jesus, that is. He had my back while I had a dagger at his.

It wasn't much of a discussion. The others were upset too, unlike me they didn't cry like big fat babies but they were obviously shaken by it.

"Poor Jeroboam," said Simon. "I loved that donkey. I wish I'd showed him more. I wish I'd made more of a fuss of him."

"Too late now," said Thad.

"Thank you Thaddeus. You are a real help, you know that?"

Phil spoke up. "With all due respect to Jeroboam, we should be talking about the wider implications of this. Of what it represents. I'm sure none of us is any doubt over who did this."

"Who?" said Thad.

"For fuck's sake, Thad," Simon shouted. "Are you completely dense or do you just pretend to be? He's talking about Antipas."

"Oh yes, that would make sense." Thad spoke all matter of fact, like he hadn't just been yelled at.

I thought about suggesting that this might have been the work of someone other than Antipas in the hope of drawing attention away from my dreadful secret, but I realised it would have sounded lame if I'd tried, even suspicious.

"Why do you think he picked you?" said Phil.

I hesitated, panicking quietly.

Jesus saved me. "I think he would have just picked one of us at random. It just happened to be Judas. He was on his own and easiest to get to, so he became the target."

"That means he's watching us," said Phil.

"Not him personally, he'll have someone doing it for him," said Thad.

From everything Antipas had said to me and what his men had done that morning I was in no doubt that he had spies on us, and the thought of it was scaring me to death already. Now the mention of it from someone else turned my insides over once more.

"Has Maximus just taken a shit?" said Phil.

"That's not donkey shit, that's worse. Someone's dropped

one," Simon bellowed.

My eyes were still burning with tears but I couldn't help but laugh. It's impossible not to when you've let a real stinker go and everyone around you is wincing in disgust.

"It could be one of us," said Thad.

"Well of course it's one of us, we're the only people here!" said Simon.

"I don't think he's talking about the fart," said Jesus. "He's talking about Antipas' spy."

Simon looked embarrassed. "Yes. Of course."

Phil shrugged. "He's right too. It could well be one of us."

"Let's not get ahead of ourselves," said Jesus. "Let's stick to what we know. Antipas wanted to send a message and he chose to do it as shockingly as he could. He must have had someone watching us yesterday. They waited until we we'd got split up."

"And pissed up," said Simon.

"Yes, us all being twatted probably helped. But as far as we know, he wasn't watching us before we came into town."

Phil wasn't having it. "He must have done, he wouldn't have known we were coming otherwise."

"I disagree," said Jesus. "You did a good job of advertising it before we came out here, all the city bigwigs knew about it. Antipas wouldn't have needed spies to find that out."

"Maybe, but cutting the head off a donkey and putting it into someone's bed while they're asleep - all without anybody else hearing - that's not something you do on the spur of the moment. Something like that's got to be planned. He knows exactly what we're up to." Phil paused and looked at each of us in turn. "We've got ourselves a traitor in our midst."

"We'll have to agree to differ on that one," said Jesus.

I didn't say a word. I couldn't get involved in a debate over whether or not there was a rat in our hole when I was the worst rat of all. I was certain that Nicodemus was working for

Antipas, but I couldn't tell the others without telling them how I knew. Nicodemus wasn't going to be staying at Joseph's, so he wasn't an immediate threat, which made me feel less guilty about keeping my thoughts about him to myself, but then I had plenty of other guilt to wallow in.

"One thing we can be sure of," said Jesus, "is if one of our crew is working for Antipas, it's sure as hell not Judas. We all know he couldn't harm a donkey, and even if he could, he wouldn't have put it in his own bed."

I felt my guilt pile grow ever larger. He wouldn't hurt a donkey but he'd give up his best mate to a bloodthirsty tyrant.

"It makes me wonder though," said Phil. "if Antipas picked Judas at random then it's quite a coincidence that his message of choice was to kill a donkey. It's a little bit too... appropriate don't you think?"

I said nothing.

Joseph's house was just outside the city and when we saw it we realised why it had been built there; it was enormous. There simply wouldn't have been room for it inside the city gates. There was plenty of space for all of us, including Aretas' soldiers, with room to spare. I turned down the offer of a comfy bed, opting instead to stay with Max so I could keep an eye on him. Joseph, not having yet heard about what had happened to 'Boam, thought I was some kind of freak, and was even more astonished when Jesus said he would keep me company. "If the stories are to be believed," Jesus said, "this won't be the first time I've kipped in a stable."

## Making a Meal of it

Jesus was as good as his word, and we both spent the night with Max. He'd bought green and wine and we got completely smashed. I won't say it felt like old times, because after everything that had happened, nothing would ever feel like old times again, but it was pretty damned close.

We chatted for hours, running through all the old material. The anecdotes were so worn that we didn't even need to say them out loud, but there's a certain satisfaction in getting the old conversational gems out and buffing them off, letting the light hit them one more time. We talked about the funny moments when we were kids, the successes (on his part) and failures (on mine) with the women we came across on our journey out of Nazareth. Towards the end we talked about how I'd found him in the desert, barely alive, and somehow brought him back from the brink.

"You saved my life, you know that don't you?" We'd drunk and smoked plenty by that stage and the sincerity beast had Jesus in its earnest paws.

"Don't be daft, mate," was my reply. I couldn't take any more guilt.

When we woke up, stiff and cold, I admitted that maybe I was being a tad over-cautious by insisting on keeping guard over Maximus. We could just as easily ask Aretas' soldiers to keep an eye on him, seeing as they were on watch duty anyway.

After a couple of days at Joseph's house, in fact let's call it what it actually was, a palace, nobody was really sure what his role in things was. I'd thought there was going to be some kind of announcement, perhaps some way of using his sway to get us some support from the Great Council, but there was nothing.

Phil had been talking to his contacts, and we learned that the entry into Jerusalem had been a bona fide triumph, making Jesus' popularity leap once again, but even in the face of this PR victory, the people who mattered were still under the influence of the Pharisees. According to those in power, Jesus' message was, at best, at odds with traditional teachings and, at worst, sheer blasphemy. Of course we all knew that all this was just a cover for what was really going on; the Pharisees were Antipas' puppets, and the wild accusations all part of his plan

In spite of this, Phil was convinced that his scheme - to make Jesus so popular with the public that he would be unarrestable - was working. But Phil's plan was based heavily on the assumption that Antipas would do anything to prevent the Romans from intervening. I knew he was only half right on that score. It was correct to say that Antipas was aware of the political implications of causing a stir, but as he'd told me outright, he'd act if he had to.

The grounds of Joseph's palace were impressive. He normally had a team of gardeners looking after them and they were immaculate, the grounds, not the gardeners. Every bush was identical, perfectly round. The lawns were trimmed like a wealthy man's beard and the ponds were obviously skimmed regularly, so if a stray leaf did have the gall to fall in and block the view of the pampered fish, it wasn't there long. The gardens were so spotless that nobody felt comfortable walking around them. If anyone fancied a stroll then the public gardens just outside the walls were more appealing.

I wasn't one for strolling, but Jesus and Mary certainly

enjoyed it. I guessed it gave them some time alone. It can't have been easy having an intimate relationship surrounded by so many other people, all of them men. The first time they went to the gardens, Phil tried to stop them, reminding them of the security risk and insisting they take some soldiers along for protection. Jesus flatly refused and said if they saw a threat coming they'd hide behind one of the olive trees. Phil wasn't amused.

We didn't see a huge amount of Joseph. I still wasn't sure about what he was getting out of putting us all up. He couldn't have been after the kudos of having the Messiah staying at his gaff, because it was made clear to him that nobody on the outside was to be told we were staying there, and even if he had been allowed to show off about it, it wouldn't have done his reputation much good. Jesus wasn't officially a fugitive but it was getting that way. It didn't occur to me that Joseph might just have been being nice.

In a place that size the lack of servants was conspicuous. Joseph explained that in the interests of discretion, he'd given them some time off to be with their families.

A few days into our stay I was playing peek-a-boo with Max, when Peter came out to see me. "We're having dinner tonight," he said. "I think it's going to be quite fancy. It's in the upper room."

"What's the upper room?"

He looked sheepish. "I don't know. I was hoping you did. Phil just said to tell everyone we're having a meal there. I didn't want to look stupid so I pretended I knew what he was talking about."

"Why can't Phil do it himself? You're not his errand boy."

"I don't mind. It gives me something to do. I'm getting a bit bored here to be honest. How's Max?"

"Ask him yourself."

"How are you Max?" Peter held out his hand.

Max replied by licking Peter's fingers. Max liked Peter.

"I reckon the upper room is a room upstairs." I said.

"You could be right, there," said Peter, pulling faces at Max, "but which stairs? I've counted three staircases."

"We'll follow the herd," I said.

"I saw Mary too. She's in the kitchen. She said that if anybody wanted to give her a hand then they're more than welcome. I've had no volunteers so far."

Even though I had my feelings for Mary under control, I couldn't pretend that the idea of some time in her company wasn't massively appealing. "I might pop over there. Max is probably fed up with me fussing him anyway."

Peter gave Max's head a final pat. "I'll come with you."

Joseph's kitchen was, of course, huge. I guessed it had to be. He was the sort of man who regularly entertained important people, and important people always have plenty of hangers on.

"There's no sign of Mary," I said.

"There is, actually. There's all those chopped vegetables and some gutted fish."

"What are you talking about?"

"We knew she was preparing food, and there's some food that's been prepared. They're all signs of Mary. You said there weren't any."

If this had been anyone else - apart from maybe Thad - I would have been sure I was having the piss ripped out of me, but this was wholesome, honest, literal Peter. I took a deep breath. "Yes, you're right, there *are* signs of Mary. I meant I can't see her."

"Nor can I."

I took another deep breath. "I know that, you're standing right next to me."

"Play nicely now, boys." We heard Mary before we saw her

flushed face rise up from behind a counter.

"Were you hiding?" I said.

She grinned. "Yes, that's exactly what I was doing. I was hiding because I'm ten years old and thought it would be fun."

Peter looked concerned. "But we might not have come in. You could have been down there for ages."

I turned to Peter. "You don't do sarcasm do you?"

He looked puzzled.

Mary answered the question of why she was crouching beneath the counter by hoisting a sack of flour noisily onto the work surface. She disappeared and quickly popped up again, bringing another equally big sack crashing onto the worktop. "Are you my reinforcements?" she said, breathing heavily.

"If you'll have us," I said.

"I guess you'll have to do."

She put us to work fetching water and mixing dough as well as helping with the vegetables and fish that she'd made a start on. We were the unskilled kitchen hands and she was the chef. She took our dough and shaped it into loaves, working on a bed of flour. We worked hard but it was good fun. As Peter had said earlier, it was a bit boring at Joseph's palace.

"I'm doing those," I said as she started brushing a plate of fish with oil, a job that I was already halfway through.

"I thought you'd left it."

"I saw that we needed some more water for the next dough mix so I went to get some."

She carried on oiling the fish. "Typical, men can't multitask."

"The reason women think men can't multitask," I said, "is that they always barge in and take over. I had it all under control, oiling my fish, popping out for water, coming back to finish oiling my fish - a prime example of multitasking - but you just leapt right in. What did you think had happened, that I'd just buggered off?"

She clasped her hands in front of her chest in mock prayer. "I'm so sorry, Judas. Please forgive me for thinking you'd left your fish oiling post."

"Where's your necklace?" said Peter.

She raised her fingers to her throat. "I don't know, I must have lost it at the party the other night, I haven't seen it since. I've no idea how it happened, I never take it off. I guess the chain broke and it fell off. I'm gutted."

The image of the blood encrusted pendant filled my head. I tried not to be sick on the fish.

The upper room turned out to be just above the kitchen, which made sense really. It had a hatch in the wall with a winch so you could pull plates of food up and send the empties down. Mary called it the silent servant and I thought it was just about the cleverest thing I'd ever seen.

We sat around the big table in the middle of the room. The fact that we'd been called together for this meal - if not formally then at least officially - gave the evening an odd kind of feel. Everyone seemed almost nervous.

After we'd set about demolishing the food that I'd spent a good chunk of the afternoon preparing, Jesus called us to order. "Can everyone shut the fuck up, please?"

We all shut the fuck up.

He cleared his throat. "The reason I wanted us all to get together like this is that things are going to change soon. I can't say how exactly but in case I don't get the chance again I just wanted to… I dunno… say thanks."

"Why?" said Thad. "Where are you going?"

"It's complicated," said Jesus.

"That means you don't want to tell us," said Peter.

Jesus nodded. "Yeah, I suppose it does."

Mary came in suddenly. "Right," she announced to the

room in general, "I'm done with serving food. There's plenty on the table and when that's gone you'll have to go downstairs and get it yourself." She opened the hatch to the silent servant. It was full of jugs of beer and wine. "Someone give me a hand with these, I'm going to sit on my fat arse and start drinking."

She had her back to us as she said this, and my eyes were immediately drawn to her backside, not for the first time. It wasn't fat, it was perfect. Everybody knew that, including Mary. At least her entrance had taken the edge off the awkwardness that hung around the table like flies around shit since Jesus' last statement.

"Is there anything we can do, Lord?" said Peter.

"You can help me with this lot," said Mary, setting two jugs of wine on the table and returning to the hatch.

Peter, obedient as ever, fetched some more wine. Andrew followed.

Jesus filled his glass and waved it in Peter's direction. "You're going to disown me." He took a bite of bread. "Three times," he said through a mouthful of food. "You'll deny me three times."

"I would never deny you, Lord," said Peter, sitting down.

"You will. Three times," he finished his mouthful and washed it down with some wine, "before the cock crows."

"Which cock?" said Peter.

"Forget the cock, I was trying to sound grand - prophetic - shouldn't have bothered. I mean it'll happen early in the morning."

"But I'd never disown you."

"So you've said, but you will. Trust me."

"I don't get it. Are you saying you want me to disown you?"

But Jesus had moved on, leaving Peter with a look of confusion on his face. "Right, this bread." He broke off a big hunk and passed it to Thad. "Everyone eat a bit of this, it's my body."

Thad broke off a piece. "Bit weird." He slowly put it into his mouth.

Simon was next. He took a piece and held it in front of him. "What's this about?"

"Something to remember me by," said Jesus.

"Where are you going?" said Simon.

"Just go with me on this, eat your bit and pass it on."

Simon shrugged, but did as Jesus said. The bread continued its journey round the table.

Jesus topped up his glass almost to the brim and made a show of taking a sip. "Now everyone have some of this wine, it's my blood."

"Now this is getting really strange," said Simon, taking the glass from Thad. "What's all this in aid of?"

"Can't you just do it?" There was more than a hint of annoyance in Jesus' voice.

"Alright, don't get your loincloth in a twist." Simon took a sip and passed it on.

It wasn't like any other night we'd all spent together. Jesus' vague but shocking statement had put the wind up everybody but nobody was sure how to act. And the ritual of bread and wine was downright bizarre. Mary acted like she'd not picked up on the strange mood in the room, playing like the whole thing was just a big piss-up, but her manner seemed forced, even fake.

Jesus cleared his throat loudly. "One more thing I need to say to you all. One of you is going to betray me."

Nobody knew what to say, least of all me.

## *In the Night Garden*

After the supper, or rather, when the drinks had run out, Jesus said he wanted some air. Nobody knew if it was an invite or not but I said I'd go along, not least because I was trying my best not to look like a back-stabber. After Jesus' final announcement, the already fraught mood in the room had declined considerably. He'd refused to take any questions on the subject and just left everyone to stew in the notion that one of us was a traitor.

It seemed that everybody else had the same idea as me, and we all followed Jesus and Mary on the short walk out of the grounds of the palace and into the olive garden.

The moonlight played tricks. More than once I thought I saw hunched figures in the shadows amongst the low trees. I had a bad feeling. Something was about to happen. Something bad.

I was baffled by how Jesus had acted. He'd obviously had a lot on his mind, and I was used to him keeping certain things to himself, but normally when we had a meeting, everybody was encouraged to pitch in with their views. Not so this time. He'd just made his announcements and cut off anybody who'd tried to contribute. Normally, even when it was a particularly delicate issue, he'd seek the counsel of at least one of us, not so much me but definitely Phil, Simon or Matt, but tonight they'd looked just as surprised as the rest of us.

It occurred to me that Joseph hadn't been at the meal. In

fact I hadn't seen him since that morning. I was about to ask Phil, who was walking next to me, where he'd got to but didn't get a chance.

The something bad was happening.

Everything felt like it had been slowed down. 'Like in a dream', would be the closest description, a dream where you know you have no control over events or yourself. In my memory I see it as if I was viewing it all from the sidelines: watching the unit of Roman soldiers, their helmets lit by the moonlight, but their faces shadowed, watching myself step towards Jesus and kiss him lightly on the cheek, watching Jesus turn and give me the strangest smile as the troops, having seen my sign, closed in around him.

Things suddenly sped up. Peter somehow managed to grab the sword out of the hand of one of the soldiers and aimed it at its owner's head. That was probably the first time Peter had ever held a sword and his clumsy swing didn't quite hit the mark, only succeeding in taking a chunk out of the guy's ear. The soldier went down screaming and suddenly all swords were drawn and pointed at heads, chests, bellies.

"Stop!" Jesus was addressing not his captors but us. "It's just me they want. There's no point fighting them. There's four times as many of them as there are of us. They're soldiers, they're trained to fight. You're not. You'll be cut to pieces. What's the use of that?"

"That one missed a few training sessions I reckon." Thad was pointing at Peter's victim crumpled on the ground clamping his hand to the bleeding hole where his ear once was.

"Can you heal him?" It was the centurion who asked the question.

Jesus looked down at the weeping man who, still on his knees, peered hopefully up at him. The soldiers released their grip and stepped back, allowing him one more miracle.

He held out a hand, palm facing the bleeding man. The wounded soldier watched as Jesus slowly turned his hand round and closed the fingers into a fist. All except the middle one which he left sticking upwards. "Do you think I'm some sort of prick? You come armed to the teeth to arrest me and you think I'm going to help you out when you get cut? If you live by the sword you can fuck off by the sword. Twat."

The soldiers around Jesus grabbed him again and their centurion barked at the earless one to stop crying and get up. I was amazed they didn't arrest Peter for his attack. I guessed they were following strict orders. They had their man and didn't need any distractions. We stood watching, as impotent as eunuchs in the last days of Sodom, as they took our figurehead away.

So that's what Antipas had meant by *somewhere private*. Phil's worries about Jesus' trips to the garden without any security had turned out to be accurate, and I half expected him to say something, but even Phil, who enjoyed being right more than anything, would have loved to have been proved wrong on this one.

It was Matthew who spoke first. "There's still time, we've got fifty soldiers next door. We can get him back."

"Absolutely not," said Phil. "We might win that skirmish but they'll just send the whole legion next time. We've got to play the long game."

"There isn't time for a long game," said Matthew. "They're not going to hang about."

Phil nodded. "Okay, not the long game then, but the less short one."

"They might not execute him. They might just lock him up." Even as I said the words I knew they weren't true, despite what Antipas had told me.

Phil looked at me with a curious expression on his face.

"What was that kiss all about?"

I could have lied, even in those awful circumstances, especially as I still felt completely numb, still in someone else's dream. I could have said that I'd just felt the urge to do it after all the weird talk that night, or that I was drunk, or even just joking, trying to lighten the mood by creeping Jesus out. But I chose an unusual path for me when I'm in a scrape. I chose to tell the truth.

"That kiss saved your life," I said. "It saved everybody's life." It all came pouring out: my meeting with Antipas, the ultimatum I'd been given, how I'd told him to go fuck himself (I stressed that part knowing that everyone in the crew was staring at me with the word traitor and betrayer ingrained on their minds like commandments on a tablet) and the fact that I'd been given no choice. Last of all I told them what I'd found in amongst the putrefying blood clinging to Jeroboam's butchered head and neck that awful morning. I held out Mary's pendant, it slowly rotated, catching the moonlight.

The silence that followed was broken by Nat. "You did have a choice - save yourself, and us admittedly, or save Jesus."

"Okay, yes, I had a choice, and I picked one. Would you have done anything different?"

"I was just saying."

"Anybody who says they're just saying isn't ever just saying, or there would be no point in them just saying it." I glanced at Simon, expecting him to notice that I was ripping off his material. He didn't look at me, so I carried on railing at Nat. "You're obviously making a point, so answer me. Would you have done anything different? And while you're at it you can fuck off."

Nat didn't answer and he didn't fuck off.

"So come on then," I said, fixing my eyes on everyone in turn, "say what you need to say, cut my throat if you think it'll help, but before you do, try and put yourself in my sandals and think about what you would've done if you'd been in the same position. Do you think I'm happy about this, or do you think that maybe, just maybe, I might feel worse than anyone could possibly imagine? Jesus is my best friend and I had to give him up. Can you imagine how that feels? If we can't get him back, and do it in a way that ends all this, that makes Jesus, Mary and all the rest of us safe - and I mean safe permanently, not until Antipas decides to strike again - then you won't have to cut my throat, I'll do it myself."

Thad frowned. "That's a really awkward thing to do."

"What do you mean?"

"To cut your own throat, it would be really hard to do, like trying to stab yourself. You'd be better off jumping in a lake, or even hanging yourself."

Despite everything, I found myself smiling, and noticed Simon doing the same. I shook my head. "For fuck's sake, Thad. Okay, you won't have to kill me, I'll do it myself. That better?"

Thad nodded.

Simon stepped forward. "Judas, I understand everything you have said, and after considering it carefully, I sympathise completely. You were put in an impossible position, and you did what you had to do. For the life of me I cannot imagine what you must have been through, or how you must have felt, and continue to feel. I can move on from this, and think even Jesus will too, although coming up with a panacea that solves everything will work a great deal towards shaping his view into a favourable one. That said, it would be remiss of me not to act upon an urge that has gripped me since you revealed what you have done. So, do you mind?"

"No, I guess not."

Simon punched me in the face, knocking me to the floor.

"Thanks," he said. "Actually, sorry old boy, just one more." He kicked me hard in the stomach.

I lay gasping for breath before he reached down and helped me up. "Now to business," he said. "Let's fix this."

# *Team Jesus*

I needed to talk to the brains behind the outfit, and with Jesus gone that was Phil. I took him into the kitchen, as good a place for privacy as any, while everybody else sat silently in what Joseph had called the entertaining area; all leather seating and low tables, ornately carved. Phil was reluctant to share my air at first, and I could see why. Right at that moment I wasn't the best person to be associated with.

We stood either side of the counter at which Mary had stood earlier that afternoon - it felt like weeks ago - looking all floury and delicious but now I was looking into the weary, worried and extremely suspicious face of Phil.

I got straight down to it. "What Matt said was right, we haven't got much time, so we have to dispense with all the stuff about me. You can have a go at me later but right now we've got to focus on what's important."

"I agree."

"Good. Now, our biggest problem - well not really our biggest, but one I happen to be mentioning first - is trust. Someone's leaking information to Antipas."

Phil burst out laughing. "Yes, I know! I said that after the donkey thing, remember? But the big man overruled me. Now I know I was right. And I know it was you."

"For Christ's sake! You can think what you like about me, but I've told you everything about my… involvement with Antipas. The donkey thing was his last warning to me after I

286

told him where to stick his threats, I wasn't in on it. And anyway, I haven't spoken to the cunt, apart from that one time at the temple and I didn't know we were coming here then. Somebody else tipped him off that Jesus would be in the garden tonight and it sure as fuck wasn't me."

"Why should I believe you?"

"What do I have to gain from lying? I didn't have to tell you anything at all, I could have kept it to myself."

"That's very big of you."

"Jesus, I didn't mean it like that, I'm just trying to make the point that I've got no reason to lie. That's not to make myself look or feel better, it's because if we're going to fix this we need to move fast, and if you don't believe anything I say then it's going to slow us down."

Phil wasn't budging. "You only came clean about it all because I asked you why you'd kissed him."

"Bollocks. I chose to tell you, I could have lied very easily," I noticed Phil's expression change, "and before you say it, I'm not saying *aren't I great because I didn't lie*, I'm saying we've got a spy in our operation."

"Apart from you."

"Apart from me, yes, but I was never a spy, fuck knows what I was but I wasn't a spy. I didn't give him any information."

"Except for the one prime piece of information his men needed more than anything else, his identity."

"Jesus! If I hadn't done that we'd all be dead now, or in a dungeon. But I'm not going to have that argument with you now, even though I know for a fact you would have done the same if it had been you."

"You reckon?"

I took a deep breath. "Fuck it, let's say you wouldn't then. Let's say you would have leapt out of your seat, taken out

Antipas' personal guards with your bare hands then ripped his head off and thrown it out the window. Let's say you're a hero, happy? Regardless of what I did and what you would have done, and whether you want to call me a spy or a dupe or a coward it doesn't matter. The point is that someone else tipped off Antipas about tonight."

He went to speak but stopped himself, finally coming to the realisation that we had better things to do with the short time we had than argue about me being a traitor. "Okay," he nodded, "okay." His face softened. "Listen mate, I've given you a hard time, and I won't be the only one, and I won't pretend I won't do it again. But I do see why you did what you did, honestly I do, and I can't say what I would have done in the same situation. Technically you saved all our lives, and with that threat about Mary, the pendant," he shivered, "fuck that's creepy. I know how important it would have been to you to keep her safe. Jesus himself might even have made that trade, his life for hers, if he'd been given the choice."

I was too embarrassed and too riddled with shame to handle his forgiveness. "Thanks, but we've wasted too much time arguing. Let's not waste any more making up. Fuck, something's just occurred to me. Fuck, fuck fuck."

"Spit it out."

"I'm going to sound like a massive prick after what I've just been banging on about but if one of the crew staying here is leaking information, then why did Antipas need me to point Jesus out? He could have just got his spy to do it. He wouldn't have needed two of us."

Phil thought for a moment. "There could be hundreds of reasons, but the one I'm guessing at is that Antipas is from a world where the leader is put on a pedestal, surrounded by a select few in his inner circle. You have to remember that to him we're a big deal, something close to a king and his courtiers.

Antipas would have applied his own standards. He wouldn't imagine that Jesus, the king in his eyes, would be happy to hang out with just anyone in the crew. So, think about it like this, he recruited someone a while ago to give him information about what we're up to, general stuff like where we're going to be, what our plans are, that sort of thing, just to keep tabs on us. Then his plans escalated and he decided how he was going to make his move. In his world, the guy already feeding him stuff was too far down the pecking order and wouldn't be guaranteed to get close enough to do the kiss thing. So he had to bring you in. He could just as easily have picked me."

"I know why he picked me," I said, ashamed. "I was pissed at Jesus. I thought he was freezing me out, making decisions, consulting you and not me. I was a dick about it. I bet he got wind of that from his little messenger and thought I was ripe for the picking."

"I wouldn't beat yourself up about it. It's quite a stretch to go from being pissed at a mate to shopping him in to his nemesis. The reason you did what you did isn't because you felt left out or sulky. It's because he threatened you."

"I won't beat myself up over it. I'll let Simon do that." I stroked my swollen jaw. "He's got a good right hand on him."

"Probably from all the wanking."

It was a bit of an obvious joke but I forced a smile to show that I appreciated his effort to relax the mood. "Right, one more thing. I know I sound obsessed with conspiracies, but I have serious concerns about Nicodemus. Antipas had access to his office while he was conveniently absent. Jeroboam was stabled at the temple. It doesn't smell right to me."

"Stables never smell right." Phil paused. "Sorry, shit joke. So you think Nicodemus is on Antipas' payroll." He thought for a moment. "He could be, I won't rule it out, but he could just as easily not be. Antipas pretty much runs the Pharisees, and probably the Great Council too. Facilities like the offices in the temple are often booked out for meetings for council business and the like, so it would be easy for Nicodemus to be told his office had been booked out for the afternoon and have absolutely nothing to do with it."

"We should look it up in the records. They keep the details don't they? We can see what name is on the booking."

"We could, but where's that going to get us? Whether or not Nicodemus is playing for the other side is pretty much irrelevant now. The game's changed. Now we close ranks and do whatever it is we need to do. We don't include outsiders. If we get through this then we can investigate all this stuff and take our revenge, if that's what we want to do, but for now we need to focus on the big picture. Forget Nicodemus. Let's just think about Jesus."

"I won't say what I was going to say about Joseph then."

"Christ, you're properly paranoid aren't you?"

"I woke up with a donkey's head in my bed."

"Point taken. What's your problem with Joseph?"

"Where is he?"

"He told me this morning that he had some business to attend to." Realisation flooded into his face. "Okay, so that's a bit strange. But again, it might not be. Even if we assume he has fucked us over, we take the same course of action as we do with Nicodemus, we forget him for now. We focus on getting Jesus back, on getting all this sorted."

"Okay, let's not waste any more time. Let's get on with it. What do we do?"

"Well we start by making a call about the leak. We don't necessarily need to know who it is, just who it's not. We need to pick the best people to thrash out a plan, so we need to leave out anyone who might be the spy. If we do come up with a move then we don't want our enemies to know what it is. In the absence of any hard facts, we'll have to go with my assumption that it's someone a bit down the pecking order. I know we don't have official rankings in this operation but I'd say that Simon would be a high ranker if we did. And he's sharp too."

"Agreed. He's in. How about Thad?"

"I completely trust Thad but I wouldn't say he's sharp. Lovely guy, but dopey as a moth."

"I think he might surprise you."

"Really?"

"And more to the point, I think he'll just barge in anyway. You know what he's like."

"Yeah, alright, Thad's in. What about Peter?"

I frowned. "He's not the most sparkling intellect in the world."

"No, he's a plodder, but he's solid, loyal, he'd do anything for Jesus."

I nodded. "Go on then. Now what about Matt? I've got to say it - I could go either way on him. In any other circumstances I'd trust him with my life but we've got to look at everything critically. It's just the fact that he's from Antipas' world that worries me. He's from the outside. We don't know much about Aretas except that he's been a profitable business partner, there might be more to the whole thing."

Phil sucked in his cheeks, thinking. "That's pretty much my view, but do we have a choice? He's the key to that army sitting downstairs, with more back in Capernaum. I don't know what our plan is yet but it's more than likely going to include soldiers so Matt's going to need to be kept in the loop. It's a risk we'll have to take."

"Yes, I suppose it is. I don't really think he'd be ratting us out anyway, especially if we use your pecking order guideline - he's a high ranker too. And once you've moved away from the trust issue and get down to the real point, which is that we need to come up with a decent plan, then he'll be valuable, he knows his shit."

"What about Mary?"

"She's no traitor and she'll want to be involved."

"Okay, so that's seven."

I shook my head. "I make it six."

Phil counted on his fingers. "Simon, Thad, Peter, Matt, Mary, me, you. That's seven."

"Absolutely not, I said. "That lot aren't going to want to be in the same room as me after what I did. I've said what I needed to say, I'll leave you lot to get on with it."

Phil waved his hand dismissively. "Don't be daft. We need you, and apart from anything else, Jesus would want you involved. And anyway, let's say we somehow manage to get everyone out of this impossible situation, which I know is very unlikely, are you going to tell me you're happy to miss out on the opportunity to be on the team that saved the day? This is your chance to make amends."

"That's very nice of you and all that, but listen. It took me and you ages to get past the fact that I shopped Jesus in, it's going to take even longer with the others. We just don't have time. I'll sit this one out."

"I'll talk to them. We'll see what happens. But let's find somewhere else for the escape committee to talk. The kitchen's not doing it for me."

Phil got the people we'd chosen and relocated to the upper room. I waited in my own room, thinking it best to keep out of the way of the others sitting downstairs.

After a while there was a knock on my door. I opened it and saw Mary. "I'm so sorry," was all I could say. I braced my face for a slap and my balls for a kick.

Instead she threw her arms around me. "We'll get through

this. I know how much you love him. I know why you did what you did. Come and help us get him back."

She was crying. And so was I.

I won't pretend that everyone was as forgiving or as welcoming as Mary, but they seemed to have settled on the fact that we had work to do. We had to hammer out a solution to this mess.

After I sat down and we prepared for business, Thad spoke. "Shall we get stoned?"

Simon answered him like a patient father with an errant child. "No, Thad, we need clear heads. We can't get stoned."

"But I do my best thinking when I'm stoned."

Simon sighed. "Okay Thad, you can get stoned."

## *Bundle of Joy*

So the question was: how does a group of blokes and one woman, already out of their depth and blagging their way as drug barons whilst doubling up as disciples of the Messiah, go about saving said Messiah from imminent execution and thwarting the most powerful man in the region?

None of us knew the answer to that but we had to give it a go.

Matthew had a simple, straightforward idea. "I say we just go for it. We've got two hundred soldiers. We hit them hard, take them by surprise."

"We've only got fifty here," said Phil. "We'd have to get the rest to come from Capernaum. That'll take days. You said it yourself. Antipas - or Caiaphus on his behalf - will act quickly. And even if we did have that many men, if we made a move like you're suggesting then we'd bring the whole Roman army down on us."

Peter spoke up. "Can someone explain something to me please? From what I've been told Antipas is doing everything he can not to catch the attention of the bigwigs in Rome, and the reason he's so careful is so his authority as tetrarch isn't threatened."

"That's right," said Phil.

"So how come it was Roman soldiers who came here tonight and arrested Jesus?"

"It's complicated," Simon said after realising nobody else

was going to take a stab at it. "There's the Roman army, and then there's the *Roman Army*. All the big decisions are taken up in Rome and there are different layers of command spiralling downwards. The local centurions have a certain level of autonomy," he saw Peter's politely confused expression and checked himself, "that is, they can make day to day decisions about how to use their men without informing Rome. It's only if they're dealing with something big that they'd have to pass it up the line. An uprising is seen as something big, but keeping law and order is business as usual."

"I'm going to make us something hot to drink," said Mary, heading for the door.

"The other thing to remember," said Simon, "is that some of the local Roman commanders are more reputable than others. As we saw when Aretas arranged for Roman soldiers to back us when the poppy factory was ransacked, it's not unheard of to buy the services of a garrison that's run by one of the more corruptible commanders. That may be what's happened tonight. Antipas, although keeping his distance and doing it all through that bastard priest, Caiaphus, might have paid for the soldiers who came here, but he probably didn't need to because he's spread word that Jesus is a bad seed. Caiaphus probably just reported this to the local garrison, along with some specific charge or other - probably blasphemy - and they treated it as they would with any other crime. They came and arrested him."

Matt was obviously losing patience with Simon's slew of background information. "Do we have any idea where he's being held?"

"It shouldn't be difficult to find out," said Phil, "but before we look into that, we need to get some sort of plan together."

"Let's stop fucking about shall we?" said Matt. "I still say we go with force. We use the soldiers we have here, send back to Capernaum for reinforcements and send a rider to Aretas to tell him we need more men, enough for a full-on battle with the Romans. In the meantime, we bed down and hold out for as long as we can until Aretas' army gets here."

"Aretas isn't going to go head-to-head with the Romans," said Phil. "You must know that better than anyone, you worked for the guy. His war is with Antipas, he'd lose everything if he took on Rome, not just thousands of soldiers but most of his trade. He'd be fucked."

"Well, we've got to do something, sitting here talking isn't helping anyone."

"I share your frustration, but be patient. We'll get there."

Mary came back in. "Drinks are ready, I've knocked up a little herb infusion, should help keep us awake." She went to the hatch and pulled at the winch. I gave her a hand unloading the silent servant.

"What have I missed?" she asked, putting the steaming jugs down on the table.

"A big fat waste of time," said Matt.

"The drink smells nice," said Thad.

We went over it again and again, trying to think of an angle. All we succeeded in doing was making Matt more frustrated. For an accountant, he was well up for a fight. As time went on, it looked like we might have to try his approach even though we knew full well it would be a suicide mission, possibly straight away, but definitely in the long term when the real Roman army arrived.

There was a knock at the door. Simon opened it to find Bart standing there, looking like he'd just been woken up, which presumably he had. "There's some people downstairs wanting to see you. One of them is the bloke who owns this place."

"Joseph?"

"That's right, but he's got two others with him."

Simon looked nonplussed. "Why is he asking permission to

come upstairs in his own house?"

"I couldn't tell you," said Bart, wearily. "Do you want me to send them up?"

Simon glanced at the rest of us, who mostly shrugged.

Phil spoke. "We can't really tell him he's not allowed in his own dining room, can we?"

"Fair enough," said Simon. "Send him up."

"Wait a minute," I said. "The other two, are they Roman soldiers?"

Bart's looked at me with contempt. "Do you not think if they were wearing helmets and carrying swords that I might not have mentioned that particular detail? Do you think I'm a complete cock?"

I swallowed the answer that came to mind.

"Send them up," said Phil.

When Joseph entered the room I immediately recognised the man next to him. It was Nicodemus. Only a few of us had met him, which explained why Bart hadn't known who he was.

And then the other one came in.

I stood up, knocking my stool flying. I was screaming, I'm not sure what exactly but something along the lines of: *what the fuck is that cunt doing here?*

It was Antipas. His hair was different and his clothes less grand but there was no mistaking him. No mistaking those eyes. My fury was matched by my fear so I could just as easily have run out the door as run towards him. I was well into the second option, which was foolhardy really because Antipas didn't go anywhere without backup. There was a big table between us so I was in the ridiculous position of having to run round the outside to get to him. There was just one thought in my head: to hurt the bastard. I careered, full pelt, round the table and was almost on him when I bounced off something and fell on my arse.

The something that had blocked my path was Joseph, and as my furious limbs flailed in a bid to get me upright he shouted in my face. "It's not him! It's not Antipas!" He stood over me, gripping my shoulders, keeping me on the floor. "Wait," he shouted. "Wait just a moment, let me explain. *Will you let me explain?*"

I stopped squirming about.

Joseph took a deep breath before speaking. "I agree he looks very much like Antipas…" In a sudden move I grabbed Joseph's arm and pulled him to the ground next to me. I pressed down hard on his back, both to keep him down and to give myself a push upwards. I was almost up, but suddenly I stopped, frozen. I was face to face with those unmistakable eyes.

"I am not Antipas. Antipas is my brother. My name is Herod, Herod the Second. Please calm down."

As soon as I heard his voice, I knew it wasn't Antipas. Okay, so apparently there was some mistaking those eyes.

"Shall we all sit down?" said Joseph. "We need to have a talk."

There was much scraping of wood on terracotta as we all did as Joseph suggested. I couldn't take my eyes of Herod, no longer out of fear or anger but out of curiosity - he looked so much like his brother. I was more than a little suspicious too, his relationship with Antipas aside, this was the son of the man who'd had Christ knows how many kids murdered thirty years ago. Talking of suspicion, I also hoped Phil had explained to the others that we didn't know if Nicodemus, or even Joseph could be trusted.

Joseph took a chair and waited for Nicodemus and Herod to do the same before addressing us. "My introductions have been somewhat pre-empted by our friend Judas, but for the sake of completeness I will carry on as planned." He gestured to his left. "Some of you already know Nicodemus. He is a business partner of yours, representing your interests in the city and in some other areas of expansion. He is respected not just in Jerusalem but far beyond." There were a few grunts of acknowledgement and Joseph continued. "My other guest, as you will now know, is Herod the Second, eldest son of King Herod the Great."

Simon spoke up. "I know we are guests in your home but I hope you will let me speak frankly. You seem to be introducing the brother of Antipas, who also happens to be the son of the babykiller, as if he is a welcome ally."

"I was getting to that," said Joseph. "Yes, Antipas and Herod are brothers, but that is where their connection ends."

Simon raised his eyebrows. "Being his brother is quite a connection, and not one that can be easily dismissed."

"I do not ask you to dismiss it," said Joseph.

"What are you asking then?

"I'm asking you to listen."

"I am listening, but you have said nothing yet."

Joseph was obviously struggling to keep his voice level. "I understand that this is a stressful time for you, for all of you. Your master has been taken and you do not know who to trust."

"He is not our master, he is our friend," said Simon.

Phil cut in. "Please, Joseph, say what you wish to say."

"Thank you," said Joseph. "Thank you, all of you, this is a difficult time for everybody but it is in your interests to listen to what I have to say."

Phil interrupted again. "I don't want to sound like I'm taking the piss but you're still talking *about* talking rather than actually saying anything. So if you wouldn't mind please can you…" he searched for the words.

"Spit it out?" Thad suggested.

Phil smiled. "That's the one."

Joseph slapped his palms on the table and stood up. "Forget talking," he said. "Come with me."

"So you can have us arrested?" said Peter.

"What the fuck is wrong with you lot?" Joseph screamed. "We're here to help you and you won't listen and you spout on at me like I'm your enemy and you won't come and see something you really need to see. You won't do anything, you just sit there squabbling." He sat down and waved his hands dismissively. "I'll tell you what, fuck off. Fuck off out of my house."

I've experienced some awkward silences in my time, but nothing came close to the one that followed Joseph's rant. I could feel the tension in the air like mist. I had a crack at pouring oil on the troubled waters. "Joseph, I would very much like to see whatever it is you've got to show us. If that's okay. And I think that on reflection, everyone else would, too." I looked around. "Is that right? Everyone?" There were embarrassed murmurs of agreement.

Joseph took a deep breath. "Please excuse my outburst. It has been a long night, and it is far from over." He stood up. "If you would be so kind, please follow me downstairs." His respectful statesman demeanour had returned.

Nicodemus and Herod stayed in the room whilst the rest of us trooped downstairs. The rest of the crew who hadn't been picked for the escape committee must have all gone to bed because they were nowhere to be seen. As Joseph led us outside, I realised that I had played straight into his hands. We were going to be seized by a gang of Antipas' cutthroats and killed. Joseph would have had it done it indoors but he obviously didn't want to get blood on his nice furnishings.

We were headed for the stable, the perfect place to round us up, kill us and dispose of our bodies. Apart from the convenience of the location, with its shedful of digging tools and - if they favoured cremation over a mass grave - plenty of straw, it would also be a perfect place for a final fuck you from Antipas. It was obvious what he'd planned. Before our grisly end, we were going to be made to watch whilst Maximus was slowly decapitated in front of us. Perhaps I was even going to be made to do it personally.

We were close enough to see the front of the stable. It was lit by the torches on either side, so I could easily see Max, grinning all over his massive face, chuffed to bits to see me. My heart broke into more pieces than I would have been able to count. I braced for the sound of daggers being drawn. I was ready for the end, and I knew it wasn't going to be quick when it came.

I was within reach of Max but didn't touch him even though his eyes were begging me to give him a big old stroke. My expression back to him said, *Don't let on that we're close mates because they'll use that against us and do something horrible to you and by the way you're the absolute business Max thanks for everything and I couldn't be more sorry that it's come to this*. Max did as I asked - he wasn't just a big face - and played it cool. But he did send me a look back that said, *Don't beat yourself up over it, mate I wouldn't change a thing*.

Joseph rested his hand casually on Maximus' head, an action that I knew was designed to strike a chill into my already shattered heart, but then he spoke to Max in a surprisingly amiable voice. "Do you want to show us who's keeping you company in there?"

He lifted one of the torches and held it over the wooden rail into the stable. He nodded towards a bundle in the corner.

"What's that?" I said.

"You mean, *who's* that? Go and have a look." He lifted the rail to allow me to step through. "I would give you the torch but that would be rather foolish with all the straw around. If you cannot see well enough then by all means just drag him out by his feet so you can get a better look. He shouldn't be able to kick you, he is rather well tied."

There was just about enough light, but I struggled to make out who I was looking at because there was so much rope and cloth, I couldn't tell one end from the other. I only knew it was a person because of what Joseph had said. I don't know if the man-bundle on the floor moved, or if I'd moved and allowed more moonlight in but something happened, and suddenly I could see a pair of eyes. Those unmistakable eyes, bulging with fury as their owner struggled against his bonds and tried to spit out the wad of cloth stuffed deep into his mouth.

I turned round and hugged Max with one arm and Joseph with the other. "You've got him, you've got Antipas!"

## Brotherly Love

Back in the upper room, Simon asked the question on everybody's excited, confused or downright terrified lips. "So, what the fuck?"

Joseph smiled. "Nicodemus, would you care to take it from here?"

Nicodemus stood up. "You will know by now why Joseph was so keen to show you the rather large package currently being stored in his stable. I will fill you in on how this came to be, and will be as brief as possible because we still have a big problem to solve."

Matt interrupted. "For the last few hours everyone's been telling me that using force to get Jesus back isn't an option because it would bring the Romans down on us. I'd like someone to explain to me how we think the Romans are going to react to us kidnapping the fucking tetrarch. I know my opinion isn't worth much, but I'm going to say it anyway. I don't think they're going to throw us a nice party."

"That's a valid concern, Matthew, but bear with me, I will come to that."

"Can't you come to it now?"

"Please bear with me."

Matt slapped the table and turned his head away. "For fuck's sake."

Nicodemus was unruffled. "Antipas was in the city tonight to ensure his operation went smoothly. As far as he was

303

concerned, I was part of that operation." He noticed Phil glance at me. "I know that some of you suspected that I was not to be trusted and, based on what you knew, you had good reason for your doubts, but there is a great deal more to this as I am sure you are now realising. Oh, that reminds me." He rummaged under the table and surfaced again holding a small cloth bag. He slid it across the table to me.

"What's this?"

"It's from Antipas. Payment for services rendered. And before anybody jumps to any conclusions about Mister Iscariot here…"

"Too late for that," said Bart.

I rounded on Bart. "Do you think I did it for the money? He said he'd kill all of you, and let's not forget the small matter of him threatening to have your niece gang-raped." I saw more than one set of eyes around the table fix on Mary and I felt suddenly sheepish. "I'm sorry, Mary." I turned my attention back to Nicodemus. "And where do you get off giving me this now, you prick? Did you think this lot weren't pissed off enough? Did you think you needed to spice things up a bit?"

"I apologise. I was using the bag of silver to illustrate the explanation I was about to make."

"Well you got it all arse about face. You should have explained first and then got the bag out, or better still not got the bag out at all." I tapped my head with my finger. "Think a bit, man." I slid the bag back across the table.

Nicodemus looked suitably chastened. "I see now. I am sorry. I would like to point out to all of you that Judas was put in an impossible situation. If any one of you had been face to face with Antipas and been given the same ultimatum, you would almost certainly have done the same." He moved on before anybody had a chance to cut in with another comment like Bart's. "Both myself and Judas were acting for a wider purpose. I was aware of this wider purpose. Judas was not. But everything that has happened has been allowed to happen for a good reason. For now we must focus on the matter in hand. Jesus currently resides in a prison cell, the hour is late," he glanced out of the window at the lightening sky. "In fact, the hour is early. We need to take action quickly. Jesus is being held in a cell beneath the courthouse in the city. Soon after sunrise somebody of sufficient rank will be sent for. Probably the Prefect himself."

"Pilate," said Joseph.

"If he can be roused," said Nicodemus. "There will be a trial, with High Priest Caiaphus as the main witness. The charge, as I understand it, will be Jesus' violent conduct in the temple grounds. Some of you here - Judas, Matthew - will remember that incident as well as I do."

"They're not going with blasphemy, then?" said Phil.

"They will not lead with that as it is a more complicated charge, but I am sure they will use it if they feel it is necessary, for example, if the witnesses provide conflicting testimony."

"Will there be any other witnesses apart from Caiaphus?"

"There will be one other witness," Nicodemus paused, "myself."

"Great," I said. "So you can put in a good word. Will that be enough?"

Nicodemus shook his head. "I will be agreeing with every word that comes out of Caiaphus' mouth."

"That's not particularly helpful " I said.

"It's all part of the plan," said Nicodemus.

"Come on then," said Matt. "What is the plan? How do we get Jesus out, and how do we stop the Romans from ripping us apart for snatching Antipas, or his own army for that matter."

"The latter part is easy." Nicodemus turned to Herod. "I don't need to tell you how much this man resembles his brother. Judas' reaction to seeing him is strong enough evidence, I am sure you will agree. The plan is that Herod takes residence in Antipas' palace and nobody ever knows that Antipas was taken."

"The old switcheroo," said Thad.

"I think you will find that the correct Latin is switcher*us*," said Simon.

"We'd have to smarten him up a bit," said Phil, "but it could work, in theory at least."

"Calm down, everyone," said Matt. "I'm all for action, but let's look at this realistically before we run away with ourselves. Even if Herod looks enough like Antipas to fool Judas, it's not going to fool anyone who knows him well. What about his servants? What about his wife?"

Herod slammed his fist on the table. "She is *not* his wife."

Nobody was quite sure how to respond to that, except Simon, who was nodding slowly to himself. "Ah, I get it," he said at last. "I see what this is about, now. She's your wife. You're doing this because you want her back."

Herod's immediate rage had subsided but he still looked pretty intense. "I do not - as you say - *want her back*. Those words would apply to a foolish teenager, not to me. I am simply going to take what is mine, take that which was stolen from me."

Peter raised his hand. "I'm confused."

"Course you are," said Simon.

Phil looked as if a torch had been lit in his head. "Of course! It all goes back to why John was killed. When Antipas divorced his wife - Aretas' daughter - so he could marry someone else, the someone else was your wife."

Herod nodded once.

"Well she's bound to notice then!" said Matt.

"She will notice absolutely," said Herod. "She will notice

that the snivelling wretch with whom she shared a bed has been replaced with a man. A real man. A bigger man."

Matt frowned. "But won't she, I dunno, raise the alarm?"

Herod smiled. "To whom will she lodge this report of which you speak? To her tetrarch?"

Matt considered Herod's words. "I see your point."

Herod looked satisfied. "And as for the servants, or anybody else in the court, they will do as I command."

"What about his personal guard?" I said. "Half a dozen hand-picked thugs. They might have something to say about it."

Joseph wore a guilty smile. "They would indeed have been problematic. But they are no longer a concern."

"You killed them?"

"How did you think we were able to seize Antipas? I cannot take the credit for the act itself. We have this household's other guests to thank for that."

"Aretas' men?" said Matt. "Why didn't anybody mention it to me? I'm responsible for them while they're here."

Joseph shrugged. "The order came from Aretas himself."

Matt's mouth fell open. "How is Aretas involved in this?"

"You may have noted that Nicodemus alluded to a wider purpose a few moments ago. Well that wider purpose encompasses Aretas, Herod and of course Jesus, all of whom have a common interest in putting an end to Antipas' reign."

Simon spoke. "We know that Jesus and Aretas share an enemy in Antipas - they made an alliance on the back of it - but Aretas has been more about support, most notably with troops. They have not been planning to eliminate Antipas. They have not even been in contact recently. We would know about it if they had."

Joseph cocked his head. "Are you sure about that?"

The answer was that none of us was sure. We'd all learned

that Jesus had his own way of doing things and only shared his plans when it was absolutely necessary.

"Why would he leave us out of something like this?" said Phil.

Matt threw Phil a derisive look. "You're just pissed because you'd got used to being the big man's go-to guy."

Before Phil could respond, Peter jumped in. "I understand that there have been some…"

"Shenanigans," said Thad.

"Thanks Thad," said Peter. "I understand that there have been some shenanigans between Jesus, Aretas and Antipas' brother here…"

"Please call me Herod."

"… Herod, but I have a question. Are you saying that Jesus planned his own arrest?"

"I am not privy to all of the details but it would be my considered opinion that yes, he allowed it to happen. I would speculate that he felt it the only way to fully resolve the situation with Antipas, the only way to prevent an eternal rearguard action."

"I agree," said Nicodemus.

"Did you know about any of this?" Bart said to Mary.

"Perhaps a little." She blushed. "I don't think we should get bogged down in Jesus' reasons for not sharing his plans though, we should just trust him and get on with it. Has he ever let any one of us down?"

She made a good point.

"We are where we are," said Matt. "There's no time to discuss the whys and wherefores. The more pressing problem is how do we get Jesus out? And how do we do it without anybody noticing he's gone? The Romans won't take kindly to a prisoner just disappearing from their custody. They'll be all over us."

"The plan is simple," said Nicodemus. "We exchange him for a prisoner of our own."

"You mean Antipas?" said Phil. "You can't solve every problem by just swapping people over. And besides, he doesn't look anything like Jesus."

"He doesn't need to look like him. The Romans, the ones who will be holding the trial at least, have never seen Jesus. The only ones that have are those who arrested him and I am sure something can be done about them."

"They might not recognise Jesus," said Phil, "but they'll recognise Antipas."

"Not if his appearance is…" Nicodemus grimaced, "…changed. It is not unusual for people resisting arrest to sustain injuries, particularly to the face."

"So we beat the crap out of him?"

Nicodemus nodded. "So his own mother wouldn't recognise him."

"I'll do it," I said without hesitation.

Phil turned to Herod. "And you're alright with that? With any of it? Not just the beating, but with your brother being condemned for a crime he hasn't committed?"

Herod pushed out his chest. "Antipas has committed many crimes, any one of them worthy of his condemnation. I will shed no tears nor will I feel any guilt over his death, he is already dead to me."

Phil's voice went up a level. "But he'll be stoned to death, it'll be horrible!"

"It is a Roman court," said Nicodemus, "so the method of execution will be in keeping with Roman customs. It will be crucifixion."

Phil winced. "That's even worse. Can you imagine?"

"Crucifixion is too good for him," said Herod.

"Charming family," muttered Thad.

"I think we should all keep in mind," said Nicodemus, "that Antipas arranged for Jesus to be arrested with the sole intention of having him executed. I am not saying that there is poetic justice in that but it should be considered when taking a moral stance against what is being proposed."

"Firstly," said Phil, "there's nothing poetic about someone being nailed to a cross, and who said I'm taking a moral stance? I'm just trying to understand how someone could be so cold towards a blood relative, even a wife-stealing blood relative."

Herod's breathing quickened and I could see that now-familiar whitening of the knuckles, but he said nothing.

"Okay, fuck it," said Phil. "I'm all for giving Antipas a beating, and so is Judas - and even Mister Herod here by the sound of it - but this plan has a massive flaw. Even after we mash up his face, Antipas will still be able to talk. And that's exactly what he'll do. He'll tell the Romans what happened and yes, I know there's a chance they'll just ignore him, but there's just as good a chance they won't."

Herod regarded Phil. "He will not be able to talk if his tongue has been removed."

Phil looked appalled. "Christ! We're not cutting anybody's tongue out. Even *his*. What is it with you?"

Herod shrugged.

"I understand," said Joseph, "that you have a plentiful supply of substances that can bring about a change in a person's state of mind. I suggest that we administer these substances to Antipas to the extent that coherent speech is no longer an option for him."

Phil laughed loudly. "We get him fucked up?" He thought for a moment. "Could we do that? Could it work?"

Everybody looked at Thad.

# Unstable Condition

Saying you'll do something is one thing. Actually doing it is something else entirely. That's true of a lot of things - promising to get up early to help out a mate, announcing that you're going to make a move on a girl. When you make those statements you really do mean them, but when it comes to actually carrying them out, well that's when reality kicks in. In the cold light of morning you don't actually want to get out of your comfy bed to help your mate lug his stuff across town, and when you realise there's a good chance that bird will turn you down, then suddenly what originally felt like a simple procedure starts to look a whole lot messier. The same applies to beating a helpless man to a pulp: fine to talk about as a theory, downright horrible in practice.

"You wishing you hadn't volunteered?" Phil read my mind as we walked slowly to the stable.

"Fuck yeah."

"Me too. We could probably get the soldiers to do it, you know. Nobody would think any less of us."

"No. I said I'd do it. I'm not going to pussy out now. I need to do this. This is the man who turned me against my best friend, the man who had John's head cut off. He's got it coming."

"You're just trying to talk yourself into it."

"Yep."

"You've made some pretty sound arguments, though. We

need to keep in our minds all the nasty shit he's done while we do it, otherwise we are going to pussy out."

"He's probably done a lot of other nasty shit too, stuff that we could never dream of."

"Yeah, we can make stuff up if it'll help. Basically, take anything bad in your life and blame it on Antipas. Now's the time for revenge…"

I stopped walking and put my hand on Phil's arm. "You don't have to get involved. I can't help but feel responsible for all of this. It's me who should step up."

"Okay." Phil started walking again.

I hurried after him. "What do you mean, *okay*? You're meant to argue with me."

"Nah, you offered. I'll let you have this one."

"Fuck you Phil."

"Fuck Antipas don't you mean?" Phil was at his worst when he was pleased with himself.

There was Max, having a bit of a doze, but still chuffed to bits to see me.

"I can't do it here. I can't have Max see it."

I'd expected a smart comment from Phil but he seemed to understand. "I'll drag him out and we'll go behind the stable."

Fair play to Phil for trying, but moving a man, even a trussed up one, is not a job for one person. It turned out to be almost impossible, even with two, but with the sun starting to rise we knew we had to hurry, or as my mum always said, *get a wriggle on.* Antipas had plenty of wriggle on and did everything he could to make it as hard for us as possible. I couldn't blame him for that. Instead I had to focus on blaming him for every evil act that had ever been carried out. By anyone, ever.

We eventually got him round the back of the stable and I could see over the wall to the garden, beyond where he'd had Jesus arrested like a common thief. I took the memory of how

I'd felt when he'd been taken, along with the image of Antipas smiling as his nefarious plans came together. I added those thoughts to the 'Things to help motivate me to beat up Antipas while he's unable to defend himself' pile, but as he lay there on the ground, coiled with twine like a piece of poultry ready for the oven, I couldn't bring myself to strike the first blow.

"We're going to have to untie him," I said after an awful silence.

"You've got to be kidding me."

"Just do it."

Phil headed back round to the front of the stable and was gone for so long I'd started to think he'd actually stormed off in a huff, but eventually he reappeared, holding a knife. He set about cutting Antipas loose.

I'd pictured a dramatic confrontation, me standing toe to toe with Antipas as we duked it out, taking heavy blows but eventually getting the better of him and winning the day. A noble bout for a noble cause, with good prevailing. What actually happened was a lot different. As soon as his arms were free Antipas started clawing at Phil in a blind fury, or perhaps panic. His mouth was still stuffed with cloth, but that didn't do much to block his screams of abuse. I leapt to Phil's aid and landed astride of Antipas, pinning him to the ground. I threw the first punch to quieten him down. And then the second because he was still making a racket, and the third because he scratched the side of my face. And the fourth and the fifth and all the rest because I hated him and everything he'd done to me and my friends and to John and Jeroboam. And with each blow it got easier and before I knew what was happening I was raining punches and spitting and screaming, and Antipas wasn't fighting back any more, and Phil was pulling me off and Antipas wasn't moving, save for the blood and spittle bubbling around his unconscious broken lips.

"I think that's about done it," said Phil.

We stood in the half-light, looking at the heap that was once the ruler of Galilee. My knuckles were skinned raw from my tirade of unanswered blows, and the shame just burned me up.

"I think we can take the gag out now," I said.

"Bugger that, he might bite us."

"I don't think he's got the strength." Without waiting for Phil's consent, I cut the string holding it in place and pulled the bloody rag out of Antipas' mouth. He retched pitifully but didn't struggle. He just lay there, breathing intermittently. "We should give him some water. When do you think he last had a drink?"

"For fuck's sake, Judas, you're like the guy in that story Jesus told that time."

"I must have missed that one."

"Well there was this traveller, and he was robbed, and nobody came to help him, including a priest, but then this Samaritan - who was an enemy of his - stopped…"

"Jesus, Phil, I don't want to hear the fucking story. And excuse me if you think it's weird to want to make a dying man a bit more comfortable."

"He'd better not be dying, we need him alive."

"Well that's even more reason to give him a drink then, Jesus!"

"Fair point."

I went round to the water trough in the stable, found a bucket and with trembling hands, rinsed it out as best I could. I was about to fill it when I was overwhelmed by the need to be sick. Aiming away from the water, I tried to unload as quietly as possible so Phil wouldn't hear. When it was over I crawled back to the trough, rinsed my mouth out and filled the bucket. I hauled the bucket back round to Phil where he took it off me. "You're done here," he said. "I'll make sure he gets a drink and is as comfortable as possible. Then I'll tie him up again, not too tight but enough so he isn't going to go anywhere. You go and see if Thad's ready, and then just, I don't know, sit down quietly or something."

"I'm okay."

"I just heard you puke. Fuck off and get Thad."

I still cringe about what I did that morning, but the thing that makes me most guilty is not my unrelenting assault on a man stiff from confinement, weak with thirst and still half-tied, but the fact that I walked straight past Maximus afterwards without so much as a pat.

I was shivering and crying and another wave of sickness hit me, making me drop to my knees and turn my empty stomach inside out a few times. I had an overwhelming urge to roll onto the ground and just lay there, but I had to ignore my body's demands because I knew I'd never get up otherwise. I forced myself back towards Joseph's house, trying to fool anyone who could see me into believing that I was absolutely fine, overcompensating like a drunk playing sober.

I heaved open the front doors and went to go upstairs but missed a step and went down, smashing my nose and nearly knocking myself out. I managed to push myself up but a wave of dizziness sent me over again and I bounced and slid down the few steps I'd managed to climb. This time I didn't get up.

I lay with my chin resting on the third stair and heard the door upstairs opening. It was Mary. She stood at the top and looked down at me in my prone, wretched position. I realised that despite the fact that everything in front of my eyes was spinning, I could actually see quite a way up her robe. I averted my eyes. "Hi Mary, can you tell Thad that Antipas is ready for him now?"

I'm glad I wasn't there while Thad did his thing. In fact I was surprised he agreed to do it at all. The idea of getting

Antipas fucked actually seemed quite funny when we first talked about it, but force-feeding drugs to someone is a rotten thing to do, regardless of whether he's your worst enemy or not. Taking someone's mind against their will is probably the worst thing you can do to a person. But then I had to remind myself that Antipas had taken John's head against his will. Perhaps that's how Thad reconciled himself with it, because he went ahead and did it.

Mary brought me round and stayed with me until the walls stopped moving. She bathed my wounds and said nice things. She's good like that. She smelled amazing, although I might have just added that detail with hindsight because my nose was properly smashed in and can't have been very efficient at doing its job of processing smells. I'm sure she did smell amazing though, she normally did, and as I felt her fingers caressing my face with a cloth and heard her angel-voice, all I could think was that Jesus was a lucky bastard. The luckiest man alive, as long as he managed to avoid being nailed to a cross.

I soon realised I could have saved myself the trouble of administering the beating to Antipas, because when I saw him again, Aretas' soldiers had had their own fun with him. His hair had been hacked off (it was a lot darker than Jesus' so I supposed it made sense but I got the impression they hadn't been particularly careful) and in its place sat a nasty looking bundle of twigs and brambles that they'd pushed down hard onto his violated scalp, drawing blood in more than a few places. "A crown of thorns for good King Antipas", I heard one of the soldiers say. I knew I'd got a bit carried away behind the stable but as I looked at his unrecognisable face, I was sure it couldn't all have been my handiwork. It was a total mess. Worst of all were those eyes. When I looked at them they were just… gone. It was like his head had been hollowed out with a spoon and filled back up with flour.

Thad's work was done.

It was time for the next part of our plan. It was time to get Jesus back.

# Do my Buns Look Big in This?

I've mentioned, more than once I'm sure, how I was constantly surprised by the direction my life had taken since leaving Nazareth and the bizarre situations in which I'd found myself. Now here I was in yet another scenario, so unlikely it should have been funny. But it wasn't funny, it was just scary. I was trundling through the back streets of Jerusalem in a wagon, Mary by my side wrapped in a shawl, and Matt, two soldiers and the battered remains of Antipas in the back, on our way, hopefully, to pluck Jesus from the brink of execution.

Mary had insisted on coming. Nobody had been able to talk her out of it, so we'd built the plan around her. Actually I can't pretend I was involved in any of the planning, what with being a total mess after what I'd done to Antipas. I was surprised to be picked to be in the rescue party at all, but I wasn't complaining. I was keen to do whatever I could to get the big man back.

Nicodemus had given us directions, which thankfully Mary had memorised. I'm hopeless with directions. I simply can't take them in. I listen to start with but after the first, *Take a left and bear to the right until you get to a fork in the road and if you see a something or other then you've gone too far*, I've completely lost interest. I know that's daft because it's in my interests to pay attention, but an overpowering can't-be-arsedness grips me in its lazy clutches and I'm helpless to resist.

Nicodemus had also given me the pouch of silver pieces I'd

previously rejected, telling me to put them to good use.

After much zig-zagging through the city we reached the jailhouse and it was time to put the plan into action. There were two guards outside. They bridled at the sight of us, gripping their swords, ready to strike at a moment's notice. I stepped down from the wagon and held my hands up to show I was unarmed.

"Good morning, gentlemen. I hope you don't mind me troubling you, but I need to ask you a favour, not for me but for my poor sister here." Mary, who'd had her head in her hands since we were in sight of the jailhouse, peeped out at the guards, all doe-eyed and sad. "She has promised our mother," I continued, "who is not long for this world, that she would pass on her love to our brother who is inside awaiting trial," I deliberately went with 'brother' rather than 'lover'. There is no underestimating the power of playing on a man's *I could be in here* instinct. Right on cue, Mary lifted her robe and *accidentally* revealed a flash of knee as she stepped down from the wagon. She threw back her hood and made a big show of shaking her hair out. She looked crazy hot and it worked like a charm, especially with the guard on the left, whose eyes nearly fell out of his head.

"Just in and out, yeah?" the other one said, probably because his partner couldn't speak through the drool.

"Just in and out," I agreed.

"It's against our orders. We could get into trouble. We'll at least have our wages docked. We've got families to feed."

At this obvious demand for a bribe I reached into my robes and pulled out the pouch of silver pieces. "That should buy plenty of bread for your families."

He rummaged through the hoard while his brother-in-arms continued to stare at Mary. Eventually, he nodded. "This all seems to be in order. I think we can grant your wish, madam."

Mary smiled pitifully through the tears. She should have been on stage. The guard turned his attention back to me. "I'd be a fool not to check you for weapons. Come on, arms up."

I did as I was told and he rummaged around my person. He came up with nothing. The other one's voice broke with excitement as he said to Mary, "I'm sorry, madam, I have to do this." Mary placed her hands on her head and put on her bravest face as the guard's hands took full advantage of the situation. "What's in there? He said when he'd finished his over-long search, his flushed face eyeing the bag slung on her shoulder.

Mary took out a loosely wrapped burlap parcel and opened it up to show half a dozen buns. "I baked these for my brother."

He took a sniff. "Cinnamon, nice. That's got my juices flowing." He looked at her with an oafish smile. "I did skip breakfast today."

"Please, help yourself," said Mary. "A strong soldier like you shouldn't be expected to do his duty on an empty stomach." She turned to the other guard. "And you of course, sir."

"Don't mind if I do."

I was surprised they only took one each.

The less horny soldier unlocked the main door and ushered us inside. "Which one's your brother?"

"Jesus of Nazareth," I answered, trying not to say too much and talk us into more questions.

"Well you'd better be quick. They're not going to spend too much time on that one. Go down these steps and follow the passage all the way to the end and turn right. His is the first cell on the left. If you get to the torture dungeon then you've gone too far."

He took a bite of his bun, stepped outside and slammed the door. We heard the rasp of the key turning.

We followed his directions which even I managed to remember. We passed rows of cells and I knew that inside each one was someone who was doomed to a grisly end. I knew we couldn't help them; we'd talked about that. We had a specific task to carry out and couldn't stray from it, difficult though that was. It sounds awful but I was glad the tiny window on each door was well above head height because if I'd seen the faces of the poor bastards inside I wouldn't have been able to live with myself. That didn't make it any better for those inside of course, they were still fucked, but if I didn't actually see them I felt somehow protected from the guilt. Selfish, I know.

We reached the outside of what had to be Jesus' cell. With some effort I slid the rusty bolt and opened the heavy door.

Jesus smiled as we entered but it was hard to tell because his face was badly battered. "You're a sight for sore eyes," he said, "and I've got to be honest, my eyes are quite sore."

Mary ran over and threw her arms round him. "What have they done to my poor baby?" She kissed him over and over.

Eventually Jesus disentangled himself from Mary's adoring arms, something that most men would struggle to do. "So what's the plan?" he said.

"We wait for a little while," said Mary.

Jesus smiled once more. "Okay, baby." If it had been me in his position I would have been falling over myself with questions and been in a rush to get the hell out of there. He must have known as well as I did that they'd be coming for him soon. The truth was simply that he trusted Mary. I was less confident, in fact I was in a state of pure terror. We had no idea if the next stage of the plan was going to work.

After the first rush of excitement on our arrival, the conversation dried up and it started to feel a little awkward.

Eventually, I spoke. "Okay, I'm going to bring up the camel in the room."

Jesus placed a hand on my shoulder. "You don't need to say anything."

"But I shopped you in to the Romans, I didn't want to, I…" he shut me up by putting his finger to my lips.

I pulled away. "Get your grubby mitts off my mouth!"

Jesus sniffed his filthy fingers. "God you're right, how did I get so dirty?"

"Being thrown into a dungeon will do that to a person," I said.

"The first thing I'm doing when I get out of here is taking a bath."

That was all it took for me to know he'd forgiven me.

Jesus looked at Mary. "Something smells good. Is that cinnamon? The hospitality in here hasn't exactly been overwhelming."

"Trust me, babe, you don't want to eat these."

I grew more nervous as time crept by, expecting guards to appear at any moment to take Jesus for trial. I panicked when I heard several sets of footsteps coming up the passage and a voice that I couldn't make out at first but soon came close enough for us to hear the words. "We're underground, we're big fat moles and this is our burrow. Feel this ground, it's hard. It's rock hard." The voice spouting the nonsense sounded familiar. We all looked at each other, our faces sharing the same puzzled expression.

The cell door opened, and there was Matt, grinning his face off. It was the first time I'd seen him smile for ages. Behind him I could see one of the guards from outside, rubbing his palms carefully against the far wall of the tunnel. "This is some hard shit." The guard didn't pay any attention to us as he continued spouting his blather.

Matt tipped his head back down the passage. "Bring him in," he hissed. He stepped back and one of Aretas' soldiers backed his way into the cell, carrying the head end of their priceless and almost lifeless burden. His buddy brought up the rear and together they bundled Antipas to the floor of the cell and cut the ropes wrapped around him. Antipas was saying the word donkey quietly to himself over and over. Jesus' face darkened as he saw the state he was in. He didn't say anything out loud but his mouth formed the words, *what the fuck?*

Mary put her arm around him, turning his head away. "Come on, babe, let's get you out of here. Don't look, but don't forget who that is, and what he's done."

We stepped into the passage, and Matt secured the door of the cell, the first guard still focusing his attention on the hardness of the tunnel wall rather than on anything we were doing. We saw his colleague, the one who'd searched Mary. He lay flat on the floor, his hands floundering in front of him. "Does he think he's swimming?" I said.

"Digging, I think," Matt said as we filed past. As we reached the turn we heard the horny guard wailing. "Where's the mole? You were going to show us the mole."

His colleague answered him. "I'm the mole, come and look at me, I'll show you the mole. The me-mole..." Their voices faded as we moved out of earshot.

We ran up the steps and were soon outside. Matt pushed the door closed, locked it, took out the key and slid it under the door of the jailhouse. "I don't know how they're going to explain what happened but after they come down off that shit they'll probably keep their mouths shut, even if they do remember anything, and that's pretty unlikely. Their superiors might piece something together but that's a risk we'll have to take."

"What about the other prisoners, they'll have heard something."

Matt brushed dust off his hands. "That's another risk we'll

have to take, there's nothing we can do about it. Let's go."

We were in the wagon and heading back to Joseph's palace, Mary and I sitting up front, back in character. We resisted the urge to hurry and both just managed to hold our nerve as around twenty Roman soldiers marched in the opposite direction, Caiaphus being carried in a litter in amongst them.

When we were out of the city, Jesus' face burst out from under the tarp. "Can I have one of those buns now? It looks like they've got a real kick to them."

# Double Cross

Back at Joseph's palace we were welcomed like heroes. Even Bart was polite to me, having seen that Jesus didn't bear a grudge. It was well into the morning now and most of us hadn't even thought about sleep, and those who had got their heads down can't have managed more than a couple of hours. The stress and anxiety that had kept us up through the night had been replaced with excitement and relief. We were buzzing, and none of us had taken anything.

Except Thad, probably.

I'm not sure if Jesus had been joking about the buns, that boy did love to get high, even first thing in the morning after having just been sprung from death row. Mary had laughingly nipped the idea in the bud, just in case. There was still work to be done although the hard part was well and truly over, for most of us at least. Mary had arguably the toughest job of all still to come.

The whole crew was in Joseph's entertaining area downstairs, hugging and high-fiving and pushing us for a blow-by-blow account of how the rescue had gone. I noticed someone was missing. "Where's Herod?" I asked Joseph.

"He's gone to his new palace."

"Do you think he and his wife are going to kiss and make up?"

Joseph laughed. "That is going to be one very awkward situation."

"He must be pretty badly hung up on her to go to all this trouble."

"I do not think it is her so much, it is more the principle. His brother stole his woman from him and at the time he could do nothing to prevent it. Antipas had the power, the position, the army. This is Herod's way to get even."

"Do you think they nicked each other's toys when they were kids?"

Joseph laughed. "Probably, and they carry a grudge like the rest of us carry…"

"What?"

He sighed. "I can't think of a thing that the rest of us carry. Damn, I was going to sound really clever then."

"Have you been drinking?"

"Maybe one or two. It's been a long night."

"I've never had a chance to thank you by the way," I said, "for putting us up here. For everything really. I have to be honest, I did think you were playing us, I thought you were the enemy for a while there."

He slapped me on the back. "Don't worry about it. I can see why you were suspicious. I'm just sorry you were put in that position."

"No harm done." I thought about Jesus' battered face, and Antipas' completely demolished one - and mind too. I even spared a thought for the two guards at the jailhouse, trying to picture what happened when Caiaphus and his mob arrived to find them seemingly having locked themselves in, crawling around the prison passages playing demented moles. "Well not too much harm done."

I suddenly noticed that someone else was missing too. Shows how observant I am. "Where's Nicodemus?"

"He's gone to court, he's a witness, remember? He's going to help condemn Jesus."

"Someone say my name?" Jesus' face loomed between us, his arms draped over our shoulders. "How're you doing fellas?"

"How are *you* doing?" I said.

I've been better but compared with how it could have gone you won't hear me complaining."

We were joined by Mary. "Your bath's ready, babe."

Jesus kissed her long and slowly while Joseph and I awkwardly studied the floor. "You're an angel, you know that?"

"Yes, I know. And you take me to heaven, babe."

"Get a room you two." Joseph took the words out of my mouth.

"Right after my bath." Jesus grinned and walked away with Mary trotting along beside him.

A few of us hit the kitchen and cooked up a storm. We brought out piles of eggs and baskets of bread, and everybody, their appetites fuelled by relief, tucked in greedily.

When Jesus came out he looked good, that is, he looked a lot better. You could still see the marks on his face but they didn't look as harsh. His hair was wet and slicked back and he wore a white cotton gown with the letter *J* embroidered on the left breast. "You do know you're not getting this back don't you?" he said to Joseph with a wink. Mary was also wearing a thin gown and the fact that her hair was also wet explained why they'd come to join us rather than going straight up to their room. They'd obviously already done what they needed to do.

Jesus was a lucky bastard.

Mary saw the food we'd laid on. "I don't believe it. Someone else has got off their backside and done something around here. So what is this, breakfast or lunch?"

"Somewhere in between," I said.

"We could call it brunch," said Phil.

"Only if we want to sound like arseholes," said Mary. She looked at me over the pile of food she was stacking onto her plate and actually fluttered her eyelashes. "You couldn't be a pet lamb and squeeze some oranges could you?" She was overplaying it a little. I could see beneath her smile that the thought of what she had to do later was weighing heavily on those perfect shoulders.

I went and squeezed some oranges.

When I returned, Joseph's comfy chairs had been pulled into a rough circle and everyone was sitting round in varying stages of exhaustion. There was a pipe going round and Thad was building a bong. I put the first tray of juice on a table in the centre and went to get the other one. When I got back, Phil was shifting a chair into place for me next to him. I flopped into it. It felt amazing, not just the pleasure of sitting down after everything I'd been through, but the feeling of all of us being together and out of danger, well almost out of danger anyway. And it felt good not to be hated by everybody.

The bong did the rounds and pretty soon everyone was either properly passed out or gazing into space wearing a soppy grin. Everyone except Jesus, Mary, Joseph and me, who'd passed on Thad's burnt offering.

"There's something I've got to ask you," I said to Jesus. "Nicodemus suggested you'd, like, planned your own arrest."

"Me being arrested," said Jesus, "was the only way to end all this. Antipas would have kept on coming otherwise."

"So is that a *yes*?"

He said nothing.

"So there wasn't a spy?"

Jesus shrugged.

"Or was it you? Were you passing information through Nicodemus to get Antipas to make his move?"

"Look mate," he said, "we're all tired, can we leave it for now?"

"But I want to know! Nicodemus also said you'd been in

328

cahoots with Aretas and Herod, working on this whole *wider purpose*."

"You can't make a move without consulting other crews. There's a delicate balance to it all. You don't want to shit on someone else's interests otherwise you find that while you're fixing one problem, you're just opening up a load of other ones. It's easy to make enemies."

"Shouldn't you let your own crew know what's going on?"

"No, not always, especially not if there's a chance that someone might do or say the wrong thing, upset the balance, fuck it all up."

Mary stood up and stretched. "I need to get going," she said, her playful manner now completely gone. "I can't put this off any longer."

Jesus stood up and hugged her tightly. "Good luck, baby. I wish I could go with you."

Mary forced a smile at me and Joseph and headed for the door. Jesus' eyes followed her out but she didn't look back.

"Joseph", I said. "Would you mind lending me a robe? Something dark, with a hood if possible."

"Of course." Without asking me why, he stood up and left the room.

Jesus looked like he could sleep for a week but his eyes were still alert. He knew what was on my mind. "Thanks mate. I really appreciate this. You're a good friend." He shook my hand.

"It's the least I can do."

I went to wait by the door and met Joseph at the foot of the stairs. He handed me a bundle of brown cloth. "Here you go."

"Thank you," I said, "for everything." I put on the robe and went outside.

I headed for the stable where I was greeted by a delighted Maximus. I fed and watered him and we were on our way.

I soon caught up with her. "Mary," I called from behind.

She put her hand to her chest and turned round. "You startled me."

I pulled up alongside her. "You didn't get very far, that donkey's no Maximus."

"I'm not in much of a hurry to be honest. What are you doing here?"

"I'm coming with you."

"No. You can't. It's too dangerous."

"It's dangerous for you, too. It's not right that you should go alone."

She thought for a moment and smiled. "Thank you, Judas. Thank you so much."

We rode, mostly in silence, skirting the city wall for a time before joining a path that led upwards. Although it was now afternoon, the sky seemed to have darkened. We could hear people and smell roasted meat. The path took us in an incline around an outcrop of rock before levelling out.

And that's when we heard the screaming.

We'd been looking down at the path immediately in front of us up to that point, officially because we were watching out for loose stones on the rough ground but really it was because neither of us wanted to see what we'd come for until we absolutely had to. But at the sound of the screams we instinctively jerked our heads up.

Crowds of people lined the path ahead, broken up by the stalls of food vendors and growing into a dense clump about half a mile further up, forming a circular clearing lined with Roman soldiers. In the centre stood three wooden crosses, and from each hung a man.

We left the path and found a good spot to tether the donkeys before carrying on up the hill on foot. Mary insisted that I stay a little way back from her, not, she said, because she was embarrassed to be seen with me but because all of Jesus' disciples - as she called us - were under threat.

"But aren't you under threat too?" I asked.

"I'm just the girlfriend."

I think I have suggested that the worst thing you can do to a person is take his mind. I hate to contradict myself but I'm not sure that's true. Not when you consider crucifixion. I'd never seen it done before but like everyone else I'd heard all about it. It was one of the ways the Romans reminded us, in the starkest way possible, that they were in charge, that they wouldn't take any kind of shit. I knew it was horrific, barbaric, unspeakable, but seeing it for real it was even more unimaginable than I could have… imagined.

Fuck.

It didn't matter that it was Antipas, it wouldn't have mattered if it was the Devil himself. Seeing a person put through that ordeal was sickening. Actually, *sickening* doesn't come anywhere near describing it but I don't think there are any words to describe it, not properly. They were already up when we arrived so we had the tiny mercy of being spared the spectacle of the poor bastards being nailed into place and hoisted up. Christ, how can anybody nail someone to a cross? I mean, in a physical sense, how can you hold a hammer and drive a great big nail into a person, hitting it again and again until it goes right through, deep into the wood underneath? They don't even do it through the hands, I'd always assumed they did but it's actually the wrists. Right through the middle of the fucking wrists. Jesus. Apparently it's because it's more secure, the hands wouldn't take the weight. They'd just tear away.

And the ankles. For fuck's sake.

Antipas wasn't screaming but the two poor fuckers either side of him more than made up for his lack of noise. I can still hear them now when I allow myself to think about it. They were naked, save for rags around their waists but their skin was so raked with lashes and smeared with blood that they could have been wearing tie-dyed tunics.

I saw Nicodemus in his ceremonial robes, his eyes fixed on the ground. Next to him was Caiaphus, eyes blazing, watching the victims suffering their unspeakable ordeal. He wasn't smiling but there was a fervour in his expression. I saw him glance at Mary and he grimaced in recognition. This was repellent but necessary. Mary was there of course because as far as Caiaphus, the Pharisees and the Romans were concerned, her lover was nailed to one of those crosses. It would have been strange, even suspicious had she not attended. But she was there, there for him, sobbing like any doting girlfriend would. And even though we both knew it wasn't Jesus hanging there in the kind of agony that nobody should ever endure, I knew her tears weren't fake.

Neither were mine.

It would have been easy not to notice Antipas finally die. After hours of torment his head just dropped and the muscles standing out on his arms and chest as they strained in an effort - that must have been as excruciating as it was futile - to take the pressure off his suspended limbs, went limp. All I can say I could feel when it happened was relief, not that the man who had threatened all our lives was finally dead, but because I couldn't bear to see him suffering any longer.

When the centurion eventually noticed, he immediately told one of his men to break the legs of the other two victims to hasten their departure. The casual way he gave the order made it clear this was no act of mercy. He just wanted to get home. As the soldier took an iron rod and approached the poor wretch on the left I was forced to imagine what his loved ones kneeling beneath must have been feeling. It was bad enough for us to see this awful spectacle when not only did we not know two of the victims, but the third had been our worst enemy.

The crowd went silent as the soldier swung the rod upwards to land a blow beneath both knees. The poor bastard was beyond screaming now and the only sound was the nauseating crunch of shattering bones. I didn't know if the guy on the other side was aware of anything around him by then and I hoped his mind had already gone as the soldier, the rod over his shoulder like he was carrying a garden spade, stepped towards him and repeated his grim task.

I don't know the science behind why this resulted in a quicker death - I've been told since that it makes the body go into shock and give up the fight for life - but from what I'd seen that afternoon the body should have been shocked to death long before then.

Caiaphus said some pompous sounding words and climbed into his litter. His bearers barked at the dispersing crowd to clear the way.

There were just a handful of us left, a few weeping loved ones of the other victims, a couple of soldiers, Mary, Nicodemus and me.

I looked back on the day, and even though we'd achieved everything we'd set out to do, completely against the odds, it still didn't feel like a particularly good Friday.

# Tomb With a View

It was over. We'd done it. We were safe. As long as we didn't do anything daft anyway.

Joseph had turned up after the crucifixion. He'd approached Pontius Pilate to ask if he could take the body and give it a proper burial in the tomb in the grounds of his house. I hadn't noticed the tomb but I guess it's not something you include when you're giving someone the grand tour - *here's the dining area, you'll see it's all open-plan after we knocked through, there's another reception room on the left there, and you see that huge rock that's blocking that cave? Well that's the tomb.*

Asking for the body was a bit of a risky move because in doing so Joseph was effectively affiliating himself with a politically incorrect figure - albeit a dead one - but the benefits outweighed the risks. If anyone had any suspicions about who was really on that cross we didn't want the body to be easy to get hold of and checked for any distinguishing marks.

Pilate had given his permission. "He was in a good mood," Joseph had said, "pleased as Pontius". So Joseph and Nicodemus had had the unenviable task of taking the body down from the cross. They had to get the soldiers to help them, not just to lift the thing out of the ground and lower it, but to get the bloody nails out. I didn't hang around for that part.

Joseph's entertaining area was pretty much as we'd left it. If it hadn't been for the snoring, burping and farting I would have believed a quick-acting plague had killed everybody right where they sat. The only difference from before was that the plates had been cleared up. Jesus had been busy.

When we sat down, Jesus cleared his throat loudly. "Can everyone listen up? I've got something to say." It took a while but eventually he got everyone's attention.

"The first thing I want to say is thank you. You guys are the best. It's been an absolute blast and it's an honour to count you all amongst my friends."

"Right back at you, big man!" said Peter.

Andrew pointed at his brother. "What *he* said."

The two of them high-fived.

"Thanks, fellas. Now, we all knew this was coming to an end - and this is it right here - the end. We've all said we'll stay in touch but you know how that goes, so let's not bullshit ourselves. There's a good chance that some of us will never see each other again."

"Judas will be glad never to see me again," said Phil.

I laughed along, but actually he was wrong. I was going to miss him more than most. And to think that for such a long time I'd thought he was a massive bell-end.

"It's not safe to carry on here, we all know that," said Jesus. "Caiaphus has tasted a bit of power. He's got an agenda now. As far as he's concerned, I'm dead, but he'll be whispering in Pilate's ear to finish the job. He'll be looking to mop up the rest of you rabble rousers."

None of this was news - it was something we'd all talked about a lot - but it was still a downer to hear him say it, like being at a party when all the beer and drugs have run out but nobody wants to be the one to say it's time to go home.

"So our little operation is over, as we know it at least. You've all got the choice of whether you want to keep your own thing going or not. That's up to you. Whatever you decide, I've got something for you. You'll have to come into the kitchen though cos I'm buggered if I'm going to carry them all out here."

In the kitchen were eleven sacks. I didn't count them but worked it out. There were twelve of us disciples and there was one for everyone except me.

Jesus carried on his speech while everyone untied their bags. "That should get you set up in whatever you want to do. For anyone who wants to take a chunk of the business with him, have a word with Peter or Andrew if it's green you're after, and Thad and Simon if you want the harder stuff. All I ask is that you sell it responsibly. Keep it away from kids for starters. And if you want to keep my word going then that would be grand. You've all heard me talk plenty of times - enough to be bored to death of the sound of my voice - but hopefully you've picked up enough of what I was trying to get across to do a pretty fair crack at it yourselves," he suddenly looked self conscious, noticing that nobody seemed to be responding to him, "erm, if you want to of course. No pressure."

The reason nobody was answering him was because each man was staring into his sack with his mouth gaping open.

Every sack was stuffed with money.

"Jesus," Thomas said eventually.

"We did have a pretty successful operation, it's only fair that the profits are shared out, but I'll level with you, I've taken more than I've given you. I'm not saying that as a fuck you, but because I want to be open about it."

"That's fair, you did more work, took more risks," Peter said, to hearty noises of agreement.

"Thank you. So, as I said, you must be bored of the sound of my voice by now so I'm going to shut up. This is it, fellas. We're at the end of the road but we had a damn good run and I wouldn't change a thing. Anyone who wants to be extra cautious is welcome to leave as soon as they want but for anyone who wants to wait until tomorrow - I suggest we get properly fucked up. Just one more time. Who's in?"

Everybody was in.

When Joseph and Nicodemus returned with their grisly cargo the party was well underway and it was time for me to find myself in yet another unlikely scenario as I, ripped to my tits on a cocktail of drugs and booze, helped them build a funeral pyre on which to burn that bad boy.

It could have been a real downer - burning a corpse isn't the first party game on anyone's list - but we resolved to make it positive, to give the bastard a good send off. Everybody came out when it was time to light it up, and we raised our glasses - bottles, mugs, whatever - and toasted the dead tetrarch. And then we toasted John the Baptist. And Jesus.

And Joseph and Nicodemus.

And each other.

And Caiaphus and Pontius Pilate.

And that's when we had to go back inside because we all needed refills.

Perhaps it was the drugs we'd slammed back. Perhaps it was the relief that it was all over. Perhaps it was the sacks of money. Perhaps we were just a bunch of saps, but every single one of us choked up like grandmothers at a Bar Mitzvah as we traded clumsy hugs and handshakes and said goodbye.

The morning after wasn't even the morning after, it was the same morning. There's no point describing the state we were in. You've been smashed, you know how it goes.

The crew left throughout the day. Those who were able took their sack of loot with them while others left theirs with Joseph for safe keeping.

Mary was obviously particularly sad to see Bart leave, what with him being her uncle and all, but he was keen to get back to Capernaum to see his daughter and to check on the bar. He had enough money never to serve a drink again but Bart liked his life and wanted to get back to it.

Matt, after picking up the rest of the army from Capernaum, was heading east. He told the rest of us that we were welcome any time we wanted to drop in at the palace.

Peter and Andrew declared they were hooking up with James and John and were going to hit the road to spread Jesus' word. Bless them. I reckoned they'd do a good job of it. Before he left, Peter called Jesus aside. "My lord," he said. "I fear I may have let you down. I have not denied you. I have not had the opportunity to."

"Have you heard a cock crow?" said Jesus.

"Not recently."

"Well there's still time then."

Peter looked none the wiser.

Thomas said he was going north to see his family. Nat left with him. He probably said what he was going to do but I don't remember listening.

Simon and Thad said they were going to check out Rome but knowing them, that plan probably changed half a mile up the road.

And that just left Phil. He asked Joseph if it was okay for him to stay on just one more night. He didn't say why but there was obviously something on his mind.

We found out what it was the next day. Early in the morning he said we should go for a walk, which with all the security implications - something he was always a massive nag about - was a bit of a weird thing for him to suggest. But we went along with it, agreeing to go for a stroll round the garden while it was still quiet.

But it wasn't quiet, not like it should have been at that time of the morning, and by that I mean it wasn't empty. We saw about half a dozen people and each one of them looked at

Jesus like they were looking at a ghost. Several uttered the phrase, 'he is risen,' while others just looked on in wonder. We quickly got out of there and headed back to Joseph's, making sure nobody was following.

"Come on, out with it," was the first thing Jesus said when we got back.

"Oh, you mean, me?" Phil said eventually, as if there'd been any doubt over who Jesus was talking to. "Out with what?"

"What was that all about? Your little stroll, those people, the stares. What the fuck?"

Phil smiled nervously. "I wanted to finish the job."

"What job?"

"My job, selling you."

"But I'm jacking it in, I'm moving on. Did you not notice all that goodbye stuff? We're done. I'm going to disappear."

Phil nodded. "I know, I know. After we did that prophecy thing I've been doing a bit of reading and I thought I'd have a go at one more."

"You're going to have to explain what the fuck you're talking about."

"People think you're dead, right?" He saw the impatience in Jesus' eyes and didn't wait for an answer. "The world thinks you're dead. They think you're buried in Joseph's tomb."

The denarius dropped. "You want me to rise from the dead? Christ, Man! Did you not think to ask me first? I'm sorry but I'm not doing it."

Phil looked properly sheepish now. "You've kind of done it already. Sorry. Those people who saw you, I... well I sort of arranged for them to be there. I tipped them off. They're massive fans of yours, totally hooked on the Son of God stuff. They'll be telling everybody they know right now. *He is risen!* You're going to be bigger than Moses."

Jesus went to say - to shout - something, but stopped

himself and visibly relaxed. "Fuck it," he said with a wave of his hand. "You do what you want mate, but I'm leaving as planned."

"You leaving is a big part of the plan. In fact," Phil looked even more awkward than before, "it's probably best that you leave right now. All we want is for word to get out that you've been resurrected. The Jesus freaks are doing that right now. We don't want anyone with a more… logical mind coming around and asking questions."

Jesus suddenly wasn't relaxed anymore. "Do you know how much I've been looking forward to my breakfast? I was going to have eggs. It feels like an egg kind of Sunday, and you're telling me I've got to get the fuck out right now? You're a piece of work you are."

"Sorry boss - couldn't resist it."

Jesus grinned. "Oh come here you great big twat." He scooped Phil up in his arms and whirled him round.

When he'd stopped spinning Phil said it was time for him to go. "I'd better make that tomb look lived in," he said.

Jesus looked at Mary. "We'd better get going too, before anyone turns up wanting to worship my ghost."

"Well good luck, you two." I said, shuffling in my sandals.

"Thanks," said Jesus, looking a bit puzzled, "I guess."

"Can I ask you something, mate?"

"Course."

"I couldn't help noticing, and I don't want to sound like an spoilt kid here, but there wasn't a sack for me."

Jesus frowned and smiled at the same time. He looked at Mary as if she was in on some joke with me. She looked as puzzled as he did. He looked back to me. "What do you mean?"

"It's okay," I shrugged, "I'm sure you had your reasons."

"Are you taking the piss?"

"Are *you* taking the piss?"

"We don't have time for this, we need to get going." He shook Phil's hand. "Good luck with your prophecy thing you daft bastard." He turned to Joseph. "We'll just get our shit together and we'll be off. But we're bound to meet again. I can't thank you enough for everything, and that goes for Nic, too, you'll pass that onto him won't you?"

"Of course, my lord," said Joseph.

"Enough with that lord stuff!" He gave Joseph a hug then headed for the door with Mary in tow.

I watched them walk away, feeling like the forgotten duckling left on the riverbank while mummy and daddy duck swim away.

As he got to the door Jesus stopped and turned round. "For fuck's sake, Judas, are you coming or what?"

"You want me to come with you?"

"Course we do. What did you think was going on, you daft prick?"

"I didn't know, you didn't say."

"Is that what all that *where's my sack* shit came from? I thought you were trying to be funny."

"You didn't laugh."

"You're not normally funny."

"I hate you."

"Yeah, I know, but you're coming anyway."

"Yeah. I'm coming."

I hurried after them like a puppy bounding after its owner.

# *Afterlife*

Being in hiding isn't really a bad life. In fact it's a pretty bloody good life. We've got more money than we need, the weather's amazing and we've got plenty of green, in fact we've always got at least one plant on the go. We don't often dabble in the harder stuff, well not too often anyway.

We do a lot of swimming, which means I see a lot of Mary wearing not very much. In any other life I would spend every day snivelling pitifully that I'm unable to consume every cubit of her delicious flesh. But this isn't any other life, this is life after death. I beat my Mary fetish some time back, and now when she comes running out of the water giggling her head off with everything bouncing along with her, I can just enjoy the show.

I still haven't settled down but there are plenty of girls here and they don't seem to find me repellent. I'm sure they're all smitten with Jesus but they know there's no way they could pry him out of Mary's delightful clutches, so they have to settle for little old me.

Maximus loves it here too. He enjoys paddling through the shallow water to cool his little hooves down. In fact that's my best chat-up line, *do you want a donkey ride?* Never fails.

I'm glad it's going to be a quiet wedding tomorrow. I'm bound to make a mess of the best man's speech, especially as there's a lot I'm not allowed to talk about so the fewer people who hear it, the better.

The big man is drifting past on a raft, a glass of wine in one hand and a pipe in the other.

"Looking good, Jesus!"

"Feeling good, Judas!"

# ABOUT THE AUTHOR

A.W. Wilson is called Alan. His middle name is William.
He hopes you enjoyed his book.

You can contact him at alan@awwilson.com

29043695R00208

Printed in Great Britain
by Amazon